LUDSECKE

Fernsby's War Book 3

J.C. JARVIS

WHERRY ROAD PRESS

Get a FREE Book!

To my wife, Glenda, who is my biggest supporter and my bedrock. Without her support and encouragement none of this would ever have happened.

My editor, Melanie Underwood, who patiently and expertly wove her magic through the pages of the manuscript and turned it into the thrilling book you see today. The deft touch and the care she poured into each page has made the book far better than it could have ever been on its own.

My cover designer, Jane Dixon-Smith, who far exceeds my expectations with the masterpieces she creates every time we work together. Jane is a true master of her art, and I am truly grateful to be able to work with her.

WHERRY ROAD PRESS

Ludsecke

Fernsby's War Series Book 3

Edited by https://melanieunderwood.co.uk/

Cover Design by http://www.jdsmith-design.com/

Foreword

Welcome to the third novel in the Fernsby's War Series, which takes the reader on a historical adventure set in the early days of WW2.

Early on in my research, I made the decision to write my books in modern (British) English. All my novels are UK centric, so it made sense to write the story using the correct spelling from that region.

Alderauge continues the story of Michael Fernsby, a young man who was forced to grow up quickly after the dramatic events of Ryskamp, the first book in the series.

Although more experienced than he was in Ryskamp, Michael retains the spirit of his youth, and I tried to convey that through the first-hand descriptions he gives us as he progresses through the adventure.

Because of his past experiences, some of the things he witnesses are intentionally vague because he either doesn't know what they are, or that was how he remembered them.

For instance, one of the vehicles he comes across frequently is described *as he remembers it*, so I have explained what it is here so the reader will know what he is talking about.

As you will discover in the pages of the novel, the unusually described vehicle was in reality a VW Kübelwagen, and a basic search of the internet will reveal why Michael would describe the vehicle in the manner that he does.

The one thing I didn't change was history itself. Any authentic events I describe are as historically accurate as possible, and when using real characters from history, I didn't have them doing anything they would have found impossible to do.

I hope you enjoy the epic adventures of Michael Fernsby and Alderauge . . .

J.C.Jarvis

Ludsecke

By J.C. Jarvis

Chapter 1

Atlantic Ocean, September 3, 1939

Seventeen-year-old Elizabeth Harper pulled the lapels of her brown woollen coat closer together as the cold Atlantic wind chilled her to the bone. Her white woollen beret was already halfway to Canada, such was the ferocity of the unpredictable transatlantic weather.

And this was a calm day according to the crew members she'd spoken to earlier!

Strong winds made it difficult to walk in a straight line, although if she cared to admit it, she enjoyed the wind buffeting through her long, wavy brown hair. The icy sting on her face made her feel alive, not something to be taken for granted in today's troubled world.

Elizabeth took her final stroll around the ship, absorbing the fading light before darkness confined her to the cabin she shared with her father, Thomas Harper.

Lieutenant-Commander Thomas Harper, she corrected herself.

Elizabeth leant against the guardrails and watched the white crests of the waves breaking against the hull of the ship far below. The sight was mesmerising, and she reflected on how she had ended up in the middle of the Atlantic Ocean as Britain once again braced for war with Germany.

The white stripe on the ship's single black funnel told anyone who knew these things that the ship belonged to the Donaldson Atlantic Line. Elizabeth only knew because her father had spent the last decade working for them as a liaison officer based out of Liverpool.

It wasn't that she didn't care. In fact, she enjoyed seeing her father's eyes sparkle and come alive whenever he talked about ships and their history. He'd served in the Royal Navy during the First World War and had seen action at the battle of Jutland in 1916.

A career officer, Lieutenant-Commander Thomas Harper remained in the navy after the Great War ended, and had been recommended for promotion to commander when disaster struck his family in the mid nineteen-twenties.

Shortly after Elizabeth was born in 1922, her mother fell ill and passed away from cancer. Her heartbroken father resigned from the navy and raised his daughter alone, supplementing his pension from his work by working for the Donaldson Atlantic Line.

It was this connection that had led to Elizabeth standing on the deck of the SS Athenia this evening.

After long conversations, her worried father had persuaded her that it wasn't safe to remain in England.

"That lunatic in Berlin will kill us all," he would say to her all the time, convincing her that nowhere was safe from Hitler's fury.

Thomas secured a transfer to Canada, where they could live a much safer life. Although Elizabeth did not share her father's fears for the future, she went along with it out of the deep love she had for him.

As darkness fell and the temperatures dropped, Elizabeth made her way to their cabin on deck B. She was still unsure of her surroundings and she found it easy to get lost, which she had several times already.

Eventually she stood outside the cabin, and she rapped loudly on the door. Moments later, her father, the man who had been her anchor through every storm, stood in front of her, tall and proud as he'd always been.

His hair may have greyed over the years, and the lines of worry might be deeper than they were before, but he stood ramrod straight as befitting an officer in the Royal Navy.

Elizabeth Harper adored him.

Immediately upon entering the cabin, Elizabeth knew something was wrong. Her father, normally chatty and upbeat in her presence, slumped in a chair and held his head in his hands.

"What's wrong?" she asked. "And don't tell me it's nothing, because I can tell from your face that it isn't."

"Sit down." Thomas beckoned his daughter to sit on the chair next to him.

While not luxurious, the cabin was spacious and well appointed, as befitting a man of Thomas Harper's stature.

Spacious and comfortable, that was how Donaldson Atlantic had explained it to them.

"Well?" she asked. "What's wrong, Dad?"

"I had dinner with the captain this evening." Thomas stared at the wall behind Elizabeth's head.

"I know. You threw me out of here and told me to eat on my own."

"I'm sorry," her father said, his faint London accent evident in his words. "He called for me, and when the captain requests your company, it isn't something you refuse."

"I know, Dad. I was just teasing you."

Thomas pulled a face and stared at his daughter. "It's finally happened. You're aware that Hitler invaded Poland two days ago, aren't you?"

"You know I am. You told me several times."

"The captain received a communication from Liverpool. The British and French governments gave Germany until eleven this morning to stop the invasion. They refused, and as a result, Chamberlain gave a radio address to the country this morning. We're at war with Germany, Elizabeth. Again."

"Just like you said would happen." The blood drained from Elizabeth's face. "Do you think we can stop it before it starts?"

Her father shook his head. "I doubt anything can stop Hitler. Europe is heading for oblivion, mark my words. He won't stop until we're all dead."

"Thank God we're getting out then. We should be safe in Canada, shouldn't we?" Elizabeth asked, fighting the rising fear that wrapped around her chest, restricting her breathing.

She noticed her hands had turned white from her grip on the chair, so she relaxed her arms and shook them to relieve some of the tension.

"We'll be safe but be careful on the ship from now on. The captain has ordered strict adherence to the blackout for the duration of our voyage. That means no external lights. Internal cabin lights have to be dim, and we are to ensure all porthole curtains are drawn so they can't be seen from the ocean."

Elizabeth thought for a moment. "Does that mean we have to stay in our cabins after dark?"

"It's not enforced, but it's a good idea. You'll get lost out there in the darkness. So, yes, stay in the cabin after dusk."

"We'll be alright, won't we?" Elizabeth asked. Her heart rate was elevated, and she could feel her chest pounding. "After all, we're not the navy."

Thomas smiled at his daughter. "We'll be just fine, Elizabeth. We're not a target, and we'll be in Canada before you know it."

Something about her father's demeanour told her he wasn't telling her everything, but Elizabeth didn't care. She didn't want to hear any more. As far as she was concerned, the less she knew, the better. All she wanted was to get safely to Canada so she could forget all about this horrible war.

Silence fell in the dimly lit cabin. Elizabeth strained to see the words of the book she'd brought with her, and she was about to put it down when she glanced at the clock ticking away on the wall.

It was 7.40pm.

Chapter 2

Her father nodded off, no doubt a result of the gentle rocking of the Athenia as she rolled with the waves far below them.

Elizabeth smiled and reached over to grab his book so he wouldn't lose his page. As she reached, her entire world shattered around her.

From out of nowhere, the peaceful serenity was destroyed by a large explosion that deafened her as it rocked the ship. The cabin seemed to jolt and shudder as books and anything else not nailed down flew from their resting places, turning them into dangerous missiles, one of which struck Elizabeth on the head, knocking her off balance.

The dim lamp flickered violently, creating shadows that danced on the walls. She gained control of herself and stepped towards her father.

A strange sound emanated from the walls of the cabin, as though they were groaning under the stress of the explosion. Elizabeth looked at her father, with a look of sheer horror on her face.

"What's that?" she asked, her voice barely above a whisper. Her ears were ringing and every noise she heard sounded like it was underwater.

Before Thomas could reply, the whole side of the cabin where Thomas was standing caved inwards, as if it were under great pressure from the other side. A large, jagged piece of metal, propelled by the explosion, suddenly cut through the space where the wall used to be. It hit Thomas squarely in the chest, knocking him to the floor.

Through the ringing in her ears, Elizabeth heard the sharp cry of pain escaping her father's lips.

The lights flickered, but by some miracle they remained on. Elizabeth rushed to her father, who was pushing frantically against the metal object trapping and crushing him.

Elizabeth fell over the broken, twisted debris that moments earlier had been their cabin. She stumbled and cut herself on the splintered remains of the wooden floor, but she didn't seem to notice the blood as she fought to rescue her father.

She cried out loud when she reached him. The sharp piece of metal was bigger than a human and much heavier. Without help, she would never be able to remove it herself. She grabbed and pulled for all she was worth, but it wouldn't budge.

She stopped and looked in horror at the scene before her. The metal had penetrated her father's chest so deeply that it protruded out the other side. Blood soaked through his clothing, and even in the dim light, she could see how pale he was.

"Dad!" she screamed, and pulled even harder.

A hand reached up and touched her cheek. Elizabeth stopped and looked at her father, unable to comprehend what was happening to him.

"Lizzie," he rasped, using the name he used to call her when she was a child. "Lizzie, be strong for me and get off this ship while you still can. You have a good life waiting for you in Canada. Remember… I love you and I always have."

Tears streamed down Elizabeth's cheeks, mingling with the blood and dirt.

"Don't die," she pleaded. "I don't know what to do without you. I need you, Dad," she sobbed, her heart pounding in her chest. "I'm going to save you. You can't die, not here. Not now."

"Lizzie," Thomas's breath laboured as he struggled to speak. "It's too late for me, but you've got a life ahead of you, so get out of here and save yourself."

His eyes widened as they locked on his daughter one last time. Then his head fell forward, and his eyes closed forever.

Thomas Harper was dead.

"No!" Elizabeth broke down and sobbed loudly. She rocked back and forth, cradling her father's hand against her body. "No!"

Shouts and screams outside the cabin snapped Elizabeth back to her senses. Crew members were yelling orders, and she heard the word 'lifeboat' shouted several times.

She knew what she was supposed to do, and she aimlessly searched for the life vest that was stored somewhere in the cabin. Wherever it was, she couldn't find it, so she slumped to the ground next to her father, his lifeless body limp underneath the metal object that had taken his life.

Two men burst through the open door of her cabin. Seeing the situation, one of the men grabbed Elizabeth under her arms and pulled her to her feet.

"We have to go, miss," he shouted. "The ship's sinking and we'll all go down with her if we don't get off."

Elizabeth didn't seem to hear as she stared at the devastation. The other man helped his companion, and together they half-pulled, half-dragged the dazed young woman from the cabin.

Strong winds whipping her face from all angles dragged Elizabeth from her dazed state. She struggled free from the grip of the two crew members and stared at the carnage and chaos all around her.

Disarray and carnage were everywhere. The outer decks were crowded with people, all of them in a state of shock and misery.

Men shouted for their wives as children screamed and clung to their mothers. Crew members shouted orders that nobody heard, and everyone was pushing and shoving their way to the lifeboats and the relative safety of the open ocean.

The ship lurched as metal twisted and wood snapped under the strain. Fires bellowed up from deep within the hull, and the ship began listing, making the people appear drunk as they struggled to gain traction on the stricken vessel.

Hands once again grabbed Elizabeth, this time steering her towards a lifeboat. She struggled initially, but then realised that her father was dead and there was nothing she could do for him.

Dying here on the Athenia won't bring him back. He wanted me to save myself, and I'll do it for him, even if I don't care if I live or die.

She allowed the crew member to guide her, and she climbed meekly into the full lifeboat, falling over a woman holding a child as she fell onto a seat.

The lifeboat creaked, and it jerked and juddered as it

descended towards the dark, black water below. It stopped with a hard crash and water poured over the sides, instantly soaking her as it did so.

Elizabeth welcomed the freezing water as it reminded her of what it meant to be alive. All she could hear were the cries of the injured and the desperate as the lifeboat, crammed full of people, bobbed and weaved on the waves as it drifted away from the sinking ship.

The salt stung her wounds, a cruel but vital reminder that she still existed in a world that had suddenly contracted to pain, loss, and survival.

"What happened?" she finally asked the woman sat next to her.

"A torpedo." The woman's eyes never left the Athenia. "A German U-boat hit us with a torpedo."

"Why?" someone else cried. "We're not the navy, or even a merchant vessel. Why did they do that?"

Nobody spoke because nobody knew the answer.

The lifeboat drifted through the darkness. The few men on board tried rowing, but with no clear direction, they eventually stopped and allowed the little boat to drift wherever the tide took them.

Elizabeth joined the other women and children and huddled together for warmth and comfort. Nobody spoke the entire night, and even the children were eerily quiet. It was as though the shock had removed their ability to comprehend what had happened to them.

As daylight broke, a silhouette approached from the distance. As it closed in, Elizabeth could see that it was a private yacht and not a naval vessel.

For a moment she panicked, thinking it was the German navy coming back to finish them off, but she scolded herself for being so foolish when she saw hands reaching down to haul her on board.

Along with the rest of her fellow survivors, Elizabeth found herself aboard the Southern Cross, a Swedish private yacht. After being given a warm blanket and hot coffee, Elizabeth found a quiet space at the rear of the ship and hunkered down. She wanted to be alone so she could process what had just happened to her.

For years, her father had tried to warn her of the perils of war. She had always ignored his rants, putting it down to shellshock from the First World War.

But now she knew different. He had been right all along. The Second World War was now here, and she had experienced it first-hand. Whatever else she did, she would no longer run off to Canada to escape it. No, she would go back to England and volunteer to fight in any way she could.

Hitler and his cronies had hurt her, and now she would do everything in her power to hurt them back.

It's war, after all.

The Southern Cross made its way to Galway in Ireland, where the survivors were greeted with helping hands and kind hearts. They helped the injured and comforted the grieving.

Elizabeth got on the first available train to Belfast and then caught a boat across the Irish Sea to Liverpool and the home she had grown up in with her father.

The day she arrived, she picked up a newspaper that had the tragic U-boat attack all over the front pages. According to the paper, 1,418 passengers and crew were onboard the SS Athenia. 128 people died, amongst them her father, Thomas Harper.

Elizabeth sat in her father's favourite rocking chair overlooking the Liverpool docks, where he'd spent most of the years of her life.

For her, and the other survivors of the cruel U-boat attack, the war had already begun.

Chapter 3

Sandwich, Kent, September 3, 1939

Michael Fernsby sat on the large, dark leather couch next to his fifteen-year-old sister, Judith, who had barely left his side since he'd rescued her from a breakaway group of Oswald Mosley's British Union of Fascists just weeks earlier.

The wounds from their ordeal were still raw, none more so than those of his father, who limped into the room with a heavy cane for support. He grimaced as he slumped into a matching Victorian armchair opposite the couch.

A dark oak coffee table, intricately carved and highly polished, sat between them.

Gerald Fernsby, the head of the household and owner of their ailing brewing empire, was struggling to recover from the automobile accident he'd been involved in alongside Michael back in May.

At least, the authorities called it an automobile accident. The Fernsbys knew the truth; that it had been an assassination attempt on Michael's life by Maureen Ingram, a Nazi spy and the trusted secretary of Unit 317,

Michael's Secret Intelligence Service (SIS) government employer.

Although Gerald was only forty-two years old, a heart condition and the severe injuries he'd received from the assassination attempt had taken a toll on his appearance. His once vibrant demeanour was gone, replaced by a sombre old man with brittle greying hair and a growing bald spot on the top of his head.

His left leg had been shattered in the accident and it was only recently that the doctors had removed the cast. He struggled to get around and couldn't walk without the aid of a cane.

To compound his misery, he'd also suffered a fractured left shoulder and several broken ribs, which made everyday tasks such as moving, sitting, and even breathing difficult and painful.

His eyes, once full of life and joy, were dulled from his pain and the loss of his eldest son, David, killed by the Gestapo a year earlier in Munich during an ill-fated attempt to rescue their Jewish uncle and great-grandfather from the Nazis.

The mission failed, and Michael returned home alone after an incredible battle for survival through the Black Forest in the dead of winter.

Dorothy Fernsby, Michael's mother, sat next to her husband in the other armchair in the room. She was three years older than Gerald, but even though recent events had aged her considerably, she still looked a decade younger than her husband.

Before their misfortune, her hair had always been styled in the latest, late nineteen thirties' fashions, and she never wore clothes from the shop racks. Everything she had was tailor made, and she always looked smart and pretty, even first thing in the morning when everyone else looked dishevelled and untidy.

After David's passing, Dorothy was close to a nervous breakdown and Michael worried about her mental wellbeing, especially after the assassination attempt and Judith's kidnapping.

Her demeanour changed for the better after Michael rescued Judith and returned triumphantly from Germany with a family heirloom that was worth a king's ransom. Finding the Brasher Doubloon was going to be their salvation, and negotiations were already under way to value the doubloon and sell it to the highest bidder.

The bank had agreed to hold off on repossessing their home and had advanced the business further funds that would carry them through to the sale of the coin.

Things were finally looking up for the Fernsbys, and it showed in Dorothy's appearance. Although greyer, her hair was back in the wavy style so popular with the ladies, and her eyes looked brighter and happier than they had for a long time.

Michael's grandmother, Giselle Fernsby, or Gigi, as she was better known, had suffered more than most. She was German, and the people of England that had once been so friendly and accepting of her after the Great War, now turned against her and refused to speak or even look at her.

Some shop owners refused to serve her, and a few shouted obscenities during her early morning walks, which she now refused to take alone.

It was Gigi who had prompted Michael and David to go to Germany after Kristallnacht, the pogrom in Germany the previous November, when thousands of Jews had their shops and synagogues burned and destroyed by the Nazi Brownshirts.

And it was Gigi who lived with the guilt of sending her grandson to his death at the hands of the Gestapo. Michael knew she would never forgive herself for sending them, no matter how much he tried to convince her it was their own decision to go.

Michael himself felt different. He'd tormented himself over David's death ever since that fateful day in Munich. The faux funeral was a turning point, and from that moment he vowed to live his life as best he could in memory of his brother, and he'd made a promise over the empty coffin that he'd stop moping around and get back to living, which is what David would have wanted.

The recent secret mission to Germany, while not a complete success, had achieved many things for him. For one, he got to see David's makeshift grave, and as the tears poured onto his grass covered resting place, Michael came to terms with what had happened.

Although unforeseen, sitting with David again had been enormously healing for him, and he'd reconciled with David's memory so that he himself could carry on living.

He'd visited Mina, the German girl who stole his heart when she sheltered him from the Nazis during his great escape. She had endured so much, and although he hated what she had been through, Michael was relieved to see her alive and still in love with him.

Whatever happened during the war, he would find her after it was over and ask her to marry him.

Working with Unit 317 had given him purpose, and although he'd considered, and even tried, to hand in his notice to Captain Sanders, he was glad he hadn't. Every able-bodied man in Britain would be required to do his duty, and Michael knew what he had to do.

Even if it killed him.

The secret appointment with the king had buoyed all

their spirits, and now Michael was the proud recipient of the Military Medal, a high honour indeed for one so young.

He was also a captain in the Intelligence Corps, although he didn't have a clue what significance, if any, that meant for him. No doubt he'd find out as the inevitable war played itself out.

That morning, they all sat huddled around the radio, anticipating and eager to hear the words of Neville Chamberlain, the British prime minister. Even Warhurst, their trusty old butler, stood in the room, looking as nervous as Michael had ever seen him.

As 11.15am approached, the room fell silent. The air felt thick with anticipation and fear, and although everyone knew what was coming, hearing the prime minister speak would bring it home with waves of fear and trepidation.

The radio crackled, and all eyes fell on the dial, waiting for the words everybody in Britain dreaded. For the older ones, this was the second time it had happened, and Michael felt pangs of sorrow for his parents, Gigi, and Warhurst.

Especially Gigi.

The radio suddenly burst into life. Judith gasped and grabbed Michael's arm. Gigi got hold of his other arm and squeezed tightly. Michael felt the blood drain from his face as Chamberlain's sultry tones crackled over the airways.

This morning the British Ambassador in Berlin handed the German Government a final note stating that unless we heard from them by eleven o'clock that they were prepared at once to withdraw their troops from Poland, a state of war would exist between us.

I have to tell you now that no such undertaking has been received, and that consequently, this country is at war with Germany.

You can imagine what a bitter blow it is to me that all my long struggle to win peace has failed. Yet I cannot believe that there is anything more or anything different that I could have done and that would have been more successful.

Up to the very last it would have been quite possible to have arranged a peaceful and honourable settlement between Germany and Poland, but Hitler would not have it.

He had evidently made up his mind to attack Poland whatever happened, and although he now says he put forward reasonable proposals which were rejected by the Poles, that is not a true statement. The proposals were never shown to the Poles, nor to us, and, although they were announced in a German broadcast on Thursday night, Hitler did not wait to hear comments on them, but ordered his troops to cross the Polish frontier.

His action shows convincingly that there is no chance of expecting that this man will ever give up his practice of using force to gain his will. He can only be stopped by force.

We and France are today, in fulfilment of our obligations, going to the aid of Poland, who is so bravely resisting this wicked and unprovoked attack on her people. We have a clear conscience. We have done all that any country could do to establish peace. The situation in which no word given by Germany's ruler could be trusted and no people or country could feel themselves safe has become intolerable. And now that we have resolved to finish it, I know that you will all play your part with calmness and courage.

At such a moment as this, the assurances of support that we have received from the Empire are a source of profound encouragement to us.

The government have made plans under which it will be possible to carry on the work of the nation in the days of stress and strain that may be ahead. But these plans need your help. You may be taking your part in the fighting services or as a volunteer in one of the branches of Civil Defence. If so, you will report for duty in accordance with the instructions you have received. You may be engaged in work essential to the prosecution of war for the maintenance of the life of the people – in factories, in transport, in public utility concerns, or in the supply of other necessaries of life. If so, it is of vital importance that you should carry on with your jobs.

Now may God bless you all. May He defend the right. It is the evil things that we shall be fighting against – brute force, bad faith, injustice, oppression and persecution – and against them I am certain that the right will prevail.

Gerald reached forward and turned the crackling radio off. His face painted a picture of how Michael knew everyone felt, not just in this room, but all over the country and indeed the world.

"We all knew it was coming." Michael finally broke the awkward silence. "It's not like it's a big surprise."

Gerald shook his head. "It seems like only yesterday we declared war the first time around. Even though we knew it was coming, we all hoped Hitler would see sense and pull back."

"You thought that lunatic would pull back?" Gigi snorted. "You've heard his speeches as much as I have. He was never going to stop."

"For some of us, the war started a year ago," Michael said softly, his mind drifting back to Munich and the apartment where so much death had happened right in front of him.

"So, what happens now?" Judith asked.

"Every man and woman must do their duty," Gerald replied. "Those of us who are older will keep the home fires burning and the younger ones will go off to war, just like before." He bowed his head as the terrible memories of the trenches creased the lines of his face.

"Women will be required to work the factories to do the jobs men normally do." Dorothy's voice was shaky. "Just like we did before, so our men can die at the hands of a crazed madman in Berlin."

"Can we beat them?" Judith asked, gripping Michael's

arm even tighter. "From what the newsreels show, the German army looks almost invincible."

"We beat them before and we'll beat them again," Gerald said. "But the loss of life will be unbearable."

"What about you, Michael?" Judith asked. "What will they have you doing?"

"I don't know, but I'm sure I'll be recalled for service soon. I know they told me to take a good break after I got back from Germany, but this changes everything. For all of us."

"How are you doing, Warhurst?" Michael craned his neck to look at their long-standing butler who'd been standing at the back of the room in silence the whole time.

"I'm fine, Master Michael. It's your generation I worry about. I remember what it was like the last time, and I wouldn't wish that on my worst enemy. I'm sorry for each and every one of you on both sides, because I refuse to believe that everyday Germans want this war any more than we do."

"Well said," Gerald replied. "I couldn't agree with you more."

Silence fell over the room as everyone got lost in their own thoughts. Michael's drifted across the continent to a farm on the edge of the Black Forest called Ryskamp and the beautiful girl who lived there.

He closed his eyes and sighed at the memories of her soft touch and how her warm smile melted his heart.

Please take care of yourself and your family. More than anything else, I hope you survive this war and will wait for me on the other side, because if I survive, and that's a big if, I'm coming to get you so we can be together for the rest of our lives. Just, please don't die.

The silence was deafening, so Michael pulled free from Judith's death grip and jumped to his feet.

"I'm going for a run."

Chapter 4

The rail service between Canterbury and London Victoria was nonstop, and at around two hours, was a faster, more direct route than it would have been from Sandwich, which involved changing trains and making more stops along the way.

So it was that Warhurst drove Gerald and Michael in the pre-dawn hours to Canterbury railway station for their first-class, direct route to London rail journey ahead of a meeting with Alistair Hargreaves, Britain's premier numismatist at the British Museum in Russell Square.

Hargreaves had been instrumental in helping Gerald with the Brasher Doubloon and had been more than excited when its discovery was first presented to him.

The atmosphere on the drive to Canterbury was sombre and tense. Warhurst looked pale and troubled, and Michael doubted he'd slept the previous night, which didn't help with the current driving conditions.

A blackout had been declared across the nation on September 1, which meant that all streetlights were turned off, and vehicle headlights had to be fitted with covers to dim them and reduce their visibility.

The order was to be strictly enforced and civil wardens were recruited to patrol the streets to ensure compliance. Anyone found violating the order, which happened a lot over the first few days, was issued with a fine for violating the law.

Accidents were already on the increase, and as would happen in any society, the lack of light encouraged a rise in the crime rate. The first thing Gerald did when the order was made was to hire two burly ex-police officers to patrol their home to make sure they were safe.

After what they had just been through, they couldn't stand the thought of anything else happening.

The journey was slow, as befitting a driver who couldn't see more than a few feet ahead. Several times, Warhurst had to swerve around parked vehicles and pedestrians wandering around doing who knows what in the early hours of the morning.

Gerald sat in the back with his leg across the back seat. He was restless, and no matter how many times he moved and shuffled around, he never seemed to get comfortable.

He too, looked pale and drawn. In fact, Michael assumed that few people in Britain had got a good night's sleep after the news the day before.

How could they?

He knew, though, that war wasn't the only thing on Gerald's mind at this early hour. Alistair Hargreaves held the future of the Fernsby family's fortunes in his grasp, and his words that morning would either make or break them for generations to come.

Hargreaves, as Britain's foremost expert on rare coins, had taken possession of the Brasher Doubloon after Michael brought it back from Germany. Gerald had decided that the British Museum, and the vaunted Alistair Hargreaves, was the place where they would be best served to discover the truth about the coin's authenticity.

All they'd heard were the stories passed down from the Guttmann family over the generations. Who knew if they were true or not? Now that Michael had found it and brought it into the open, the stories that had become a legend in the Guttmann family were about to be exposed as either truth or fantasy.

And the entire future of the Fernsby family rested on the outcome.

No wonder his father was pale and worried. Michael just hoped his heart didn't give out before the meeting took place later that morning.

He spent the one-hour drive talking to Warhurst, keeping him awake. More than once he caught him dozing off at the wheel, and although he offered to drive, the ever-proud Warhurst refused.

As dawn broke and daylight returned sanity to the streets of Britain, Warhurst dropped the tired travellers off outside the railway station in Canterbury.

"What will you do until we return?" Michael asked him.

"I was thinking of driving back to Sandwich, Master Michael. It won't be as bad in daylight, and I have chores to do when I get there."

"No, you don't," Michael said firmly, handing over an envelope with some money in it. "I am ordering you to take the day off and find a hotel somewhere close by. Get some rest and meet us here this afternoon. It will be dark when we drive home and you need to get some sleep, so you won't kill us all."

Warhurst hesitated and looked at Gerald, who smiled and nodded at his long-serving butler. "Michael is right.

Don't worry about Sandwich, just take care of yourself and get some rest. We'll be back later and then we can all go home together."

"Very well, sir. Thank you." Warhurst nodded his head and smiled at Michael.

The train ride was as sombre as the car journey had been. Gerald stretched out his leg across the seat in the first-class carriage and tried getting as comfortable as he could. He spread out his copy of *The Times* in front of him and spent the next forty-five minutes reading the news.

Michael dozed off. He was tired of the headlines, which were, unsurprisingly, all about the declaration of war and what it meant to Britain and its allies.

As he drifted off, his mind focused on the speech he'd heard late the previous afternoon. The radio address by King George VI aroused more patriotism and national pride than Michael had ever imagined he possessed.

Like everyone else, he knew the very public issues the king had with his speech impediment, and he'd heard it first-hand just a few short weeks earlier. And yet, in some strange way, the very thing that was a major cause of embarrassment for the king garnered him great sympathy from the people, endearing him to the British public and bringing home the fact that he had problems and issues just like everyone else.

Coupled with the way he ascended to the throne, being thrown under the bus, so to speak, by his elder brother, King Edward VIII, when he abdicated to marry the American divorcee, Wallis Simpson in 1936, King George VI was close to the hearts of many Britons, and Michael felt a special connection to him after unexpectedly receiving the awards from him a few weeks earlier.

The first few words from the king had resonated with Michael, and he played them over and over in his mind as he lay back with his eyes closed. Perhaps it was the awkward silences as the king fought for the words, or maybe it was the emotion he portrayed as he said them.

Whatever it was, the king's speech penetrated Michael's heart and filled it with pride and the will to fight for his country against the tyrannical madman in Berlin who threatened Europe in a manner nobody had since the days of Napoleon.

In this grave hour, perhaps the most fateful in our history, I send to every household of my peoples, both at home and overseas, this message, spoken with the same depth of feeling for each one of you as if I were able to cross your threshold and speak to you myself.

For the second time in the lives of most of us, we are at war.

The opening words of his speech played over and over in Michael's head, and he drifted off to sleep, happy and proud to be in a position to be able to play his small part in saving the country from the ravages of Nazism.

His father woke him, calling his name repeatedly. "Michael, wake up. Can you hear me? Wake up!"

Michael stirred. "Are we in London?"

"Not yet, but we're close. Have you read the paper today?"

"No. I heard enough last night, and I don't want to read the doom and gloom again today. I know we're at war, and it'll become obvious to everyone in the country soon enough when German bombers are pounding us into submission."

"You underestimate the RAF, but that's not why I was asking you."

"What is it then? What's in there that isn't about the war?"

"Not much, to be honest."

"That's why I didn't read it."

"Did you hear about the passenger ship last night?" Gerald ignored his son and continued. "It's terrible."

"A passenger ship? No, what happened?"

"According to the newspaper, the Athenia was heading for Canada from Glasgow… no, let me read this properly. It left Glasgow, went to Ireland, and then Liverpool. It left Liverpool and headed out across the Atlantic for Canada."

"What happened to it? Surely you aren't going to tell me it was attacked and sunk last night, are you?"

"Unfortunately, that's exactly what I'm telling you. Nobody knows exactly what happened yet, but apparently it was out in the Atlantic when it suddenly exploded. From what the paper says, unlike the Titanic, most of the passengers got off safely, but they are anticipating several hundred or more are dead."

"What happened to it?" Michael asked. "I'm sure it didn't hit an iceberg out there. Was it the Germans?"

"They don't know for sure." Gerald furrowed his eyebrows as he squinted at the small print on the page. "They think it was a U-boat that did it. When you think about it, it couldn't really be anything else."

"Why would a U-boat sink a passenger ship?" Michael asked. "What could they possibly gain from that?"

"The U-boats were a major problem in the last war, and they nearly brought Britain to its knees. My guess is that they'll use them to great effect in this war and try to destroy us in the Atlantic. If they get the upper hand, we'll lose this war. Just mark my words."

"Are they that dangerous to us?"

"Perhaps more than anything else, including the bombers that will inevitably come. Think about it, Michael. If they sink enough of the merchant ships bringing supplies to our shores, we won't be able to fight them. The entire fate of the war could be decided in the Atlantic. We simply have to defeat the U-boats."

"That's a frightening proposition, but it doesn't explain why they attacked a passenger ship." Michael shook his head. "I know from experience how cruel and uncaring the Nazis are, but surely even they wouldn't attack innocent people like that?"

"Germany has remained silent so far, and they'll probably deny it when they do speak about it, but I am in no doubt it was a U-boat that did it. They are deadly, Michael. Deadly and dangerous."

"I feel for the passengers, and I hope not too many died out there." Michael closed his eyes as he felt the pain of the incident wash over him. "I hope the Royal Navy does its duty and protects our shipping from the U-boat menace before it gets too bad."

"I do too. I'm sure the PM will say something about it in his address to parliament today."

"He should. The Nazis need to know that we won't tolerate them attacking passenger ships for no reason. There must be repercussions for their actions."

"They've done it before." Gerald looked up and stared at his son as he remembered the events of the First World War. "A U-boat sank the Lusitania in 1915. Over a thousand people perished in that attack, and it led to a large public outcry against the Germans. Hopefully, not as many died in the attack on the Athenia, but I hope it brings the same public outcry."

Michael opened his mouth to speak, but a penetrating whistle from outside the train told him they were entering the packed Victoria station. It was time to meet their moment of destiny.

Chapter 5

Gerald fell silent, his face even paler than before. The forty-minute taxi ride to Russell Square was taken in silence, both men lost in their thoughts.

For Michael, it was a mixture of excitement and trepidation about the upcoming meeting, and he was sure his father was feeling the same. There was more riding on the outcome for Gerald, as he was the one who'd overseen the loss of the shipping business during the Great Depression when he'd been forced to sell it to his hated rival, Sir Robert Stourcliffe.

It was Gerald who had presided over the demise of their once powerful brewing empire which now sat on the brink of collapse, and it was Gerald who was threatened with the repossession of their home as the losses mounted and the debt levels had become impossible to manage.

For Gerald Fernsby, the next hour would be one of the most important moments of his life, and the pressure his father faced was not lost on Michael, especially after he added in all the personal turmoil the family had faced over the past year.

Michael squeezed his father's right arm and looked him in the eyes. "Everything is going to be alright, Dad. Whatever happens today, I make enough now to keep the house in Sandwich. Even if the coin is a fake and the stories weren't true, we won't be homeless."

Gerald threw a weak smile towards his son. "Nice try, Michael, but you know as well as I do what's riding on this. My heart can't stand much more of it, so let's get in there and get it over with."

Michael helped his father up the steps of the British Museum and stopped at the top to admire the Romanesque pillars and elaborate figures carved above them. He was imagining columns of Roman legions marching down the ancient streets of Londinium when his father poked him in the ribs.

"Before you make the mistake of thinking this is Roman, it isn't. It's themed on the Greek Empire, and it wasn't built until the middle of the last century. It's impressive, though, don't you think?"

"It's incredible," Michael answered, craning his neck so he could see the figures carved high above his head. "I can't wait to see what's inside."

"It holds one of the largest collections of ancient artefacts in the world, including the Rosetta Stone, carved in 196BC! It was that discovery that allowed us to finally decipher the Egyptian hieroglyphics."

"How did it end up in London?" Michael asked.

"We took it from Napoleon after we defeated him in Egypt over a hundred years ago. Now it's all in danger of being destroyed by Nazi bombers."

Gerald shook his head, his cheeks flushed bright red. "I'm sure they have made contingency plans to protect their priceless artefacts, but I find it sad that we've come to this in our lifetimes. Like everyone else in my generation, we hoped the last war would be the war to end all wars."

"It was supposed to have been that way," Michael said. "The peace has only lasted twenty-one years, so what does that say about us and our generation?"

"It doesn't say anything. This is all down to the whims of one man who, like Napoleon before him, wants to rule the world. We have no choice other than to stand against him so that others in the future can be free of tyranny. I only hope that we are strong enough to survive it this time."

"Come on," Michael said, gripping his father's arm tighter. "Like you said, let's get this over with."

After finding the information desk, the two men were led down a series of narrow corridors that led deep into the bowels of the museum.

Gerald struggled with the steps, and Michael couldn't help him because of the narrowness of the stairways.

"Excuse the mess, gentlemen," the lady escorting them to their destination told them. "The museum is undergoing major changes because of the war."

"Will it remain open?" Michael asked, genuinely interested. He loved history, especially historical architecture, and he could have explored this magnificent building all day if the circumstances were different.

"To the public? I believe so, but in a much more limited capacity. There won't be a lot to see because our most important artefacts have already been removed and safely stored somewhere else."

"What about the Rosetta Stone?" Gerald asked. "Is that still here?"

"Oh no," the lady laughed. "That was the first thing we moved. Please don't ask where, because even I don't know where they took it. It's a secret."

"I'm glad they moved it," Gerald said. "It would be a travesty if we lost priceless artefacts to the senseless bombing that is surely coming our way."

"I certainly hope not," the lady replied sternly. "The Germans have nothing to gain by bombing our cities. And if they do, we'll bomb theirs in return, so I think we're all perfectly safe from any of that nonsense."

Gerald glanced at his son and gave him a wry smile. Michael nodded back, understanding what he meant. The people of Britain needed hope, and they needed to believe they would be safe in their beds at night.

Eventually, the lady stopped outside a closed door in the dimly lit corridor. She knocked and waited with Gerald and Michael until the door opened.

A tall, middle-aged man with a head full of grey hair combed back over his head stood before them. He wore gold-rimmed glasses that made his eyes look a lot bigger than they really were, and Michael suppressed a smile when he looked at him.

He's the wise old owl!

"Good morning, gentlemen. It's good to see you again, Mr Fernsby." The man had a deep, guttural voice that wouldn't have sounded out of place reading BBC's world news on the radio.

He turned to Michael. "I'm Alistair Hargreaves and I've been looking forward to this meeting. You must be the young man who found the Brasher Doubloon?" Hargreaves asked, looking at Michael.

Gerald indicated towards his son. "This is indeed the man who found the doubloon. Please allow me to introduce you to my son, Captain Michael Fernsby."

As the men shook hands, Michael reflected on his father's introduction. It was the first time he'd ever been introduced as Captain Michael Fernsby and it felt strange, as if it was somebody else they were talking about, not him.

I guess I'd better get used to it.

Alistair Hargreaves waited until the lady left and then turned to Gerald and Michael. "Please, come with me. My office is being used to store all kinds of documents that are about to be removed for storage and there isn't much room, I'm afraid. We'll be much more comfortable in the conference room up the hall."

Hargreaves led the way along the narrow hallway, taking the time to slow down to allow the struggling Gerald Fernsby to keep up. Michael walked behind his father, ready to catch him if he stumbled.

Five minutes later, Hargreaves opened the door to a large room that was bathed in light from the expansive windows. Michael shielded his eyes for a moment while they got used to the change.

Gerald's forehead was covered in sweat and Michael could see that he was exhausted from the effort. His heart sank as he saw his father struggle to carry out the everyday tasks most healthy people took for granted. He tried helping him to his chair, but his father refused, as stubborn as ever.

Michael took the seat next to his father as Hargreaves sat opposite. He waited patiently as Hargreaves pulled a box from his pocket and gasped when the contents were revealed.

It was the Brasher Doubloon! He hadn't seen it since handing it to his father after his mission in Germany weeks earlier.

Seeing it brought back all the memories of the fateful operation, and try as he might, he couldn't get the blood-stained images of Friedrich Halmer and Karl Lutz out of his head.

The Brasher Doubloon looked different and Michael stared at it, trying to work out what had changed. Then he realised: probably for the first time in decades, perhaps even centuries, the coin had been cleaned and polished.

Michael glanced at his father, who stared at the doubloon like it was the Lost Ark of the Covenant. To him, it probably was.

"Captain Fernsby..." Hargreaves broke the silence, staring at Michael. "Tell me again how you came across the doubloon?"

"May I?" Michael reached for the coin, ignoring the question.

"Absolutely. It's yours to do with whatever you desire."

Michael took the coin from the box and held it in his hand. Once again, vivid memories of how he found it flooded back, and he forced them away with images of his beloved Mina melting his heart with her smile on her farm in Bavaria.

He stared at the inscriptions that were much clearer now it was clean and shiny. On one side, an eagle clutched an olive branch in one claw while holding a set of arrows in the other. The initials EB stood out to the left of the eagle, telling the world who had made the coin way back in 1787.

Ephraim Brasher.

On the other side, he saw the sun rising over a series of mountains, and he studied the words, so much clearer now:

NOVA EBORACA COLUMBIA EXCELSIOR.

New York in America.

As far as Michael was concerned, this was the real deal. He looked at his father, who refused to handle the coin. Instead, he stared at it as though his life depended on it, which in many ways it did.

"Well?" Gerald's voice croaked as the words struggled to leave his throat. "Is it genuine?"

Michael's heart thumped in his chest and he was sure Hargreaves could hear it across the conference table. Sweat broke out all over him, leaving his body clammy and damp. Even his legs felt strange and wobbly as he waited for the words that would either make or break the Fernsby family.

Hargreaves stared at them both in turn, milking the moment as much as he could. Michael wanted to reach over and shake him, but he didn't.

He again glanced at his father, who by now had sweat running down his face and neck. He was a strange shade of grey, and Michael was genuinely worried his heart was about to give up.

"Sir," Michael turned to Hargreaves. "Our family has a lot riding on this. Although we only recently heard about it, the German side of our family has held this secret for centuries."

His eyes held the gaze of Hargreaves as he spoke. "You know the stories as well as we do, but that's all they are, stories. Did Brasher really mint an eighth coin and give it to his friend? Or is it all a sham and the coin's a fake? Please tell us, because I don't believe my father's heart can take much more."

Hargreaves cocked his head and looked Michael up and down. "I've heard the story of how you came across the coin, but I'd like to hear it straight from the horse's mouth, so to speak. Tell me, Captain Fernsby, exactly how did you find the doubloon?"

"Not until you tell us what we came here for." Michael was losing patience with Alistair Hargreaves.

Hargreaves sighed. "Very well, if you insist."

To prolong the drama, he looked over at Gerald. "I know this means a lot to you, Mr Fernsby, but tell me…"

"Tell us what we want to know!" Michael cut him off. "Now, Mr Hargreaves."

"Please," he added in a gentler tone.

Hargreaves smiled and cocked his head again. "I can see why you are so formidable for one so young, Captain Fernsby. Very well, I'll tell you what you wish to know, and then you must promise me you will tell me how you found it."

He raised his eyebrows at Michael and paused, waiting for his response.

"Agreed. Now please, tell us if it's genuine or not."

Gerald reached over and gripped Michael's arm. Michael could hear his rasping breath emanating from his chest.

"Please, Mr Hargreaves, before my father has a heart attack!"

Hargreaves leant back in his chair and crossed his hands. He looked Gerald in the eyes and broke into a wide grin.

"We compared your doubloon against one of the seven known ones. The owner of this doubloon kindly allowed us to use it as a source of reference. I can tell you that after an extensive investigation by me and my team, your doubloon is the genuine article. Mr Fernsby, your son uncovered a previously unknown and uncirculated eighth Brasher Doubloon. Congratulations."

Silence filled the room for a moment as it sank in. Michael bellowed like a moose, or at least that was how he'd describe it later. Gerald stared at Hargreaves as though frozen in time.

Tears fell down his face, and it broke Michael's heart to

see his father so shocked. He placed his hand over his father's and squeezed.

"Everything will be alright," he said softly.

Gerald sprang to life. "Tell me again, Mr Hargreaves. Did you say it was genuine?"

"I did, Mr Fernsby. Congratulations."

"How much is it worth?" Michael asked the inevitable question.

"A coin as rare as this? Considering it was previously unknown and therefore changes everything we ever knew about Ephraim Brasher's doubloons, I'd say that you are sitting on a king's ransom."

"What does that mean?" Gerald squeaked.

"It means that whatever financial issues you may or may not be having, this doubloon will solve all of them and keep your family safe for generations to come. If you're sensible, of course."

Gerald, his eyes full of tears, turned to his son and clasped his hands in his. "You did it, Michael. You saved our family."

Before he could respond, Hargreaves cleared his throat. "Now it's your turn, Captain Fernsby. Tell me how you found it."

Chapter 6

Michael spent the next ten minutes giving Alistair Hargreaves a watered-down version of how he found the Brasher Doubloon in the Nazi doctor's home in Munich.

He left out the gory details and avoided any mention of Gustav Adler and the real reason he was in Germany in the last days before the war broke out.

After he'd finished, Hargreaves sat back and once again crossed his hands together.

"That's an interesting story, young man. However, I don't believe you have told me everything that happened. If you're worried about security, let me assure you that I am well trusted by His Majesty's government. In my capacity as numismatist to the British Museum, I am the curator of many pieces of information that would damage the country should they ever get out."

"That may well be the case, Mr Hargreaves, and I am grateful for your loyalty to our nation, but much of what I do is bound by the Official Secrets Act, as I am sure you must be too. So, you know I cannot discuss the reason I was in Germany."

Hargreaves paused and stared at Michael for longer than was comfortable, but Michael's eyes never left his. Eventually, Hargreaves looked away, and he broke into a smile.

"Your youth belies your maturity. Whatever it was you were doing over there, I am sure it was dangerous and that you risked your life for king and country. Please let me be one of the first to thank you for your service, because God knows we're going to need brave men and women like you if we're going to win this war."

"Thank you, Mr Hargreaves. And we are grateful to you for keeping our national treasures safe."

"What do we do next?" Gerald changed the conversation. "We want to sell the doubloon, so in your capacity as a numismatist, can you recommend a good place for us to start?"

"Actually, I can. During our investigations into the doubloon's authenticity, I received a few enquiries from well-heeled clients as to what your plans would be should the doubloon prove to be authentic."

"Really?" Gerald looked surprised. "Who were they?"

"As you know, Mr Fernsby, families of a certain level of wealth prefer to conduct their business out of the public eye. They would rather keep whatever agreement you come to between yourselves, if you know what I mean."

"I know exactly what you mean," Gerald said. "The less anyone knows about it, the better. I am perfectly happy with such arrangements. In fact, that's my preferred method of doing business as well."

"Very good. We can proceed then, as that was their biggest demand."

"I have one stipulation," Michael interjected. "And as I found the doubloon, this is not negotiable."

Hargreaves raised his eyebrows and his father looked at

him in horror. Michael knew his father had to sell the doubloon if he was going to save the family and their business from financial disaster, but there were some things more important than money, and this was one of them.

"What would that be?" Hargreaves asked.

"Under no circumstances is the Brasher Doubloon to be sold to Robert Stourcliffe or anyone associated with him. I will not have that stuck-up snob holding that over us as well as our shipping business. I'd rather die in poverty than allow that ferret to get his hands on it."

His father suppressed a wry chuckle, which broke the tension in the room. Hargreaves laughed and shook his head.

"Ironically, Sir Robert was one of the first to enquire, but I told him it was doubtful you would sell to him. Your spat is well known, as is the reason you were expelled from Cambridge University last year. After being on the wrong end of Sir Robert's sense of entitlement many times, I must admit to enjoying the stories of how you roughed up his equally entitled offspring."

Michael smirked at Hargreaves. "That smack was a long time coming, believe me. I'd do it again in a heartbeat if I got the chance. We can sell the doubloon to anyone else but them."

"Except the Nazis," Gerald corrected his son.

"Except the Nazis." Michael echoed his father's words.

"Gentlemen," Hargreaves leant forward. "The existence of a previously unknown Brasher Doubloon has caused quite a stir. If it wasn't for the war, this discovery would be front-page headlines all over the world."

"I am aware of the interest, Mr Hargreaves," Gerald said. "And from what I gather, it has created great interest in the United States, which is understandable given the doubloon's history."

"Quite," Hargreaves answered. "And ironically, that is where the buyer I have in mind comes from. The family is very private and doesn't want any publicity about this. Depending on what you are asking for it, this family has both the means and the desire to purchase it from you."

"Who is it?" Gerald asked, his voice higher in pitch than a moment before.

Tension filled the room again as the conversation became serious. Hargreaves, who seemed to enjoy the discomfort on Gerald's and Michael's faces, took a while to look at them both as if to emphasise his importance in the matter.

"I will act as a broker for the sale," he said finally. "For a small commission, of course."

"Who pays that?" Michael asked. "And what do you call a small commission?"

"My commission is ten per cent, and it will come from the agreed upon sale price."

"So, we're paying it then." Michael's comment was more of a statement than a question.

"You are free, of course, to make your own arrangements, but I think you will find my commission is standard across the board. I doubt many will have the connections I have made over the years, but that is your choice, Mr Fernsby."

"I know how this works, Hargreaves," Gerald said. "We accept your terms. Who is the buyer?"

"The buyer wishes to remain anonymous, but if you were to assume it might be a wealthy American family, I wouldn't deny it."

"What valuation would you place on a coin so rare and valuable?" Gerald asked.

Hargreaves sighed. "It is difficult to place a monetary value on such a rarity, Mr Fernsby, because the value ultimately lies in the amount a collector is willing to pay. But something like this would fetch a lot of money, so I wouldn't ask less than forty to fifty thousand pounds if it were mine."

Michael let out a low whistle. "That's serious money. There aren't many who could afford it."

The blood drained from Gerald's face once more. "Fifty thousand pounds?" he asked. "That's far more than I imagined it would be worth. I was thinking more like twenty thousand. Twenty-five at most."

"Fifty thousand is at the top end, I must admit, but it's somewhere in that region," Hargreaves said.

"The average annual wage for factory workers is less than three hundred pounds." Michael's voice was hushed. "Even the PM only gets around ten thousand a year, so this is a lot of money by any standards."

Gerald cleared his throat and spoke slowly and clearly. "Tell the Astors, or the Du Ponts or whoever your client is, that we will accept not a penny less than fifty thousand pounds. And they are to pay half of the commission as well. If they agree, then we will agree to the sale."

"Mr Fernsby, that is on the top side of the valuation. I would recommend a little flexibility in your negotiations if you want a successful sale."

"No negotiations." Gerald held firm. "The price is fifty thousand plus half of the commission. If your client doesn't accept, then I will take my business elsewhere."

"You drive a hard bargain, Mr Fernsby. I will relay your offer to my client and I will be in touch in the next few days."

"Thank you for your time, Mr Hargreaves. My family appreciates the outstanding work you have done for us." Gerald struggled to his feet. "Now, if you'll excuse me, I need to get home so I can rest."

The men shook hands, and as they filed out of the conference room, Alistair Hargreaves whispered in Michael's ear. "I am good friends with Claude Dansey, and although he doesn't talk about his work, when I mentioned you were coming to see me, he smiled and said that I should be glad you are on our side. Whatever you are, young Michael Fernsby, please know that *I am* glad you are on our side."

Michael smiled. "Thank you, Mr Hargreaves. I appreciate your kind words. However, I believe we will all need each other by the end of this war. It's going to be long and difficult, and if we are to beat the Nazis, it will take a great effort from every one of us. We're all in this together. You, me, and every single man, woman and child in this country."

Alistair Hargreaves bowed his head. "I will be in touch, gentlemen. I wish you a safe journey home."

Chapter 7

The journey home was a mad dash to beat the sunset. British weather is famously grey and overcast, and some days it seems as if it never gets fully daylight. This was one of those days, and by the time their train pulled into Canterbury, it was already showing signs of dusk.

Warhurst was waiting for them, and he made sure the headlights were fully covered before beginning the dangerous drive home.

Michael likened driving in the blackout to being on the dodgem cars at a fairground, where adults and children alike purposely drove at each other as fast as they could with wild excitement on their faces.

Warhurst dodged and weaved through the streets at a snail's pace, but eventually he got the two weary men home in time for a late dinner.

They ate in silence, but the looks and fidgeting of the ladies left nobody in doubt what they wanted.

As soon as Gerald placed his fork onto his empty plate, Dorothy piled into him. "For God's sake, Gerald. You've kept us waiting far too long. I was expecting a telephone call from London, so spit it out, man, and tell us what happened. Is the Brasher Doubloon real or not?"

Gigi remained calm and stoic, but Michael could tell that behind her demeanour, she was as anxious as Dorothy and Judith to know what they had found out.

Gerald cleared his throat. "I'm sorry, I was starving. It's good news," he said. "The Brasher Doubloon is genuine."

Noise erupted as everyone spoke at once. Dorothy, with tears flowing freely down her face, ran to her husband and threw her arms around him.

Judith did the same with Michael, and even Gigi grabbed the tablecloth and squeezed tightly.

Gerald held his arm in the air and winced as pain shot through his shoulder. He quickly lowered his arm and rubbed his aching body.

Michael felt sorry for him, because after all the family had been through over the past year, this was a rare moment of triumph and Gerald wasn't able to enjoy it like he should because of his broken body.

His mind briefly cast back to the accident Maureen Ingram's treasonous group of Blackshirts had instigated. The driver of the vehicle that almost killed his father had been captured alive after Michael and Captain Sanders rescued Judith from their clutches, and Michael wondered how the interrogation was going.

He'd wanted to be involved in the man's questioning, but Sanders had deemed him too close to the matter after Judith's kidnapping. Dansey ordered Michael to go home and rest while Unit 317 took care of the traitor.

His father's cheerful voice pulled him back to the present, and he stared at his beaming face holding a glass in the air as a toast to their good fortune.

"The Brasher Doubloon is not only genuine," he told the excited group staring at him. "But we also have a buyer."

"Who?" Dorothy asked.

"How much?" Gigi asked at the same time.

"They wish to remain anonymous, but we believe it's one of the wealthy American families. It makes sense, seeing as the coin originated in America."

Gerald paused and looked at his wife before breaking into the happiest smile Michael had seen since he and David left for Germany all those eventful months ago.

David! Michael's heart dropped as he thought of how much he missed his brother at this moment. He'd have loved this.

"The numismatist valued the doubloon… Are you waiting for this?"

"Get on with it, Gerald, and stop teasing us." Dorothy playfully slapped her husband. "What's it worth?"

"He valued it between forty and fifty."

Michael smiled. He knew his father was teasing his family. He enjoyed seeing his playful side again.

"Forty to fifty pounds?" Dorothy looked downhearted.

"Forty to fifty *thousand.*" Gerald emphasised the thousand.

Dorothy's jaw dropped.

"I told Hargreaves we wouldn't accept a penny less than fifty thousand, and the buyer has to pay half the commission, which is ten per cent."

"So, we get forty-seven thousand, five-hundred pounds?" Dorothy's eyes were wider than the saucer beneath her teacup.

"If the buyer agrees," Gerald said. "Hargreaves said he'll call us in a few days with their answer."

"What if they refuse?" Gigi asked. "Surely you agreed to negotiate with them?"

"I did not." Gerald looked at his mother. "Hargreaves stands to make five thousand pounds from this sale. He doesn't need any more incentive to keep the price as high as he can."

"But what if the buyers refuse?" Judith asked. "That's a lot of money, even for them."

"I told Hargreaves that if they declined our offer, I would take my business elsewhere and find a different broker. That made him sit up and take note."

"I hope you didn't ask for too much," Gigi said.

"We'll find out, won't we," Gerald answered. "The worst-case scenario is that we find a different broker and accept a little less for the doubloon. Either way, we win."

Michael rose to his feet. "I propose a toast," he said.

All eyes turned to him as he looked at the empty seat across the table.

"To David, who would have loved this. He is still here with us in spirit, even if he can't be here in person."

Everyone's faces looked solemn as they raised their glasses. "To David," they all said in unison.

"I wish he was here," Judith pawed at her cheek. "I really miss him."

"We all miss him," Dorothy said. "But he's here. I can feel him."

They all raised their glasses one more time to their missing son, grandson, and brother.

"Now, if you'll excuse me," Gerald said. "It's been a long day and my body is about to give out on me."

"One more thing…" Gigi stood up. "What happened to the doubloon? You didn't leave it with the broker, did you?"

"Do you think I'm stupid?" Gerald asked his mother.

"Of course not. It's right here in my pocket and it's going to the bank vault first thing tomorrow morning."

Gerald limped off to bed with Dorothy right behind him. Judith went to her room and Michael could hear her playing up the stairs with Lucy, their black Labrador who had become her faithful companion ever since Michael had brought the dog home after taking it from Robert Stourcliffe Junior for neglecting and beating the animal.

Michael retired to his room and reflected on what the day meant to his family and how the sale of the doubloon would change their fortunes.

As he drifted off to sleep, his mind focused on Germany and a mixture of David's resting place and Mina's beautiful smile. How he longed for them both, and in his half-awake state, he reached out to them.

What came back at him forced him to sit bolt upright and gulp large lungfuls of air. Instead of reaching either David or Mina, he saw the tall, angry features of Albert Kreise, the Gestapo chief who had almost captured him at the railway station in Ravensburg.

He would be dead if it wasn't for the brave woman from the resistance who had given her life so he could escape.

Michael never knew her real name. All he knew was her codename: Mother. And yet she had saved his life and given him the means to escape Germany with a briefcase full of Nazi secrets.

Whoever she was, Michael would never forget the brave sacrifice Mother had made for him.

Kreise's image wouldn't leave him, so he focused his mind towards the one place that always seemed to soothe him when the nightmares became too much: Ryskamp, the picturesque farmhouse on the edges of the Black Forest in

Bavaria, and the beautiful German girl who had stolen his heart.

He said a prayer that she was happy and safe, and as he drifted off to sleep, he kept his mind focused on her and refused to allow the evil Gestapo agent to invade his thoughts.

Chapter 8

Early the following morning, the shrill ring of the telephone in the spacious hallway of the Fernsby home in Sandwich caught everyone off-guard. By the time Gerald struggled to his feet from his study, Dorothy was already picking up the receiver and yelling into the mouthpiece.

"The Fernsby residence. This is Dorothy Fernsby. To whom am I speaking?"

Judith led the charge to the hallway, with Michael not far behind. He'd have beaten her to it if he hadn't tripped over Lucy half a dozen times as she ran between his feet, making him stumble.

Lucy thought it was a game, and her loud barks added to the comedy as everyone rushed to hear what the numismatist had to say.

Gigi came down the stairs and reached Dorothy at the same time as Gerald arrived, and they all stood there impatiently, waiting to hear if the buyer had accepted Gerald's terms.

"Oh, yes. Please wait a moment." Dorothy turned, her

features downtrodden and solemn. "It's for you." She looked at Michael. "It's Major Sanders."

Michael felt the bile in his stomach rise to his throat. He'd known the call was coming, but he was hoping for a few more days at least so he could be there when the doubloon was sold. It would be a momentous occasion for the family, and he didn't want to miss it.

"Major Sanders?" Michael asked as he waved everyone away from the hallway. He watched as dejected faces turned and walked away with their heads bowed as if in prayer.

"Did you get a promotion?"

"Good morning, Captain Fernsby. What did you expect? They couldn't really have me running the department at the same rank as the men underneath me, could they? I was promoted the day after you were, albeit in much more humble surroundings."

"Congratulations, Major. To what do I owe the honour?"

He knew, but he wasn't ready to hear it. Not yet.

"It's time, Michael. I'm sorry to cut short your well-earned rest, but we need you back. I'm sure you know that the war is finally here and we need everyone back on duty."

"I understand," Michael answered. "When? Is it the same location as last time?"

"Tomorrow by noon. And we have a new headquarters. I can't tell you over the telephone, but you'll be receiving a letter, hand-delivered by a uniformed soldier from the Intelligence Corps. Follow the directions given and be here no later than noon tomorrow."

"Yes, sir," Michael said. "I'll be there."

"We have a war to win, Captain, and we need to be ready."

"Yes, sir. I'll see you tomorrow."

Michael replaced the receiver and made his way to the sitting room, where he knew everyone was waiting for him.

"You're leaving, aren't you?" His mother couldn't hide the distress in her voice as it wavered and cracked.

"I'm afraid so," Michael said. "Major Sanders needs me back by noon tomorrow. I'm sorry, and I hate to leave again, but you know I have to go."

Dorothy threw her arms around Michael's neck. "Every mother in the country will have to go through this. I'm so proud of you, Michael, and I know how brave you are. But please be careful and take care of yourself. I can't lose another son."

Dorothy broke away, her sobs escaping in loud gasps as she struggled for air.

"We all knew this moment would arrive," his father said from the chair as he struggled to get to his feet. "Now I know how Gigi must have felt when Frank and I were called up in the Great War. I'm so proud, and yet at the same time, I'm frightened for you."

Michael's father looked fatigued and pale. The ordeal of dragging his battered body all the way to London the day before had been too much for him, and he looked tired and in pain.

"I'm sorry to leave you like this, but I'll be back as soon as I can. I'll write, although if you don't hear from me for long periods, don't worry. You know they send me to places where letters are impossible. I'll be back before you know it."

Gigi was about to say something when the shrill tone of the telephone sounded again. Michael was glad, because he was losing control of himself, and the lump in his throat was getting bigger with each breath.

He ran to the hallway and picked up the receiver. "Fernsby residence, Michael speaking."

Several nods and thank yous later, Michael turned to face his family crowded around him.

"Sitting room," he ordered, gesturing to everyone to follow him.

Dorothy's eyes were bright red and puffy as she stood holding onto her son's arm. Judith's eyes, too, looked swollen and red from the tears. Even Gigi looked pale and drawn as she blinked back the tears that fought to escape.

But the one Michael worried the most about was his father, who looked shattered and devastated all in a single expression, if that was even possible. He hoped the news he'd just received would cheer him up.

"Well?" Gigi asked. "Were those your orders for tomorrow?"

"No, they're being delivered by hand later today. That was Alistair Hargreaves, the numismatist."

The room fell silent and all eyes were on Michael.

"The buyer has accepted our offer. Well, almost. They'll pay the fifty thousand, but we have to cover the commission. They want a quick deal and it can be completed as early as next month if we agree to their terms."

"It's a reasonable request, Gerald." Dorothy looked at her husband. "Don't allow your pride to stand in the way of rescuing our family. We need to sell the doubloon, and we need to sell it fast."

"Hargreaves said it was their only offer and we can either take it or leave it," Michael said. "I think we should take it, but the decision is yours, Dad. I told Hargreaves that you would return his call within the hour with your answer."

Now all eyes were on Gerald, and he blinked back at them and scratched at his chin.

"We'll accept the offer," he said at last. "I'll telephone Hargreaves right away and inform him of our decision."

Loud chatter broke out in the room as everyone spoke at once. Michael took the opportunity to back out and retreat to his room for a few moments so he could gather himself for what was to come.

Whatever it was, he knew it would be dangerous, and the chances of him surviving the war were at best slender to none. He changed into his running shoes and headed outside for a run.

Chapter 9

As promised, a uniformed sergeant from the Intelligence Corps arrived at the Fernsby home later that afternoon. After checking Michael's military ID against his papers, he handed over a sealed envelope.

"Sir, Major Sanders requests that you be at the location contained within that document by noon tomorrow. In addition, he ordered me to tell you that the letter is for your eyes only and that nobody else, not even family members, may read the contents."

"I understand, Sergeant. Please inform Major Sanders that I will comply, and that I'll be there tomorrow."

"There's just one more thing, sir," the sergeant said. "You are to travel in civilian clothing and are to sign here that you understand your orders and will adhere to them."

The sergeant handed Michael a clipboard with a document stating what he'd just told him. Michael read it over and signed it. "Is that all?"

"Yes, sir, thank you." The sergeant stepped back and saluted Michael, which took him by surprise as he hadn't been expecting it.

The sergeant got back into his vehicle and drove off, leaving Michael alone with the documents Sanders had sent over.

He went to his room and digested what he had to do the following morning. He gathered his train tickets and placed everything in the rucksack that 'Mother' had given him in Munich.

He put the letter from Sanders into one of the secret compartments and sealed it. Then he threw the few clothes he was taking into a suitcase and stored them at the bottom of his bed.

He was ready.

Dinner, or the last supper as Michael referred to it, felt forced and difficult. Everyone acted as though nothing was different and that the war wasn't changing their lives as it inevitably would for every family in the country.

Nobody spoke a word about Michael leaving and instead focused their attention on the Brasher Doubloon and the ways it would change their lives.

Michael sat back and looked around the dining table at the strained faces, doing their best to show anything other than concern for him going off to war the next morning.

"Come on, people," he said. "Finding and selling a rare coin such as the Brasher Doubloon is a historic event and the money we're getting for it is an enormous amount. We should be sitting here talking about how bright our future is, and instead you look like you sold the doubloon and discovered Stourcliffe swooped in and took all the money from us. Cheer up and celebrate! This is a life-changing event and we should be happy it's happened in our moment of need."

"What good is money when there's a war on?" Dorothy asked. "When the people we love are taken from us? I'd give every penny from that doubloon to have you and David back here with us again. Every single penny."

Her eyes filled up again, and Michael felt helpless as they rolled down her face. "No mother should have to put up with this. I can't stand it."

She rose from her chair and rushed to her son's side. "I don't say this enough, Michael, but I love you very much, so please come back to us when this is all over."

Dorothy's chest heaved with her sobs, and Judith joined her from across the table. Even Gigi's eyes were red and swollen, and Michael fought back the emotion as hard as he could. He didn't want to be an emotional wreck on the last night with his family.

Gerald sat with his eyes closed, fighting back just like Michael was. He threw his hand in the air and pushed himself slowly to his feet. He raised a glass in the air and looked around the room at the solemn faces staring back at him.

"Let's make a promise to ourselves here and now that we'll take great care with the money from the sale of the doubloon so that when Michael returns to us, which he surely will, he will return to a family that is secure and proud of what we have achieved through our times of adversity."

"Cheers!" he roared, raising his glass high in the air.

"Cheers," came the replies and everyone fell silent while they drank.

After dinner, Michael returned to his room and prepared to leave the next morning. He studied the letter from Sanders, taking care to memorise every detail so he wouldn't have to take it out in the middle of London with thousands of people around him.

It was late by the time he finished, so he lay back on his

bed and thought about what he'd been through already in his young life.

I'm still only nineteen and I've lived three lifetimes already!

Whatever lay ahead, he was ready for it. Nothing could be worse than he'd already been through, and the memories of all those he'd lost would never leave him, especially his brother, David. The guilt tormented his soul every night, a feeling he would never lose, no matter how long he lived.

As always, when he closed his eyes to sleep, he pictured Mina in his mind's eye, and for a moment he lost himself as he relived their brief times together. But as always, the tall figure of Albert Kreise invaded his thoughts, and he fought him in the shadows of his mind over and over and over.

However many other victims this war would claim, Michael hoped that Albert Kreise was one of them. Men like him didn't deserve to survive and live as though nothing had happened afterwards.

Albert Kreise had to die.

Chapter 10

Berlin, September 7, 1939

Admiral Ludwig von Ludsecke strode through the corridors of the Bendlerblock building in the heart of the Reich like he owned the place.

At the age of fifty-nine, Admiral Ludsecke carried the weight of a lifetime in the navy. Even in retirement, he remained a figure of unwavering discipline, never stepping outside his home without donning his naval uniform.

Prominently displayed, the Iron Cross took centre stage on his attire, a symbol of his dedication and service. The array of medals adorning his chest stood as a testament to his valour and steadfast commitment to the German navy.

While short in stature at five feet eight, his lack of height starkly contrasted with his oversized ego and sense of entitlement. Born into the Prussian aristocracy, Admiral Ludsecke was used to feeling superior over the masses, which included just about everyone other than the deposed Kaiser Wilhelm II.

On this afternoon, he was in a foul mood after a tongue-lashing from the Führer regarding the recent sinking of a British passenger ship heading to Canada. Hitler left him in no doubt that heads would roll if it transpired that a German U-boat was responsible for the loss of life and the international condemnation that followed.

The Bendlerblock shared office space between several military and intelligence departments, but the one he was aiming for was the Office of the Naval High Command, or the OKM, as it was better known.

"Good morning, Admiral," one brave general said, nodding as they crossed paths in the narrow corridors of military power and prestige.

With his customary disdain for anyone born outside of the Potsdam aristocracy, Admiral Ludsecke sneered at the general and ignored his pleasantries.

"Heil Napoleon!" the general said out loud. "Great job your U-boats did, sinking an innocent passenger ship. You must be very proud of them this afternoon, Ludwig."

Ludsecke stopped dead in his tracks and spun around. He wasn't used to being spoken to like that, especially by a low born soldier who lived above his station. Although he knew his nickname of Napoleon was whispered in the corridors of power, few ever dared say it to his face.

"Speak to me again in that manner, Köenig, and I'll have you removed from office and stripped of your rank. You will address me as admiral and will not speak to me again unless I ask you to."

General Köenig's face turned red but he held his tongue. Like everyone else, he knew the admiral had the ear of the Führer, and although insufferably aristocratic and self-absorbed, the man was a war hero and beloved by everyone in Germany.

Well, everyone that didn't know him at least.

Admiral Ludsecke spun on his heels and stomped off

towards the naval conference room and the two hapless men inside who were about to feel his wrath.

He stormed past the SS guards, ignoring their salutes in his rush to get into the room.

Purposely late, the decorated war hero from the battle of Jutland in World War One glared at the two high-powered men waiting for him inside the conference room.

"Good morning, Admiral." Two voices spoke at once, but Ludsecke ignored them. He enjoyed watching powerful men squirm in his presence, and his self-importance didn't allow him to see any of them as his equals, no matter their stature or achievements. After all, he, Admiral Ludwig von Ludsecke, was not only a decorated admiral, but he had also been a close friend and confidante of the late president and Great War general, Paul von Hindenburg. More importantly, he had been a close ally and adviser to Adolf Hitler ever since he'd been made Chancellor of Germany back in '33

Neither of the men in the room dared question him, not even the grand admiral of the Kriegsmarine, Erich Raeder, who stood rigid as Ludsecke strode to his seat at the head of the conference table.

"Sit down," he ordered.

The two men did as they were told. To his right sat Großadmiral Raeder, the head of the German Navy, and the man ultimately responsible for the disaster in the Atlantic.

To his left sat Kommodore Karl Dönitz, the man about to be promoted to the rank of Konteradmiral, or rear admiral, as it was known in English. Along with the promotion, he was also to be awarded the title of commander of the submarines.

Ludsecke threw the newspaper he'd been carrying on the desk in front of Dönitz and glared at him.

"What happened?" he demanded. "Please tell me our U-boats had nothing to do with the sinking of that ship."

Both Admiral Raeder and Admiral Ludsecke stared at Karl Dönitz, who looked back with a look of defiance.

"As you are both aware, the U-boats work with a large amount of autonomy, and it isn't until they get back to Wilhelmshaven and hand in their reports that we know the details of their mission."

"Was it us or not?" Ludsecke demanded.

"There's no way of knowing," Dönitz replied. "At least not at this point in time. Until we know for sure, I think it is safe to believe that we didn't have anything to do with it."

"As the naval adviser to the Führer, I can tell you he is furious." Ludsecke spat the words out. "He called me personally and told me he was considering firing both of you if it was one of ours that did it. And I'll tell you, if the Americans join the war, that's exactly what he'll do."

"Or worse," he added.

"We don't even know if it was us," Raeder said. "So, let's not jump to conclusions before we know all the details."

"Let's be honest," Ludsecke said. "A British passenger ship suddenly explodes and sinks in the middle of the Atlantic, killing hundreds of people. If it wasn't a U-boat, then what was it? Moby Dick?"

"You will know as soon as we do, Admiral," Dönitz said. "The U-boat commander will report to me when they get back to port, and I'll deal with it personally."

"The Führer wants to conduct a gentlemanly war and incidents like this, on the very day the British and the French declared war on us, won't show us in a good light, will it?" Ludsecke continued. "I don't need to remind you that sinking passenger ships goes against both international law and more importantly, our own rules of engagement."

"Of course we are aware, Ludwig, but it's war, and mistakes happen in times of war. You know this yourself," Raeder said. "We need to prepare ourselves just in case and deny any involvement, whether we did it or not."

Ludsecke bristled at being addressed by his first name, but he remained calm. He could tell by Raeder's face that he'd enjoyed the barbed attempt at equality.

"I want answers, Raeder, and I want them now." The admiral put the head of the German navy firmly in his place.

Raeder rose to his feet, his face a mask of fury. "I understand your anger, Ludwig, and I will apologise and explain everything to the Führer when I know all the facts, but right now, we don't even know if we were responsible."

Ludsecke glared at Raeder and was about to respond when Dönitz cut in. "Gentlemen, we have a pressing issue to address, and baiting each other will do none of us any good. We need to plan our response, both to the Führer and to the people of the world, who are no doubt waiting to hear what we have to say. So please, sit down and let's act like adults and stop this nonsense."

Admiral Raeder sighed and shook his head. "He's right, Ludsecke, so let's get on with it."

Admiral Ludsecke snorted but took his seat. "What are we going to do about it then, gentlemen? The Führer needs answers."

Admiral Raeder cleared his throat and looked at Dönitz. "This is your department, Karl, so tell us your thoughts."

"I think we can agree that until we know for certain, we need to act as though we are innocent, which we might well be. If, as it certainly appears, we are responsible for sinking the Athenia, then we need to deny it wholeheartedly, both internally and to the wider world."

"I agree," Raeder said. "We need to put a lid on this and deny any involvement. I'm meeting with Goebbels later this week, and I'll make sure he goes on record denying any German involvement."

"Very good," Ludsecke said. "But how are we going to make sure this never happens again? I might appease the Führer this time if he believes we didn't do it, but if it happens again, he'll have you removed."

Raeder shot a quick glance at Dönitz before answering. "We're aware of that, Ludwig, and I'll see to it personally that it never happens again."

Admiral Ludsecke glared at Admiral Raeder for a long moment. "Call me Ludwig again, and I'll see to it that you are sent out on the next U-boat yourself, Raeder."

Admiral Raeder's face turned purple, and he opened his mouth to put the retired war hero in his place. Dönitz grabbed his arm and shook his head.

"It isn't worth it, Erich. Let it go. We all know what a pompous old fool he is. Let him wallow in his own self-importance, because we've got more important work to do."

"As always, Karl, you are the voice of reason." Raeder stood up. "If there's nothing else, then I declare this meeting over."

Ludsecke stared at the two men who weren't fit to lace his boots. "We'll meet again as soon as you hear from the U-boat captain. I want to know immediately they return."

"Yes, sir," Raeder said sarcastically.

Ludsecke started to say something before changing his mind. He stormed out of the conference room, throwing the door open and almost hitting the SS guards standing outside.

The guards saluted the admiral as he stormed past, but as usual, he ignored them and stared straight ahead.

AS SOON AS the aristocratic admiral was out of sight, Karl Dönitz turned to Admiral Raeder. "I doubt Napoleon himself had an ego that big."

"I wouldn't let him hear you say that," Raeder replied. "I've seen him destroy a man's life for calling him Napoleon, although if he were still alive, he'd probably agree with you."

Dönitz laughed and picked up the telephone. After a brief pause, he asked the operator to put him through to the naval base in Wilhelmshaven.

"This is Kommodore Dönitz. Inform me immediately on the arrival in port of U-30. Tell Captain Lemp that he is to report to me personally."

"Yes, Kommodore. I'll convey your command to the captain as soon as he's back in port."

Dönitz hung up the telephone and turned to his superior officer. "I hope it wasn't us, but we both know it was. Let's prepare Goebbels to do what he does best and tell the world what we want them to hear."

"I'll take care of that," Raeder answered. "You rein in the U-boat captains and get them under control. We can't go around attacking passenger ships, not if we don't want the entire world joining the war against us."

"I'll see to it, Admiral."

Kommodore Karl Dönitz saluted the admiral and marched out of the room, making sure to salute the SS guards standing by the door.

Chapter 11

Admiral Ludsecke looked on with pride as his chauffeur swept into the grounds of his secluded, private mansion in the upscale area of Dahlem, in the southwest of Berlin. The large, grandiose house was a three-storey villa that was as imposing and majestic as he himself was.

The first thing that anyone noticed when they approached his home was the complete isolation and privacy provided by the woods surrounding his property. Unless a visitor knew it was there, it would be almost impossible for a trespasser to find it.

The second thing they'd notice were the ornate wrought-iron gates that guarded the entrance. If there was any doubt before, the experience left them in no doubt that the admiral was a man of both power and means.

The gates opened to reveal a meticulously landscaped garden with perfectly trimmed hedgerows and an assortment of plants and shrubs that led up to a grand staircase.

The garden, his wife told him, mirrored Ludsecke's need for order and dominance.

She's probably right, he mused.

Finely crafted stonework was highlighted by rows of windows that the admiral knew promised lavishness within. The inside was as opulent as the outside, and Ludsecke was as proud of his Berlin home as a man could be.

As he stepped out of his vehicle, gardeners and servants stood to attention as he passed. As a testimony to his authority, he ignored all but one – the loyal SS guard who had been with him since the very beginning.

He nodded curtly at the SS guard, which was about as gracious as the admiral could be.

The SS guard opened the door and followed him into the house. He strode through the large, opulent foyer, ignoring the household staff and dismissing their greetings.

The briefcase he carried in his right hand was the only thing he paid any attention to, and he held it to his body as if it were the holy grail. None of the staff knew what was in it, but they knew it meant more to the admiral than any person ever would.

Once safely inside his private study, Ludsecke let out a loud sigh and slumped into his chair. He threw the briefcase onto the ornately carved mahogany desk that was so highly polished that he could see his reflection staring back at him.

Lost in thought, he pondered his life briefly, and wondered how he would ever extricate himself from the embarrassing position of servitude he found himself in.

Servitude. That's for others to provide to me, not the other way around!

Ludsecke slammed his fist onto the desk, sending a pile of neatly stacked papers flying. He'd pick them up later because no servant was ever allowed inside his private study.

In fact, the only other person who ever went in there

besides himself was his wife, Katharina, who stood behind him now, coughing gently to get his attention.

"Good evening, my dear," she said softly. "Did you have a good meeting?"

"A good meeting?" Ludsecke snorted. "How can I have a good meeting with two half breeds who don't have a single brain cell between them?"

"Come now, husband. The admiral and his Kommodore are distinguished men who will lead the Reich to glory. I heard you say so yourself."

"That was for the benefit of Adolf Hitler. You don't think I really believe that, do you?"

"You really don't like him, do you?"

"Who? Raeder?"

"No dear. Adolf Hitler."

"He's nothing but a vulgar little corporal, and to make it worse, I have to bow down to him every day and treat him like he's the new Messiah or something. I don't think I can stand it much longer."

"What did you think would happen? Once Hindenburg died, you knew he'd take over and declare himself Führer. You said so yourself."

"It doesn't mean I have to like it," Ludsecke snapped back.

"You just don't like being subservient to anyone, not even Hitler. Just look at what he's provided for us, Ludwig. He's given us a life we could never have dreamt of before, so you just need to keep bowing to him and putting up with it. If you don't, he'll drop you faster than a hot poker."

"I know, Katharina, believe me, I know. I'm stuck in this situation for as long as he's alive."

"Which will hopefully be a long time, because if

Hermann Göring takes over, he'll have you shot. He hates you."

"A mutual feeling, my dear, I assure you. Now, if you'll excuse me, I have work to do."

"Don't stay up too late. You have a meeting with the Führer tomorrow morning."

"That's why I'm working late."

Alone again, Ludsecke locked the door to his study and opened the briefcase. As he emptied the contents onto his desk, he shuddered as Reinhard Heydrich's words echoed in his mind.

If I discover you are taking top secret documents home, I will personally come to your house and arrest you myself. Believe me, Ludsecke, you don't want to end up in one of my SS interrogation rooms. A spoiled brat like you wouldn't last five minutes before you begged for your mother.

Ludsecke shuddered again. Heydrich. The peasant with the icy heart, who had Hitler's trust, and who worked alongside that other madman, Heinrich Himmler.

The Blond Beast was one of the few men Ludsecke genuinely feared. The last thing he ever wanted was to end up on the wrong side of Reinhard Heydrich and his criminal SS.

Still, Heydrich had been right in his assessment and Ludsecke took even greater care of the documents he carried around with him.

He hated the Bendlerblock, and the small office the navy had provided for him was barren and unfit for a man of his stature. Uncontrolled men and women ran around all day like headless chickens and he didn't trust anyone. The secretary he'd been assigned was incompetent and he'd fired her the first morning she showed up to work for him.

The only person he trusted was himself, and he worked

better when he wasn't distracted. Or at least that was how he justified to himself the reasons why he walked around with the navy's top secret plans for the war.

They were safer in his study than they ever were in the Bendlerblock. That ferret Canaris and his intelligence department, the *Abwehr*. He didn't trust them as far as he could throw them. As far as he was concerned, Canaris had his spies searching through every office in the Bendlerblock during the night when all the senior officers were at home with their wives or mistresses.

The navy's secrets are safer with me than they would ever be in that building. It's probably full of British spies and French thieves, if the truth be known. Heydrich can go to hell, where he belongs.

Ludsecke stared at the documents spread out on his desk. The one that got his attention was the plan put forward by Dönitz to use the U-boats in hunting packs he called Wolfpacks. In Dönitz's opinion, if the submarines hunted British shipping in packs, they could bring Britain to its knees in double-quick time, and it would leave the Wehrmacht free to concentrate on Russia, which everyone knew was Hitler's ultimate target.

He may not like Dönitz, but he admired him. He actually believed that Dönitz was correct in his assessment, and he'd told Hitler he supported the idea in private meetings. Göring was the one who objected, telling Hitler that his Luftwaffe would take the British out of the war on its own.

Göring is an imbecile, and Hitler would do well to listen to me rather than that overblown fighter pilot.

He read Dönitz's plans until after midnight, at which point he gathered them up and placed them back in his briefcase.

In his bedroom, Admiral Ludsecke looked at himself in the full-length mirror. Liking what he saw, he knew he was ready for the morning meeting with Adolf Hitler.

Chapter 12

It was evident that something was different about London from the moment the train pulled into Victoria station.

For one thing, it was busier than Michael had ever seen it. People in and out of uniform were scurrying everywhere, and the platforms were full of weeping mothers trying to get hysterical children onto packed trains heading to countryside destinations all over the country.

Fear of German bombers pounding British cities pushed the government to shut down schools, and they encouraged parents of school-aged children to evacuate them to rural areas where they would be less likely to be attacked from the skies.

Although not mandatory, over one million children had been evacuated by worried parents in the days following Germany's invasion of Poland, and although not all of them were from London, a great many were. Michael watched as tired looking members of the Women's Voluntary Service helped devastated mothers send their children off to live with strangers in a countryside many of them had never seen.

The scene before him humbled Michael and made him feel ashamed of the emotional outburst he'd experienced before Warhurst drove him away from his family that morning.

Although he'd tried to hold it all together, the look of abject defeat on his mother's face sent his emotions spiralling, and he'd been unable to contain himself as his mother and sister broke down in tears.

Watching these terrified children being wrenched from their equally terrified mothers sent shivers down his spine, and a feeling of anger at Hitler and the Nazis for what they were doing to the people of not just Britain, but the whole of Europe – especially the poor Polish people right now – pierced his heart.

A new resolve coursed through him, and even if it killed him, which it probably would, he would never rest until the evil shadow of tyranny was removed forever.

"Mummy, Mummy, where am I going?" a little girl who couldn't have been more than seven years old wailed at her visibly distraught mother.

"You're going to a nice big house in Derbyshire, where they have sheep and cows and dogs running around everywhere. The nice people who own it are going to take good care of you, Helen, and they'll keep you safe and let you play with the animals."

"Why aren't you coming with me? I don't want to go. Mummy, please, I don't want to go."

The little girl screamed and clung to her mother in a scene that broke Michael's heart. A volunteer lady helped prise Helen from the grip she had on her mother, who sobbed for all she was worth.

"I'll write to you every day, little one, and I love you so much. This will all be over soon, and I'll come and get you, I promise."

"I dooon't... want... to... go..." The little girl screamed and sobbed alongside hundreds of others nearby.

"It's for your own good, Helen. I know you don't understand, but it's too dangerous right now."

Michael had heard enough. He hurried his steps and left the station as fast as he could. His heart broke for the parents who were sending their children away, and he was full of gratitude for the families far away that were taking in the kids from the cities. It was not easy for them either.

He wondered if his family would take any in. Was Sandwich far enough away from London? Or was it deemed too dangerous because it was on the south coast, which was the most likely location of any invasion, should it ever get to that?

Like everyone else, Michael hoped it wouldn't.

He took a taxi to Westminster Abbey, and as the driver wove slowly through the crowded streets, he watched the changing face of one of the world's premier cities as it prepared for war.

Never before in Britain's long history had the threat of aerial bombardment been like this. There had been fears in the Great War from the zeppelins, but this was different. The newspapers and newsreels were full of images of what the Luftwaffe was doing to Polish cities, and there was little doubt that, in the near future, Britain's cities would get the same treatment.

It was a horrifying thought.

Posters from various agencies covered windows, doors, lampposts, and everywhere else with enough space to take them. One took his eye because it showed a man pointing forwards with the words 'YOUR COUNTRY NEEDS YOU' in bold letters. It reminded Michael of the ones he'd seen from the Great War, where Lord Kitchener was recruiting men for the front lines.

Others reminded Londoners of the importance of the blackout, showing images of drawn curtains with the message 'Blackout at Night – Keep Lights Out!'

Posters designed to boost morale or to remind civilians of their civic duty were interspersed with the others, leaving Michael in no doubt as to what the government was trying to get across.

He got out of the cab outside the famous old abbey and set off on foot for his final destination, which sounded exciting when he was reading about it the night before.

Whitehall was about half a mile from Westminster Abbey, and he enjoyed the iconic sights of Big Ben and the Houses of Parliament as he walked by.

A thought struck him as he passed. What would happen to these world-famous buildings in the coming months? What about St Paul's Cathedral, one of his favourite structures anywhere in England? Would the German bombers desecrate them with their bombs?

The thought of London flattened and devoid of its historic icons made Michael feel uneasy, so he turned his thoughts to the hustle and bustle all around him.

Men and women in uniforms were everywhere, which was a sight he hadn't seen before in the city. At least not to this extent, and he imagined it would become even more noticeable as the war progressed.

As long as Britain remained free.

The familiar feelings of butterflies erupted in his stomach as he neared Whitehall and the government buildings that occupied it. The closer he got, the more he saw people in uniforms coming and going from the various buildings lining the famous street.

He slowed as he crossed Horse Guards Avenue and approached the War Office on his right. He was there.

Chapter 13

He walked past the War Office and turned down the next street. He followed the building down about halfway until he saw two large doors a few feet apart from each other.

In the centre of the doors was another, single unmarked door that was painted a dull green and looked as if it hadn't been used in years.

The two larger, more official looking doors were guarded by uniformed men, but the one in the middle was not, or so it seemed. Michael looked around and noticed two plain clothed men a few feet away.

He approached the one closest and spoke softly, making sure he wasn't overheard by anyone casually passing by.

"Good morning. Bush House sends their regards."

"Name?" The man produced a clipboard with a list of names on it.

"Fernsby. Michael Fernsby."

The man looked down the list and found his name. After showing his military ID, the man unlocked the door and allowed him entry.

The door closed behind him, leaving Michael in a dark, narrow, dimly lit corridor that stank of mould and stale tobacco. Pipes and cables lined the walls, which stood in stark contrast to the grandeur he imagined people would experience if they entered the War Offices from one of the main entrances.

He shuddered and pulled the lapels of his jacket closer. The air was noticeably cooler than it had been outside, and it wasn't that warm out there.

The corridor was long and narrow, and the stone walled tunnel reminded Michael of a medieval castle full of secret escape routes.

After a long walk down the steeply angled corridor, he came to an abrupt stop. Warning signs were plastered on the walls to look ahead and to watch your step.

Now he was looking at a series of stone steps that led deep into the bowels of the city. He took a gulp of stale air and grabbed the narrow handrail before beginning his descent into the abyss below.

Intermittent lights illuminated the steps just enough so he didn't stumble, and as he descended deeper and deeper, he thought about how much effort the government had gone to in order to build what he assumed was an underground city below London.

After what seemed an age, the steps ended, and Michael found himself in another corridor, this one wider and lined with doorways and offices on both his left and right.

He strode past closed doors, the echoes of his boots mixing with muffled voices to create an eerie atmosphere that seemed out of place with the everyday life going on above his head.

Military brass walked in and out of the offices, the pips and crowns on their lapels showing their rank and authority. Interspersed with them were men and women in civilian clothing.

Michael was passing one room as a young woman opened the door. The room was larger than he'd imagined, and it was full of women hard at work typing, and perhaps doing other clerical duties.

There was a complete underground command centre down here.

He walked past one set of rooms that were heavily guarded and sealed off from the rest.

These must be the PM's war rooms, Michael thought as he strode by.

He turned a corner beyond the heavily guarded rooms and counted. Eight further closed doors down, he stopped.

This was it.

He knocked and entered, not sure what to expect. The well-lit room was small, at around twenty-five by twenty-five feet. A man sat at a desk at the far end, and the walls behind him were covered with maps of Europe.

A woman sat at a desk against the wall to Michael's right. Her desk was full of papers and radio equipment that crackled and popped, adding to the already surreal and tense atmosphere.

Two more men in civilian clothes sat at desks to his left, and they nodded at him as he walked past them towards the lone man at the back of the room.

"Major Sanders, it's good to see you again."

With his round face and short brown hair, Sanders was the only person Michael recognised. At the sight of Michael, Major Sanders rose to his feet and offered his hand.

"Welcome back, Michael. Welcome to our new home. It's not exactly a suite at the Savoy, but it serves our purpose well enough."

"It's good to be back," Michael lied. Well, half-lied. He would much rather be with his family at home, or even better with Mina somewhere, but he knew he had a role to play in the war, and he wanted to get it over with as soon as he could.

"So, Major Sanders, what am I going to be doing?"

"Let's drop the official shit, Michael. I might run the unit, but in here we're all equals. Please, call me Tony. I'm only Major Sanders when we're in public."

"Fair enough," Michael said. "Thank you, Tony."

"Allow me to introduce everyone else in the room. This is Alison, our new unit secretary. She is in charge of administration and communications."

Michael smiled at Alison as she waved at him from her desk. He gave an inquisitive look to Tony Sanders.

"I know what you're thinking," Tony said. "Don't worry. Alison has been heavily vetted, and she's clean. We won't make the same mistake we made with Maureen Ingram ever again."

"That's good to know. Will Alison be the point of contact for us wherever we are in the world?"

"She will, and even if she's off duty, one of us will man the radios at all times, so we'll get your communications no matter when you send them. It's a lot more streamlined than it was before, and a lot more direct. There'll be no misdirecting your messages from now on, so don't worry about it. We learned our lessons the hard way."

"I thought Dansey didn't like radios because the Germans could hear them as well as us."

"He doesn't, but we need faster communication if we're going to make a difference in this war. We'll be using radios as and when we can, so you'd better get used to it."

"A bit of training wouldn't go amiss," Michael said.

"We're on it."

"The man closest to you is Richard Keene, one of the founding members of 317, and our top agent."

Keene rose from the desk and shook Michael's hand. He was tall at over six feet and was trim and athletic. Michael guessed he was in his late twenties or maybe early thirties, with collar length brown hair and friendly blue eyes that sparkled in the bright lights of the secret underground office.

"I've heard a lot about you, Michael." Keene spoke with a northern accent which Michael placed around the Lancashire area. "It's good to finally meet you. Tony here thinks very highly of you, and it's good to have you on our team."

"Thank you," Michael answered. "I hope I can live up to everyone's expectations."

"From what I hear, you've done more than that already," Keene said. "You have nothing to prove to us, Michael."

"Thank you."

Something about Richard Keene's demeanour told Michael he was as ruthless and efficient as he himself had been when the chips were down in Germany during his missions. Keene looked like he was a man you could rely on, which they may well need during this war.

"Last but not least, that guy over there is Lieutenant John Palmer. He's my new assistant, as things are about to get busy in here and we need all the help we can get. He'll be the liaison officer for all the unit's operatives, so you'll be getting familiar with each other over the coming months."

The two men shook hands. John Palmer was shorter than Michael and had a more stocky, muscular frame that spoke of someone who took care of himself.

"I won't let you down, Michael," Palmer said in a

broad London accent. "Like Richard said, your reputation comes before you, and I will do all I can to help you."

Michael nodded. "Thank you."

Richard Keene looked at Sanders. "I'll be going then. I'll check in as soon as I get to Warsaw. Michael, it was good seeing you. Take care of yourself."

And with that, he was gone. Warsaw. Although Michael didn't ask any questions, he knew that whatever he was doing, it was about as dangerous as it gets.

"Sit down, Michael." Sanders gestured to a chair in front of his desk. "We've got a lot to discuss."

Chapter 14

Michael got comfortable in his chair while John Palmer pulled another one up and sat next to him, facing their leader, Tony Sanders. Palmer unlocked a metal container and pulled out a set of files Michael recognised immediately.

Adler's files!

"You might recognise these." Palmer nodded his head at the files that now lay on Tony's desk. "They're the ones you took from Gustav Adler in Germany."

"I know what they are," Michael said. "But before we talk about them, I want to know what you found out from Maureen's Blackshirt that we captured."

He stared at Sanders, holding his gaze with an intense stare.

Sanders pulled a face and sat forward, resting his arms on the desk in front of him. "We, that is me, John here, and Richard Keene, questioned Geoffrey Tunney at length. He's an avid Nazi who believes Hitler will march through the streets of London by the end of next year."

"Who was giving them their orders?" Michael asked.

"Who was the wolf at the door that Maureen talked about? You were there, Tony. You heard what she said."

"Tunney was a hired thug who enjoyed the rough stuff. We've interrogated him thoroughly and I'm convinced he was telling the truth. Whoever Maureen was communicating with, it wasn't someone on this side of the North Sea."

"Who was it then?"

"Tunney doesn't know because Maureen kept it to herself. We'll perhaps never know who it was for sure but we suspect it was a member of the Abwehr, the German intelligence agency."

"What was their aim?" Michael asked. "And you still haven't told me anything about the wolf at the door. Her words have kept me up at night worrying that someone high up is passing secrets to the Nazis."

"They had already achieved their primary goal of infiltrating the top secret Unit 317 of SIS. Maureen Ingram saw to that, and as such, she was a traitor of the highest order. God alone knows how many vital secrets she passed on to the Nazis about our operations, and it's no wonder we lost so many of our best agents to seemingly bad luck or bad timing. Maureen must have been behind all of it."

Michael scowled. "She got what she deserved then."

"That she did," Sanders replied. "As for the wolf at the door, from everything we learned from Tunney, and from turning over her flat in London – where we found copies of our most secret files – when she talked about the wolf at the door, she was referring to herself and the fact that she was there and we didn't even know it."

"Are you sure?" Michael asked. "We need to be one hundred per cent certain about this."

"Believe me, Fernsby, we turned over every stone and

we investigated every lead we found. There was absolutely no evidence that anyone else was involved."

"Did you find out where she was transmitting from, at least?" Michael asked.

"We did." Palmer joined in the conversation. "We found the radio set in a rented house in London and we found her code book in a secret compartment behind the wall in her flat. Obviously, the Abwehr won't be using those again, so any channel of investigation we had is now closed."

"Are you sure?" Michael asked. "I mean, are you *really* sure?"

"One can never be fully sure," Sanders said. "But I'm as sure as sure can be that she was the wolf at the door."

"If you're satisfied, then I am too." Michael took a deep breath. "I know she did a lot of damage to our organisation, but at least we got our own back with Adler's documents."

"That's what forced them into the open," Sanders replied. "If it wasn't for you getting hold of Adler's files, we may never have known about Maureen's treachery."

"That makes sense," Michael said. "Adler told me how important his files were and how it would disrupt the entire German High Command if I were successful in getting them out of Germany. Somebody high up the food chain must have ordered Maureen's handler to go to any lengths to recover them, even as far as exposing herself and her gang of traitors."

"That's exactly what we think happened," Sanders said. "We think the German High Command were furious that highly sensitive documents had been compromised by a defector, and they threw Maureen to the gallows to get them back."

"Luckily for us, we had you," Palmer said. "If it wasn't

for your prompt and brave actions, we would have lost them, and who knows what else the Germans would have found out about us."

"I did what I was supposed to do," Michael said. "I brought Adler's briefcase back and then I did everything I could to save my sister. Anyone in my position would have done the same thing, and in any case, I couldn't have done it alone. Without Tony's help, I couldn't have done it."

"Modest to the end, Michael," Sanders replied. "And while I wouldn't expect anything less, you showed incredible bravery and valour, which is why the king rewarded you with those well-deserved honours."

"It was nothing less than anyone in this room would have done," Michael corrected him. "So, if we're satisfied there isn't a mole in our midst, what else do we have going on? I'm sure you discovered a lot of useful intelligence in Adler's files, but is there anything you want me to work on?"

"Adler's files provided us with much needed, top-rated intelligence that we are still digesting and working on. Several departments, both military and intelligence, have benefitted and are even now, as we speak, changing their approach based on the information you recovered."

"So, what do you want from me?" Michael asked.

"You are to stay here in our underground office. We have sleeping quarters close by, and everything you need is down here, except good old-fashioned sunlight, of course. We want you to sit with Alison and become conversant with our radio procedures, as you will be issued a code book and will be expected to write and code your own messages from now on."

"Will I be getting a radio set?"

"Highly unlikely. They are heavy and bulky, and will not only slow you down, but you can hardly be fast and stealthy when you're carrying a suitcase full of heavy equipment."

"Am I learning Morse code?"

"Yes. It is a skill every one of our operatives needs to learn, although it won't be something you will use every day. We'll continue using the dead letter box system, or DLB as we refer to it, as it allows you to remain anonymous and you don't have to lug around heavy equipment that would give you away faster than anything. You will learn how to code your messages, though, so the operators can send them without knowing the true meaning of what they are transmitting."

"What's the ultimate goal with this? In other words, where are you sending me and what will I be doing?"

"I have an important meeting in the coming days and we'll know more after that. For now, sit tight and study what Alison teaches you. It might save your life one day."

"When do I start?"

"This afternoon. Alison will show you around so you don't get lost, and then you'll get down to business."

Sanders rose from his chair and headed for the door. "I'll be back, Michael, and I want you ready when I do."

Michael nodded and closed his eyes. Whatever Sanders had in mind for him, he knew it would not be good.

Chapter 15

Tony Sanders sat at the small desk in an empty office in the cramped underground complex. Unit 317's busy office was a distraction, with the radio crackling and people talking all the time.

He needed a quiet place where he could concentrate on his work undisturbed, and the small office at the end of the corridor worked well for him.

Equipped with a desk, a chair, and a lamp, the tiny office was perfect, and he spread out Adler's files across the desk and looked at all of them in turn.

Operational Intelligence
Operational Personnel
Policy and Strategy
Eugenics Programme
European Network Contacts

Each of them was of vital importance, and Tony knew them as well as he knew the way around the tiny flat above a bookstore overlooking the River Thames in the heart of London that meant so much to him.

He had to because the information within the files was

of such national importance that they had taken almost his every waking moment.

Tonight was even more important because he had a meeting with Colonel Claude Dansey the following afternoon at Bletchley Park.

Dansey, or Colonel Z as he preferred to be known, was the deputy chief of Britain's SIS and as such, Unit 317 of Section V, SIS, came under his jurisdiction. He was the man Major Sanders reported to as the supreme head of the secretive operational intelligence department.

The next day's meeting would decide what Unit 317 would focus on in the coming months, and for all the operatives, their decisions would mean life or death.

Of course, winning the war and gaining an advantage over the Nazis took precedence over everything, including the lives of the agents and staff of every department within the SIS, but Tony Sanders felt personally responsible for the lives of those serving under him, and he wouldn't send them off on suicide missions unless there was absolutely no other way.

Most of his time had been taken with the two files marked Operational Intelligence and Operational Personnel, and he had learned a lot about the hierarchy of the Third Reich and its key personnel from those files.

Important, no doubt, but there wasn't anything 317 could act upon, other than to perhaps assassinate some key figures that would upset the German war effort.

The problem with that was the Germans would no doubt reciprocate, and Britain would end up losing key men at a time when she could ill afford to, so that wasn't the best use of 317's time and resources.

However, after studying the files over and over, two things stood out to Sanders that were noteworthy. First, the Policy and Strategy file was most enlightening, as amongst other things, it outlined the strategies proposed by Karl Dönitz, the commander of the German U-boats.

The U-boats had been a major problem for the British during the Great War, and there was good reason to fear them even more this time.

Although they hadn't admitted it, the sinking of the Athenia demonstrated the full power and ruthlessness of the U-boats. Once the German's got their act together under Dönitz's guidance, the U-boats had the potential to turn the tide of the war in Germany's favour.

As First Lord of the Admiralty, Winston Churchill had the utmost respect from Sanders, and he knew he would take the U-boat threat seriously.

Although it was outside 317's remit, the submarine threat was one that every intelligence agency had to be aware of.

Sanders looked at his watch and gathered his files. It was well after midnight, and he had to be on the train at six the following morning. He walked the mile or so to his flat and collapsed onto his single bed.

Sleep was all but forgotten in the early days of the war, and he longed for the long summer days he'd enjoyed with his beautiful Martha back in the carefree days of 1936.

As he drifted off, he clung to the memory of them picnicking in Hyde Park before spending the night together in her tiny flat above her bookstore overlooking the River Thames.

He woke drenched with sweat as the nightmare tortured his dreams. It was always the same nightmare over and over. After breakfast together, they'd left for their office jobs. He was a manager in the civil service transportation department, and she owned the bookstore overlooking the Thames.

They said goodbye with a promise to meet later that

evening when they would take a train to Surrey, where her parents lived, for the weekend. He would ask her father for her hand, and they planned on an autumn wedding in her hometown.

It never happened, because as she crossed the road to buy a newspaper, a truck delivering fresh goods struck her head-on. Martha died instantly, and Tony's life was forever changed.

He wiped the sweat from his forehead and reached for the torch he kept by the side of the bed. His watch said it was three forty-five.

That's enough.

Tony Sanders got out of bed and made himself a cup of tea by the light of the dim lamp he had in the kitchen.

Chapter 16

Bletchley Park had changed since the last time Tony Sanders had been there. Security was on a much higher level, and several more wooden huts had been erected.

The security was similar to that of the secret war rooms underneath the War Office, and the once grand stately home with its expansive gardens was now a secret hub of clandestine wartime activity.

After showing his ID at several checkpoints where his name was verified against a clipboard roster, Tony was finally escorted to a hut in a secluded corner of the mansion's grounds.

The hut that had once briefly served as 317's headquarters was visible between the trees and Sanders watched as men and women in civilian clothing entered the wooden structure.

He knew from private conversations with Dansey that the ultra-secret Government Code and Cypher School had taken over Bletchley Park, or GC&CS as it was better known in clandestine circles.

While Sanders didn't know the full extent of the role GC&CS played in the war effort, he knew they were tasked with breaking the codes the Germans used to transmit secure messages to their military deployments.

He knew the naval codes differed from the ones used by the Wehrmacht and Luftwaffe, so the code breakers had their hands full trying to crack the heavily encrypted secret orders and messages.

As far as he knew, they hadn't yet broken the codes sent from the German encryption systems that were based around the Enigma machine, the typewriter-looking device they used to encrypt their messages.

Getting hold of an Enigma machine was at the top of the list for all intelligence agencies but, so far, they had been unsuccessful in getting their hands on one, at least as far as he knew.

If that wasn't enough, the GC&CS was also tasked with analysing Germany's security and counterintelligence operations, and they worked with SIS to uncover espionage networks and provided information on enemy and double agents.

It was in this area that Sanders worked closely with them, and it was probably why he'd been summoned to the meeting that morning, along with Colonel Dansey and Alastair Denniston, the Scottish head of the Government Code and Cypher School.

A circular table stood in the middle of the hut and when Sanders walked in, he jumped back in surprise at the men staring back at him.

Dansey and Denniston he already knew, having met them many times before. A woman he'd never seen before sat at a table at the rear of the room. To Denniston's right sat a woman he'd never seen before. She had a notebook, a pencil, and was ready to record the pertinent minutes from the meeting.

What Sanders wasn't expecting, and why the blood drained from his face in shock, was the sight of the First Lord of the Admiralty staring back at him.

The unmistakable smell of cigar smoke should have warned him as he entered, but he was taken aback, nevertheless.

The rotund figure and receding hairline faded into the background as the face, recognisable all over the world, glared at him as he walked into the room.

"Good of you to join us, Major Sanders. Now, please take a seat so we can get this meeting started."

Winston Churchill!

Sanders sat meekly in the empty seat and fidgeted as he tried to control the landmine that had just exploded in his stomach.

"Right, now that we're all here, let's get down to business." Churchill's huge personality took over the wooden hut and everyone, even Dansey, fell under his spell.

"I'm sure we are all familiar with the files the operative from Unit 317 obtained from Gustav Adler?" Denniston spoke in his distinctive Scottish accent.

Heads nodded around the table.

"There is information in those files that pertains to each of our individual departments and we will pursue them both collectively and independently, but there is one overriding issue that we can work together on that, if successful, has the potential to turn the tide of this war in our favour."

"What's that?" Dansey asked. "There is a lot of information in those files, so what in particular are you talking about?"

Churchill pulled on his cigar and leant forward in his

chair. "Gentlemen, the biggest threat we face apart from an invasion is the U-boats. Adler's files show Dönitz is planning to use them in packs to attack both our naval vessels and our merchant ships."

He paused to relight his cigar.

"You don't need me to tell you the severity of the threat the U-boats pose for us. As First Lord of the Admiralty, the U-boats represent my greatest fear for the survival of our nation, and it must take top priority over everything we do."

"What do you require from us?" Dansey asked. "As much as I agree with you, sir, surely this is a matter for the navy, unless you have specific intelligence on the ground that we can act upon?"

"That's why you are here." Churchill waved his hand at Dansey and Sanders. "We have a task for you."

Dansey raised his eyebrows.

"I agree that while the U-boats are specifically a naval issue, there are areas where we can work together to nullify their threat," Denniston said. "I believe my department has identified a situation where we can do just that."

"You have my full attention," Dansey said.

Denniston looked at Churchill, who nodded back at him. He took a file from his briefcase and spread the contents out in front of him.

"I'm sure you recognise the documents that your operative retrieved from Adler." He looked up at Dansey and Sanders, who had remained quiet so far.

Both men acknowledged they had read the files he was presenting.

"If you look at this document in particular." He handed over a sheet of paper.

Canaris indicated several times during our meetings that the biggest threat to the security of the Kriegsmarine wasn't Britain or her allies cracking Enigma, but that absurd, out of touch admiral in Berlin who has the ear of the Führer.

This relic from the past wallows in his own self-importance, and if the Führer knew what he really thought of him, he'd have him executed on the spot.

Although he's been warned multiple times by such eminent men as Canaris, Raeder, and Dönitz, he continues to break security protocol and take home files and documents so sensitive that they could break the Reich if he was ever compromised.

His aloofness and conceited behaviour are, in Canaris's opinion, the biggest threat to the Reich since Ernst Röhm, the head of the Brownshirts, who the Führer executed during the Night of the Long Knives in 1934. According to Hitler, Röhm had been plotting to *take over the army and seize power for himself.*

Hitler took care of him with ruthless efficiency, so the question remains as to why he doesn't do the same with this incompetent fool.

Denniston sat back and looked at both Dansey and Sanders.

"Canaris is the head of the Abwehr, and I know first-hand what a shrewd operator he is. Our paths have crossed many times and I can tell you he is a man to be taken seriously. Admiral Canaris served in the German navy in the Great War, and the Kriegsmarine is close to his heart. If what Adler says in the document is true, it's worth us taking a closer look at it."

"I know who Canaris is," Dansey snapped. "But do we know who he is talking about? Who is this admiral he's referring to?"

"I set my department to task on proving the veracity of Adler's document and whether Canaris ever uttered these words," Denniston replied. "I was shocked when we discovered that not only were they true, but if anything, they were understated. That's when I approached the First Lord of the Admiralty with it."

Winston Churchill cleared his throat and looked around the room. “Please continue,” he said to Denniston.

“We narrowed our focus to older, retired admirals who had Hitler’s ear, and we came up with one name: Admiral Ludwig von Ludsecke, a Great War hero from a Prussian aristocratic family who is about as elitist as they come.”

“I know the name, but I didn’t have him down as a big player in the Nazi regime,” Dansey said. “From what I know of him, he’s arrogant, stuck up, and his only claim to authority is that he is Hitler’s spy in the Kriegsmarine, although everyone seems to know it.”

“You are correct,” Denniston confirmed. “Both Raeder and Dönitz despise him, but with his close ties to Hitler, there is nothing they can do about it.”

“You must have learned something more about him, or we wouldn’t be here discussing him this morning.” Sanders broke his silence. “Although I can see where this might be going, please tell us what Unit 317 has to do with any of this.”

“I’m getting to that,” Denniston answered. “My department focused on his communications and his movements, and from what we learned, he regularly takes home ultra-secret documents, even though he’s been warned against it numerous times by Raeder, Dönitz, and countless others.”

He cleared his throat before continuing.

“We intercepted a communication from a colleague who is close to Ludsecke. According to him, Hitler puts up with his indiscretions against the advice of his top commanders because he is useful to him. Ludsecke sits in on all the naval policy meetings and throws his rank around, alienating everyone around him. Then he goes to Hitler and tells him what is really going on at the head of the Kriegsmarine. That makes him invaluable to Hitler and infuriating to Raeder and Dönitz, who cannot have a meeting without Ludsecke being present."

"This is getting interesting," Dansey said. "Please, carry on."

"Our intelligence indicates that he does, indeed, take home top secret information regarding the Kriegsmarine's strategies and policies."

Denniston stopped and looked at everyone in the room for effect.

"Including, we believe, Dönitz's detailed plans for the U-boats in the Atlantic. This, gentlemen, is vital information that we need to get our hands on."

The room fell silent while Denniston's words sank in. Finally, after a long pause, Winston Churchill chimed in.

"This is where you come in," he said, looking at Dansey and Sanders. "We know from the information Bletchley Park has been able to ascertain and verify that the Kriegsmarine high command, which comprises Raeder, Dönitz, and Ludsecke, amongst others, has a meeting planned in Berlin in early November."

Churchill looked Sanders directly in the eye.

"We want your unit to relieve Ludsecke of those documents after the meeting is over. If we pull this off, then at best we can win the war in the Atlantic, and at worst, lessen the threat of the U-boats in our shipping lanes."

Sanders closed his eyes. "You want me to send my agents to Berlin, the very heart of Nazi power and government, and somehow steal the Kriegsmarine's secrets from under their noses?"

"In a nutshell, yes, that's what we're asking."

"It's a suicide mission," Sanders retorted. "Even if we manage to get an operative into Berlin, the security will be so tight after the heist that it will be impossible for them to get out."

"Yes, Major Sanders." Churchill's tone was soft and understanding. "I'm well aware of the risks, but I wouldn't be here if it wasn't so vital for the war effort. It's extremely high risk, but the potential prize makes the undertaking worth the sacrifice."

"Sir, it's an impossible mission."

"That's why Unit 317 exists, Major Sanders." Churchill spoke with more authority. "To carry out impossible missions. You've already proven you can do it, and now we need you more than ever. We wouldn't ask if it wasn't so vital."

"Make plans to send in your best operative," Dansey said. "Meet with me in the war rooms at six tomorrow evening to present your plans."

"Yes, sir." Sanders felt numb. He knew it was a risk worth taking, but he also knew it was a one-way mission.

"That's it then." Churchill rose to his feet and grabbed the cane that he was famous for. "I'll leave the details in your capable hands, and I expect to be kept up to date with your progress."

Winston Churchill strode out of the wooden hut, allowing daylight to stream in and temporarily blind the men and woman left behind.

Sanders turned to Denniston. "I need everything you have on this Ludsecke sent to my office in the war rooms by the time I get back this afternoon."

He turned to Dansey, who still remained seated for a further meeting with Denniston. "Sir, I'll have our initial plans ready for your approval by tomorrow afternoon."

Sanders strode out into the rare September sunshine and with a heavy heart, began making mental assessments about who was best suited for the job.

Two men came to mind, but his preferred operative, the one with the most experience and ability to pull off something like this, was already on another extremely dangerous mission in Warsaw.

That left one other. The youngest member of Unit 317, and yet in many ways, the one who had already demonstrated his skills and bravery the most.

Michael Fernsby.

Chapter 17

Tony Sanders sat at his desk in the war rooms in the early hours of the morning. At four am, the only other person present was the radio operator monitoring the radio frequencies for any messages from the unit's agents scattered across Europe.

The hiss of the radio was a welcome background noise that calmed the arguments raging inside his head. Along with the powdered aspirin he'd taken earlier, the radio hum helped ease the splitting headache that had taken hold on the train ride back to London after his meeting at Bletchley Park.

His eyes felt heavy, and he massaged his temples. He knew he looked tired and haggard, but sleep was impossible when he knew he was about to send one of his best men on a suicide mission for king and country.

For king and country, he repeated several times before forcing himself back to the papers spread out before him.

Denniston had dispatched an armed courier to the war rooms with everything he had on Admiral Ludwig von Ludsecke, which wasn't much.

But it was enough.

Sanders spent the early hours formulating a plan for the impossible mission he'd been tasked with. By the time Alison took over the radio from the night girl, he'd come up with a plan that might just work.

Might.

The bigger problem was getting the operative out of Berlin and safely back to Britain, but that was a problem for later. For now, he was concentrating on Admiral Ludwig von Ludsecke and the secrets he carried.

As the war rooms filled up with men and women, the smell of fresh tobacco stung Sanders' nose. He'd never understood the need to smoke and yet almost everyone did it. He hated it because it made his eyes sting, his clothes stink, and he found it hard to breathe.

He enjoyed the fleeting moments when he could go outside and breathe fresh air into his lungs, and it was during one of these rare moments when he bumped into Michael Fernsby making his way towards Alison's desk and his crash course in Morse code.

"Good morning, Major," Michael said as he approached. "You look like you didn't get much sleep last night."

"Is it that obvious?" Sanders laughed. "How's the Morse code coming along?" He changed the subject.

They walked along the dimly lit corridors and started down the stairs, going deeper and deeper underneath the vibrant city streets far above their heads.

"It's going well," Michael answered. "I'm good with the basics and I'm concentrating primarily on decoding messages sent in Morse. I can do that pretty well already, which is a big surprise if I'm being honest."

"That's good to hear," Sanders said, "because you will be needing it soon."

Sanders saw the change in Fernsby's features, and his heart dropped. He knew he was sending a good young man with a lifetime ahead of him to a near certain death and it was this, along with the other excellent agents like him, that kept sleep at bay.

How can I sleep when I'm sending men I consider friends to their deaths?

Sanders looked away, so Michael wouldn't see the pain in his eyes.

"I'm able to decipher Morse some but it will take me a lot longer to transmit it with any accuracy. That's going to take a lot more training, I'm afraid. Weeks, if not months more."

"You won't need to send any messages, so concentrate on decoding them. For now, that's all we need from you."

"Yes, sir."

Michael held the door to the office they shared for him, but Sanders stood back. "You go on. I've got to go see someone."

Sanders watched the door close and stood for a moment. His heart was heavy and his breathing felt laboured. He knew he needed rest, but he didn't have a clue when he was going to get any.

He stood outside Dansey's office, which wasn't much bigger than the one the unit shared, and he entered. He helped himself to a cup of coffee and turned to the secretary.

"Is the boss in?" He aimed his head at the closed door at the back of the room.

"Not yet," the secretary answered. "I haven't heard from him this morning, so I don't know where he is."

"May I?" Sanders asked, gesturing to the pot of coffee close to Dansey's door with his now empty cup.

"Help yourself, Tony. You drink more of it than we do."

"That's because you have a coffee grinder somewhere and the ground coffee beans end up in this office. We have to make do with Camp coffee made with chicory. There's a world of difference in the taste."

"Colonel Z gives me the beans to grind and I bring them fresh each morning. He told me to keep it a secret, but you seemed to know right off the bat."

"I promise I won't tell anyone if you let me have a few cups every day."

The secretary laughed. "You're doing a good job of that already, I see."

Sanders smiled at the secretary and left Dansey's office with his fifth cup of the morning. He made his way back to Unit 317's space and stood for a moment outside before taking a deep breath and opening the door.

He had work to do.

Chapter 18

At six sharp, Tony Sanders knocked on the door to Colonel Dansey's office and entered. The secretary looked up and smiled, nodding her head towards the closed door at the back of the room.

"He's expecting you," she said.

Sanders helped himself to his umpteenth cup of coffee that day and shook the tension from his shoulders. He knocked, and after hearing a gruff sound from within, he entered and closed the door behind him.

The ageing man with a receding hairline and round glasses that looked too small for his head sat at his desk staring at Sanders with eyes that looked sharp and somehow all knowing.

Recently, Sanders had taken to calling him the hawk, but he kept that to himself.

He lowered his gaze to avoid eye contact and approached one of the two chairs placed across from Claude Dansey.

"Good afternoon, Colonel Z."

"Sit down, Major." Dansey was never one for small talk. "We have a lot to discuss."

Sanders did as he was told and laid down the file Alison had typed up for him an hour earlier.

"Do you have a plan?" Dansey asked. "I don't think much of Denniston's ideas and I don't rate our chances of success, but if the First Lord of the Admiralty wants us to do it, then we'll bloody well do it."

"Yes, sir, I agree." Sanders pushed the typewritten notes over the desk. "These are the preliminary plans I have come up with that, in my opinion, give us the best chance of success."

Dansey fell silent as he digested the ten-page report. After reading it, he lowered the papers to his desk and spoke with a calmer, more concerned demeanour.

"It might just work," he said. "That's good work, Tony."

"Thank you, sir," Tony replied. "I still haven't worked out how to get him out, but at least we have a starting point."

"Have you told him yet?"

"No, sir. I wanted to see what you thought of the plan first."

Dansey picked up his telephone and held the receiver to his ear. "Call 317's secretary and get Michael Fernsby in here," he said sharply to his secretary. "And bring me three coffees when he gets here."

"Yes, very good," he said after a brief pause. "Thank you, Irene. When Fernsby gets here, you can leave for the day."

He replaced the receiver and sat back with his hands interlocked behind his neck. Tony Sanders fidgeted in his chair, his stomach tied in knots because of what he was about to do.

Five minutes later, a knock on the door preceded the entry of Michael Fernsby, the nineteen-year-old sensation who had pulled off the incredible mission earlier that year in Germany. It was still the talk of intelligence circles, and the king had rightly rewarded him for it.

This time, he was being sent on an even more dangerous mission.

"You called for me, sir?" Fernsby asked as he entered.

"I hope you have taken the training on board, Captain, because we have a mission for you." Dansey got right down to it. "It's more dangerous than anything you've done before, and before Major Sanders says anything, I'll tell you that the mission we are about to give you is vital if we're going to win this war. The risk is worth taking, Captain, even if you don't survive."

Sanders felt the tension ratchet up in the room. He took a deep breath and fought back the nausea creeping up inside him.

Michael Fernsby sat upright in his chair and calmly looked at Claude Dansey. Sanders thought he looked paler than usual, but otherwise, he looked as calm as ever.

"What do you want me to do, Colonel?"

"We want you to go into Germany and relieve an old admiral of his belongings," Dansey said. "Then we want you to get out safely and bring them back here."

"That sounds familiar," Michael said. "But something tells me you're leaving something out." It was more of a question than a statement.

Dansey looked at Sanders. "Tell him."

Sanders cleared his throat and looked Michael in the eye.

"You already know the grave threats the U-boats present to us, and you are also aware that unless we contain them, they could potentially win the war in the

Atlantic. They will bring Britain to her knees and force us to surrender."

"Yes, sir. I'm fully aware of the U-boat threat."

"You saw what they did to the Athenia not even two weeks ago?" Dansey asked.

"Is it confirmed that a U-boat sank the Athenia?" Michael asked.

"Not yet, but all indications point to a U-boat attack," Dansey said. "That's what they will do to our merchant ships and our navy. We have to stop them."

"I understand, sir, and I'll do whatever I can to assist."

"Whatever the cost?" Dansey asked.

"Whatever the cost," Michael answered.

"Read this." Sanders handed him a copy of the file he'd presented to Dansey. "It explains everything."

The room fell silent while Michael read the ten-page brief. When he'd finished, he placed the pages on the desk and looked first at Sanders and then Dansey.

"You want me to go to Berlin, somehow steal whatever documents this Admiral Ludsecke has in his possession, and then waltz out as if nothing has happened?"

The look on his face told Sanders everything he needed to know.

"We wouldn't be sending you if it wasn't so vital," he said. "You're resourceful, so I leave it up to you how you get out of Berlin, but my advice would be to create a diversion somewhere that allows you to slip out unnoticed."

"Create a diversion in the midst of the enemy so I can slip out unnoticed?" Michael repeated. "What exactly do you think I should do? Burn down the Reichstag? Oh, wait. That's been done already."

"That's one of the many things we will work on together over the coming days," Sanders said. "We'll make sure you have an exit plan that gives you the best possible chance of success."

"When?" Michael asked. "Your report didn't give me a timeline. How long do I have to prepare for this?"

"The Kriegsmarine has a strategy meeting at their headquarters in the Bendlerblock building once a month," Sanders said. "We know from our intelligence reports there is a meeting scheduled for the eighth of November. As the ninth is a day of remembrance for the Nazis who died during Hitler's failed attempt to take over the government in Munich in twenty-three, many Germans will be celebrating."

Sanders looked at Michael. "We think it's a good day to carry out the mission. The Germans will hopefully be a little off-guard because of the anniversary, but the admiral should still be in possession of documents pertaining to whatever was discussed at the meeting the day before. The U-boats, as vital as they are to their naval strategy, will surely be on the agenda."

"The ninth is also the anniversary of Kristallnacht," Michael said, his eyes focused and fierce. "It will be exactly one year since my great-grandfather and uncle went missing, never to be heard of again."

"There are many reasons we have to win this war, Captain Fernsby," Dansey said. "And that is most certainly one of them, especially for all the people who suffered because of that dreadful night."

"They won't stop there," Michael added. "Mark my words, Colonel, they'll destroy the Jewish population in Poland as soon as the military invasion is complete. Then they'll turn their attentions to Western Europe. None of us are safe, not Holland, not Belgium, not France, and not us."

"We know, Michael." Sanders spoke softly. "And that's why we have to stop them."

"I'll do it," Michael said. "Let's finalise the plan and I promise to do my very best to carry out the mission."

"I knew we could count on you, Captain Fernsby," Dansey said. "Now, get some rest, because the serious planning begins tomorrow morning at six sharp."

Michael stood up and left the room. Sanders rose to follow him, but Dansey called him back.

"This has to be successful, Major. Our futures may very well depend on the success of this mission, so don't mess it up."

Sanders shook his head and walked out.

Chapter 19

The thunderous autumn storm showed no sign of abating. Heavy rain had pelted the old Bavarian farm on the edge of the Black Forest in Bavaria for days, and the forecast warned of more to come.

This was the kind of weather that Mina Postner, the nineteen-year-old daughter of the farm's owners, Tim and Irma Postner, despised. She was soaked to the skin, and mud clung to her shoes and splattered her legs from her ankles to her calves.

The temperatures were in that horrible place where it was just above freezing, and everything was soaking wet. Inside the barn where she worked, collecting eggs from the chickens running freely around the hay covered floor, Mina's mood mirrored the dreary scene outside.

Her long blonde hair was soaked and it stuck to her face as she bent forward to collect the eggs before she stood on them and broke them.

She looked up as her younger sister, Senta, entered the barn. As the door opened, Mina got a glimpse of the mid-afternoon sky that was full of dark, heavy clouds that looked as though they were going to burst open above Ryskamp, their farm.

Senta was two years younger than Mina, and if it wasn't for her youthful innocence, she could easily be taken as Mina's twin. Both had the same features passed down from their mother, from the long blonde hair to the deep blue eyes and full lips.

"This foul weather will be the death of us," Senta complained as she raced inside the barn. "I'm freezing."

"If we hurry, we can get back in front of the roaring fire Papa has ready for us." Mina offered some comfort.

"I doubt it," Senta snorted. "We have a house full of people and there are hungry mouths to feed. Papa will have us running around out here all night."

Mina smiled at her always complaining sister. "No, he won't, Senta. Once we've gathered the eggs and fed the animals, there won't be any reason for us to go outside again."

"Until tomorrow, when we have to do it all over again."

"That's our job."

"Well, I wish it wasn't."

"Here, take these." Mina passed a basketful of eggs to Senta and grabbed the empty one from her. "I'll finish this and you can help Mama prepare dinner."

"Are you sure?" Senta looked sheepish. "I don't mean to complain too much."

"It's alright." Mina laughed. "I'm used to this weather. We live in Bavaria, after all."

"I wish we didn't."

"Don't we all." Mina looked towards the ground, her mind far away from the heavy clouds and the rain.

"Well, if you're sure…"

"Yes, I'm sure. Go inside and get warm. I'll be right behind you."

Senta giggled and ran out of the barn. Mina watched as she squelched through the mud as fast as she could. The driving rain pounded her body, but Senta didn't slow down.

An instant later, she was gone, leaving Mina alone with her thoughts. Her mind drifted to the previous winter that seemed a lifetime ago, when she'd found the English spy, Michael Fernsby, hiding in their barn.

She glanced upwards at the hayloft above her head and smiled to herself, remembering the stolen moments they had shared together in the hay.

Her heart yearned to feel his arms around her again, and she closed her eyes to allow the emotions to flow through her. She sat on the hay covered floor, right on the spot where she'd shot Alwin Lutz, the ardent Nazi who had designs on her.

She shuddered at the memory, and although she'd been over it so many times in her mind, Mina knew she would never get over it. Taking someone's life is a terrible thing to do, no matter the circumstances.

Michael took the blame for Alwin's death and he'd convinced her and her parents to lie to the Nazis so they wouldn't be punished.

It worked, or at least it did for her parents and sister. Mina hadn't been so lucky.

The memory of Alwin made her shiver as she blocked out the images of his older brother, Karl, who had forced himself onto her after Alwin's death.

She'd rejoiced when she heard the news of Karl's death at the doctor's house in Munich. The Nazi radio broadcasts reported Karl had died heroically protecting the doctor from a crazed, undesirable intruder. Unfortunately, they had both died, but not before Karl killed the intruder.

The newspapers had been full of the story of the great

SS hero, Karl Lutz. Pictures of him were on every page, and he'd been awarded several medals of honour that were given to his parents in a formal ceremony performed by Heinrich Himmler himself.

It's all lies.

Although she didn't know for sure, Mina knew the story wasn't true. A part of her hoped it had been Michael that had killed Karl, but if it was him, why did he kill the doctor? Surely, he was someone who saved lives, not took them?

Whoever it was, Mina knew there was more to it than was reported in the papers. At the end of the day, Karl was dead, and he couldn't harm her anymore.

She forced the memories of the Lutz family from her mind and concentrated on Michael Fernsby, the man who had appeared out of nowhere and stolen her heart. Wherever he was, she hoped he was safe and well, but more than anything else, she couldn't wait until the moment they could be together again.

Who am I kidding? We're at war with the British and soon we'll all be dead. For all I know, he could be dead already.

Soft tears fell from her eyes. Damn Hitler and his stupid war.

Whatever Michael was up to, it would have to wait. She had more pressing things to worry about right now.

Like the Jewish family of four that had arrived the day before from Frankfurt.

Chapter 20

The Goldberg family had arrived at Ryskamp the previous afternoon in the back of a delivery wagon from Glatten. They had been on the road for over a week, moving from truck to truck, always moving at night, and often on foot to avoid the Gestapo.

The Goldbergs made their final journey to Ryskamp in the back of a coal truck. Although only eight kilometres, the last leg of their long journey had been fraught with danger.

The truck was stopped at a roadblock where dogs and guards searched every vehicle passing through. The family buried themselves deep inside the mound of coal to avoid detection and arrived at Ryskamp filthy, frightened, and starving.

The first thing Tim Postner, Mina's father, did when they arrived was to order them to take a bath and change their clothing. Although they possessed little themselves, her father insisted on giving Mr and Mrs Goldberg a set of old clothes belonging to him and his wife, Irma.

Their son and daughter were both under ten years old,

and they had to make do with what they already had, so Mina and Senta had spent the evening scrubbing their clothes as clean as they could.

All of this wasn't only for the benefit of the Goldberg family. There was a large element of self-preservation because if the Gestapo ever got wind of their resistance operations, they would raid the farm immediately.

If they discovered coal dust all over the house, they would be arrested and sent to one of the ever-growing number of concentration camps that were popping up all over the country.

After a good meal, the Goldbergs slept in a downstairs room at the rear of the farmhouse where they could escape quickly out of the back door if the need arose.

Thankfully, so far, it hadn't, and the Goldbergs were just one more family in an increasing number of Jewish men, women, and children the Postners helped escape the Nazis.

The Postners' role in the resistance was nothing more than sheltering escaping families until transportation could be arranged to pick them up and take them across the border into France.

So far, everything had gone smoothly, and nobody had been caught, but Mina and her family knew they were only one slip-up away from disaster.

If Michael can come all the way from England to rescue his family, then I can help a few Jews cross the border.

Mina was defiant.

Her best friend, Anna Rosenberg, was a Jew, and Mina had seen first-hand how the Nazis had treated her and her family. They'd owned the once-thriving general store in nearby Glatten until the Brownshirts attacked it, painting terrible slogans and signs on the outside of their store.

On Kristallnacht, the Brownshirts smashed the

windows and burned the store to the ground. Then they went in a frenzied search for Anna's parents, but they never found them.

They had been at Ryskamp, hiding from the brutality aimed at them by the brown-shirted army of hate. Two weeks after Kristallnacht, they found a way out of Germany, and as far as Mina knew, they had settled in Amsterdam, where they would be safe.

Mina sighed and pulled herself from her thoughts. She shivered and shook, trying to warm herself up from the cold, damp conditions.

Her feet were like blocks of ice, and she couldn't feel her fingers as she hurriedly picked up the remaining eggs from the chickens clucking around under her feet.

She fed the animals as fast as she could and then opened the barn door. Thick, black clouds were unloading what seemed like a year's worth of rain over their farm. Rivers of water streamed down the sodden, muddy road past the house and away from the farm, and she wished she was just about anywhere than Ryskamp at that moment.

I want to be wherever Michael is.

She pictured him safe in a flat in London, working in an office far from the dangers of war. She knew that wasn't likely but it helped her sleep at night.

Frowning at her crazy ideas, Mina braved the terrible weather and stepped outside. Her breath caught as the freezing rain immediately soaked her to the skin once again. She closed the barn door and ran as fast as she could towards the warm fire and dry clothes she knew were waiting for her.

After dinner comprising of pork, cabbage and potatoes, Mina and Senta played games with the two Goldberg children while the adults talked privately.

Finally, after what seemed like forty days and forty nights, the rain slowed down to a normal torrent, rather than the biblical one they'd been experiencing all day.

The Goldberg children were already asleep and their parents were about to join them. Senta and Mina had separate rooms and Mina lay on her bed drawing sketches of her and Michael together in a house by a large lake somewhere.

She enjoyed drawing, but she would never be as good as Senta, who had a natural talent. Senta's dream was to go to art school, where she would thrive. She could look at anything just once and be able to recreate it perfectly from memory, hours or even days later.

Her artistic talents were in evidence all over the farmhouse, as her mother had framed many of her drawings of Ryskamp and hung them on the walls.

Mina had asked her to draw a scene of her and Michael by the same lake she always imagined, and the result had been astounding. That drawing now took pride of place on the wall opposite her bed so it would be the first thing she saw in the morning and the last thing she looked at before falling asleep.

As she drifted off, her eyes shot open with a start. Something wasn't right, and through the fog in her brain, Mina struggled to work out what it was.

Then it dawned on her. The sound of vehicles – more than one – was getting louder and closer.

Someone was coming!

Chapter 21

Everyone else in the house must have heard it too, because a flurry of panicked footsteps and urgent, hushed voices sprang up outside her room.

A shiver ran down her spine as her bedroom door burst open, and her father rushed in, his face a canvas of terror and urgency.

"Mina," he panted, his voice trembling with fear. "The Gestapo are here! Gather the children and get to the barn right now."

"What about you, Papa?" Mina stammered, her world erupting into a hive of fear and desperation. She hurriedly threw on as many warm layers of clothing as she could muster.

"There's no time for that," her father snapped. "They're here now. We have to go."

Mina had one last, longing look at the drawing on the wall of her and Michael by a peaceful lake. Then she ran down the stairs to the door at the back of the house.

She arrived to a crescendo of chaos. Senta was already there, trying her best to pacify the Goldberg children. Mr and Mrs Goldberg, their faces ghostly white in the dim light, looked like figures trapped in a nightmare.

"Silence them," her father barked at Mr Goldberg. "You know what will happen if the Gestapo find you here. Stick to the plan and get to the barn. Now!"

As Senta thrust the rear door open, the howling gale outside seemed to echo the turmoil within. The Goldbergs, burdened with their children and their fear, stumbled after her. Mina hesitated, her heart torn.

"Papa, Mama, where are you?" she called back into the house, her voice a blend of desperation and urgency.

"Go, Mina, we're right behind you." Her parents appeared, laden with heavy rucksacks.

The night air was thick with the sound of danger drawing nearer. The last thing Mina heard before plunging into the dark was the frightening thud of fists against the farmhouse door.

Scrambling to catch up with Senta and the Goldbergs, Mina felt her parents close behind. Once they were in the barn, her father secured the door with practiced urgency, using a heavy plank as a makeshift barricade.

The storm blocked any moonlight from entering through the windows, and for the first time, Mina was grateful for the foul weather.

"Go!" her father hissed. "We've rehearsed it a thousand times. Go!"

Senta, moving with a confidence honed by countless rehearsals, led the way. They followed her to the barn's darkest corner underneath the low ceiling of the hayloft.

Even in the darkness, she knew exactly what to do. She fell to her knees, moved the hay away from the floor, and reached down, grabbing the handle of a wooden trapdoor hidden in the corner. This was a secret the Postners had kept to themselves – not even Michael had been told about it during his time of need a year earlier.

Fearing for his life, he spent two years building a concealed escape route from the farm that led into the darkness of the Black Forest. The tunnel could be used as a hiding place until it was safe to return home, or at worst, it was an escape route out of Ryskamp.

Ever since the First World War ended, the tunnel had been largely forgotten about, but during the rise of the Nazis, especially after Kristallnacht, Tim Postner had revived the old relic and spent weeks clearing it out in readiness for a disaster. The family dreaded the day they would ever have to use it, but right now, it might just save their lives.

The sound of banging on the barn door dragged Mina from her thoughts. Senta was already in the hole at the back of the barn, and the Goldbergs were passing down their two children, who were crying uncontrollably. Their mother tried to console them, but it wasn't working. Luckily, the wind buffeting the barn smothered the noise they were making.

"Mina, go!" Her father pushed the heavy rucksacks towards the escape tunnel.

"I'm not going without you, Papa."

"Mina, go now before we're all caught. Go! Now!"

Mina dropped to her knees and crawled to the hole in the ground. She sat on her rear and slowly clambered into the tiny escape hole. The hole was only a few feet deep, and Mina could stand on the bottom and see out into the barn.

Mina waited for her parents, and as her father approached, he said, "Go! We're right behind you."

Mina moved deeper into the tunnel, grabbing one of the rucksacks. Mr Goldberg had the other one. She waited for her father, but all she heard was the banging of the secret compartment lid coming down and then the sound of hay being scattered back over the entrance.

"Papa!" Mina screamed. "No!"

The Gestapo's relentless pounding on the barn door jolted Mina to her core. Each loud bang on the door sounded like a shot being fired into her body, and she shivered at the thought of what was going to happen to them once they were in captivity.

The tunnel was narrow, not much wider than a person's body, and was no higher than three feet. The children were sobbing and as Senta was leading the way, she didn't know what was going on behind her.

Mina knelt in the darkness, not knowing what to do. Her parents were sacrificing themselves to save them and the Goldbergs, but that didn't make her feel any better. She pushed up the corner of the trapdoor to hear better what was happening in the barn.

Chapter 22

Mina pressed her hands over her ears and silently screamed. As the barn doors smashed open, she couldn't see much from her hiding place, other than several pairs of feet.

Above the storm, she distinctly heard the raised voices of angry, storm-ravaged men screaming at her mother and father.

"Why are you here?" her father shouted.

"You know why we're here," a gruff voice snapped back.

"We're simple farmers who keep to ourselves."

"Why are you hiding in the barn then?"

"We're not hiding," her father said. "We're repairing the leak in the roof over there in the corner, see." Her father pointed to a place opposite the trapdoor, where water was leaking in.

"I don't believe you. You're hiding a Jewish family. You're helping them escape."

"I don't know what you're talking about," her father responded.

"You've been helping Jews for the last year," retorted the agent seemingly in charge. "Your time is up, Tim Postner."

"I don't know what you're talking about," her father repeated. "We're just trying to mend a hole in our roof."

Mina's heart raced as she saw her mother's legs next to her father's as they stood close together.

"Bring him in," the man in charge ordered.

Mina couldn't tell how many men were there, but from the sound of the voices and shuffling feet, there must have been at least half a dozen. A few minutes later, she reeled in horror when she saw the coal merchant flung to the floor in front of her parents. He'd been badly beaten, and she could tell his face was battered, bruised, and bloodied.

"We know everything, Postner," the chief Gestapo agent snarled. "We know who you helped escape, who you work with, how they got here, and where they went after they left. Your entire network is exposed, so stop lying and tell us where they are."

The ensuing silence was as loud as any thunderstorm Mina had ever heard. She knelt in the darkness, wondering what to do. She didn't possess any weapons, and even if she did, the Gestapo agents were better armed.

If she tried anything, they would mow them all down within seconds. Her parents had sacrificed themselves so she and Senta could live, and Mina, heartbroken, was not about to jeopardise that.

She observed the unfolding scene with a surreal detachment, as if she were absorbing the words of a novel rather than witnessing reality. Yet the harsh truth was undeniable. The coal merchant revealed eyes swollen from the Gestapo's boots, a stark reminder of the grim reality before her.

"I'm sorry," he gasped. "They've got my family. They

took them. My wife and daughter, the Gestapo took them. I had no choice."

"It's not your fault," Mina's father said. "We know how cruel they are. We're supposed to be fellow Germans, yet these people act like animals."

One of the Gestapo agents struck her father on the side of the head, knocking him to his knees and Mina flinched at the sound.

"Where are the Jews?" the man in charge asked.

The coal merchant broke in, "It's the Shaefers' fault, I'm sure of it. They're the ones who betrayed us."

Her father was on his knees, and from her hiding place, Mina could just about see the back of his head. He was looking down at the coal merchant, probably with as much sympathy as Mina felt for him.

The man in charge snapped again. "Shut up!" Boots crashed into the coal merchant's body. Mina cringed as the sound of boots on bone cracked the night air. "Last chance, Postner. Where are they?"

Her father rolled to his feet. "By now, they're far from here, out of your reach, and safe from the Gestapo's clutches. You're not fit to call yourselves German."

Another heavy thud as the butt of a rifle slammed into her father's midriff, sending him once again sprawling to the floor. Irma, her mother, sobbed, "Leave him alone. Stop this now."

"Where are your daughters?" another Gestapo agent asked. "You have two daughters, Mina and Senta. Where are they? Are they with the Jews?"

"Long gone," her father hissed through the agony.

"You know the penalty for helping Jews," the chief agent said menacingly. "When we catch them, and we will, they will be sent to a concentration camp and into forced labour. Do you really want that for your daughters?"

After a moment's silence for dramatic effect, the agent continued. "Tell us where they are, and we'll spare them. You will take the blame and your daughters will be allowed to live here, on your farm, unharmed."

Neither of her parents said a word. They knew he was lying.

"Take them back to headquarters. They'll talk there."

Mina watched helplessly as hands dragged her father roughly to his feet. As they were about to move, someone else entered the barn and Mina's blood turned ice cold when she recognised the voice.

"Good evening, Herr Postner," the voice said calmly. "I always knew we would one day meet in these circumstances."

It was Dieter Lutz, Carl and Alwyn's father, and the leader of the local branch of the Nazi party in nearby Glatten.

"Herr Lutz," her father said, "you know we are innocent. Tell these men to stop this now."

"You're innocent?" Lutz's voice rose. "My son, Alwyn, died in this barn, perhaps even on the very spot where I'm standing right now. I always suspected that you murdered him and sheltered the British spy. And even if it was he who pulled the trigger, it was you, Tim Postner, who was responsible."

Her father was silent, the tension palpable in the air.

"Do you know who killed my other son, Karl?" Lutz asked, his voice menacing. Mina trembled from her hiding place under the hayloft.

"Everybody knows," her father answered. "It was all over the newspapers and newsreels at the cinema. Karl died a hero protecting the doctor from an undesirable who broke into the doctor's home."

A choking sound emerged from Dieter Lutz's throat.

"That's the official story, released because we didn't want the local population to worry in their beds at night. Do you want to know what really happened?"

Silence.

"I'll tell you. Karl's job was to protect Dr Halmer, which he did with his life. It was the British spy, Michael Fernsby, who broke into Halmer's home and murdered both the doctor and my son in cold blood. The same British spy you sheltered here, and who murdered Alwin in this very barn!" Lutz screamed the words out.

"I'm sorry," her father said. "But that had nothing to do with us."

"Nothing to do with you?" Lutz screamed.

Mina shuddered.

"If you'd done as you were supposed to do, the British spy would have been apprehended as soon as he set foot in your barn. Alwin and Karl would be alive today if you'd done your duty. No, Herr Postner, Alwin and Karl may have died at the hands of the British spy, but you may as well have pulled the trigger."

A loud gunshot rang out, deafening Mina and taking her by surprise. She almost let out a scream but stopped herself just in time by placing her hand over her mouth. Her mother did scream, however.

Her father crumpled to the ground in a heap, dark liquid oozing from the side of his head. Lutz had shot her father in the temple, murdering him in cold blood.

Mina was about to climb out of her hole. *To hell with saving myself. He isn't getting away with this.*

"That's enough!" the Gestapo chief yelled. "Put the gun away, now! We need them alive so we can question them."

There was silence. Mina couldn't see what was happening, but from the sound of it, the other agents were leading Herr Lutz away from the scene of his crime.

"Take these two!" the Gestapo chief ordered. "I'll send someone back for Postner's body."

The coal merchant was dragged sobbing out of the barn alongside her mother, who was hysterical with grief. Mina held herself together until the sounds of the vehicles faded into the distance and the farm fell quiet.

She'd completely forgotten about the Goldberg family and Senta behind her, and she was surprised when she felt a tug on her leg. It was Mr Goldberg.

"Senta wants to know what happened," he whispered.

"Stay there, and don't make a noise," Mina whispered harshly. She clambered out of the hiding place and, remaining on her hands and knees, crawled over to her father. Wind roared through the broken barn doors, banging them back and forth in the darkness.

Her breath stuck in her throat as she approached her father. Warm, sticky liquid covered her hands, making her want to vomit.

She turned her father over, and even in the barely discernible light, she could see the blood oozing from the wound at the side of his head. Tim Postner was dead. His lifeless eyes stared back at Mina, and large tears rolled down her face. Her chest heaved, and she sobbed for all she was worth.

"I'm sorry, Papa," she said. "I'm so sorry I couldn't save you."

She threw her arms around her father's chest and held him tightly, praying for the miracle she knew wouldn't come.

A scuffling sound in the corner got her attention. Senta was forcing the Goldbergs out of the secret tunnel so she could see what was going on.

Mina couldn't let that happen. She left her father, giving him one last longing look, and scooted back over to the corner.

"Get back in there," she hissed. "Now!"

Mr Goldberg was already out, and the first of the two children were halfway out of the hole when Mina got there.

"Get back in there, now," she said again.

"But I want to see what's going on," the child yelled from behind.

"There's nothing to see," Mina lied. "We have to get out of here now. The Gestapo will be back any minute. Get back, go!"

The child reluctantly backed down into the small hole, followed by Mr Goldberg. Mina took one last longing look at the devastating scene around her and closed her eyes, forcing back the tears. Now she had to be strong for Senta and the Goldbergs. She pulled the cover back over the hole, made sure she had one of the two rucksacks, and yelled forward to Senta.

"Did you get one of the rucksacks?"

"Yes," came the terse reply. "Where's Mama and Papa?"

"I'll tell you later. Now move."

Mina knew the Gestapo would be back in force.

Chapter 23

For half an hour, Mina painstakingly manoeuvred through the cramped, dark tunnel. Carved in haste by her grandfather, it was a rough-hewn passage, barely wide enough to allow her to kneel and push forward.

The tunnel's narrow confines forced her to move cautiously, feeling her way in the absence of light. Her only point of reference in the enveloping darkness was the occasional touch of Mr Goldberg's feet ahead, guiding her through the tight space that seemed to echo with the urgency of its creation.

The children had indiscriminate outbreaks of fear and fatigue, which distracted Mina from the heartbreak she battled with over the death of her father.

Senta cursed and yelled in front, and Mina had to remind her to remain quiet several times. What seemed to take all night, in reality only took about thirty minutes, and there was great relief when cool, fresh air rushed down the stuffy tunnel after Senta opened the hidden trapdoor close to a group of trees on the edge of the Black Forest.

One by one, they clambered out of the tiny dark hole and leant against the trees, gasping for air, and taking in deep breaths while they surveyed their surroundings with wide, cautious eyes.

The forest, dense and unyielding, seemed to watch them in return, its silence offering a stark contrast to the frenetic escape they had just endured. Each of them, still grappling with fear and exertion, allowed themselves a moment of respite, their chests heaving in the cool, earthy air of freedom.

The rain felt good on Mina's skin as it cooled her sweat-soaked body from the effort of crawling over half a mile in the darkness.

After a few minutes, Senta walked over and slumped down beside her older sister.

"What happened?" she demanded. "Where's Mama and Papa? What was all the shouting about? Did the Gestapo get them?"

Mina closed her eyes and grimaced. She put her arm around her younger sister's shoulders and pulled her tightly towards her.

"Back there," she said, her voice barely a whisper. "I couldn't see much, but I heard it all. It was terrible, Senta."

"Where are they?" Senta asked again.

"They're gone." Mina's voice broke in the darkness.

Senta pulled away from Mina's grip and spun around to face her. "What do you mean, they're gone? Did the Gestapo take them?"

The look on Mina's face told her it was worse.

"What happened?" she wailed.

"The Gestapo caught the coal merchant and threw him to the floor in our barn. He lay there, covered in blood, and he looked as though they'd beaten him badly.

The Gestapo questioned Papa, and he stood up to them, Senta. He was so brave."

"What did he tell them?" Senta's voice was close to breaking and Mina squeezed her arm to comfort her.

"The Gestapo asked where we were, but he wouldn't tell them. They were about to take them away for questioning when Dieter Lutz entered the barn."

"Dieter Lutz?" Senta asked, her eyes wide with trepidation. "What did he want?"

"He's the head of the local Nazi party, so he would have known about the raid on the farm. If you want my opinion, he probably organised it," Mina said.

Mina took a deep breath before continuing. She glanced around and noticed Mr Goldberg in the half light of the forest. His furrowed brow and slumped shoulders spoke of his guilt at what he'd done to the Postner family. She turned to face him.

"It's not your fault, Mr Goldberg," she said. "Don't blame yourself for what they did to us."

"What happened to Papa?" Senta demanded, yanking Mina back to face her.

"He accused Papa of being responsible for Alwyn's death. And then he told him what really happened to Karl."

"Karl?" Senta asked. "I thought he died a hero."

"He died, but he was no hero," Mina said. "He did some things…" Her voice broke off. "Some terrible things."

Senta reached out to her sister. "I know," she said softly. "We all knew. But there was nothing we could do about it. I'm so sorry, Mina."

Tears fell from both girls' eyes. The Goldbergs sat, holding onto their children, listening with anguish as Mina explained what had happened.

"Lutz told Papa that it was Michael who killed Karl and the doctor, not some undesirable who wandered in off the street. And he blamed Papa for it, because he said he should have turned Michael in when he came to Ryskamp last year. He said that none of this would have happened, and both Alwyn and Karl would be alive today if it weren't for our treachery."

Senta stared at her sister.

"Papa didn't say a word." She hesitated. "He shot him in cold blood in the middle of the barn. Papa was dead before he hit the floor."

Senta threw her hand to her mouth and rocked back and forth. "Mama?" she asked.

"The Gestapo took her and the coal merchant for interrogation. When they're finished, they'll send them to a concentration camp."

"At least she's alive," Mina added.

"Papa…" Senta rocked back and forth. "No."

Mina once again hugged her sister, and this time, she refused to let go. They held each other for a full five minutes until Mina released her.

"The Gestapo will be all over this place," Mina said. "Our parents sacrificed themselves for us, so we need to live so we can tell their story when this nightmare is over. We have to get out of here, Senta."

Clearly in shock, Senta nodded.

"I need you to be strong," Mina said. "There'll be time to grieve later, when we're safe."

She looked over at the Goldbergs. "Are you ready?"

Mr Goldberg nodded. "We're very sorry about your parents," he said.

Mina ignored him and turned to her sister. "Grab that rucksack," she ordered. "And let's get going."

"Where are we going?" Mr Goldberg asked.

"We have a plan for emergencies," Mina answered. "Everyone who helped Jews escape had a plan of their own that we kept private. We hoped we'd never have to use it, so let's hope it works."

"Where are we going?" he asked again.

"Out of Germany," Mina answered.

Chapter 24

After passing around a bottle of water, Mina led the bedraggled group through the dark, wet, Black Forest on a well-rehearsed journey she'd hoped never to make.

The thunderstorm and heavy rain that matched her mood were both a blessing and a curse. It was a blessing because the footsteps and the chatter of the children would be difficult for anyone searching for them to hear.

It was a curse because it was also difficult for them to hear anybody approaching, although Mina doubted the Gestapo would be out in the Black Forest on such a filthy night.

It was much more likely that they would perform house-to-house searches in the area over the following days after interrogating their mother and the coal merchant. At least that's what Mina told the Goldbergs when they asked if they were safe.

She was thankful for the detailed plans her father had made for a situation like this, and although she'd complained as much as Senta at the number of times he'd forced them to rehearse, right now she was grateful.

And heartbroken.

"Where are we going?" Mr Goldberg asked for at least the fifth time.

"As I keep saying," Mina answered, "Everyone involved in aiding you had a rescue plan of their own, and this is ours."

"But what if the Gestapo know where we're going?" Goldberg pressed on. "Then what do we do?"

"Then we're in serious trouble," Mina said. "There is no other alternative."

The group fell silent, even the children, as they made their way through the dark, dense, and soaked Black Forest. Mina's mind drifted to how Michael must have felt the previous year when he was being pursued by what seemed like half of Germany.

At least she knew where she was going. Michael didn't.

The three-mile route was ingrained in Mina's brain, such was the amount of practice her father had made the two sisters perform over the previous months. They could make this trip in their sleep.

In fact, she did. She'd dreamt about it several times, but in her dreams, she always seemed to end up by the side of the lake with Michael at her side.

She shook herself back to reality and, clinging to the belief, or at least the hope, that the Gestapo would wait to search for them until after the interrogation, she led them out of the Black Forest and into the outskirts of the small town of Freudenstadt.

After spending the next forty-five minutes skirting around buildings and keeping out of sight as much as they could, she eventually stopped in the middle of a dense group of trees that formed a square between two rows of houses.

"Stay with the Goldbergs. I'll be right back," she whispered to Senta, who hadn't said a word during the entire trek through the Black Forest.

Mina knew she was suffering from shock at the sudden loss of their parents, and she made a mental note to comfort her sister as soon as they got a moment to relax together.

"Did you hear me?" She shook Senta's shoulders. "Stay with the Goldbergs. I'll go and make sure everything's all right."

Senta nodded, her face as pale as snow.

"Good. I'll be right back."

Mina left her rucksack with her sister and left the safety of the trees. She climbed over a small fence into the rear garden of a house that faced Ringstrasse, one of the main streets in the town.

Peering through the darkness at the side of the fence, she ran to the rear windows, placed her ear to the glass, and listened. The curtains were drawn tight and it was impossible to see inside.

As it was the middle of the night, she didn't expect to hear any voices. If she did, it would mean the Gestapo were already there waiting for them, so she held her breath and listened.

Everything seemed quiet, so she stepped back, picked up a handful of small stones from the side of the garden, and threw them gently at the upstairs window. After the third try, the curtain fluttered, and a face appeared at the glass.

Mina sighed in relief. The Gestapo hadn't learned about the Stummer family yet. The face at the window spotted Mina in the garden below and pulled away, allowing the curtain to drop back into place.

A few minutes later, Mina heard the locks on the rear door being drawn back, and the door creaked open.

"Mr Stummer," Mina whispered when she got close. "It's Mina Postner. We're in trouble. The Gestapo killed my father and they've taken my mother. We need your help."

Mr Stummer looked around to make sure nobody was watching, and then signalled with his hand for her to approach.

"I'm not alone," Mina said. "I'll be right back."

She jumped over the fence and ran to the trees where Senta sat with the Goldbergs.

"Come on," she whispered, indicating everything was clear.

She picked up the rucksack, threw it over the fence, and jumped after it. Senta followed, then Mrs Goldberg, and finally Mr Goldberg, who had taken the other rucksack from Senta, came last after helping his two children over the fence.

The soaking wet, bedraggled group shuffled into the Stummers' living room. Mr Stummer's wife had now joined him in her dressing gown.

Although she left the light on over the stairs, she purposely didn't turn on the overhead light that would have given the signal to anybody watching that something was going on in their house in the middle of the night.

"The Gestapo don't need any excuses to raid homes," Mrs Stummer said as she guided them into the darkened room.

"We're sorry to put you in danger," Mina said, standing near the door.

She glanced at her sister, who had still not spoken since Mina had broken the news to her.

"What happened?" Mr Stummer asked.

Mina turned her head and looked towards the elderly couple who were risking their lives helping them escape.

Mr and Mrs Stummer were in their mid fifties and had known the Postner family for as long as Mina could remember.

Although not directly involved in smuggling Jewish people out of Bavaria, the Stummers had occasionally stepped in to help when things had gone wrong.

It was the Stummers who helped Anna Rosenberg and her family escape to Holland once the furore of Kristallnacht had died down a little. Mina's parents sheltered them for almost two weeks before the Stummers took over and organised their escape from Germany.

"What happened?" Mr Stummer asked again, gently.

"We always knew this might happen," Mina said. "Papa warned us about it, but we hoped it would never come to this."

She wiped her eyes before continuing. "Somebody betrayed us, and the Gestapo showed up this evening with the coal merchant, who had brought the Goldbergs to our farm a few days ago. They were going to leave tomorrow morning, but now our entire network is in danger."

Mina suddenly looked up, realisation and panic in her eyes. "Mr Stummer, you might be in danger too."

Mr Stummer held his hands up. "Relax, child, we're not a part of your group, and nobody outside of you and your parents knows anything about us. The Gestapo have no business with us."

"You don't understand," Mina said, blinking heavily, trying to stop the tears from flowing down her face. "They've taken Mama, and you know what they'll do to her."

"Your mother is made of sterner stuff than that," Mr Stummer said. "Don't worry about us. So, tell me, what happened exactly?"

All eyes fell on Mina, and she spent the next ten

minutes telling everyone what had happened in the barn. Senta just sat, expressionless and motionless, staring forward. Mina wasn't even sure if she'd heard a single word she'd said.

When she finished, she went and sat next to her sister and put her arm around her, trying to comfort her.

Senta never moved.

"You need to get out of the country," Mr Stummer said eventually.

The elderly couple looked at each other, and Mina could see the pain on their faces. She knew how close they had been to her parents.

"We're sorry about your parents," Mr Stummer said. "But we need to think about you now. The Gestapo won't stop until they find you, especially now they know that you've been helping Jewish families for the last year. We need to get you out, all of you." He waved his hand around the room to include the Goldbergs,

"How?" Mina asked. "How are we going to get out?"

"The same way we helped your friend last year," Mrs Goldberg said gently. "Leave that to us. In the meantime, you'll hide in our basement and not come out under any circumstances. We'll bring you everything you need, and we'll come and get you when everything's arranged."

"What will you do?" Mina asked.

"We'll get you out of Germany."

"To where?"

"Holland."

Chapter 25

As daylight faded, Sir Robert Stourcliffe found himself staring at his reflection in the full-length window of his office, which overlooked the Nieuwe Maas River in Rotterdam.

The light outside was dimming, but the troubles in his eyes were clear as day. It had been a terrible week, and today had just added to the weight of it all.

His reflection showed an ageing man worn down by anger and frustration, standing amidst the luxury that felt more like a gilded cage than a prestigious office.

He glared as four hefty men struggled to lift the solid mahogany desk from his private office and carry it through the extra-large doorway towards the lifts.

"Be careful with that desk, damn it." Stourcliffe spoke in a cultured accent that was several centuries out of date. He sounded as though he came from the time of Henry VIII and Elizabeth I rather than modern-day Europe.

Robert Stourcliffe, once a star athlete at Trinity University, held the distinction of being Britain's wealthiest man. But that wealth did not bring with it a modicum of humility or empathy.

Stourcliffe was a shipping magnate and, after he used the Great Depression as an opportunity to buy the shipping business from his struggling rivals, the Fernsby family, he was now the owner of the largest private shipping company in the world.

He drew himself to his full six-foot height and looked woefully at his ageing features reflected in the pane. His once trim figure that had won many awards was now portly, some might even say chubby, due to his overindulgence in the finer things in life.

He spun away from the depressing image of himself and focused his ire on the men struggling to carry the heavy desk to his exacting standards.

"I said be careful with that," Sir Robert snapped in his cultured, aristocratic voice.

He'd been like that all week, short fused and on edge as he barked orders at the men he'd handpicked to empty his prized offices of his valuable belongings.

Each piece of furniture, whether it be the large mahogany desk, the leather-bound chairs, the rare oak bookshelves, or the paintings on the wall; each one was worth several times, indeed many times, an average man's lifetime earnings.

And he wasn't about to have them damaged by these imbeciles who could barely talk, never mind understand the true value of what they were carrying.

Stourcliffe was in the process of emptying his Dutch office and closing up shop. It was a major inconvenience, because Rotterdam was one of Europe's busiest, and therefore most lucrative, shipping ports for the Stourcliffe shipping line.

Closing it was the last thing Sir Robert wanted to do, but with the shadow of war hanging over Europe, he had no choice. Facing the prospect of either moving his offices out of Rotterdam or losing everything he'd ever worked for, he chose the former.

Unable to take the rough handling of his favourite European desk, he stormed past the workers, out of his private office and into the boardroom, where more men struggled to dismantle the long, highly polished oak table that weighed more than any two men could carry.

This office also overlooked the Nieuwe Maas River, and Sir Robert stood there, allowing the impressive sight to calm his frayed nerves.

The European offices of the Stourcliffe shipping line stood in the Boompjes district of Rotterdam, which was a prestige area if ever there was one.

The well-to-do of Europe coveted the Boompjes area, and true to form, Sir Robert owned the largest building on the entire strip of land. And now, he was having to give it up for that lunatic in Berlin. Sir Robert wasn't happy.

Half of his office was being moved to Marseille in the South of France, well out of the way of the Nazis, to another one of Sir Robert's European offices.

The rest was being sent back to London, where it would remain in mothballs until he could once again reclaim his prime real estate in the exclusive district of Rotterdam.

As darkness fell, Sir Robert had seen enough. He was hungry, tired, and out of patience. Before he ended up slapping someone, he ordered his chauffeur to meet him by the riverfront. He was done for the day.

His driver was taking him to a dinner meeting at seven pm at the private, upmarket Royal Maas Yacht Club overlooking the waterfront. For this important occasion, Sir Robert had booked the entire building.

Stourcliffe needed privacy. He couldn't afford to have any prying ears listening in to what he had to say.

Chapter 26

He was about to have dinner with Wilhelm Zobart, the Dutch Minister for Maritime Affairs. He knew Zobart very well and had, in fact, paid him handsomely over the years in return for favourable contracts, reduced rents, and preferential treatment in various maritime projects in the port of Rotterdam.

Their relationship, a well-guarded secret, was the cornerstone of Sir Robert's success in the industry, at least in Holland.

As he prepared for dinner, Sir Robert reflected on how Zobart's influence had opened doors that would have otherwise remained firmly shut to him, paving the way for lucrative deals and a significant expansion of his shipping empire.

The dinner, unlike the many before, took on more significance because as much as he didn't like it, Stourcliffe was going to have to trust Zobart.

And that was one thing he'd never done.

Zobart had benefitted handsomely from Sir Robert's

generosity over the years, and now it was time to call in those favours.

Sir Robert took his seat, and while enjoying a glass of wine, he leafed through the exclusive menu.

The waiter came over and announced the arrival of his honoured guest. Normally, men rose to meet Zobart, but not Sir Robert Stourcliffe. He remained seated and looked up over the rim of his gold-rimmed glasses. "You're five minutes late, Zobart," he snorted.

"It's nice to see your manners haven't improved, Robert," Zobart replied before taking a seat opposite him. Stourcliffe peered over the menu at the man who'd joined him.

Similar in age to himself, in his late fifties, Wilhelm Zobart had mousy grey hair that curled over his ears, and thick, bushy eyebrows that were untidy and drove Sir Robert crazy.

Every time he thought of Zobart, all he could think about were his disgusting, bushy eyebrows that needed to be seriously trimmed.

"I'll have the oysters for an appetiser and the Dover sole à la meunière for my main course," Sir Robert said.

"And what would you prefer, Minister?" the waiter asked in perfect English.

"I'll have the same as he's having," Zobart said. "Considering he hasn't given me the courtesy of reading the menu."

"You should have got here on time," came the curt reply.

As soon as the waiter left, Sir Robert got down to business. "Zobart, I've been good to you over the years. I've crossed your palms with more silver than you've ever deserved. And now I need you to repay my loyalty."

Zobart laughed. "Repay your loyalty? Sir Robert, the

only person you're loyal to is yourself. You wouldn't know how to care for someone else if your life depended on it."

Sir Robert's pockmarked cheeks turned red. "Be careful how you speak to me, Zobart. You owe me. I've made you a very wealthy man."

"After all the favourable business deals you've received in the port of Rotterdam, I believe it's you who owes me, Sir Robert. Now, enough of that. Why have you summoned me here?"

Zobart lifted his hand to stop Stourcliffe from answering.

"Let me guess. You're moving all your priceless paintings out of your offices, and you're worried about them sitting empty with the threat of Nazi Germany hanging over us. You want me to somehow take care of your precious assets until this war is over. Am I correct?"

"You're close," Stourcliffe said. "When the Germans invade, and believe me, Zobart, they're coming, I want you to cut a deal with whoever's in charge here in Rotterdam."

"You want me to cut a deal with the Nazis?" Zobart's eyes grew wider. "For what, exactly?"

"I want you to cut a deal and make them promise to take care of my property, which must remain in pristine condition until I return at the end of the war."

"Let me get this straight," Zobart said, his face a mixture of disbelief and anger. "You want me to fraternise with an enemy that is about to invade my country, and above everything else they might do to both the city of Rotterdam and our people, you want me to prioritise your office building to make sure they don't damage it?"

"That's the gist of it."

"You disgust me," Zobart said.

"That may be the case," Stourcliffe responded, "but I've paid enough for your treachery and deceit over the years to know there's no level you won't stoop to if the price is right. So, how much is it going to cost me?"

Zobart's face turned purple. Sir Robert had never seen him angry before because he'd always had him in his back pocket. He was stunned when Zobart slammed his fists on the table, stood up, and threw his napkin at the aristocratic British businessman.

"You can shove your office building up your pompous rear end, Stourcliffe," Zobart snarled. "My people are facing annihilation, and all you're concerned about is your precious building. I don't care what you say or do. You can shove it where the sun doesn't shine."

"How dare you speak to me like that?" Sir Robert leapt to his feet.

"Go to hell, Stourcliffe. I hope the Germans bomb your precious office to the ground."

And with that, he spun on his heels and stormed out of the restaurant.

Sir Robert slumped in his chair, stunned. He wasn't used to being spoken to like that. He reached for his glass of wine to calm his frayed nerves and was about to ponder how he was going to ruin the corrupt minister when the waiter brought his oysters.

"I've brought them for you and your esteemed guest, who seems to have left in a hurry, sir. What shall I do with them?"

"Leave them," Sir Robert snapped. "And bring me another bottle of wine."

"Yes, sir, right away." The waiter scurried off, leaving Sir Robert to stew on his options.

Chapter 27

Robert Stourcliffe ate in silence after the waiter brought his main course. Although furious, he decided to give the minister for maritime affairs one more chance to accept the more than generous offer to take care of his property in Rotterdam.

Failing that, he would report him to Queen Wilhelmina herself and destroy his career. The choice was simple for Willem Zobart: either take his money, which he'd had no problems doing before, or pay the price.

Satisfied, he dabbed his mouth with his napkin and emptied the remainder of the bottle of wine into his glass.

Slightly tipsy, Sir Robert felt smug and quite pleased with himself.

As he placed the empty glass on the table, he was surprised when a tall, slender man in his early forties entered the yacht club he'd rented in its entirety and took the seat that Zobart had occupied.

"Who are you?" Sir Robert asked, put out by the man's impertinence. "I've rented this entire building for myself this evening, so you're in the wrong place. Get away, go, and leave me alone."

The man, Sir Robert noticed, had a fading scar on the bridge of his nose, and for reasons he couldn't understand, Sir Robert took comfort in knowing that the man had suffered some kind of injury.

I hope it hurts.

"Sir Robert Stourcliffe," the man said in perfect English, although Stourcliffe detected a slight trace of a German accent. Butterflies fluttered in his stomach.

What does a German want with me?

Panic set in. *Are they going to kidnap me? I know I'm a valuable asset to the British government.*

"Relax, Stourcliffe," the man said, as if reading his mind. "I'm not here to kidnap you. I'm here to do business with you."

"You want to do business with me?" Stourcliffe snorted. "Who the devil are you?"

"My name is irrelevant. What is important is that you listen to me very carefully. Otherwise, your life is about to take a very bad turn."

"Are you threatening me?" Stourcliffe asked, his face turning red again.

"Your reputation does not do you justice," the man said, leaning even farther forward in his chair. "Everything I've ever read and heard about you doesn't go far enough from what I see."

Stourcliffe glared at the impertinent man sitting opposite him.

"I know all about you," the man said with a sneer. "You're a shipping magnate, and you own the largest private shipping company in the world. I also know you're the most arrogant, conceited, aristocratic imbecile in the

British Isles, whom everybody despises. Particularly your old nemesis, Gerald Fernsby."

"Fernsby? Did he put you up to this?" Stourcliffe raged. He rose to his feet and pushed his chair back. "I wouldn't put it past that impertinent inbred twit."

"Sit down, Stourcliffe. Gerald Fernsby knows nothing about this, although if he did, I'm sure he'd find it very entertaining."

Stourcliffe sat and stared at the man who'd invaded his personal space in the most obnoxious of ways.

"What do you want?" he asked again, this time a little less angrily. He was curious as to what the man was up to.

"During your frequent trips to Europe, under the guise of your shipping business, you carry out, shall we say, certain duties for your acquaintance, Claude Dansey, the deputy head of SIS and the leader of Z Organisation."

"I don't know what you're talking about," Stourcliffe said. "Have you been drinking, sir?"

"No, but clearly you have," the man replied. "You're slurring your words."

"I am not," Sir Robert said indignantly.

The man smiled. "Made you think, though, didn't it?"

Stourcliffe sat stony-faced.

"I know you deliver messages for Dansey to his network of SIS agents throughout Europe. I know who they are, where they are, and I know what they do every day of the week. You have met with them several times."

Stourcliffe didn't deny it. Instead, he sat completely still.

The man stared at Robert over the table in a clash of wills that reminded Stourcliffe of Wild West gunslingers walking out into the street with their guns strapped to their thighs, staring each other down before drawing their weapons.

"What do you want?" he asked finally.

The man said nothing. Instead, he reached inside his jacket and pulled out a large white envelope.

"Before we begin, you might want to take a look at these."

The man placed the sealed envelope on the table in front of him. "I'd be careful if I were you, because you wouldn't want anyone else to see the contents."

Sir Robert scrunched his nose and grabbed the envelope with his right hand. As he opened it, he looked at the man, who stared back, expressionless.

With dread, Stourcliffe pulled a wad of papers out of the envelope. Immediately, he closed his eyes tight and screwed up his nose.

"What is this?" he demanded.

"You know exactly what it is, Stourcliffe. You met Nina Janson a year and a half ago at the art gallery in Amsterdam. Surely you haven't forgotten her already?"

Stourcliffe closed his eyes. "Oh no," he groaned.

The sophisticated, ravishing Dutch beauty of aristocratic birth, who was related, according to her at least, to Queen Wilhelmina herself. Her flowing brown wavy hair, high cheekbones, and seductive, smouldering beauty had taken him in completely.

He leafed through the photographs of him and Nina in the main bedroom of his private villa in the exclusive Kralingen area of Rotterdam. His body trembled as photograph after photograph revealed them together in what could only be described as exceedingly compromising positions.

And world ending! For him, at least.

"She's convincing, isn't she?" the man asked.

Stourcliffe glared at the man across the table. "I'll have you shot for this," he snarled.

"No, you won't, Stourcliffe." The man sighed. "Of course, Nina Jansen isn't her real name. She isn't an aristocrat, and she certainly isn't related to Queen Wilhelmina. In fact, she isn't even Dutch. She's one of the top agents of the Sicherheitsdienst, or SD as you might better know it. She's extremely good at what she does, wouldn't you agree?" the man asked pleasantly.

Stourcliffe closed his eyes. "What do you want, and who are you?"

"My name is irrelevant," the man answered. "But here is what I want. You will give us regular updates on British shipping plans, both military through your connections with Dansey, and commercial. We need to know where the British ships are, what their plans are, and particularly, we need to know about the Royal Navy."

"I don't know what the Royal Navy's plans are. I have nothing to do with them," Stourcliffe stammered.

"You have contacts, Stourcliffe. You have connections all the way to Neville Chamberlain himself. How you get what we need is up to you. All I care about is that you get it."

"Why would I do that?" Stourcliffe asked.

"Because if you don't, I will destroy you," the man said, pointing at the pictures. "And don't think these are the only copies we have, because they're not. And if you stray just a little from our agreement here this evening, these photographs will be on the desks of every newspaper in Great Britain the following morning."

"We don't have any agreement," Stourcliffe said, his eyes wide with panic, his face as white as a ghost.

"Oh, I think we do," the man said. He passed over a second, smaller envelope. "Inside there, you'll find the details of several dead letter boxes you will use, both in Europe and in Britain. In them, you will place the information regarding the Royal Navy and the Merchant Navy. In addition, one of our agents will contact you in London. What we need to know is in that envelope, and you will reply by noon tomorrow with our first requests. Otherwise, well, you know what's going to happen."

Stourcliffe sat stunned in silence.

"Oh, and that's not all..." —the man smiled— "There's one more thing."

Stourcliffe stared at him.

"We know Dansey is in charge of the British Special Operations Group called Unit 317."

"What the hell is Unit 317? What are you talking about?" Stourcliffe asked.

"I believe that you may not know who they are," the man said. "Unit 317 is a Special Operations Unit within the SIS that carries out deniable operations on foreign soil. And although not involved in the day-to-day activities of this unit, Dansey is in overall command of them. We want you to find out about this Unit 317, who the operatives are, where they are, and, more importantly, what they are doing."

"You're asking me to commit treason," Stourcliffe stammered. "I won't do that."

"Yes, you will, Stourcliffe. Your vanity and pride won't allow you to do otherwise. Just imagine how your wife and son would react if they saw those photographs."

The man paused for effect, seemingly enjoying Stourcliffe's impossible predicament. His face had turned a shade of green, and he thought he might retch at any moment.

"I'll be shot as a traitor or hanged," he moaned softly, not believing what was happening to him.

"Not if you handle it correctly. We won't tell if you

don't." The German SD agent smiled pleasantly as if they were discussing something as benign as the weather.

"Please don't think we're totally cruel and one-sided," the man said. "There are benefits for you."

Stourcliffe cocked his head and stared.

"If you deliver on your promises today—"

"I've made no promises!"

"You're about to, and don't interrupt," the man ordered, his face suddenly serious and intimidating.

"If you deliver on your promises, the German High Command guarantees the Stourcliffe shipping line will remain intact throughout the war, and we will not damage your ships. Once the war is over and the British are defeated, your company will benefit, because you are the man who will transport goods from the Greater Reich to the British mainland. You see, we're not all bad."

Stourcliffe stared at him.

"So, what's it to be, Stourcliffe? Ruination and disaster, or thrive and become even wealthier and more important?"

Stourcliffe said nothing while the man gathered up the photographs.

"I need your answer before these are back in the envelope. If I leave without your agreement, you know what's going to happen."

Stourcliffe sat green-faced, unable to believe what he'd just heard. The man placed the envelope inside his coat and rose to his feet.

"Last chance, Stourcliffe."

As he began walking away, Stourcliffe yelled out, "Stop!"

The man turned. Stourcliffe sighed.

"I'll do it."

STURMBANNFÜHRER ALBERT KREISE settled into the comfortable leather rear seat of his Renault Primastella. He sighed and allowed a small wave of accomplishment to wash over him.

His first mission as a new member of the Sicherheitsdienst had gone well; even better than he'd anticipated. He'd expected the pompous Englishman to put up more of a fight than he'd shown, but that was down to the meticulous way he had conducted and controlled the conversation.

Sir Robert Stourcliffe had powerful connections going all the way to the very top of the British government, and he would be a valuable resource for German intelligence.

SS Obergruppenführer Heydrich will be pleased.

Chapter 28

Berlin, September 28, 1939

The Bendlerblock was busy that morning as Admiral Ludwig von Ludsecke strode towards the meeting room within the headquarters of the Office of the Naval High Command with Hitler's words ringing in his ears.

"Find out what happened with that British passenger ship and report to me at once. I'm going to hold you personally responsible for this, Admiral, so make sure you get to the bottom of it and find out what happened."

Admiral Ludsecke understood the price of failure, and he had no intention of failing the Führer. He despised the vulgar little corporal, but Hitler held all the power, and Ludsecke was milking the influence of his association with the man for all he was worth.

He strode along the narrow corridors of the Bendlerblock building in full uniform, proudly displaying his Iron Cross prominently at the top of his chest as he passed several high-ranking military officers.

He knew full well the generals behind him were turning their hats sideways in a reference to Napoleon, but none of them dared do it to his face. His access to Hitler gave him almost unlimited power at the top of the military command, and although he was hated for it, no one dared challenge him.

Ludsecke thoroughly enjoyed the power and prestige he commanded, and in his mind, it was nothing less than his breeding and rank deserved. As far as Admiral von Ludsecke was concerned, he was in the position his destiny demanded.

Two men greeted him in the meeting room. One he already knew, as it was the Supreme Head of the Kriegsmarine, Großadmiral Erich Raeder.

Ludsecke smiled as the two men rose to their feet.

Even the great Erich Raeder shows deference to me.

The other man was Oberleutnant Fritz-Julius Lemp, a junior officer in his mid twenties, who had earlier that day received the Iron Cross Second Class from Kommodore Karl Dönitz in Wilhelmshaven before his hastily arranged trip to Berlin to meet with Grand Admiral Raeder.

And Admiral Ludwig von Ludsecke.

"Sit down," Ludsecke barked.

Erich Raeder scowled at the man who was junior in rank to himself and took his seat to Ludsecke's right. Ludsecke himself sat at the head of the table, and Lemp sat to his left.

"Gentlemen, the Führer demands answers, and you will tell me the truth of what happened to the Athenia."

Grand Admiral Raeder cleared his throat and began to speak, but Ludsecke cut him off.

"The Führer wants to hear it from the man himself." He pointed at Lemp. "Tell me what happened, Oberleutnant Lemp."

"Sir, I was patrolling the Atlantic, as per my orders from Kommodore Dönitz. We spotted what we believed to be either a troopship or, more likely, an armed merchant cruiser. We engaged, and the ship sank after being struck by our torpedoes."

"When did you realise you had made a mistake?" Ludsecke asked.

"When we watched the passengers getting into the lifeboats, sir. I realised straight away that it was a passenger ship and not a military target."

"What did you do next? What were your orders to your crew?"

"What members of my navy say to their crew is none of your business, Ludsecke," Erich Raeder snapped, his face almost purple with rage. "Whatever my men do, they will answer to me, and then I will answer to the Führer. You have no right to question my men, and you will desist at once."

Ludsecke was enjoying the sight of the grand admiral frothing with anger before him.

"May I remind you, Grand Admiral, that I am here on the express orders of the Führer himself. I am granted liberty to conduct the investigation into the unlawful sinking of the Athenia as I see fit. If you have any reservations as to my methods, Erich, I suggest you take them up with the Führer."

Ludsecke stared at his rival. "If he'll spare you the time, that is."

Raeder's face turned an even deeper shade of purple, but he bit his bottom lip and remained silent.

Ludsecke smiled at his victory and continued. "Well, Oberleutnant, what did you say to your men?"

Lemp looked at Raeder, who gave a slight nod of the head for him to continue.

"Sir, I left a blank space in my logbook and didn't record what had happened. I ordered my men to never say a word about the event. As far as U-30 and her crew are concerned, we were never involved in the sinking of the British passenger ship Athenia."

"You are aware that Americans and Canadians were amongst the casualties?" Ludsecke asked. "What you did violated maritime law, and the fact that you fired without warning on an unarmed passenger ship makes you guilty of war crimes, Oberleutnant. And that was on the very first day of the war."

Lemp looked at Raeder before looking back at Ludsecke.

"My crew are innocent, Admiral. I alone was responsible, and I will take whatever punishment the Führer deems fit. But please spare my men, because they were only following my orders."

Ludsecke sat back and crossed his hands. "You did the right thing by not reporting it in your logbook. The Führer believes it is best if we deny any involvement and keep it to ourselves. You will alter your logbook to show that you were somewhere other than near the Athenia, and you will deny forevermore that you were responsible."

Lemp's eyes almost shot out of his head, such was his surprise at Ludsecke's words. From his demeanour, he appeared to have been expecting the worst.

"We will deny it," Ludsecke continued. "And Joseph Goebbels will blame the British for sinking their own ship in the hope of enraging the Americans enough to enter the war, just as they did with the Lusitania in the last war. Our task is to ensure that doesn't happen."

"Yes, sir, I understand. Thank you, sir."

"Fill out your entry in the logbook. You'll find the words to use with the secretary outside this room. Leave the logbook with her along with your report to the großadmiral of what really happened."

"Aye, sir."

"You are free to go, Oberleutnant Lemp."

Oberleutnant Fritz-Julius Lemp rose to his feet and thrust his right arm out in front of him. "Heil Hitler," he roared, clicking his heels and puffing out his chest as far as he could.

Both admirals rose to their feet and repeated his salute. "Heil Hitler," they bellowed in unison.

Lemp left the meeting room, leaving the two admirals alone.

"What happened to Dönitz?" Ludsecke asked. "He should have been at this meeting today."

"He had business to attend to in Wilhelmshaven. Other U-boats are heading back to port, and he is there to oversee their next missions."

"Make sure he knows what we discussed today," Ludsecke ordered his superior officer. "I'll report back to the Führer and tell him what happened and what we are going to do about it."

"Will he be satisfied?" Raeder asked.

"Yes, I believe he will. We will deny it and blame the British. Nobody can prove otherwise, so it's our word against theirs."

Raeder took a deep breath. "So be it then. We deny it,"

"A word of warning, Erich. This cannot happen again. If it does, I cannot promise the Führer will be so lenient."

Raeder's face turned purple again, but he held his tongue and kept his thoughts to himself.

"It won't happen again. I'll make sure of it."

Ludsecke hung back until Grand Admiral Raeder left the meeting room. Then he turned to the secretary at the back and gathered the minutes of the meeting, along with Lemp's handwritten explanation of what had happened. He went outside and took the U-30 logbook with its new entries from the secretary who'd helped Lemp file the false information.

Ludsecke went to his office and waited until his own secretary had typed up the minutes of everything he'd gathered. He had her take the logbook and all the original paperwork back to Raeder's office for distribution to Dönitz and Joseph Goebbels.

The rest he placed into his briefcase and headed for home.

Chapter 29

Over the previous two weeks, Michael Fernsby had thrown himself into training and preparing for the most important mission of his life. He pounded the busy streets of London, which were a far cry from the breezy, open greens of Kent's golf courses he preferred.

He knew he was in good shape physically, so in the evenings he reflected inwards, trying his best to harden his resolve so he would be ready when the moment arrived.

Morse code training had gone well, and although he still wasn't very good at sending messages, he could encode and decode with few problems.

Although Colonel Z had a dislike for radio transmissions, and preferred using dead letter boxes and live contacts, Michael knew there would come a time when he would need to use a radio set.

The remainder of his time had been spent with Tony Sanders, planning and preparing for every eventuality they could think of. The final details would be discussed in the upcoming briefing with Colonel Z, but until that moment arrived, Michael and Tony worked on finding solutions to every scenario as it cropped up.

He lay awake at night, wondering what it would be like for him in Germany, knowing how much he was despised by Kreise and the SD, who wanted nothing more than to see him dead.

Getting Gustav Adler's briefcase out of Germany was one thing, but going to Berlin, the home of the Third Reich, and stealing the most secret documents in the realm, was something else.

Getting them out of Germany seemed impossible. So, Michael had lain awake at night, writing his final wishes that would go to his family in the event of his demise.

In the field, the best he could hope for was to find a friendly radio operator. Perhaps, through the resistance, he would transmit the encoded secrets back to London, because for the life of him, Michael could see no way of getting out of there alive.

Two weeks after his first meeting with Dansey, Tony Sanders strolled over to him late in the afternoon. He laid his hand on his shoulder and said, "Tomorrow morning, seven sharp."

Michael nodded. This was it.

The following morning, Michael walked into Dansey's office right on time. Dansey and Tony Sanders were already there, waiting for him. The atmosphere felt chilled, and a shiver ran down Michael's spine as he realised this was it. He was about to get his orders on what was likely a one-way mission.

"Sit down, Michael," Tony Sanders said. "I'll get you a coffee."

While Sanders was pouring Michael a coffee, Dansey looked over his desk at the young operative.

"I know we're asking a lot, Captain Fernsby, but you

have proven more than once that you're able to rise to the occasion. This is quite possibly the most important mission of the war, because if we can get our hands on Dönitz's plans for the U-boats, we can change the course of the war in the Atlantic and defeat Hitler. At the very least, it will force Dönitz to rewrite the strategy for the U-boat campaigns, and that will put them back several months, if not years."

"I understand, sir," Michael said. "I won't fail you."

He wished he felt as confident as he was purporting to be.

Dansey sat back and touched his fingertips together. "You leave a week from Monday, which is the ninth of October. This gives you a month to enter Germany, make contact with the resistance, finalise your plans, and be ready after the Naval High Command's meeting on the eighth of November."

Michael closed his eyes and took a deep breath.

"There is added risk to this mission," Sanders said. "German intelligence knows who you are, but the last place they would expect to see you would be in Berlin."

"I hope you're right," Michael said. He didn't need Sanders or anyone else spelling it out. He already knew.

"The RAF will take you to Holland," Sanders continued. "And from there, you'll make your way to Hamburg, where the resistance will be expecting you. After training together and completing your plans, you will travel to Berlin and carry out the operation."

"I assume I won't be alone?" Michael asked. "I'm going to need help with this one."

"You won't be alone," Dansey said. "You'll be accompanied by the resistance members from Hamburg."

"Can they be trusted?" Michael asked.

"The man you will be working with has a long history

with SIS," Dansey answered. "He has his own reasons for wanting to get at the Nazis. He's trustworthy, Captain. You don't need to worry about that."

Michael wasn't completely convinced, but the image of the woman he'd known as 'Mother' ran through his mind. That incredibly brave woman had given her life to protect Michael, so if this man was half as dedicated as she'd been, it would be an honour to serve alongside him.

"The exit, as you know, has been the subject of deep discussions." Sanders pulled Michael from his thoughts. "And here's what you'll do. You'll make your way to Denmark, and we'll get you out from there."

"Nothing to it then," Michael said sarcastically. "How am I getting back from Denmark?"

"You'll get all the details, but you'll travel back on a merchant ship." Sanders looked away, avoiding eye contact with Michael.

"Who owns the merchant ship I'll be travelling on?" Michael asked, tension gripping his chest. "It's not who I think it is, is it?"

"Sir Robert Stourcliffe does a lot of work for SIS; more than you'll ever know, Captain." Dansey took a deep breath. "He's a patriotic British man who loves his country, and he'll put aside any personal grievances for king and country."

"Are you sure about that?" Michael asked. "He hates my family."

"Not as much as he hates the Nazis," Dansey snapped. "I trust Sir Robert explicitly, and in this instance, you should too."

"You won't even see him," Sanders said. "It's not as though he'll be waiting dockside for you when you get off his ship."

"True enough," Michael said. "He'll be too busy

complaining to the PM that I've contaminated one of his ships."

Sanders snorted and smiled. "Now that I can see happening."

Even Dansey forced a half-smile. "Don't worry about Stourcliffe. We'll take care of him."

Dansey opened the filing cabinet behind his desk and pulled out a thick file. He tossed it on the desk in front of Michael and held his gaze.

"Study this carefully," he said. "Your life and the future of this country depend on it."

Another shiver ran down Michael's spine. The responsibility Dansey was putting on his young shoulders pressed against his soul, making him feel small and unworthy of such a mammoth task.

"We wouldn't send you if we didn't think you could pull it off." Sanders seemed to read his thoughts. "You are more than capable of doing this, Michael. We have every confidence in you."

"Study the file." Dansey was serious. "It doesn't leave the war rooms. Do you understand?"

"I understand."

"Everything you need to know is in that file. Read it, digest it, know it back to front and inside out. Today's Friday, so you have the weekend to visit your family and say your goodbyes. I want you back here Monday morning, and from then on you are to remain down here until your departure."

"Yes, sir." Michael and Tony Sanders rose to their feet.

"That will be all," Dansey said. "Good luck, Captain Fernsby."

Chapter 30

Although he was free to go, Michael didn't immediately leave for Sandwich after walking out of Dansey's office. The weight of the mission played heavily on his mind, and he couldn't face the look of sorrow on his mother's face when she realised he was going off to war.

He dedicated the entire day to poring over the file, etching every detail into his memory. As night fell, he sprawled on his bed, the day's information replaying like a loop in his mind.

Every so often, he'd spring up, a burst of realisation prompting him to scribble down notes, a safeguard against the morning's forgetfulness.

His orders were clear, yet flexible. They granted him the liberty to adapt his plans as necessary, as long as the mission's objective was met.

He was well aware that when, not if, things went awry, the responsibility to improvise would fall squarely on his shoulders. It was *his* life on the line, and he was determined to handle it his way.

He rose extra early the next morning and, as it was

Saturday, the streets weren't quite as busy as they were during the week, although that was changing now Britain was at war.

He caught the early morning train to Canterbury and took his seat in the half-empty carriage with other men, women, and children going about their daily lives.

Because of the blackout, they travelled in total darkness for the first hour, which felt strange to say the least. Michael sat back with his eyes closed, going over and over the plans for his upcoming suicide mission.

To console himself, he thought of Mina and wondered what she was doing right now. He imagined her in the barn feeding the animals, and pictured her smiling at him, which gave him goosebumps all over his arms.

Now that Karl Lutz was dead, he hoped Mina had found peace in her little corner of Bavaria. The war could pass her by, and she would be there, safe and sound, waiting for him when the war was over.

A shrill whistle sounded, informing the passengers they were approaching Canterbury, so Michael pulled himself together and got ready to disembark.

He had less than ten minutes to change platforms and make his connection to Sandwich. With any luck, he'd be there in time for a late breakfast.

Gerald Fernsby was resting after a painful night. His leg bothered him, and it often kept him awake at night. Rather than wake him, Michael told Warhurst to keep his arrival quiet until his father was awake.

He crept to his room and changed into his running gear. The one thing that had always calmed his mind was running, and there was nowhere he'd rather run than around the sandy lanes of the golf courses in Sandwich Bay.

He ran for miles, enjoying the cool wind from the sea

in his face. He felt alive, and he ran harder and harder, gasping for breath and enjoying every step as he struggled against his body in a battle of will over fatigue.

In the end, fatigue won, but not before he'd run at least ten miles. He slumped onto his bed, covered in sweat but content, which was more than he'd ever felt cooped up in the war rooms the last few weeks.

For some reason, the voice of David drifted into his mind, and he had an imaginary conversation with his deceased brother, something he often did when he was alone.

Mum and Dad need you, so don't do anything stupid. You can't win the war on your own, so stay safe and do something else. Join the army or the navy but get away from the SIS. Our family would be destroyed if you were to die as well as me.

Michael stood up. "This conversation is over, David. I'm doing it and that's it. If you were alive, you'd have seen what the U-boats did to the Athenia on the first day of the war. They'll keep doing it over and over, killing hundreds, if not thousands, of people. I have to go. I have to at least try to stop them, or at least slow them down."

His bedroom door flew open, and Lucy threw herself onto him, knocking him onto his bed. She licked him all over, and Michael laughed and played with her for several minutes.

Rescuing Lucy from that arrogant arsehole Stourcliffe was one of the best things he'd ever done, and he loved Lucy to the core of his soul.

So too did Judith, and she and Lucy were rarely separated.

"Michael, you're here!" Judith squealed, throwing herself next to him and Lucy on his single bed. "Why didn't you say anything? How long have you been here?"

"Not long," Michael laughed, trying to extricate

himself from the frenzy. "I didn't want to wake anyone, especially Dad, so I went for a run, and I just go back a few minutes ago."

"Michael's here!" Judith's yells went around the house, and soon everyone was packed into his bedroom, which was far too small for a family gathering.

"Okay, everyone," Gerald Fernsby shouted from the doorway. "Let's all go to the sitting room, where we can sit down and talk."

Michael's mother, Dorothy, led the way, or at least she did until Lucy jumped off the bed and almost knocked her over as she bundled past.

"Judith, get control of Lucy," her mother demanded.

Judith giggled and ran past, clapping and beckoning Lucy to follow, which she did eagerly.

Michael changed out of his sweat-drenched running clothes and joined the rest of his family in the sitting room, where they were all eager to ask him questions at the same time.

"Whoa." He held up his hand to stop the incessant chatter. "I can't hear anyone for all the noise."

They all began talking again at the same time, so Michael threw his hands in the air and waved them around.

"Alright, stop! I arrived this morning, but Dad was sleeping after a rough night, so I went for a run. I hadn't been back more than a few minutes when Lucy threw herself on me, and the rest you know, because you were there."

He looked over at his father, who looked pale and uneasy. Michael could tell he was having trouble sleeping, and he'd aged noticeably in the few weeks that Michael had been in London.

"How are you feeling, Dad?" Michael asked.

"I'm good, son. Don't worry about me," he lied.

"How long are you here for?" Dorothy asked.

"Only tonight. I have to go back to London tomorrow morning." Michael felt a tug inside his chest as he realised this might be the last time he ever saw his family.

Nobody complained, because every family in the country was experiencing the same thing. Military conscription was in force, and every fit and healthy man between eighteen and forty-one had been called into service.

"Are you staying in London?" Gigi asked.

"As far as I know," Michael lied. He didn't want to worry his family, and in any case, he couldn't tell them anything even if he'd wanted to.

"Warsaw fell the other day," Gigi continued. "It won't be long before Poland surrenders. Between the Germans to the west and the Russians to the east, they haven't got a chance."

"No," Michael agreed. "They don't."

"It's Western Europe's turn next," Gerald said.

"The French will stop them," Dorothy said. "With our help, we'll stop them and send them back to Berlin with their tails between their legs."

"I hope so," Michael said, although he worried it would not be that easy. "How's the sale of the doubloon going?" He changed the subject.

"Very well, actually." Gerald's eyes lit up. "The sale is arranged for October eighteenth at our bank in London. I'd like you to be there if you can."

"I don't think I'll be able to, sorry." Michael blinked at his father. "I have something important coming up."

"I understand," Gerald said after a pause.

"Did you ever find out who the buyer was?" Michael asked, keeping the subject away from the war. He was genuinely interested in finding out who was buying the Brasher Doubloon, as there weren't many families in the world who could afford such a sum.

"No," Gerald shook his head. "The condition of the sale is that the buyer remains anonymous."

"I don't blame them," Michael said. "Have you decided what you're going to do with all that money?"

"Much of it is going to save the business, and another sizeable chunk is going to pay the bank off, so this house will be safe for you and Judith after we're gone."

"I'm glad, but do it for yourselves, not me and Judith."

"Excuse me a moment." Gerald struggled to his feet and left the room.

A short time later, he limped back in, carrying a large envelope in his hand. "I meant to do this before you left, but I didn't get around to it."

"What's that?" Michael asked.

The room fell silent as Gerald placed his hand on his son's shoulder. "None of this would have happened if it wasn't for you, and we, that is your mother and I, want to thank you for it properly."

"You already did," Michael said. "I don't want anything, Dad. I'm benefitting from this just as much as you are."

"Please, allow us to do this one thing," Gerald pleaded. "It's the least we can do."

"What is it?"

"As you know, I can't get around like I used to, and it isn't going to get better anytime soon. Your mother and I are very happy here in our home in Sandwich, and now it's saved, we don't see ourselves moving around much."

"What are you getting at?" Michael asked. "I don't want you to move away from here. This is your home, not mine or Judith's."

"It's your home too, but that isn't what I'm talking about," Gerald said.

He looked at Dorothy, who rose from her chair and took the envelope from Gerald.

"Michael." Her eyes filled as she approached.

Michael stared at his mother. He had no clue what she was about to say.

"You saved us, and this is our way of showing our gratitude. You're a grown man now, and once this wretched war is over, you will need a place of your own, especially if you decide to go back to university."

Michael still didn't have a clue what was going on. He looked at Judith, who stared back with an equally blank look. She didn't know either.

"We went to our lawyer and had these documents drawn up. All you have to do is sign them and return them to us so they can be filed."

"What are you talking about, Mother?" Michael asked.

"We're giving you the house in Cambridge. It's yours, Michael."

The blood drained from Michael's face. His jaw fell so far open he was sure it hit the floor.

"Mum, Dad! No, I can't possibly accept that, at least not yet."

"We know you can't live there right now, son," Gerald said. "But it's there for you when the war is over."

"It's the least we can do," Dorothy added.

"I don't know what to say," Michael stammered. His chest tightened, and he struggled to breathe as bile rose in his stomach.

They don't know I'm going on a suicide mission, and I won't be back. They'll be in the cemetery in London wearing black clothes, mourning me as they lay a second empty coffin beside David's.

And they're trying to give me the house in Cambridge?

Michael felt completely overwhelmed and inadequate. He gripped his mother tightly and didn't utter a word, for if he did, he feared he wouldn't be able to contain his emotions.

Finally, after a long silence, he uttered two words.

"Thank you."

It was all he could manage.

Chapter 31

It had taken Mina and Senta three weeks to get out of Germany. The Goldberg family left the Stummer's basement first, a week before the sisters.

They were headed for Belgium and before they left, they held a candlelight vigil for Tim and Irma Postner, Mina and Senta's parents.

After the vigil, Senta had come around a little. She was still quiet, but her anger was directed at the Nazis, and she vowed to Mina that she would one day take her revenge.

Mina agreed and vowed alongside her that their parents would not have suffered in vain.

Mr and Mrs Stummer had risked everything to get them to safety, and it was a great relief when they finally left their basement and headed for the border.

The relief didn't last long. The over three-hundred-mile journey north in the back of a freezing truck underneath sacks of carrots and turnips was both uncomfortable and dangerous.

Several times they were stopped at checkpoints, but the secret compartment the Stummers had installed underneath the wooden bed of the covered truck held firm, and the searches came up empty.

By the time they reached the small border town of Gronau, both Mina and Senta were ready to get out of the tiny hiding place.

Mr Stummer unloaded the final sacks of produce at a grocery store in Gronau, and when he'd finished, he drove the truck to a quiet country lane outside the town.

After turning off the engine, he banged on the floor of the truck bed above Mina's and Senta's heads.

"It's time, girls. This is as far as I can take you."

Mina led the way, her limbs stiff from lying in the cramped hiding place for two days.

She shouldered the rucksack she'd brought with her from Ryskamp.

"You have enough food and supplies to last for a couple of days," Mr Stummer said. "Remember what we talked about? The border is one mile that way," he pointed to the west.

"Cross the border and go to Glanerbrug after dark tonight and look for the green door at number twenty-three Uilvlinder. It's a house by itself at the corner of the street."

"We know, Herr Stummer," Mina said. "We've been over it a thousand times."

Stummer smiled. "Tell the man you are from the grocery store. Pay him, and he will take you to your friend in Amsterdam. You have the address, don't you?"

"I do," Mina said. "Herr Stummer, we can't thank you enough. You risked everything for us, and we won't ever forget you."

"We've known your parents for as long as we can remember and helping their daughters was the least we could do. Take care of each other. Do you understand?"

Stummer looked at Senta.

"We will. Thank you, Herr Stummer, for everything."

Senta threw her arms around the old man and hugged him tight.

"We'll be back when this is all over," Mina said. "Please take care of yourselves and whatever you do, be careful of the Gestapo."

"We'll be alright, don't worry about us. You take care of your sister and make sure you survive this war."

After one more hug, Mr Stummer was gone, leaving Mina and Senta alone in the late afternoon gloom. They huddled together in a copse of trees by the side of a river and waited for darkness.

Mina surveyed their surroundings, which were nothing but farmland. Aside from a few trees scattered here and there, there wasn't much cover if they had to hide.

A couple of trucks passed them by, but they kept their heads down and remained unseen.

Mina was glad when darkness fell. She was cold, damp, and worried about getting Senta to safety. Whenever she felt overwhelmed, she allowed herself to imagine what it must have been like for Michael when he was being pursued by the German authorities through the Black Forest in the middle of winter.

He made it out alive, so if he could do it in those conditions, she could get Senta to safety now.

"Let's get going." Senta stood up. "It's dark enough, and by the time we get into Holland, it'll be bedtime for most people."

An excellent artist, Senta could see something and draw it perfectly from memory. Although warned not to by Herr Stummer, she'd drawn a map from the directions he'd had them recite over and over.

She put the map in her coat pocket and faced the darkness.

"Well, sister, it's now or never. If we survive this, it will be a miracle."

"We'll survive," Mina answered. "We have to, or Papa will have died for nothing. And Mama…" Her voice trailed off, unable to finish what she was saying.

Senta squeezed her arm and pulled her forward. "For Mama and Papa," she said.

"For Mama and Papa."

Chapter 32

They followed the country lane for a mile or so until they came to a sign at the side of the road that told them they were entering the Netherlands and leaving Germany.

Senta, who was leading the way, turned to her sister and clasped her hands. "We've made it, Mina. It's going to be strange no longer being in Germany, but there's no turning back now."

Mina squeezed Senta's cold hands. "We're not there yet but it will feel different."

Senta consulted her map by torchlight, and they turned right at the end of a field and walked past a farm on their right. As they walked past, a truck's headlights illuminated the darkness as it drove down the lane that ran parallel to theirs on the opposite side of the border.

Mina grabbed Senta and pushed her into the ditch on the opposite side of the road from the farm.

"We don't know who it is," she panted. "It could be the Gestapo looking for us for all we know."

The truck slowed, but didn't stop, and after everything fell quiet, the girls continued on their journey.

Mina's chest tightened as Senta followed her map to the street called Uilvlinder. They found number twenty-three and walked up the tiny path leading to the front door.

"Is it green?" Mina whispered.

"How would I know? It's dark."

Mina shone the torch she'd taken from the rucksack and confirmed the door was, indeed, green.

Senta stepped forward and knocked softly, although in the quiet street it sounded as though a series of gunshots were going off.

After a few moments, the door opened, and an elderly man in his late fifties peered out.

He said something in Dutch that neither girl could understand. Mina stepped from behind her sister and spoke in broken English.

"Do you understand English?" she asked.

The man nodded.

"Good. The grocery store sent us."

Mina could see the whites of his eyes, and he stepped aside. "Come in, quickly."

He looked around after the girls entered and quickly locked the door behind him.

"Were you expecting us?" Mina asked. Her English was better than Senta's, but it wasn't good enough to hold a proper conversation.

"Perhaps. Do you have something for me?"

Mina handed over an envelope full of Dutch guilders. "We go to Amsterdam."

The man showed them to yet another basement. "Wait there."

The next morning, he fed them a hearty breakfast and ushered them into the rear seat of his car. Three hours later, he dropped them off in the middle of Amsterdam.

"Now what?" Senta asked.

"We find Anna."

Using the Dutch money Herr Stummer had exchanged with them before they left, Mina bought a street map of the city. Anna had sent a letter to Mina after their escape, telling her where they were and that they were happy and safe.

"Anna's going to be surprised, don't you think?" Senta asked. "We're the last people she'd be expecting to see in Amsterdam."

"You're not kidding," Mina agreed. "She'll be really shocked."

They found the house in Westpoort, and Mina's stomach knotted when they knocked on the door.

A woman in her thirties answered, and she stared at the bedraggled girls standing on the street in front of her.

"We're looking for Anna Rosenberg?" Mina asked in her broken English. "Is she here?"

The woman looked shocked. "Come in," she said.

Mina and Senta were ushered into a sitting room and sat on a couch.

"What do you want with Anna Rosenberg?" the woman asked in German.

"She is my best friend. My name is Mina Postner and this is my sister, Senta. Anna may have mentioned us?"

"Indeed, she did, but what are you doing in Amsterdam? You're not Jews."

"We helped Jewish families get out of Germany," Mina said. "The Gestapo caught us. Our mother was arrested and our father…" Her voice broke.

"I'm so sorry." The woman's voice softened. "What is happening there is terrible. I'm sorry, but you've come all this way for nothing. Anna and her father aren't here."

"What?" Mina's spirits dropped like a stone. "Where are they?"

"They stayed here for a few months and then moved to Rotterdam to be nearer to people they knew."

"Do you know where they went?" Mina asked.

"I know the area, but that's all. I'm sorry."

"That will do. Where is it?"

"It's called Overschie, and all I know is that it's in Rotterdam somewhere."

By late afternoon, Mina and Senta were in Rotterdam. Lost and alone and running out of money, they worried about what they would do if Anna couldn't be found.

They purchased a map of the city and found Overschie to be slightly north of the city centre. Not knowing the language and not wanting to draw attention to themselves, the two tired girls walked for over an hour through the city streets until they reached the area where Anna was supposed to be living.

By now it was dark, and although the Dutch didn't have blackout regulations in force, they didn't want to be caught on the streets alone at night.

They found a guesthouse and checked in for the night, explaining to the owner that they had left Germany to find their best friend, who they now believed to live in the Overschie area of Rotterdam.

"Is your friend Jewish?" the wife of the owner asked after she had shown them to their room.

"Yes, why?" Mina was cautious.

"I ask because a few Jewish families moved here recently. Your friend might be one of them."

"Do you know where I might find them?" Mina asked.

"Some of them moved to the apartments on Lemkensstraat. That's as much as I can tell you."

Mina thanked the woman and waited until she'd left before turning to Senta.

"What are we going to do if we can't find her?" Senta asked.

Mina sighed. "We'll find a cheap place to live and find jobs so we can support ourselves. That will have to do until we find something better."

"Like what?" Senta asked. "What else do we know besides farming?"

"Then that's what we'll do," Mina answered. "We'll find a farm and offer to work for a room and food."

Senta shrugged. "It's a plan at least, although I'm not sure how welcome two German girls will be in a Dutch farmhouse."

"We'll find out," Mina answered.

Chapter 33

At dawn the next morning, Mina and Senta set off for Lemkensstraat using the directions given to them by the owner of the guesthouse.

They found it just two streets from one of the many waterways in Rotterdam and although it wasn't a big street, it contained two large two-storey blocks of apartments.

"She could be anywhere in here," Senta complained. "We'll never find her."

Mina ignored her sister and started knocking on doors. Senta saw what she was doing and joined in. Multiple apartments later, a door opened, and a face Mina thought she'd never see again appeared in front of her.

The two girls stared at each other for several moments, each unable to believe what they were seeing.

"Anna!" Mina shouted, alerting Senta, three doors down on the opposite side of the corridor.

"Mina? Is that you?"

"Yes, it's me and Senta."

The girls embraced tightly. Senta joined in and

together the three of them hugged each other for a long time.

"Anna, who is it?" a man shouted from inside the apartment.

Anna pulled the girls into the sparsely furnished flat. "Papa, you wouldn't believe me if I told you. Look who's here."

Her father came out of his bedroom and his jaw almost hit the floor when he saw Mina and Senta stood before him.

"Mina Postner?" he asked, his voice several pitches higher than normal. "What on earth are you doing here? Has something happened?" His expression suddenly changed from cheerful to a look of despair.

Mina looked at her best friend. Anna was now twenty years old and her once flowing brown hair was cut short. She'd always been on the larger side when they'd owned the general store in Glatten, but now she looked thin and pale.

She looked as though the weight of the world rested on her and her father's shoulders and she wondered if she and Senta appeared the same to them.

"What happened?" Anna asked.

Mina slumped in a chair and, with the help of her sister, told Anna and her father everything that had happened since they'd last seen each other after Kristallnacht a year earlier.

"Your mother and father were great people and I'm sorry to hear this," Anna's father said after they'd finished. "We don't have much, as you can see, but you are welcome here as long as you want."

"You can share my room," Anna offered. "I never thought I would see you again, so please stay with us."

"We have a little money," Mina said. "And Senta and I

are willing to work anywhere so we can help. Are you sure we won't burden you?"

"After what you did for us?" Mr Rosenberg said. "Never. You must stay here with us until we can all return home once the Nazis are defeated."

"We've got much to talk about," Anna said, her eyes ablaze with excitement and happiness at seeing her best friend again. "We read about the British spy at Ryskamp and I can't wait to hear what happened."

Mina smiled, her heart jolting at the mention of Michael. "It's a long story," she said.

Senta tutted and pulled her face. "You have no idea, Anna. Mina's in love."

"With a British spy?"

"I hate to break this up," Mr Rosenberg said. "But we're going to be late for work if we don't leave. Please make yourselves at home and we'll be back later, after work."

"What are you doing now?" Mina asked.

"Papa works in the general store about half a mile away. I clean and help at the radio station in the city centre. I'll miss my tram if I don't hurry, but I can't wait to see you later."

Anna and her father left, leaving Mina and Senta to get familiar with their new home in Rotterdam.

Chapter 34

The time for planning was over. Michael and Tony Sanders had gone over the plans multiple times, day and night, and every scenario had been discussed in depth.

Now it was time for action.

Secrecy was vital to the success of the mission, so all normal channels of communication and transport were off the table.

Although Michael had spent countless hours learning how to create and decrypt messages sent in Morse code, he was under strict orders from Colonel Z not to use it unless it was a last resort, and even then, it had better be a major emergency.

Instead, he was to stick to Dansey's tried, tested, and preferred method of communication, which was a series of dead letter boxes, or DLBs as they were better known, and live agents.

He had a codebook that was unique to Unit 317 stashed in one of the secret compartments of his rucksack, and this was what he was to use in his communications with London.

Over the course of the previous week, he'd been given the locations of the DLBs available to him in Holland, Germany, and then in Denmark for his extraction.

The two men filled the time it took to drive from London to RAF Tangmere on the south coast near Chichester by going over the details, making sure no stone had been left unturned.

By the time they arrived in the late afternoon, Michael was sick of talking about it. All he wanted now, in the final hours before leaving British soil for perhaps the last time, was to be left alone with his thoughts.

Sanders sensed this and after dinner in the officers' mess, he presented Michael with a key to a room he'd organised for him.

"Get some rest before you leave," he said, sliding the key towards him. "Meet me at the front entrance at midnight sharp."

"See you then."

Michael rose from his chair, grabbed his rucksack that he hadn't let out of his sight from the moment he'd packed it several days earlier, and found his way to the private room where he could be alone in the final hours before departure.

Although sleep was impossible, he lay on the bed and closed his eyes. His mind drifted from page to page of the mission brief, and with a splitting headache forming, he forced them out of his mind.

He replaced them with thoughts of Mina smiling at him in the hayloft at Ryskamp.

What are you doing? Are you safe now Karl Lutz is dead?

Images of her came to him and he immersed himself in her beauty, allowing the smells and sounds of the farmyard to consume him. He pictured her feeding the chickens and the pigs, and collecting the eggs they would use for breakfast the next morning.

Whatever she was doing, Michael wished with all his heart that he was doing it with her. He'd never imagined himself as a farmer, but right now he'd happily settle for being just that for the rest of his life.

With Mina by his side, of course.

His thoughts drifted to his family, and to his father in particular. He worried that his health was failing him and hoped he would live to see him again before the inevitable moment came.

He yearned for the comforting embrace of his mother's words, that never failed to soothe his restless soul, and he smiled at memories of playing fetch with Lucy in their back garden.

His smile vanished at the memory of Judith just two short months earlier, when he'd rescued her from kidnappers intent on ending her young life.

Is she going to be safe with me gone?

Another bout of guilt made him choke and he momentarily contemplated finding Sanders and telling him he couldn't go ahead with it.

He forced the thoughts from his brain and tried to think of nothing.

I need to calm down or I'll mess this up before I even start.

As soon as he thought that, images of David flooded his mind, and once again, he began an fictious conversation with his dead brother.

Stop this! Every mother in Britain is going through the same thing right now, wondering if they'll ever see their sons again. You can do this, Michael, so stop feeling sorry for yourself and keep that stiff upper lip!

"A few days ago, you were telling me to leave the SIS

and join the army," Michael said out loud. "Make your mind up. Do you want me to go or not?"

David didn't answer and the voices in his head fell into silence.

Chapter 35

As the clocked ticked towards midnight, Michael pulled on his black woollen trench coat and waited for Major Sanders at the front entrance of the officers' mess. Two tipsy officers in uniform walked past them, eyeing him suspiciously.

The older of the two, who looked to be in his mid thirties, looked Michael up and down, and pulled his face in disapproval at the choice of civilian attire he was wearing.

"Who are you?" he asked in an accusatory manner. Michael thought he sounded just like a younger version of Robert Stourcliffe, such was the upper crust accent he used.

Michael ignored him and looked away.

"Don't ignore me, soldier," the tipsy officer sneered again. "I asked you a question. What are you doing at the officers' mess at this hour? The privates' quarters are over there." He pointed to his left in the darkness.

Michael slowly turned to face the angry, drunken officer. "Who are you?" he asked.

"I'm Major Arnold of the Blues and Royals, Household Cavalry." The officer pulled himself to his full height of around five feet eight inches. "I ask again, who are you, soldier, and what are you doing outside the officers' mess?"

Michael was already highly strung because of what he was about to do, and he felt the anger rising in the pit of his stomach. Resisting the urge to slap the arrogant officer, he instead stepped backwards so he was out of range.

"I'm waiting for someone."

"Who? What is someone like you doing here at this time of night? I think you're up to no good."

"I will be if you don't sod off!" Michael snapped and stepped towards the major, who stepped back in surprise.

"I'll have you court martialled for this," the officer stammered. Michael could see his nose turning red and he held himself back from smacking him on it.

"God help us if you're the kind of officer who's going to lead us to victory," Michael answered back.

As the argument raged, Tony Sanders joined them. "What's going on, gentlemen?" he asked. "Is there something wrong?"

"I asked who this scruff was and what he was doing outside the officers' mess. He answered me back terribly rudely and I'm going to have him court marshalled," the man spat over Sanders, who wiped his face with the back of his hand.

"No, you won't. You're drunk and you're making an arse of yourself, so I suggest you go inside and sleep it off. You have no idea who this man is but I assure you, you wouldn't want to find out."

Sanders stood between the major and Michael, but Michael stepped past him. "Hey, Rupert," he said. "If you hadn't noticed, this is an RAF base, not an army one. You're either drunk, lost, or stupid, and I'd place my bet on the latter."

"How dare you? My name's not Rupert!" the officer raged, his nose even brighter than before.

"Be careful." Michael laughed, enraging him even further. "You'll be breaking blackout rules if that nose gets any brighter."

"That's enough," Sanders snapped. "Wait here and don't say another word," he said to Michael.

He grabbed the officer's arm roughly and dragged him off to the side. His friend started after them, but Michael stood in the way.

"Don't," he said, and something in his voice told the quiet man he meant it.

The man stood aside and watched his friend from a distance.

Tony Sanders spoke in hushed tones to the cavalry officer and although Michael couldn't hear what he was saying, he could tell from the man's demeanour that he was getting a good rollicking from Sanders.

After a few minutes, the cavalry officer let out a loud noise that sounded like the harrumph from a horse, glared at Michael one more time, and stormed inside the officers mess with his friend in tow.

"What did you say to him?" Michael asked.

"I told the drunken fool that if he didn't shut up, I'd call the commanding officer and have him locked up for interfering in a top secret, highly sensitive, and vitally important visit from the prime minister, and that you were his personal assistant and had arrived early to get things ready for him."

"He believed that?"

"I also told him that you were an expert in close quarter combat and that if he didn't leave, I couldn't promise that he'd still be in one piece tomorrow morning."

Michael snorted. "Do I look that intimidating?"

"You do when you're angry," Sanders answered. "I've seen it first-hand and I wouldn't want to get on the wrong side of you."

"Rubbish," Michael said. "I wouldn't have hurt him too much."

"We're here for a sensitive mission, Michael. You can't go around beating up an officer in the Household Cavalry, no matter how drunk and obnoxious he is."

"Fair enough. Let's get on with it."

Michael strode off towards the hangars at the other end of the airfield.

Chapter 36

Sanders gripped Michael's hand. "It seems like we've been here before, but I mean it Michael. Remember your training and take care of yourself. This mission is probably the most important one you'll ever go on, so may God protect you."

Sanders surprised Michael by grabbing his arm and lowering his head towards the ground. He understood what he was doing and joined him in prayer.

"Almighty Father, as I stand on the brink of battle, I humbly seek Your protection and guidance. In the shadow of conflict, grant me the courage to face the uncertainties ahead, the strength to uphold the honour of our nation, and the resolve to stand firm in the face of adversity.

"Watch over my comrades and me, shield us from harm, and lead us to victory. And in the quiet moments, remind us of the love and peace we fight for. For King and Country, I place my trust in You. Amen."

"Amen," Michael said.

With one last handshake, Michael turned and walked

towards the intimidating black hulk that sat silently waiting on a short piece of runway at the rear of the RAF base.

At first glance, the small, single-engine monoplane seemed unremarkable in the darkness; at least compared to the sleek beauty of the spitfires he'd seen in the propaganda leaflets on every desk in the war rooms.

Yet, as he drew closer, Michael couldn't help but admire its utilitarian beauty. The Westland Lysander's sturdy, high-wing design and its oversized, bulbous canopy gave it a distinct, almost quirky appearance.

Its short take-off and landing capability was evident in the broad, stubby wings that were perfect for landing on clandestine airstrips, hidden in fields and small clearings in the middle of nowhere.

The fuselage, painted in a dark, camouflage pattern, hinted at its primary role for operations such as this. The unassuming Westland Lysander was fast becoming legendary in Unit 317's world, as it provided a lifeline to agents operating behind enemy lines, capable of slipping in and out of enemy territory under the cover of night.

Michael circled the Lysander in the moonlight, brushing his hand against the rugged exterior, feeling the rivets and seams that held it together. For the next couple of hours, it would be his home in the sky, whisking him off to places unknown and enemies all too real.

Michael took a deep breath, trying to control the shivers that pervaded his body.

A man Michael assumed was the pilot approached from inside the hangar.

"It's a perfect night for us." The pilot pointed towards the full moon that shone brightly down on them. "With the clear weather, we should have you on the ground inside an hour and a half."

Michael nodded. One and a half hours from now, he'd

be closer to the German border than he'd ever wanted to be again, at least until the end of the war when he could visit Ryskamp to see Mina.

The pilot laid out a map of Holland on the floor of the plane behind the wing on the left side of the fuselage.

"This is where we're heading." The pilot pointed to a circled area on his map. Michael didn't need to look too closely because he knew it like the back of his hand from the maps and drawings he'd studied over the previous weeks.

"When we land, I'll slow down as much as I can. I'll give you the nod, and you've got less than a minute to open the door, jump out, and close the door again. I won't stop completely, and if you're not out by the time I indicate, the landing will be aborted and you'll be coming back to Blighty with me. Any questions?"

"No." Michael shook his head.

"Good." The pilot checked his watch. "Let's go."

Michael settled on the uncomfortable floor at the rear of the modified Lysander while the pilot readied the plane for take-off. He fastened his safety harness and took a deep breath as the engine spluttered into life and the Lysander rolled forward.

The rear Browning machine gun had been removed and Michael took the place normally reserved for the gunner, or the observer, as he was often called.

This second crew member assisted the pilot with navigation and observed the terrain to help him spot enemy positions and artillery. He would also be required to operate the Browning if the need arose.

Tonight, it was just the pilot and Michael.

Michael sat back against the cold hull and went through his rucksack, using the light from his torch to see what he was doing.

The rucksack was crammed full and was as heavy as it had ever been. Most of the weight and bulk was ammunition for his favoured Walther PPK, which had been his weapon of choice ever since he'd used one in an apartment complex in Munich a year earlier.

The main reason he chose the PPK over British made weapons was that so far, every mission he'd been on was in Germany and getting his hands on the 7.65mm rounds the PPK used was never a problem.

One of the secret compartments in his rucksack contained the codebook, which wasn't the best way to send and receive messages securely.

A one-time pad would have served him much better, but the time constraints on his training meant he'd not had the time to work with the more advanced methods.

The other significant problem with one-time pads was that they were bulky and heavy as each transmission required a new pad.

The other two secret compartments of the rucksack were filled with Dutch guilders, German Reichsmarks, Danish krone, and the three false identification documents supplied by Sanders.

The first identity was Dutch, which he was supposed to dispose of before crossing into Germany. He only had this in case the Dutch authorities stopped him during his run to the German border.

Once there, he would use the German ID he'd been given, and then finally, he would be a Swiss national for his crossing into Denmark.

Anything related to Michael Fernsby was left behind with Sanders, who had strict instructions to hand them to his parents in the event of his death.

The only other items were a set of maps and a few

sandwiches that would tide him over until he connected with the SIS in Holland.

Michael put everything back in place and sat back, taking deep breaths to control the rising tension that sent sharp pains through his chest.

One and a half hours later, the pilot turned on a red overhead light, telling Michael they were approaching the drop zone.

He was ready.

Chapter 37

The pressure in his ears increased as the Lysander dropped from the sky towards the empty field in the middle of nowhere. Michael massaged his ears to ease the discomfort and craned his neck to see out of the windshield.

A series of red lights illuminated the landing strip on the outskirts of Austerlitz in the Netherlands. The importance of this mission demanded total secrecy, so landing at a regular airport, even a military one, was out of the question.

The Abwehr had eyes and ears everywhere, and Unit 317 couldn't risk compromising the operation before it had even begun. So, they chose a small, private field close to Utrecht, where the stealth of the Lysander shielded them from their enemy.

As soon as the wheels bumped and rocked on the uneven ground, Michael unbuckled his harness and watched the red light over his head.

The Lysander slowed and a moment later the light turned green, which was Michael's cue to act. He had one minute to open the door, jump out, close the door, and get out of the way before the Lysander circled around and took off again.

A rush of cold air stung his eyes as he jumped out of the door. The plane had slowed to a crawl, but it still required quick reflexes to stay on his feet. He grabbed the door handle, slammed it shut, and ran for the cover of the trees nearby.

He watched as the pilot sped up and took off, heading back to southern England and a nice warm bed. Quietness descended as the Lysander faded away, leaving Michael alone in neutral Holland.

He lay low for ten minutes, watching all around him for signs of human activity. Gradually, the forms of two men appeared from his right.

Michael gripped his gun as they approached, and when they were less than twenty feet from him, they stopped and dropped to the floor.

"What are you here for?" whispered a voice in English.

"Strawberries and cream," Michael replied, uttering the code words he'd rehearsed with Sanders.

"I'd prefer a good cup of tea myself," came the reply from one of the two men.

Michael rose to his knees. The two SIS agents were genuine. Their job was to take him to Utrecht and set him up for the next leg of his journey.

"We're glad you could join us," the lead agent said. No names were offered or asked for; they were just ships that passed in the night. Whatever Michael's mission was, they didn't want to know.

Such were the requirements of operational security within Britain's Secret Intelligence Service.

Without uttering another word, the two men, with Michael's help, gathered the landing lights to remove any evidence of them being there. They led Michael through the trees to a narrow country lane where a third agent waited for them in a vehicle.

Michael jumped in the back, and they drove off without speaking towards the lights of Utrecht, forty-five minutes away.

Chapter 38

The tiny house on Hartingstraat was less than half a mile from the railway station, a move by SIS that hadn't gone unnoticed by Michael.

"It's late," said the agent who'd driven them to the safe house. "Get some sleep and we'll talk in the morning."

Michael was shown to a small room at the top of the stairs and he collapsed onto the soft bed with his rucksack by his side.

He awoke to the smell of bacon cooking downstairs. He ran down and entered the kitchen, where an agent was cooking bacon and eggs on the gas stove.

Michael's stomach grumbled. He hadn't realised how hungry he was until the smell of sizzling bacon entered his nostrils.

Other than Michael, the agent was the only man present. The other two were nowhere to be seen.

"Our orders were to keep you safe and take you to the border. Whatever you're doing is hush-hush, so let's keep it that way, and not talk about it."

"Agreed," Michael answered. "Although I must say that bacon smells rather good."

"I thought you might be hungry after your short hop over the Channel."

After they'd cleared their plates in silence, the agent gathered the dishes and washed them in the tiny sink.

"If you wait in the other room, we'll discuss what comes next."

Michael sat in one of the two chairs and was happy when the agent walked in with two cups of steaming hot tea.

"You read my mind," Michael said. "This will go down a treat."

The man sat next to him, set his cup down, and reached into his jacket pocket, pulling out a map of Holland.

"We're here," he said, pointing to a circled area around Utrecht.

"And I'm taking you here." He pointed to a spot near the German border.

"Let me see," Michael said. "I was under the impression that I was taking the train to the border."

"That's what was originally relayed to us, but we think it's too risky. Whatever you're here for, they want to keep it quiet. The railways are full of spies, especially around the border, so we thought it would be more prudent to take you there ourselves, so you won't be seen in public."

Michael mulled it over for a minute. "Makes sense," he said. "Where are you taking me?"

"Here," the agent passed the map over to Michael. He'd circled a small town east of Arnhem, right on the border with Germany.

"Why there?" Michael asked.

"It's rural and not heavily patrolled for one thing," the

agent said. "It's woodland, so you can cross through unseen and be in Germany without any drama."

Michael studied the map. What the agent said made sense, and he agreed with his assessment.

"How far is it to the nearest railway station in Germany?" he asked.

"Bocholt is six miles from the border and there's nothing in between. If we drop you off at night, you can walk to Bocholt by daylight and the Germans won't be any wiser."

Michael fell silent while he digested the agent's plan. In the end, he deferred to the SIS unit's greater local knowledge and agreed to go with it.

"I like it," he said. "I agree it's safer than using the train. When are we leaving?"

"Midnight. It's about seventy miles to the border, so when you take into consideration crossing into Germany and walking to Bocholt, if all goes well, you'll get there in time for the first train to wherever you're going."

Michael spent the rest of the day in his room, going over the altered plans in his head. He saw no need to report the changes to London, so he ruled out leaving a message at the DLB in Utrecht. He reasoned that he'd only use them when he had something useful to report.

After his experiences with the German railways the last time he'd been there, Michael decided to use slower trains that stopped at every town, rather than the express trains that were likely to be under heavier scrutiny.

He'd make his way to Hamburg via Dortmund, Bielefeld, and Bremen, and not worry about meeting up with the German resistance until he was in Hamburg.

It was going to be a long time before he got any more rest, so he slept most of the afternoon before joining the SIS agent downstairs for dinner.

They made small talk until eight o'clock, at which point the SIS man rose from his chair and went to his room.

"It's going to be a long night, so I'm going to get some sleep. Meet me down here at midnight."

Michael went back to his room and tried to sleep, but it wouldn't come. As the moment neared, he couldn't control the rising tension. What they were asking of him was virtually impossible, and he felt as though he was being sent to be slaughtered in the name of king and country.

He sat up and read the English newspaper the agent had brought for him earlier so he wouldn't dwell on his mission, but no matter what he tried, the nagging feelings of doubt and fear wouldn't leave him.

I can walk out of that door right now and be back home in three days.

Michael exhaled deeply. He wasn't doing that, and he knew it. Whatever he was these days, whatever he'd become, he wasn't a coward.

Chapter 39

Although the Netherlands were officially neutral, everybody knew there was a lot of spying around the border towns. The SIS agent kept to the back roads and took his time, being careful not to give the Dutch police any reason to pull them over.

The uneventful journey took two hours, and by the time the agent pulled over beside a wooded area to the south of Dinxperlo, when Michael checked his watch, it was two fifteen in the morning.

"I don't know what you're up to, but I can tell it's a big one. Be careful, and whatever you do, get back safely. This is going to be a long war, and we need every good man we can get."

The two men shook hands.

"Thank you for your help," Michael said as he exited the vehicle.

He waited in the trees until the sound of the engine faded away, leaving him alone in the middle of the night. He pulled his trench coat tighter around his neck and sat in the trees until he was sure nobody had followed them.

When he was satisfied he was alone, Michael pulled the torch from his rucksack and studied the hand drawn directions one last time. Then he strode out of the woods, emerging on the other side along the banks of the Bocholter Aa River. The border was smack in the middle of the river.

Keeping to the riverbank, Michael followed the river a third of a mile until he reached a bridge. At this point, the border left the river and swung north, dissecting the conjoined towns of Dinxperlo in the Netherlands and Suderwick in Germany.

He went under the bridge and followed the road for another mile until he found a country lane off to his right, then turned down the lane and headed east into the darkness.

Bocholt was six miles down the road, so he kept to the side and made his way towards the town he knew was ahead of him.

The country lane followed the Bocholter Aa River, and Michael knew from the rough map the SIS agent had drawn that the river went right through the centre of Bocholt. As long as he stayed by the river, it was impossible to get lost.

After a couple of hours, the open fields gave way to civilisation, and the next thing he knew, he was on the outskirts of the town. He still had a few hours before daylight, so he found a quiet place in a copse of trees and rested.

It was cold, but at least it wasn't raining, so he pulled his coat tight and closed his eyes. It was going to be a long day and he needed to keep his wits about him.

As soon as dawn broke, Michael rose from his resting place and followed the rough map provided by the SIS agent. The railway station wasn't hard to find, so he bought a copy of the Nazi Party's official newspaper, the *Völkischer Beobachter*, or People's Observer as it would be called in English, and waited for the ticket office to open.

The paper was filled with the news of the victory in Poland and as he leafed through the pages, he read story after story of how the Nazis were cleansing German soil of the evil Jews. Every page praised Adolf Hitler as though he was the Messiah of Germany, and the stories of praise and hate made Michael want to vomit.

He tensed his hands into a fist, crumpling the newspaper in his lap. A couple of passengers looked at him, so he quickly smoothed it out and made sure he looked as though he was thoroughly enjoying it.

He smiled, but underneath he was silently cursing for bringing attention to himself. If he messed up now, his mission would be over before it started.

As he'd done once before, he bought a small suitcase from a shop on a street close to the railway station and put his rucksack inside. Any little thing he could do to avoid attention was a good thing, and details mattered.

Holding his new identification papers, he approached the ticket office.

The ticketing went smoothly, and he purchased a ticket for the first train to Dortmund.

One thing that stuck out to him was the absence of soldiers on the train. It wasn't as though there weren't any, because there were, but compared to the last time he'd been in Germany when the trains were full of uniformed soldiers, the lack of them was noticeable.

They must be in Poland, he thought and considered sending a message to London telling them that now would be a perfect opportunity to invade Germany from the west, as most of their troops were in Poland.

We could end this war quickly and I could get to Mina sooner.

If only it were that simple, he thought. Britain wasn't ready for a major offensive, and in any case, he was sure minds far superior to his own had already considered such a possibility.

He shook the thoughts from his head and concentrating on what he was there for, he took his seat on the train and kept his head down.

A man three rows down in a civilian suit watched as men and women boarded the train. He stared at each person for a long moment before casting his gaze onto the next one.

He had Gestapo written all over him.

A chill ran down Michael's spine as he remembered all his encounters with the Gestapo, few of which had ended well. He looked away as the man's gaze fell in his direction.

The carriage was around three-quarters full when the train pulled away from the station. Michael pretended to read the *Völkischer Beobachter* as he kept his eye on the Gestapo agent in front of him.

The agent gave a perceptible nod of his head towards someone behind Michael, and the next thing he knew, another man wearing a crisp civilian suit sat on the seat beside him.

The man leant over and touched Michael on the shoulder. "Why aren't you in uniform?" He spoke softly, although the other passengers within earshot must have heard his words. They all turned away, looking anywhere except at the man from the feared Gestapo.

Michael had been expecting the question and his cover story had been rehearsed many times in the war rooms in London. But now it was happening. It was real. His stomach tied in knots, and he gulped in fear.

"Sir?" he asked innocently, as though he hadn't heard properly.

"Show me your papers," the man barked.

Michael slowly removed his identification papers from his jacket pocket and handed them over to the Gestapo agent.

"Who are you?" the man asked, switching seats so he was now opposite Michael where he could get a better look at his face.

"Gerhard Hoffmann, sir." Michael spoke in fluent German, a skill he'd learned as a young boy. He pretended to be nervous, but in reality, he wasn't pretending.

"What are you doing on this train and why aren't you in uniform?"

"Sir, I was in Poland with my brother Gunther, who was killed in Mlawa. I'm a medic, and after our glorious victory, my commanding officer allowed me to come home so I could comfort our mother, who is beside herself with grief."

"Your brother died in Poland?" Michael saw a flicker of empathy in the man's eyes.

"Yes, sir." Michael lowered his head in grief.

"What unit were you serving with?" the Gestapo agent's face was cold and ruthless again.

"The First Infantry Division, sir."

Michael handed over a signed document from his commanding officer, allowing him two weeks' compassionate leave to spend time with his grieving mother.

"I didn't know the Wehrmacht handed out leave documents to bereaved soldiers," the man snapped.

"It was only allowed because of our glorious victory." Michael's voice rose as if in celebration of the Polish collapse.

"Where are you going now?"

"To see my uncle in Dortmund, sir. He was very close

to Gunther. He doesn't know yet and I'm dreading telling him."

The Gestapo agent studied the papers for far too long, making Michael sweat underneath his heavy coat.

The Gestapo man rose from his seat and turned to the soldier sitting before him. "I'm sorry about your brother. Long live our glorious Führer. Heil Hitler!" he bellowed.

Everyone on the train jumped up and screamed back at him, including Michael, who didn't dare do anything else.

"Heil Hitler!" The collective shouts of a train full of people made the carriage vibrate.

Michael sat down as the Gestapo agent moved on to his next victim. Although he appeared calm on the outside, Michael was a nervous wreck and he couldn't wait to get off the train in Dortmund.

Not that any of his future train journeys would be any better.

He picked up the *Völkischer Beobachter* and pretended to bask in the glory of the Führer, all the while keeping his eye on the two Gestapo agents who had brought so much discomfort to the train ride.

Chapter 40

Michael was relieved when the train finally reached Dortmund. He waited patiently to get off, all the while watching the two Gestapo agents to make sure they weren't going to ambush him on the way out.

The train was continuing to Cologne, and thankfully, the Gestapo agents remained on the train. Michael heaved an enormous sigh of relief when he realised they weren't following him.

He'd worked hard with Tony Sanders on his cover story and they'd changed their plans at the last minute after the collapse of the Polish forces. Now he was a bereaved brother, returning home to comfort his mother.

He'd hoped to keep his identity to himself, at least until he reached Hamburg, because if the Gestapo agent reported his run in with Gerhard Hoffmann, any future identification checks would result in his immediate arrest.

I'll cross that bridge when I get to it.

The train ride to Bielefeld was packed with soldiers, which negated his earlier assumption that the entire German army was in Poland. He barely found a seat, and when he did, he ended up next to an old lady who didn't want to talk, for which he was grateful, because she left him alone.

From Bielefeld, he bought a ticket to Bremen, and from there, he boarded a train to his final destination of Hamburg.

It was late afternoon by the time he arrived in Hamburg and it was nearing time for the blackout. Michael wondered if the Germans had as many problems with it as the British did.

I'm sure they do.

He quickly boarded a bus outside the Bahnhof and bought a ticket for Eimsbüttel, a quiet residential area to the northwest of the city centre.

He'd chosen this area because it was far away from the busy main streets, and he could melt into the neighbourhood without arousing any suspicions.

Darkness descended as he knocked on the door to the Lindengarten Pension, which was the name of the guest-house. The curtains were drawn tight, and there were no lights outside to illuminate the large house, but Michael was sure he'd found a suitable place to rest his head until he contacted the resistance.

After a few moments, the door opened, and a heavy-set, middle-aged man in his late forties stood in his way.

"Can I help you?" he asked, looking anxiously around to see who else was present.

Michael felt sorry for the Germans, having to live in the shadow of the Gestapo every day.

"Good evening," he said in flawless German. "I've just arrived in Hamburg, and I'm looking for a room for the evening."

"Are you alone?"

"Yes, I'm alone."

"Just one night?"

"Yes, sir."

"Are you with the army, or the navy?"

"The army. I have to report back tomorrow, but I wanted a night on my own, away from the base, before we head east."

"I don't blame you. Come in, son."

The man gave Michael a tour of the large house, proudly showing him pictures on the walls of his army unit in the trenches during the First World War.

"We'll win this time," the man said. "Now the Führer has removed the traitorous Jews who sold us out in the Great War. He'll lead us to glory in this one."

"Let's hope so." Michael forced back the anger rising from within.

The man showed Michael to a sparsely furnished room that overlooked a garden at the rear of the house. All it had was a bed, a wardrobe, and a chair, but it suited Michael fine.

As soon as he was alone, he opened the window and looked for escape routes. He was on the first floor and the jump to the grass below was ten feet or more, which could lead to injuries if he landed wrong.

To his left was a drainpipe so, in a push, he could climb down a few feet before jumping the rest of the way.

The garden was dark because of the blackout, but from the shadows he could make out a six-foot fence at the edge behind a row of bushes. He didn't know what was on the other side, but it was probably a road.

He could get out if the need arose and, satisfied, he locked his bedroom door and sat on the bed. He pulled his rucksack from the suitcase and took out the stale sandwiches the SIS agent had given him before they left the safe house in Holland.

While he ate, he went over the plans to make contact with the resistance the following day.

This was the first stage of the mission that worried Michael. So many things could go wrong, and any of them could lead to a painful death. He had to make sure he wasn't walking into a trap, and he vowed to be on high alert for the slightest thing that looked out of place.

Despite the lack of sleep, Michael slept fitfully, tossing and turning all night, and constantly waking up soaked in a cold sweat. As always, images of Mina, as well as the conversations with David kept him sane – or insane if anyone heard him speaking to a dead man.

He was glad when the morning finally arrived, and he was downstairs, ready to go, as the city burst into life with the dawning of a new day.

The owner's wife provided a tasty breakfast of bread, jam, and hard-boiled eggs, which Michael greedily wolfed down. After thanking them for their generous hospitality, he headed for the door.

The male owner and former soldier stood in his way, and as Michael approached, he threw his right arm in the air and clicked his heels together.

Michael groaned inwardly. He hated this, but he had no choice. As the man bellowed the two words he loathed, Michael reciprocated.

"Heil Hitler," he yelled back, thrusting his arm high in the air.

The man moved aside and opened the door for him. Michael thanked him again and stepped onto the street, hoping that was the last time he'd have to give the Nazi salute.

Something told him he wouldn't be so lucky.

Chapter 41

The park where the first contact was to be made was about two miles from the guesthouse, and as the first attempt wasn't supposed to happen until the afternoon, Michael decided to walk.

He kept to the busier main roads and even with his small suitcase, he didn't look too much out of place. He'd have much rather ditched the suitcase and carry his rucksack on his back, but it was better kept away from prying eyes.

Michael bought himself lunch in a cafe facing the Planten un Blomen, a colourful, picturesque park well known for its extensive gardens and floral displays.

The seating outside the cafe offered a good vantage point where he could watch people come and go from the busy and popular outdoor spot where people could walk, meet, and otherwise enjoy a peaceful floral haven in the middle of the bustling city.

Michael watched as men sauntered together in small groups, discussing whatever was important to them on this particular day.

He overheard several people as they passed. One group discussed the war, and at least one man seemed concerned for the safety of their city as it was a naval hub and he was worried the British and the French might bomb it.

He watched as a teenage boy met a similar aged girl by a park bench, smiling and looking uncomfortable as they held hands and strolled around the pond together.

It could be a scene from Hyde Park in London, or Central Park in New York. Everyday Germans were no different from anyone else, and Michael wondered how they had allowed a crazed lunatic to lead them into another war against a people that weren't so different from themselves.

He ordered another cup of coffee and scrutinised the park for anything out of place. Nobody seemed to linger suspiciously, and no men were waiting in the shadows for a British spy to show up to a meeting with a resistance member.

Michael relaxed. The serene setting calmed him and nothing seemed out of place.

His mind turned to the people he was about to meet, a relatively new resistance group that had been put together with the help of the SIS.

The group originated from Munich but moved to Hamburg at the behest of the British to spy on the dock-yards and U-boat activities in the famous port city.

From what Sanders had told him, the leader was a brave, patriotic German who had good cause to hate the Nazis, and although Michael wasn't privy to that reason, he'd been assured that he was trustworthy and efficient.

He was also the only person who knew the true purpose of Michael's mission, other than the SIS agent who had set everything up for them. As the SIS agent was only acting as a liaison and wouldn't have any direct involvement in the mission, Michael was worried about putting his trust in a German he knew nothing about.

What if he's a Nazi spy?

That was a genuine possibility, and although Sanders had reassured him several times that the resistance leader was dedicated to the cause and trustworthy, Michael had his doubts.

Unlike Sanders, his life depended on it.

Fighting his unease, Michael checked his watch. It was ten minutes to two, and as the first contact was supposed to happen at two precisely, it was time to act.

He crossed the road and entered the peaceful park, picturing a different time when he and Mina could walk together amongst the flowers, hand in hand, enjoying the wonderful floral displays that seemed to be everywhere.

With two minutes to spare, he sat on a bench close to the water's edge and pretended to watch the ducks. At precisely two o'clock, he opened his copy of the national daily newspaper, the *Frankfurter Allgemeine Zeitung*, and turned to page four, his heart thumping in his chest and the hairs on the back of his neck prickling.

He felt as though everyone in the park was staring at him, knowing he was a British spy, and he struggled for breath as he fought the urge to flee.

A minute later, a man sat on the bench beside him. Michael didn't look up from the newspaper, but from the corner of his eye, he could tell the man was in his mid thirties, and underneath his long coat, he looked trim and in good shape.

"Do you have the time, please?" the man asked.

"I'm sorry," Michael replied, his heart thundering against his rib cage. "My watch is broken and is stuck on twelve noon."

Michael placed his newspaper on the seat between them and looked straight ahead at the ducks.

"Enjoy your day," the man said, and got up to leave.

Michael watched as he strode off towards the street on the far side of the park. He picked up the newspaper, folded it in half, and walked the opposite way.

Chapter 42

He walked back to the Eimsbüttel area, stopping along the way to buy some supplies. When he got there, he chose a different guesthouse far away from the one he'd stayed at the previous night, and used the same story to secure a room for the evening.

Once inside, he locked the door and closed the curtains. His shoulders quivered as he unfolded the newspaper and retrieved the blank piece of paper the man had slipped inside.

Michael took the candle and matches he'd purchased and lit the candle. As he held the paper over the flame, words magically appeared in gold ink.

He pulled the paper from the flame and held it up so he could read it.

Underneath the old clock at the Hauptbahnhof at 10 sharp tomorrow morning. A woman wearing a red scarf will drop a brooch on the floor. Hand it back to her and tell her you saw it fall from her lapel.

She will say 'Thank you kindly, sir.' If she uses any other words, we are compromised and the mission is off.

You are to ask if she knows where you could purchase a stuffed toy for your niece's birthday.

If everything looks good to our operative, she will give you directions on what to do next.

After memorising the note, Michael held the paper over the flame and burned it to a cinder. He gathered up the ashes and flushed them down the toilet in the bathroom he shared with all the other guests.

Early the next morning, he took a forty-five-minute bus ride to the north of the city, getting off outside one of the largest cemeteries in Germany: the Ohlsdorf Cemetery.

The weather wasn't as good as the last few days had been. The skies were gloomy, and rain drizzled over the city, matching Michael's mood that morning.

He'd purchased an umbrella before getting on the bus and he was glad of the protection it gave him, not just from the rain, but also from prying eyes that might have been watching.

Ohlsdorf Cemetery was massive, bigger than any he'd seen before in his entire life. Without prior research or knowledge, there would be no way to ever find the grave of a relative or close friend.

Michael walked down Cordesallee, one of the main pathways that crisscrossed the graveyard. Men and women sauntered around, many of them carrying umbrellas just as he was.

Most of them appeared elderly, although one or two looked younger. None, however, gave Michael a second glance, and he felt comfortable that he wasn't followed.

He counted to the fourth lane on his right and turned down it as though he'd been there many times before. He walked between the trees, reflecting on the peacefulness of graveyards in Europe, and probably the world over.

Images of David flooded his mind. He lay in an

unmarked, unconsecrated grave near a town called Erding, a few miles northeast of Munich. A sudden urge to go there and pay his respects entered his mind, and he winced as he pushed it away.

"One day, David, I promise. One day, I will return and take you home for a proper burial with all our family there to say goodbye." Michael whispered the words out loud, his heart hurting at the thought of his brother lying under the ground, alone in enemy territory.

Returning his focus to the reason he was there, he paused when he reached a junction. He turned left and then left again into another lane. From there, he paced to his right and looked for a gravestone marked Marlene Braun.

After searching for a few minutes, he found the weatherbeaten, arched gravestone leaning to its side in an overgrown plot close to the trees.

This was one of the older sections of the cemetery and not many people ventured here anymore. He was alone, and after one more glance to make sure he wasn't being watched, he wiped at the old headstone and read the inscription.

Marlene Braun, 1818-1843. Loving wife, mother, sister, and daughter.

Underneath were two other names: Marlene Braun, 1840-1843, and Katharina Braun, 1842-1843.

Michael's heart dropped at the young ages of the two girls, who were obviously Marlene's daughters. He had no way of knowing what happened to them, but it saddened him to see the lives of young children snatched away so early.

He knelt at the side of the leaning headstone and gently removed a few handfuls of dirt and grass. He took the message he'd written using the codebook he'd brought from London and read it one more time to make sure he'd not missed anything.

Deciphered, it read:

Made contact. Meeting later this morning. Operation is a go.

He signed it with his codename, *Harbour.*

Michael placed the message in a flat tin box he'd emptied of tobacco and buried it behind the gravestone, being careful not to disturb the grave itself in front of the stone.

He rose to his feet and wiped himself down. With one last look at the sad grave, he turned to leave.

Then he stopped and turned back around. Bowing his head, he pressed his hands together and spoke a few words in German for the young family that had been taken far too soon.

"Heavenly Father, in this quiet place, I pause to remember the lives of those who rest here. Though I knew them not, I acknowledge the bond of humanity that unites us all.

"Bless this mother and her young children, taken too soon, and enfold them in Your eternal peace.

"May their spirits find rest in Your loving embrace, and may their memory be a reminder of the preciousness of life.

"In this moment of reflection, I honour their existence, however brief, and pray for the comfort of all souls who have departed.

"Amen."

For some reason, the ages of the perished family bothered him more than it should have. After all, he didn't have any connection to them, and they were German, Britain's hated enemy.

And yet Michael couldn't think that way. He was in love with a German girl, and he intended to marry her once the war was over. Several brave Germans had already given their lives for him, so how could he hate them?

The answer was that he didn't. All he wanted was for them to be able to live in a Europe that was free of tyranny and hatred, and if that meant waging war against the Nazis, then so be it. Hopefully, one day they would all be able to live together as neighbours, in peace and prosperity.

Michael snorted as he left the cemetery.

Who am I kidding? That's a long way from reality right now.

Chapter 43

By the time the bus reached the Hauptbahnhof, it was approaching ten o'clock, so Michael hurried towards the old clock that was unmissable, as it towered over the station, reminding everyone not to be late for their trains.

At exactly ten, Michael spotted a woman in her mid twenties, and wearing a red scarf, approach the clock. She looked straight ahead and as she walked past, he saw something drop from the lapel of her coat as she brushed her hand against the side of her face.

Michael waited for her to walk by.

He made sure nobody was watching and picked up the brooch. He hurried after her, catching up as she was about to leave the railway station.

The brooch carried a tiny image of an old sailing ship, which was apt as they were in one of the major port cities of Europe.

"Excuse me, miss," he said as he caught her up. "I think you dropped this near the old clock."

The woman looked him up and down and smiled. "Thank you kindly, sir."

"I'm sorry to bother you, miss, but could you direct me to where I might buy a stuffed toy for my niece?" Michael asked.

The woman looked around and lowered her voice. "Follow me from a safe distance. Don't look around and don't speak to me again."

She hurried off into the busy streets.

The red scarf made it easy for Michael to follow the woman through the busy streets of the city. She hopped on a tram, and Michael followed suit.

The tram took them to Hamburg's eastern side and she got off by a small park. Michael followed a safe distance behind.

The streets became more and more residential until eventually the woman turned onto Griesstrasse. Michael made a mental note of every turn they'd made in case he had to find it again on his own, and he trailed her through a dense clump of trees to a gated fence at the rear of a house.

The woman opened the gate and walked through, not looking behind her once. She left the gate ajar and Michael followed, closing the gate behind him.

At the door to the house, she knocked, and when a man opened to let her in, she finally turned to face Michael, who quickly followed her into the house.

The man led them into a rear room on the ground floor. The curtains were drawn and a dim light hung from the ceiling. Three weary-looking men in their late thirties were sitting at a square wooden table by the window, a two-seater couch sat against the opposite wall from the door, and large-scale maps of Berlin hung from the walls.

The woman Michael had followed from the railway station strolled over to one of the men at the wooden table and placed her hands on his shoulders in a show of affection, indicating to Michael that they were more than just members of the same resistance team.

The man who'd led them into the room stood by the table and turned to face their new guest.

"Agent Harbour, I presume?" the man asked in broken English.

"The one and only," Michael replied in flawless German.

"Konrad, Hans, and Matthias." The man waved his hands at the three men at the table. "My name's Martin Heinze and you've already met Kirsten."

Michael nodded towards the faces that stared back at him.

"Now the formalities are out of the way, let's get down to business. Please, sit."

Michael shook his head. "I'd rather stand, thank you." He remained by the door, still unsure of the situation.

"Are you sure you weren't followed?" Martin asked Kirsten, who shook her head.

"Totally sure. I watched all the way back and nobody followed us." Hans reached up and gently stroked her arm, confirming what Michael had already suspected.

"We weren't followed," Michael assured them. "I was watching too."

Tension rose as the room hushed. Michael looked at the men around the table. Martin was the obvious leader, and he got the distinct impression that all four were former soldiers as their faces displayed the battle-hardened and world-weary look of time spent in the trenches.

Martin was of medium height and had a stocky build. He was in his mid forties and had short, jet-black hair that was brushed to the side.

All the men had cropped, military-style haircuts, another indicator that they were former soldiers.

From what he'd learned in London, and from the little Sanders had told him, Martin Heinze was a quiet, determined man, driven by a strong desire to rid his country of Hitler and the Nazis.

Michael had asked what drove this man to risk his life, but Sanders either didn't know or wouldn't tell him. Whatever it was, he'd been assured that he was the type of man you'd want by your side when things went south.

Kirsten was a pretty, petite woman with shoulder-length brown hair that was curled and wavy. Her piercing blue eyes bored into Michael, making him feel as though she were reading his mind.

"Everything is good as long as you weren't followed," Martin reassured everyone in the room. "From now on, nobody leaves this house until we go to Berlin."

"Who else knows about this?" Michael asked.

"Other than your man in British intelligence, nobody but us," Martin answered. "And that's how it will remain."

"How was your journey?" Kirsten asked.

"Uneventful, which is how I like it," Michael said.

"Were you questioned by the Gestapo at any time?" Martin asked.

"One time, on the train heading to Dortmund."

"Did you show him your identification papers?"

"Yes."

Martin looked at his comrades around the table. They nodded back at him in silent agreement.

"You'll need a new set of papers before we leave," Martin said. "Keep the old ones in case you need them after the operation is over."

Michael understood. He'd been worried about that himself.

"Hans will arrange that after this meeting."

Hans acknowledged his orders with a curt bow of his head.

"Now to business." Martin wasted no more time. "We have a lot to discuss and not much time to get it done."

He walked to the wall and pointed at the large-scale map of Berlin that had areas circled in ink.

"What your government is asking is difficult," Heinze said. "But not impossible. Konrad and Matthias have been watching Admiral Ludsecke ever since this operation became a reality and his movements are as regular as clockwork. He's a stickler for routine and he always takes the same route wherever he goes. If what they say is true and he's carrying the Kriegsmarine's U-boat secrets with him, then he's a fool, but from what we've learned about him, he's so arrogant and entitled that he believes he's untouchable."

"I know someone just like that in England," Michael said, thinking of Robert Stourcliffe. "Although the man I'm thinking of doesn't run around carrying state secrets. Or at least I don't think he does."

"We have no way of knowing what is inside his brief-case, obviously," Martin continued. "But ambushing him won't be a problem."

"That's not entirely true." Konrad spoke for the first time. "Finding him might not be a problem but ambushing him won't be so easy. He has an SS guard with him at all times, and when he goes to the Bendlerblock, at least four SS guards escort him."

"He lives here." Heinze pointed to another circled area to the south of Berlin. "It's a mansion surrounded by dense woodland. There are no neighbours nearby and it's about as isolated as they come."

"That might be the best place to get to him then?" Michael asked. "It's not close to any main roads, so if we can get to him at his home, we won't have to worry about a member of the public reporting it to the authorities."

"That's correct," Konrad said. "But his house is also guarded by a squad of SS. We're not sure how many, but there are at least four outside, and that doesn't include the gardeners and other workers who are there most of the time."

"We have to assume there are more SS inside the house, but it does look like our best bet if we're going to get to him." Martin looked at the people gathered in the cramped room. "We've been tasked with the impossible, and there is a good chance this is a suicide mission, but if it helps end this war and stop Hitler and his Nazis, then I'm in. What about you?"

One by one, Konrad, Hans, Matthias, and Kirsten all signalled they were in. Even if it meant their deaths.

"Good." Martin turned to Michael. "We make our plans here and we leave two weeks today."

Butterflies fluttered in Michael's stomach as he realised things were about to get dangerously serious.

"Now, go with Hans and he'll take care of your new identification papers."

Michael followed Hans to an upstairs room to pose for a photograph.

Chapter 44

SS Sturmbannführer Albert Kreise sat by the window in a small cafe in downtown Rotterdam. He ordered a coffee and watched people rush by as they went about their daily lives.

He'd purposely got there early to make sure he found a suitable table by the window so he could watch anyone approaching from across the street. The methodical SD officer liked to be punctual and was always early for important meetings such as this.

Kreise smiled at Robert Stourcliffe's lame attempts at disguising himself. He crossed the street with his coat lapels pulled all the way up, so they met the fedora hat covering his head.

This was the second meeting they'd had since that fateful dinner nearly four weeks earlier. Although Stourcliffe choked on his words, the information he'd passed on had already led to the sinking of two British merchant ships owned by his rivals.

Reinhard Heydrich was pleased with his contributions so far, and he wanted Kreise to press him even further to see what he knew about the inner workings of the British government.

Stourcliffe slumped into a chair opposite Kreise without saying a word.

"Good afternoon, Sir Robert," Kreise said in English. "You know you're making yourself stand out by trying so hard not to be seen."

Stourcliffe scowled. "I don't care. I hate you and everything you stand for."

"And yet you willingly pass on information that leads to the sinking of your rival's ships. Everyone has their price, Sir Robert, and it seems we have found yours."

Stourcliffe scowled again.

"What do you have for me?" Kreise dabbed his mouth with his serviette.

"I'm not giving you anything else until you hand over every copy of those photographs. After this, we're done, and I mean it."

Stourcliffe sat back, his face as red as a beetroot. "Well? Where are they?"

Kreise leant forward. "Let's be clear, Stourcliffe," he said, his tone menacing. "We are in control here, not you. Walk out right now if you wish, but be warned, those photographs will be on every front page tomorrow morning."

"I don't care." Stourcliffe spat the words at Kreise. "Go ahead, publish them. I'm done with you and I won't do any more harm to my country ever again."

"You don't get it, do you?" Kreise stared into the frightened eyes of the British aristocrat. "The photographs are the least of your worries. How do you think your government would react if they discovered you were responsible for the sinking of those cargo ships? I doubt they'd be very lenient with you, Sir Robert."

Stourcliffe glowered but his eyes filled. Kreise would have felt sorry for him if he had a heart.

But he didn't. He had a job to do, and if he said so himself, he was very good at it.

"Well?" he asked.

Stourcliffe reached into his coat and pulled out a large envelope. He held it back for a few moments before looking Kreise in the eyes.

"This is the last time we shall meet. I'm leaving Europe for good this evening and I shall not return until the Nazis are defeated. This is the last thing I'm doing for you, so go ahead, ruin me if you must, but I'm not giving you anything else after this."

Kreise took the envelope and quickly hid it inside his own coat. "What is it?" he asked.

"I don't know the exact details because, regardless of what you think, I'm not privy to the inner secrets of the British intelligence community."

"So, what is it then?"

"All I know is that I've been ordered to send one of my ships to Denmark to pick up one of their operatives after a covert mission somewhere. He is to be concealed aboard my ship and taken back to Britain unseen by any of the crew. That's all I know, I swear."

"When is this happening?" Kreise's ears pricked up at this information.

"I don't know. They'll let me know when to send it. Soon, I think."

"You will let me know the minute they tell you to send your ship, and if you find out who it is, or even better, why, you will inform me straight away."

"I shall not," Stourcliffe snapped. "I already told you, I'm leaving for London this evening, and I am never meeting with you again."

"Do you think we don't have agents in London?" Kreise sneered. "We have eyes and ears everywhere, Sir Robert. My people will be in touch, and when they are, you'd better have something for me."

Kreise rose from his chair, leaving Robert Stourcliffe staring at the window in despair.

Chapter 45

Martin Heinze was the first to leave. Using the cover of darkness, he slipped out of the house they'd holed up in since Michael's arrival two weeks earlier, and headed to Berlin in one of the two vehicles they had bought with the generous funding supplied by the British government.

Travelling at night, Martin would drive the two hundred miles via the back roads to avoid the bigger cities that carried greater scrutiny. If all went well, he'd arrive in Berlin in three days' time, where he'd set up the safe house provided by a family sympathetic to their cause.

Four days later, Matthias left. He was travelling by rail and would arrive the day after Martin.

Konrad left the same day as Matthias, and he also drove, taking a different route to the one Martin was taking. He would stay at a separate location known only to the resistance team. This would operate as a backup to the Berlin safe house, and it was where Konrad would gather the supplies and equipment they needed to carry out the operation.

Where he got them from, Michael didn't know.

Once everything was in place and everyone accounted for, the mission would move to Konrad's location until it was over.

Hans and his girlfriend, Kirsten, stayed behind to clear out the safe house and remove any traces of the resistance's time there once the mission was complete. They were to monitor the activities of the Gestapo in Hamburg as best they could in case they got wind of their operation.

During their reconnaissance missions, Konrad and Matthias had used a radio set to transmit updates to Martin in Hamburg and they'd hidden it before leaving Berlin. Konrad would retrieve it, and they would use it to communicate with Hans and Kirsten in the coming days if the need arose.

Michael was the last to leave, four days after Matthias and Konrad. He was travelling by rail, and like Matthias before him, he would take the long route to avoid the more direct, heavily scrutinised express trains.

Despite their age differences, Michael and Martin had developed a bond during their time together in the safe house. Although he never spoke of his reasons, it was clear to Michael that Martin hated the Nazis with a passion, and he would go to any lengths to stop them.

Michael grew to trust him, and together they developed the plans first formulated in London.

Each of them had new identification papers, and Michael was now Ingo Meier, a twenty-year-old student at the prestigious Friedrich Wilhelm University of Berlin, where he was studying law as a precursor to joining the Gestapo after completing his studies.

None of them knew the identification of the others for security reasons, so outside of Michael and Hans, nobody knew what his alias was as he made his way to the Ohlsdorf Cemetery to leave a message for SIS, updating them on the situation.

After leaving a message for London, he felt a tingling sensation down his spine when he realised that his next report would be from Berlin.

From the cemetery, he took the bus to the railway station and passed underneath the old clock that towered above his head as he found his way to the platform for his first train.

A breakdown on the line forced him to stay in a guest-house in Wittenberg, so he didn't arrive in Potsdam until noon the next day.

The train from Potsdam to the Berlin Hauptbahnhof was packed, and the ticket conductors worked tirelessly, making sure every passenger was properly ticketed.

Security personnel selected a few passengers for closer inspection as a steady stream of people tried to exit the station. Michael kept his head down and tried to control his limbs as they shook and wobbled beneath him.

Fortunately, he wasn't chosen, and they waved him through without further inspection.

He took a bus to the Tempelhof airport, and from there, he walked twenty minutes to the safe house at the end of Kanzlerweg.

Like other safe houses he'd seen and used, this one sat at the end of a cul-de-sac, so they were spared from potential Gestapo vehicles driving past without their knowledge.

One of them would be on constant watch, and if a vehicle approached either day or night, they would know immediately.

The rear of the house led into a thicket of trees, and from there they had several directions they could go in, depending on what the emergency plans were, and that was what he was about to find out.

He rapped on the front door. There was no need for any kind of secret codes or knocks because whoever was on watch would have spotted him a mile away.

Similarly, if he'd been followed, the others would be long gone by now, and Michael would be left to deal with the Gestapo alone.

This was the nature of the operation. They all knew it, and they were all at peace with it.

Matthias opened the door and stepped aside. There were no formal greetings, just a curt nod of the head to assure Michael he hadn't been followed.

Martin was waiting for him in the living room. "Glad you could finally join us," he said, clapping his hand into Michael's in a firm handshake. "You were supposed to be here yesterday. What happened?"

"There was a breakdown on the line and I had to stay at a guesthouse for the night."

"Were you asked for your identification papers?"

"No," Michael shook his head. "Other than when I bought the ticket, of course."

"Good," Martin said. "We're all accounted for and none of us experienced any major problems."

Martin looked at Michael and Matthias. "Our operation is a go."

Heinze obviously had contacts in Berlin because he'd got hold of a new vehicle, and enough food to last them for two weeks or more if they were careful.

Konrad was at the other safe house, the whereabouts still unknown to Michael. Once again, operational security demanded the utmost secrecy, and the less they knew about each other, the safer they would be in the event of capture.

The following morning, Heinze and Michael drove the twenty-minute drive to the Bendlerblock, where the senior officers from the German military planned their conquest of Europe.

The area was full of security, so Heinze didn't hang about. They drove past, then left and headed for the upmarket area of Dahlem, where Admiral Ludsecke resided.

They didn't go to the admiral's house because it was so secluded, and their presence would not have gone unnoticed. Satisfied with the route the admiral would take, Heinze headed the vehicle back to their safe house.

Chapter 46

The following morning, Heinze gathered them all together. He'd already pulled all the food jars from the cupboards and assembled everything they'd brought by the front door.

"This place was just the staging post for us to meet. If any of us were followed, we'd have led them right to Konrad if we'd gone straight there, and our mission would have been over before it started. Now we're all accounted for and sure we've not been tracked, we can go to our safe house outside the city. Although it's quiet here, there's a strong possibility that a neighbour might find our presence a bit suspicious. We leave this morning."

"We're meeting Konrad?" Michael asked.

"We're meeting Konrad," Heinze confirmed. "He's already prepared the safe house for our mission and we'll be a lot safer than we are here. It's out of the way in a place where we won't be under so much scrutiny."

Michael and Matthias helped Heinze load the Opel Olympia, and when they were done, Matthias climbed into the back seat.

Michael watched Heinze lock the door and hide the

key under a stone near the front door before grabbing a suitcase.

The Olympia wasn't as sleek as the Opel Kapitan Michael had driven once before, but it fit in with the other vehicles on the streets of Berlin. The black Olympia was compact and streamlined, which was perfect for their purpose.

The seats had matching black leather upholstery, and the wood-grained dashboard gave it an air of luxury to complement its otherwise understated appearance.

Michael climbed into the passenger seat next to Heinze, who took the wheel. The drive out of the city made Michael nervous, and he remained quiet while he watched the roads for any sign of a roadblock or other activity that could threaten their freedom.

He relaxed when they finally left the concrete behind and headed into the countryside on the outskirts of Berlin.

"Where are we going?" Michael asked again.

"To a farmhouse about an hour out of Berlin. It doesn't have any neighbours, and it's perfect for our purpose."

"How did we get a farmhouse this close to Berlin?" Michael asked.

"It belonged to a Jewish family." Matthias spoke for the first time that morning. "They were displaced when they built the Olympic Village for the games in thirty-six."

"I thought the Olympic stadium was in the city?" Michael asked, perplexed. "I know they removed Jews from everywhere in Germany, but what did that have to do with the Olympics?"

"The Olympic Village is in Elstal," Heinze said. "And so is the farm. The Nazis didn't want a Jew living so close to the athletes, so they confiscated it and gave it to the

Gestapo to use as their headquarters where they could monitor the athletes."

The blood drained from Michael's face. "The farmhouse is a Gestapo headquarters?"

Both Heinze and Matthias laughed. "Not anymore," Matthias answered. "They abandoned it after the games were over. A general owns it now, although he never goes there."

"What is the Olympic Village used for now?" Michael asked.

"It's a training area for the Wehrmacht," Heinze said.

"Are there barracks there?" Michael asked, his voice rising with anxiety.

"Yes, but don't worry," Heinze said. "We spent a lot of time staking the place out before we moved in. The Wehrmacht never go near the farm because it's owned by a general, and if they damaged it, they'd probably be shot. The farm is out of the way and far from the village, so we're safe."

Michael forced air from his nostrils. "That's a relief," he said.

"We wouldn't use a place that wasn't suitable." Matthias sounded offended. "Who do you British think we are? Amateurs?"

"I meant no offence, Matthias," Michael said. "We all know how professional you are. I've seen it enough times with my own eyes to know how brave and efficient the resistance is in Germany."

Heinze looked at Michael but didn't say a word. Instead, he drove the rest of the way to their destination in silence.

When they reached the town of Elstal, Heinze made a series of left turns onto ever smaller country lanes. Eventually, he turned onto a narrow lane that ended half a mile farther along by the side of an old farmhouse.

A second building stood off to the side, which Michael thought wasn't too different from Ryskamp, where his beloved Mina was safe from the war.

Trees were abundant, but not like they were in the Black Forest. These were more sparse and were numbered in their hundreds instead of the thousands as they were in the forests.

The field to the south of the road was large and barren, and was probably a fertile field just waiting for someone to plant crops so it would be a working farm again.

Heinze pulled the Opel into the empty barn, and from there he walked to the rear door of the farmhouse. The door opened before he could knock, and the three comrades embraced like long-lost friends.

After their reunion, Konrad looked at Michael and shook his hand vigorously. "Welcome to our humble headquarters, Sir Englishman."

The comment seemed to be funny to the men of the resistance and Michael left them alone to enjoy their playful dig at the British while he explored the old farmhouse.

The kitchen was well stocked with jars of preserved food, and along with what they'd brought, they had enough to last them for the duration of the mission.

Most of the rooms were empty, but Konrad had converted the main living area into their control room. Four chairs sat around a rectangular wooden table in the middle of the room, and a large map adorned the wall opposite the door.

Pens and paper covered the desk, many of them presenting drawings and neat, handwritten notes.

The Germans joined him while he looked and Heinze gently slapped his arm. "We like to make fun of the British," he said. "We mean no offence by it."

"None taken," Michael answered.

"The bedrooms are upstairs," Konrad said. "There's four, so we have one each. There aren't any beds, but I managed to get hold of some straw and blankets. They're comfortable enough."

"That's all we need," Martin Heinze said. "We'll be here for as short a time as we can. Now, let's complete our plans so we can get it done and get out of here."

For the next three days, the men went over every detail meticulously, analysing every move and every possible scenario. By the end, each of them knew their roles inside out and back to front.

Heinze proved himself to be a strong leader and Michael fell in behind and allowed him to take the lead. The only thing he insisted on was that he would take charge of the admiral's files once they had them, and although there was some discussion about it, Michael's insistence won the day.

The last thing they discussed were their escape plans. Like before, they would each travel alone, except this time, they would go their separate ways. The Germans would meet in a pre-arranged place unknown to Michael for security reasons, and Michael would make his way to Denmark, and then Britain via one of Stourcliffe's ships, again unknown to the resistance.

That night, Heinze surprised them all by producing a bottle of Scotch whisky. As they had no glasses, they took turns passing it around and taking a swig. After a couple of rounds, Konrad and Matthias retired to their rooms, leaving Heinze and Michael alone in the living room.

Michael took a few swigs, but the liquid burned his

throat as it went down. He felt lightheaded and at that point he knew he'd be physically sick if he had any more. He refused when Heinze offered him the bottle.

They made small talk for a short while, and as the whisky kicked in, Heinze began opening up more about his life.

"You know I hate the Nazis, don't you?" Heinze asked. His eyes were a little glazed, but he was still coherent enough to hold a conversation.

"That's obvious," Michael answered. "But why do you hate them so much? What did they do to you?"

"I know all about you, Michael Fernsby. I know what you did in Germany."

"How?" Michael suddenly sobered up. "What do you know about me? That's classified information."

"I was close friends with Gustav Adler once. I used to be in the Abwehr."

Michael's jaw dropped.

Chapter 47

Martin Heinze took another long slug of whisky from the bottle. He placed it on the table and looked straight at Michael, who stared back at him in a mixture of shock and anger.

He was shocked because if he was telling the truth, Heinze was too valuable an asset for Britain to be allowing him to run around Germany with the resistance. He should be in Britain, teaching them all about German intelligence and how it operated.

He was angry, because Sanders should have told him about Heinze's history. Gustav Adler was a senior member of the SD, the intelligence wing of the SS.

Michael's previous mission had been to assist Adler and his family in their defection, and although he'd failed to get them over the border, he'd delivered Adler's files to SIS, where they'd proven vital to the war effort.

The one thing Michael was most proud of was that he'd rescued Adler's disabled son from the clutches of the Gestapo and delivered him to safety.

All of this was top secret, and Michael was astounded that Heinze seemed to know all about it.

"Well?" he demanded.

Heinze sighed. "Gustav Adler and I were friends for a long time. Our families had dinner together whenever we could, and we shared information, especially after we learned what Hitler was really doing to the Jews and the disabled."

"Why was this not in any report I was given?" Michael's cheeks flushed red.

"I can see you are angry, but do not worry. I specifically requested that my history be sealed when I began working with the British. They wanted me to go over there and advise them."

Heinze waved his arms around in the air, demonstrating his resistance to the British demands.

"I refused. I would work with them, but only on my terms."

"Which were?"

"My history was to be buried and never told to anyone, especially you, once I found out you were to be on this mission with us."

"Why?" Michael didn't understand. "And why tell me now, if you were so adamant you didn't want me to know?"

"That's a good question." Heinze drank another long mouthful. "I wasn't sure having someone as young as you on the mission was a good thing. I objected to the British agent who was my contact in Germany. In the end, the only way I agreed to go ahead with this was after they'd told me what you did over here."

"They told you? Who else knows?" Michael didn't believe him.

"Just me, my men, and Kirsten. They told me everything. I wouldn't have allowed you anywhere near us otherwise. You may not know it, but you are a hero to many people in Germany, at least those who know of your exploits. They may not know your name, but many people know what you did."

Michael shook his head. "What? How? I don't believe a word you're saying."

"None of my men know it's you, but they know what you did."

"No one can possibly know what I did," Michael snapped. "Not even SIS knows what I did, except maybe a few senior officers at the top."

"I have sad news though." Heinze reached over the table and grasped Michael's arm. "The boy you saved, Heinrich Adler. I knew him very well, and he often stayed with me and my wife before Hitler destroyed everything."

"You're married?" Michael asked.

"I was." Heinze looked away. "I mean, I am. My wife is in a prison in Nuremberg, waiting to be executed." He stared at Michael. "I'm going to get her out if it's the last thing I ever do."

Michael remained silent. The whisky had made Heinze talkative, so he sat there and allowed him to speak.

"Your rescue of Heinrich Adler is the action of a man who can be respected. Not many have dared take on the Gestapo and come out alive."

"Is he alive? Do you know where he is?" Michael demanded.

Heinze didn't say a word.

"Where is he?" Michael asked. "Is he safe?"

"No." Heinze's face filled with pain. "He's dead."

Chapter 48

The room fell silent. Michael stared at Heinze as he took another long swig from the half-empty whisky bottle.

"What did you say?" he asked, after a long pause.

"I still have friends in the Abwehr who share my fears that Hitler is going to destroy Germany. However, unlike me, they are too afraid to voice their opinions in fear of retribution against themselves and their families."

"What happened to Heinrich Adler?" Michael thumped his hands on the table.

"From what I was told, a truck was searched during a border crossing into Switzerland. One of the occupants was Heinrich Adler. The Gestapo took him straight to Alderauge, the facility in Munich that you know about."

"How do you know they killed him?" Michael asked, his heart about to burst with a mixture of anger and remorse for not finding a way to take him back to England with him.

"I don't for sure," Heinze answered. "But you know full well they don't take kids to Alderauge for no reason. If he went there, he's dead and we both know it."

Heinze reached for the whisky and offered it to Michael, who joined him by taking a long drink.

"Who's the doctor there now?" Michael asked.

"I don't know, but just because you killed Halmer didn't mean they shut down the facility. All they did was replace him with someone else."

Michael lowered his head. "I should have taken him with me."

"It's not your fault." Heinze tapped his arm. "You performed miracles by getting him away from Halmer in the first place. You gave him a chance, so you should be thankful for that."

"I'm not," Michael said. "I should have taken him with me."

"You wouldn't have made it over the border." Heinze glared at Michael. "You did all you could, so if you want to do more, help us win this war and defeat Hitler."

"Believe me, Heinze, I do." Michael sat bolt upright. "Even if it takes my life, I will never rest until the Nazis are defeated."

Silence fell as both men became lost in their thoughts. A profound sense of loss hit Michael, and he forced back the emotion as best he could. He hadn't felt like this since David had died outside Munich the year before.

"Why did you leave the Abwehr?" he asked Heinze, changing the subject so he wouldn't descend into a blubbering wreck in front of him.

"I refused an order." Heinze looked up at Michael. "My superiors knew I was friends with Gustav and Maria. Heinrich was a frequent visitor to our house, so they ordered me to investigate and report on anyone in the Abwehr or SD who was hiding life-unworthy adults or children."

Michael stared at Heinze and shook his head. "It sounds like they were setting you up."

"They were testing my loyalty to the Reich. When I refused, they arrested me. I was to be sent to a concentration camp, where I would have probably been quietly executed."

"What happened?"

"Adler got me out," Heinze answered. "But not before Eva, my wife, was arrested on charges of treason for conspiring to assassinate a senior member of the Abwehr."

"Did she really do that?"

Heinze pulled a face. "I'm sure she wanted to, but no, she was as innocent as I was. The Nazis wanted to make an example of me, so they made up serious charges so they could execute us as an example to anyone else who thought they might resist."

"Where was this?" Michael asked. "In Munich?"

"I was based in Munich, which is why I knew where Alderauge was."

"What happened to your wife?"

Heinze took another gulp of Scotch and passed it to Michael, who shook his head.

"I don't talk about this to anyone," Heinze said. "My men know the gist of it, but not the details. I don't know why I'm telling you."

"I'm not forcing you," Michael said. "I know what it's like to hold secrets. They tear at your soul and torment your dreams. They make your life a living nightmare, so I know how you must feel."

"You describe it exactly," Heinze said. "Perhaps that is why I tell you this now."

"Only if you want to." Michael would not try to force him.

"I only learned of Eva's arrest after Adler got me out.

He organised a group of anti-Nazis to grab me during a transfer to another facility while I awaited the sham trial. They sprung me out and Adler hid me for weeks until I was ready to go it alone."

"That sounds similar to what I did the first time I was in Germany," Michael said. "I hid under the floor in a church for weeks while the Gestapo searched for me above. I owe everything to the man who saved my life."

Michael would be forever grateful to Father Eise and after the war was over, he was determined to thank him properly.

If he survives, that is.

"Adler told me Eva had been arrested and was in a secure facility where she was being questioned – or tortured more like, for information on my whereabouts. She was in the basement of the Gestapo headquarters in Munich, which was so secure that even Adler couldn't get her out."

"Kreise." The name fell from Michael's lips, and he scowled as he spat it out. "She wasn't arrested by Albert Kreise by any chance, was she?"

Heinze bowed his head. "You know him? He is the cruellest man I know. He's very good at his job but he's as ruthless as they come."

"I know him." Michael's lips curled downwards.

"The last I heard, Heydrich had him transferred to the SD," Heinze said. "I was told that by a close friend in the Abwehr who knew him."

"I'm not surprised," Michael said. "He's the sort of man Heydrich would want to work for him."

Heinze fell silent for a moment, his eyes distant and lost in painful memories.

"She's in prison in Nuremberg and I'm sure she'll be executed if I don't find a way to get her out. She thinks

I'm dead, and as long as I'm free, they will never let her live."

Heinze rummaged around in the lining of his jacket and pulled out a photograph.

"This is Eva." He passed the photograph to Michael. "It's the only thing I have left of her."

Michael picked up the photograph and looked at a woman who stood next to Martin with a radiant smile on her face. She looked to be in her forties, and although the photograph was in black and white, he pictured her wavy, shoulder-length hair to be brown in colour.

He choked when he saw her face.

It couldn't be! No, that's impossible.

Michael looked closer, struggling to get air into his lungs. He closed his eyes and the terrible memories that had caused so many sleepless nights flooded back into his mind.

Here. I haven't read it, so they can't force it out of me. Take it and go.

Those words would forever be etched into his mind. They were the last words of the woman he knew only as Mother. She'd passed him an envelope containing a set of false identification papers at Ravensburg railway station right before she was gunned down and murdered by the Gestapo.

"No!" The words escaped Michael's lips, and he grabbed the bottle of whisky from the table. He took a deep swig, failing to notice the burning sensation as it went down.

"What is it?" Heinze asked, confusion written all over his face.

"This is Eva?" Michael finally asked.

"Yes. What is it? Do you know her? Have you seen her?"

Michael let out a loud sigh. "Martin, I'm sorry. If that's Eva, she isn't in prison in Nuremberg. She's…" he tailed off, not wanting to finish the sentence.

"Tell me what you know of her!" Heinze raised his voice and grabbed Michael's arm roughly. "What do you know about Eva?"

Michael sighed again and looked into Heinze's pained eyes. "Eva worked for the resistance in Munich. She was my contact when I was sent to help Adler defect. Her code-name was Mother, and she pretended to be my mother while I waited for Adler to contact me."

Heinze's face turned white. "Why didn't I know any of this?"

"I don't know," Michael answered gently. "Maybe she didn't try to find you because she thought you were already dead."

"Then why didn't Adler tell her I was alive? No, you are mistaken. The woman you met wasn't my Eva. It couldn't have been."

Michael looked hard at the photograph one more time to make sure he wasn't hallucinating.

"No, it's definitely Mother, or Eva, as I know now." He passed the photograph back to Heinze. "That's her, Martin."

"Are you sure?"

"Absolutely. It's definitely her."

"Where is she then? If she's free, I'll find her once we're done here."

Michael shook his head, and the look on his face told Heinze that something bad had happened to her.

"What happened?" Heinze gasped.

"The Gestapo were onto me. They tracked me down to the railway station at Ravensburg. Mother, or Eva, she tracked me there as well, and she handed me an envelope containing a new set of identification papers so I could escape with Adler's briefcase."

Michael grasped Heinze's wrist. "I'm sorry, Martin. Kreise and his men opened fire, and they shot Eva. She died right in front of me, but not before she'd killed at least one of them."

Heinze glared at Michael as though he were Kreise himself.

"Why didn't you help her? Did you run away like a coward? Why didn't you stay and fight with her?"

That very question had kept Michael awake at night ever since.

"I've been over and over that ever since it happened," Michael replied as Heinze pulled away. "Eva gave me the papers so I could get Adler's secrets back to Britain. If I'd stayed, there's no doubt they'd have killed me as well. Eva, Adler, Gerda, David, everyone that had given their life for me would have died for nothing if I'd stayed that day to die alongside Eva. That's why I ran, Martin. That was the reason, although it has haunted me ever since, and will probably do so for the rest of my life."

Heinze reached for the Scotch and emptied it in one slug. He slammed the bottle on the table and rose unsteadily to his feet.

"Well, now I know," he said.

Heinze stormed off up the stairs. Michael waited a while before following. He could hear Martin's sobs, and at that moment he'd have given anything to change places with Eva.

Chapter 49

The next morning, Heinze was quiet and remained alone for most of the day. He looked pale, and Michael knew it wasn't only the hangover that was causing it.

If Konrad or Matthias had heard anything, they kept it to themselves and carried on as if nothing had happened.

Heinze avoided Michael all day, and he began to wonder if the operation would go ahead at all, or if it did, would Heinze shoot him in the confusion and pretend it was an accident?

I shouldn't have told him.

Michael was furious with himself for letting his guard down and telling him about Eva. He should have waited until after the mission was over and told him at the end.

The next day, they had their final meeting before the operation. Everyone took turns going into detail about their particular role.

Heinze, as the leader of the operation, had to make sure everyone knew what they were doing and had what they needed.

When it came time for Michael to speak, Heinze

looked away and seemed disinterested. Matthias held up his hand and jumped into the conversation.

"I don't know what happened between you two the other night but whatever it was, it has to stop now. If we're going to pull this off, we need to work together and do our jobs as we planned. If you can't sort out your differences, then I'm out and the operation is off."

"I agree." Konrad backed him up. "I've never seen you like this before, Martin. If there's something you're not telling us about the operation, or about the British involvement, then tell us now, or I'm with Matthias and I'm gone."

Michael was about to speak when Heinze waved him off.

"You're right and I'm sorry. I allowed my emotions to cloud my judgement. I'm fully engaged and this won't happen again."

Michael could see he was still holding back, so he stood up. "Perhaps it's better if I do this alone. You have all risked enough and I can't ask any more of you."

He looked at Heinze. "I'm sorry I told you about Eva, but I'd rather you know the truth. She died trying to make Germany a safer, better place, and you should be proud of her for that."

Konrad and Matthias stared at their leader.

"What happened to Eva?" Konrad asked.

Heinze slumped to his chair and told them what Michael had said about Eva. They, too, stared in disbelief and questioned if he was really sure.

"I'm one hundred per cent positive," Michael told them. "I wish I wasn't, but if the woman in that photograph is Eva, then it was Eva who saved my life at that railway station in Ravensburg. She died to save Germany, not me, and if that's what we're doing here, then we either work together and get it done, or you go home and let me do it myself."

Heinze stood up. "He's right. I'm sorry, Michael. I allowed anger to cloud my judgement, but it won't happen again. If Eva died for Germany, then I will fight as well. The operation continues."

Heinze offered his hand to Michael. "Eva died with a good man by her side. I'm glad you were there in her final moments."

Michael shook his hand vigorously.

"Let's do this for Germany and Eva."

Heinze agreed.

Chapter 50

Robert Stourcliffe sat on a bench by the side of the River Thames, close to Lambeth Bridge, and stared at the dull, grey water as it rushed towards the North Sea.

He'd left the comfort of his nearby luxury office with every intention of ending it all by throwing himself into the murky water, but now he was here, he couldn't do it.

Fear, pride, and the thought of abandoning everything he'd strived for his entire life held him back, forcing his tormented mind to rage even harder.

Guilt ate at his consciousness and he hated himself for what he'd done to his family, his country, and to his legacy.

Why did I let that woman near me?

That question burned in his mind day and night, and the dark lines underneath his eyes told of troubled, sleepless nights worrying about what was going to happen to him when the authorities discovered his treachery.

He, Sir Robert Stourcliffe, the wealthiest man in Britain and proud recipient of the king's knighthood, had betrayed the country and family he loved so much.

And it was killing him.

A middle-aged man wearing a grey raincoat sat next to him on the bench and fed the birds with bread from his pocket.

Stourcliffe closed his eyes tight, hating every fibre of his being for what he was about to do.

Without a word passing between the two men, Robert Stourcliffe slid an envelope to the stranger. Then he stood up and walked away without a second glance. He wouldn't, indeed he couldn't, look the man in the face while he was committing treason to his beloved country.

He shuffled back to the prestige offices of his company headquarters, a shadow of the brash, outspoken, confident, and entitled aristocrat he'd been just weeks before.

Now he was broken, and he saw no way back.

He knew the Nazis had him where they wanted him. No matter how much information he gave them, it would never be enough. All he was doing was digging an ever-deeper hole for himself, and there was no way out.

He'd set his considerable resources to finding out everything he could about the man in Rotterdam who had become the tormentor of his life. This man had seen his weakness for young women and he'd exploited it perfectly by sending the pretty German spy to trap him.

He'd discovered the man was called Albert Kreise, and he held the rank of Sturmbannführer in the Sicherheitsdienst. He was a favourite of Reinhard Heydrich, who many considered the most ruthless of all the Nazis.

Kreise was smart and determined and had a strong reputation for being something of a Rottweiler. He never stopped until his orders were successfully completed, and as far as he could ascertain, he had only failed one time to deliver.

In 1938, when he was still a Gestapo commander in Munich, he'd allowed the British spy, Michael Fernsby, to escape custody in Germany, and he'd failed to capture him as he escaped through the Black Forest into France.

The irony of that failure wasn't lost on Sir Robert. The Fernsby family were his sworn enemies, and although his rivalry with Gerald was his primary one, his offspring was equally despised by both himself and his son, Robert Junior, who'd experienced several unsavoury altercations with the younger Fernsby during their time at Cambridge.

Until Sir Robert used his considerable influence to have him expelled.

Now it appeared Fernsby would have the last laugh on him. Their fortunes had changed for the better with the discovery of that blasted doubloon, while his had dropped off the face of the earth because of his own stupidity.

Sir Robert Stourcliffe hated himself.

Stourcliffe stomped past his secretary without giving her a second glance. He ignored her questions, closed the door to his private office, locked it, and slumped into his chair in front of the full-length window overlooking the Thames.

The opulence surrounding him suddenly made him feel sick. He'd spent his whole life striving for wealth and prestige, and where had it got him?

His large mahogany desk was covered with circular acanthus leaves, woven in gold thread against a deep blue background. It had cost several times an average man's annual wage, and he'd always enjoyed seeing the reaction on people's faces when they saw it for the first time.

Right now, he'd trade it for just about anything that would wipe his indiscretions from his life.

Dour faces stared down at him from the walls, goading and ridiculing him. Portraits of the Stourcliffe family going back generations seemed to stare at him, accusing him of betraying everything the family name had ever stood for.

He turned around so he couldn't see them.

Then he sat still, unmoving and unknowing what to do. Eventually, as darkness fell over London, he opened the drawer and removed his suicide note. Spreading it out in front of his shaking hands, he silently read it.

My dearest Eleanor,

As I write this, my heart is heavy with a burden that words can scarcely convey. The man you knew, the husband you loved, is not who he seemed. I have made choices, terrible choices, that have led us down a path with irreversible consequences.

In a moment of egregious folly, I allowed myself to be ensnared in an affair that was nothing more than a ruse. A young woman, whom I believed I had feelings for, was in truth a member of the German intelligence.

Our liaisons were not just a betrayal of our love, but a trap that led to my ultimate undoing. They have photographs, Eleanor, evidence of my indiscretions, which they have used to blackmail me into betraying our beloved country.

The information I have given them has already resulted in unspeakable tragedy. Two merchant ships, innocent lives, lost to the ocean's depths because of my treachery.

The guilt weighs on me more than you can imagine. Each day, I am tormented by the faces of those who perished because of my actions.

The Germans have me ensnared in a web from which I see no escape. Each piece of information I pass on saves me from exposure but plunges me deeper into the abyss. The only way to stop this cycle, the only way to ensure no more lives are lost because of me, is to end my own.

Eleanor, my heart breaks as I write this. Not for the end I face, but for the shame I bring upon you and our family. You are the innocent in all this, a bystander caught in a crossfire of my making. I can only hope that in time, you will find it in your heart to forgive me, though I do not deserve it.

I have written to the authorities, explaining your innocence in these matters. I pray they will show you mercy and allow you to keep our home and fortune in England. You deserve that much, at least, for the suffering I have caused.

I leave this world with only one consolation: that in doing so, I protect you from further harm. My love for you remains undiminished, a single light in the darkness of my actions. Goodbye, my dearest Eleanor. May you find peace and happiness in a life far removed from the shadows I have cast.

Yours always and forever,

Robert

He wiped his face with the back of his hand and pulled out the second letter he'd written to his good friend, the First Lord of the Admiralty, Winston Churchill.

Holding both letters over the rubbish bin, he set fire to them and watched them turn to ash.

I'm too much of a coward. I can't even kill myself.

The secretary banging on his door dragged him from his dark thoughts. He wiped his eyes again and stumbled to the door to let her in.

"I'm sorry to bother you, Sir Robert," Gladys said in her distinctive East London accent that had always annoyed the aristocratic businessman.

But not today.

Today, he embraced her friendship, even if it was one born of fear of her entitled boss.

"What can I do for you, Gladys?" he asked.

He must have sounded as bad as he looked, because Gladys stared at him for a long moment.

"Are you alright, sir?" she asked.

"I'm fine, Gladys. I'm just having a bad day, that's all."

"Is there anything I can help you with?" she asked, seemingly genuinely concerned for his wellbeing.

Normally, he'd have brushed her off gruffly, but instead

he looked at her as if he was about to break down in tears in front of her.

"I got a call from the Thames Police, sir," Gladys said apologetically. "They noticed a light from your office, and they want me to draw the curtains."

Stourcliffe looked at Gladys as though he were confused.

"It's the blackout, sir. I have to draw the curtains."

"Oh, yes. Of course."

Stourcliffe stepped aside to allow Gladys access to the windows. She sniffed the air as she closed them.

"Has something been burning in here, sir?" she asked.

"Just some old papers I no longer needed."

"Are you sure you're alright, Sir Robert?" Gladys's looked genuinely concerned, which was surprising, bearing in mind how badly he'd treated her over the years.

"I'm fine, Gladys, thank you."

"Is there anything else you need from me this evening?" she asked.

"No. Go home and embrace your family. I'll see you in the morning."

Gladys looked at Stourcliffe as though he was a different man. He'd never shown the remotest interest in her life before.

"Thank you, Sir Robert. I'll see you tomorrow then." Gladys stared at her boss as she left the room.

"Wait!" Stourcliffe startled his secretary as she reached the door.

She turned and looked at the floor, waiting for the inevitable bollocking for some perceived wrong she'd committed during the day.

"How long have you worked for me, Gladys?" Stourcliffe asked.

"Ten years, sir, give or take a few weeks."

"You have a family?"

"A husband and two little ones." In ten years, Stourcliffe had never once asked about her family. "Are you sure you're alright, sir?"

"Are the children with you? Or were they sent away from the city?"

"They've gone to stay with me aunt in Blackburn, sir. I miss 'em every day, but at least I know they're safer there than they are in London. Am I in trouble, sir?"

Stourcliffe opened his wallet and pulled out a wad of money.

"No, Gladys, you're not in trouble. I fear that over the years, I may have mistreated you somewhat. You've been an excellent secretary and I'm sorry if I've caused you any harm."

Gladys frowned.

"Christmas is coming, and with the war on, we're going to need all hands at the pump if we're going to defeat the Nazis. Tell me, Gladys, when was the last time you had a holiday?"

"I don't know, sir. Years ago. You threatened to fire me the last time I asked for some time off."

Stourcliffe sighed, another dagger blow piercing his heart. "Why don't you go to see your children in Blackburn? I'm sure they'd love to see you."

"I… I…"

"Take this," Stourcliffe held out the thick wad of pound notes. "It should cover your expenses and allow you to spoil your children a little."

"Sir?" Gladys stammered. "I don't understand, sir?"

"The world is changing, Gladys. With whatever time I have left, I'm going to change with it. You deserve that and more, so go with my blessings and have a good holiday while you can. I fear things are going to take a turn for the worse soon, so enjoy your life while you can."

"Sir Robert, there must be over a hundred pounds here." Gladys's face was as white as a ghost. "It's nearly a year's wage."

"It's no less than you deserve. Now go, before it's too dark to see outside because of that infuriating blackout."

"Thank you, sir. I don't know what to say."

"Don't say anything. Just go and enjoy yourself. I'll see you two weeks from today."

"Th-thank you, sir," Gladys stammered as Stourcliffe ushered her out of the door.

As soon as she'd gone, he locked the door again and slumped back into his chair. He opened the bottom drawer of his desk and took out a bottle of brandy, filled a tall glass to the brim, and downed it in one. Then he poured another. If he wasn't brave enough to throw himself into the Thames, perhaps he could drink himself to death instead.

After the second glass, he stopped drinking. He returned the brandy to the drawer and sat back in his chair with his arms behind his head.

An idea came to him. One that turned his stomach and went against everything he'd ever stood for.

What do I stand for? Treason? I have no pride left to preserve.

In his half-drunken state, Sir Robert formulated a plan that would go some way towards redeeming himself, at least in his own eyes. If this turned out to be the last thing he ever did, at least he'd die on his own terms, trying to repair some of the damage he'd caused to his family and his country.

Chapter 51

SS Sturmbannführer Albert Kreise hurried into the offices of the newly formed Reich Security Main Office, or RSHA, at Prinz-Albrecht-Strasse 8 in Berlin.

In the recent reorganisation, the Gestapo, SS, and the SD were brought together under the central leadership of SS Reichsführer Heinrich Himmler and his second in command, SS Obergruppenführer Reinhard Heydrich.

The new headquarters brought under one roof the entire Nazi security apparatus, and it was the most feared building in Germany.

Kreise had been summoned at a moment's notice to report to Heydrich in Berlin. Although he suspected it had something to do with his last report regarding the information provided to them by the Englishman, he could never be sure.

Butterflies flapped around in his stomach as he walked up the staircase to the offices on the top floor. Although he worked for Heydrich, he knew he couldn't trust him. He was just as likely to have him tortured and executed in the basement interrogation rooms as he was to promote and praise him.

Kreise just didn't know which of these it was going to be that day. He'd heard of other men holding similar ranks to his own who had disappeared after meeting with Heydrich.

The rewards of being closely associated with Heydrich were great, and Kreise had already benefited enormously. He owned three houses in Munich alone, along with a further two in the countryside that he used for rest and recuperation.

All had been confiscated from Jewish owners, but Kreise saw nothing wrong with that. As far as he was concerned, they were Jews, and had no legal right to any property or business in the modern Reich.

Along with the potential rewards of being closely associated with Heydrich, the downside could be swift and brutal, as others had already discovered. If you crossed him or failed to carry out his orders, Heydrich's retribution could be fatal.

Kreise knew, because he'd seen it with his own eyes.

He hesitated before knocking on the door marked SS Obergruppenführer Heydrich. Kreise took a deep breath and entered.

"They're waiting for you," Heydrich's secretary said. "Go straight in."

They're waiting for me? Kreise's stomach did a couple of nausea-inducing somersaults. That could only mean one thing. *What have I done wrong?*

He gulped in a mouthful of air and entered the large, opulent office occupied by the Blond Beast. Two men sat side by side behind an ornately carved desk. One was Heydrich.

Kreise was stunned when he realised who the other one was.

With short cropped dark hair, round glasses and moustache, the black-clad figure of Heinrich Himmler was unmistakable.

Kreise stood to attention, threw his right arm out in front of him and screamed the two most used words in Germany. "Heil Hitler!"

Himmler raised his hand in a half-hearted wave, while Heydrich lifted his above his head.

"Sit down, Kreise."

Albert Kreise did as he was told. As experienced as he was at handling powerful men, these two wielded almost God-like power over the people of Germany, and he felt like an ant about to be stamped out of existence.

"Your recent report has caused quite a stir in Berlin," Himmler said.

"I was merely reporting what I discovered from the British shipping owner, Reichsführer Himmler. I didn't mean to cause any concern."

"How sure are you of its veracity?" Himmler pressed him. "Do you believe him?"

"Everything he's told us so far has proven to be accurate, sir, culminating in the successful sinking of two merchant ships. I have no reason to believe he's lying to us now."

"You have done well, Kreise," Heydrich said. "We think he's telling the truth, which is why we summoned you here today."

"It's an honour to be here, sir," Kreise lied, trying to stop himself from throwing up.

"Why do you think this Stourcliffe has been ordered to send one of his ships to Denmark to pick up a British intelligence agent?" Himmler asked.

"I'm not sure, sir. I pressed Stourcliffe on that, and I believe he genuinely doesn't know. Obviously, the British are sending someone in to carry out a mission, and I believe it's in Germany somewhere, but what it is, or where, I don't yet know."

"We agree with your assessment," Heydrich said. "The question is, what do we do about it?"

"Sir, it could be for a number of reasons. They could be setting up a resistance cell somewhere, and they're sending an agent over to recruit and train. Or it could be a sabotage mission. At the opposite end of the spectrum, they could be planning to assassinate someone. There are just too many possibilities."

"While I agree"—Himmler's cold eyes bored through Kreise—"I believe it is the latter end of your spectrum."

"You believe they are going to try to assassinate someone?" Kreise asked. "Forgive my bluntness, Reichsführer, but what brought you to that conclusion?"

Himmler leant forward and rested his forearms on the desk. "Why would the British go to such lengths to risk their operatives on a resistance group? We already have several of those, and while they might be a minor inconvenience, that's all they are, and nothing more. No, Herr Kreise, if they are going to all that trouble to send one of their agents into Germany, they are doing it for a far greater reason."

"I agree with you, sir, but why an assassination? Who would they try to kill? The Führer?"

Himmler and Heydrich stared at Kreise without saying a word.

Kreise's eyes fell wide open as the implication of what they were suggesting hit home. Not that he hadn't considered it – he had. But Hitler was too well protected, and any assassination attempt would be a suicide mission.

"Your reaction tells me you've considered the possibility," Himmler said. "The British may believe they can end the war before it's even begun by killing the Führer. I'm convinced this is what they are planning, and we must act accordingly."

"Absolutely, Reichsführer Himmler. I'm at your disposal to do whatever you need."

"I want you to keep pumping your source for information. Threaten him, do whatever you have to do, but get him to find what they're up to."

"Yes, Reichsführer, but while Stourcliffe has extensive knowledge of the merchant shipping operations in Britain, and he is friends with Winston Churchill, as far as the inner workings of SIS, I doubt he'll know much about that."

"Churchill!" Himmler spat the words out. "That man has a big mouth. Lean on this Stourcliffe and find out what you can."

"Yes, Reichsführer. I'll do everything I can."

"In the meantime, the Führer is going to work from the Berghof in the Bavarian Alps near Berchtesgaden," Himmler said. "His SS security will be increased, and he'll be better protected there. A British assassin won't be able to get close enough and we'll have eyes and ears everywhere. We'll be ready, and he won't get out of Germany alive."

"Very good, Reichsführer Himmler. If I hear anything different, I will inform you immediately."

Kreise left the RSHA office and headed straight for the railway station. He didn't want to be in Berlin a second longer than was necessary.

As he relaxed in his first-class carriage on the long journey to Munich, he mulled over the meeting and

Himmler's insistence that the British were planning an assassination attempt on Adolf Hitler.

The more he thought about it, the more he disagreed with Himmler's conclusion. But who was he to argue with the head of the SS?

No, the British were here for a different reason. If pushed, he'd put his money on them trying to set up a resistance group to harass and slow down the German war machine.

As far as he was concerned, whatever the British were trying to do was akin to using a single matchstick to set the entire world on fire. It was too little, too late. The British, the French, the Russians – they were all at the mercy of the Third Reich, and one by one, they would fall at the feet of the almighty Führer.

Chapter 52

On the eve of the operation, the four men gathered for one last meal together. Tension was high and there was little conversation.

Like the others, Michael had little appetite. The dinner, composed of hard bread and soup, felt like the Last Supper, and each of them was lost in their own thoughts.

After dinner, Heinze broke the solemnity by turning on the radio he'd modified to receive short-wave broadcasts from outside Germany. Anyone caught listening to foreign broadcasts was subjected to heavy punishment, up to, and including, execution in some cases.

"This is depressing," he said as he looked around the room at the dour faces staring back at him. "Let's liven it up a bit. We're on the brink of a moment that will go down in history and we should be celebrating, not moping around like scolded toddlers."

He turned the dial until he found a station playing music. The sultry tones of Lale Anderson singing her newly released song Lili Marleen filled the room, and all three Germans seemed to know it well as they joined in with the words.

Michael hadn't heard it before, so he remained silent, enjoying the sudden camaraderie and joy.

When the song was over, the music stopped and the presenter went into a rant about how great the all-knowing Führer was, and how lucky they were to live under his great leadership.

Heinze tutted and turned the dial. "That's enough of that," he said.

He spun the dial through a few other stations playing the same old propaganda, and as he slowly tuned past a woman telling a story, Michael stopped him.

"Go back," he said, his attention focused on the voice he'd just heard.

"Why?" Heinze protested. "It's just more Nazi propaganda."

"I don't think it was," Michael said.

His breath caught in his chest. *I've been cooped up in here too long and I'm hallucinating.*

The radio crackled to life, breaking the monotony of propaganda with a voice that sliced through the air like a beacon of truth in a sea of lies.

This is Elise, broadcasting from a place that knows and understands freedom from persecution. To my fellow Germans, I bring the truth that has been veiled by the shadow of Adolf Hitler and the Nazis.

The speaker's voice was laced with a resolute calmness that belied the gravity of her words.

Michael, huddled in his Berlin hideout, froze. The voice, though using a different name, was unmistakably hers. He leant in, his heart thumping against his chest, disbelief and hope intertwining in his mind.

"What is it?" Heinze asked, noticing the sudden look

of shock on Michael's face. "You're acting as if you know this woman."

"Shhh." Michael waved his hands so he could hear her words.

I speak to you today, not as a traitor, but as a daughter of Germany, who has witnessed unspeakable horrors committed in our name. My family, simple farmers in Bavaria, dared to defy the inhumanity of the Nazi regime.

After being shown the way by a brave and courageous man who I love with all my heart, we sheltered those who were persecuted. We helped them escape the clutches of tyranny.

It *is* her! Michael wasn't hallucinating.

Mina's voice cracked with emotion, and Michael could feel her pain as he listened to her story in horror. His chest heaved in staccato movements, and although he was aware of the three resistance men glaring at him, he ignored them, focusing his entire being on Mina's words as they spoke to him across the void of space.

Our compassion was met with brutality. My father, a man of peace, was murdered for protecting the innocent. My family, once safe on our farm, is now scattered in the winds of war.

Let my story be a testament to the true spirit of our nation – a spirit not of hatred and oppression, but of courage and compassion. Do not be swayed by the lies of those in power.

Open your eyes to the atrocities committed in our names. It's time to stand for what is right, for the Germany we truly love and remember…

As her voice faded into the static, Michael's heart sank. He'd been holding onto a flickering hope that Mina was safe, away from the turmoil, living a quiet life at Ryskamp.

The truth shattered that illusion, leaving him with a hollow ache. Her voice, though steady, carried a profound sorrow that resonated with his own, and it broke his heart to feel so helpless in her time of greatest need.

"What happened to her?" he asked out loud. "Where is she?" He gasped for air, conscious of the fact that tears were streaming down his face.

Heinze turned off the crackling radio. "We can't leave it on too long because the Nazis monitor the airwaves."

"How do you know that woman?" Matthias asked. "It's obvious that you do, so don't lie to us."

"Her name is Mina Postner." Michael closed his eyes as visions of her simmering beauty washed over him. "She is supposed to be safe on her farm in Bavaria."

"Is she the girl who helped you during your escape last year?" Konrad joined the conversation.

"I have to get to her," Michael ignored the question. "I have to find out what happened to her."

He rose to his feet, but Heinze gently pushed him back into the chair.

"There's nothing you can do, Michael. You don't even know where she is. You know I understand how you are feeling, but the best way to help her is to win this war so we're all free from Nazi tyranny. Use this mission to drive a stake through the heart of Hitler and his henchmen, and when you do, do it for your Mina."

Michael sat in stunned silence. Mina, his Mina, was out there, fighting a battle far greater than he'd ever imagined. After he'd killed Karl Lutz, he'd pictured her living a life of peace and tranquillity, far removed from the dangers of war.

By extending the hand of kindness to those oppressed and dehumanised, Mina and her family had put themselves in grave danger.

Too much danger. Her father was dead, and who knows what had happened to her mother and Senta? The blood in his veins ran cold at the thought of her alone in a foreign country.

In that moment, Michael knew that the fight was not just against an external enemy, but also for the soul of their nation. And in her courage, he found a renewed sense of purpose.

Even if it cost him his life, he would not fail.

Chapter 53

At dawn the next morning, Heinze gathered the men together one last time in the control room that was now as empty as the day Konrad had moved in.

"As long as everything goes to plan, we'll be out of here tonight. If we get separated, make your way back here, if it's possible. If not, get out any way you can and follow your extraction plans. We all know what to do, so gentlemen, it's been a pleasure serving with you."

Martin Heinze shook hands with each of the men vigorously, leaving Michael for last.

"You will have the documents, so take care of them. I wish you well, Englander, and I'm glad you told me about Eva. I hope you can one day find your Mina, but until then, stay alive and win this war."

The two men shook hands, the bond between them stronger for Michael's revelation.

Heinze, Michael, Konrad, and Matthias climbed into the Opel and set off on their well-planned, long-winded route to Dahlem in the suburbs of Berlin, and their date with destiny.

They left Elstal and headed south on narrow lanes through the woods towards Potsdam. As usual, they were trying to avoid the busier roads where they would be more likely to run into a roadblock, and instead crisscrossed between the Brandenburg and Berlin state lines.

The traffic was heavier when they reached Potsdam, where they left Brandenburg for good. They drove north-east around the southern edge of the lakes formed by the Havel River and after passing through Wannsee, Heinze turned north and got back onto the country lanes in the thick, quiet woods.

The men remained silent throughout the journey, each lost in their own thoughts. Michael, still stunned from hearing Mina on the radio, was filled with a mixture of fear, excitement, and resentment.

He'd expected fear and excitement to be his biggest emotions, and perhaps they would be once the operation began in earnest, but right now he was overwhelmed with resentment and hatred towards the Nazis for what they were doing to the ordinary, good people of Germany.

His body shook, not with fear, although he was sure that would come later, but with an intense desire to inflict as much damage on the regime as he could. If his actions, or even his death, could lead to a small victory over the Nazis, then he'd give his life gladly.

Here and now.

By mid afternoon, the vehicle was hidden in the trees at the side of a country lane half a mile from the mansion Admiral Ludsecke called home. The men checked their equipment for the umpteenth time and got out of the Opel.

They made their way on foot, silently, stealthily, through the trees to the rear of the grand house. Michael checked his trusty Walther PPK and checked the extra magazines in his coat pockets.

The main compartment in his rucksack was empty, waiting to be filled with the top secret U-boat plans Admiral Ludsecke was supposed to be carrying home from his meeting with the Naval High Command.

"I hope this is worth it," he muttered as he checked the straps were secured around his waist.

"Even if it isn't," Matthias said. "It will put the fear of God into them."

Michael wanted more than that, but he didn't answer.

The line of trees ended outside the six-foot-high walls surrounding the mansion. After hiding his rucksack in the foliage, Michael climbed the tree closest to the wall and looked down into the rear courtyard with its large greenhouse growing vegetables, fruit, and plants.

He dropped to the other side and lay on the ground facing the house, his gun drawn.

One by one, the others joined him, and they spread out as they moved with well-trained efficiency towards their targets.

The SS guard hut was at the front of the house near the wrought-iron gates. From what Heinze had learned about Ludsecke, he hated it with a passion, because they disturbed his perfectly manicured lawn.

Heinze's contacts in the Abwehr told Heinze that Ludsecke had been involved with countless arguments with Himmler over this, and he'd insisted the SS be moved to the rear of the house where they wouldn't be seen.

Himmler had refused, and instead ordered the SS guards to patrol wherever they saw fit around the outside of the admiral's property. Ludsecke threw a fit and only survived arrest after the direct intervention of Hitler himself.

The men split up, and Michael kept close to the fence where he was protected from view by the bushes. When he got near to the house, he checked his watch and waited for the SS guard to patrol the rear grounds.

They had about forty-five minutes before Ludsecke was due to arrive from his meeting.

Konrad had staked out the mansion and timed the SS as they patrolled. The one advantage Michael and the others had was the German insistence on efficiency. If their orders were to patrol around the perimeter every fifteen minutes, then Konrad found he could almost set his watch by the precision of the SS guards.

Right on time, a young man clad in the all-black uniform of the SS appeared from the side of the mansion. He paced across the rear of the house, checking windows and doors along the way.

Although he was thorough, the young man looked disinterested as he went about his duties. Ludsecke's protection was considered low risk, and probably the worst any of the guards had experienced were a few squirrels breaching the perimeter fencing.

Unknown to the guards on duty, all this was about to change dramatically on this cold, grey afternoon.

The guard walked around the fence, keeping to the ground between the greenhouse and the bushes. He fell out of sight as he patrolled the opposite side, and Michael used that time to prepare himself for what he was about to do.

The fear he'd been expecting finally kicked in, and his legs shook as he struggled to control the tingling in his spine. No matter how many times he did this, he would never get used to it.

His stomach was churning with nausea, but he forced everything from his mind and took a few deep breaths to steady himself.

The guard reappeared from the side of the greenhouse. Michael was sure he could hear his heart thumping out of his chest, and no matter what he did, he couldn't get it to calm down.

The guard sauntered past him, oblivious to the danger lurking in the bushes. As soon as he'd passed, Michael leapt into action. He jumped out from the bushes and grabbed the young SS guard around the neck, yanking him backwards and knocking him off balance.

Holding his hands over his mouth, Michael dragged the guard behind the bushes and hit him hard over the head with the stone he'd readied earlier.

Blood spurted from a large gash on the guard's head, but he still struggled and tried shouting for help. Michael knew he didn't have long before he was missed, so he struck him again.

And again.

The guard fell silent, and Michael saw his face for the first time. He didn't look any older than he himself was, and for a moment he felt pangs of remorse for what he'd just done.

But as thoughts of what the SS and Gestapo had done to David, Gerda, Mother, and now Tim Poster, as well as countless others, flooded Michael's mind, any feelings of remorse he'd harboured quickly fell away.

He stripped the limp guard and used the telephone wire from his pocket to tie him to the bushes. The SS uniform was tight, but it would do. He pushed the disgust to the back of his mind and changed quickly, leaving his own clothes hidden in the bushes.

He looked at the guard lying still on the ground with his eyes closed. He'd allowed him some decency by leaving him in his underwear and boots.

Was he dead? Did I use too much force?

There was no time to look, and if he was, then so be it.

Michael brushed the dirt off the uniform and hurried towards the front of the house. His eyes drifted to the cut telephone lines, and he silently acknowledged the professionalism the resistance members displayed.

At the corner of the mansion, he paused for a moment to compose himself and get his bearings. He took another deep breath and pulled the peaked cap over his eyes as far as he could. Then he marched out as though nothing had happened.

"Mann Keller, you're late. Where have you been?" an SS officer barked as he walked towards the SS guard hut.

Mann was the SS equivalent of a private in the British army, so the man Michael had assaulted was at the bottom of the pecking order in terms of rank.

"I'm sorry, sir," Michael mumbled.

The officer stared at Michael. "Remove your headgear, Keller."

Michael knew he had to act before the SS officer raised the alarm. He checked around to see if anyone else was watching and noticed a gardener on the opposite side of the massive lawn staring at them.

He placed his left hand on the cap as though he was complying with the order and approached the officer.

The officer stepped back and went for the gun that was attached to his belt. Michael jumped at him, closing the gap between them. As he jumped, he pulled the knife from his belt and pointed it at the SS officer.

His other hand reached for the gun in the man's hand, and they collided in a frenzied physical assault. The SS officer shouted out, but Michael quickly silenced him by ramming the point of the blade into his neck.

Blood spurted everywhere, and Michael had to jump aside to avoid it. He grabbed the lifeless officer and dragged him quickly to the fence so he wouldn't be seen by anyone entering the mansion through the wrought-iron gate.

Michael didn't have time to reflect on what he'd done. He spun around and started after the gardener, who'd watched it all happen. He was charging towards the SS hut, and whatever happened, he had to be stopped.

Ludsecke was due home in the next fifteen minutes, and there was no time for anything to go wrong.

Michael momentarily contemplated shooting the gardener, but he didn't.

What would that make me if I shot a gardener in cold blood?

The gardener ran into the hut, screaming and yelling at the top of his voice. A moment later, he staggered out, clutching his chest. He fell to the ground, lifeless.

Michael got there seconds later and ran into Matthias and Heinze, standing over the dead bodies of four SS guards. Like Michael, they were both now clad in the black uniforms of the SS.

"We had to do it," Matthias said. "He gave us no choice."

Michael glared at Matthias and was about to say something when Heinze intervened.

"He'd have given us away and compromised our mission if we didn't silence him."

"Did you have to kill him?"

"Do you really think he's just a gardener?" Matthias spat the words out. "Don't be so naïve, Englishman. Look!"

Matthias tore open the dead gardener's shirt pocket and pulled out a card showing his picture and the rank of SS-Sturmmann, which was above the rank of Mann.

"See?" Matthias said. "He's SS. Everyone here's SS, so don't feel too sorry for them."

Michael immediately calmed down. "I apologise. I didn't know that."

"There's a lot you don't know," Matthias said. "Complete the mission and leave your sentiments behind, or you will get us all killed."

"Lesson learned," Michael said. "Where are we up to? Are we ready?"

"The guard hut is secured. Konrad cut the telephone lines so nobody inside can call for help, and none of them have tried to get out to raise the alarm, at least not yet."

"Good," Michael answered. "Ludsecke will be here shortly."

Michael waited in the guard hut for the admiral to arrive. Matthias took his place in the bushes on the opposite side of the gate, and Konrad was inside the house securing the admiral's wife and the servants who took care of them.

Chapter 54

Konrad joined them moments before the sound of an approaching vehicle disturbed the silence surrounding the mansion. Heinze and Matthias manned the elaborate wrought-iron gates, ready to open them and salute the admiral on his arrival.

Michael watched from the guard hut as the sleek, shining black Mercedes 770K came into view. This was the same model that was used by Hitler, Himmler, and Göring, as well as other top ranked Nazis. By using such a vehicle, Admiral Ludsecke was displaying his power and prominence in the Nazi hierarchy.

The top of the convertible was up, making the long wheelbase Mercedes look even bigger. The spare wheel was attached to the car in front of the passenger door, fitting nicely in the groove between the stretched bonnet and the large front wings.

Flags fluttered on either side of the two headlights. One was the unmistakable swastika, and the other had the Iron Cross over a white background. A golden eagle with a swastika in its claws, also in gold, sat in the centre of the Iron Cross.

The presence of the flags meant the admiral was in the vehicle, so Michael shook the tension from his body and readied himself.

Heinze opened the gates as the Mercedes approached. The chauffeur waved as he drove slowly past the SS men guarding the entrance to the huge stately mansion.

The bodyguard closest to the admiral sat in the front beside the chauffeur, and he watched unflinching as the car passed through the gate.

As usual, the admiral sat in the back, ignoring the men who protected him. He ignored Heinze's salute, instead staring out of the window at his magnificent palatial home.

As the vehicle drove through the gate, Heinze jumped in front to block its path. He held up his arm to halt the driver.

Konrad, also clad in a black SS uniform, jumped out of the bushes and opened fire with an MP 38 sub-machine gun. The folding stock was perfect for transportation and concealment, and Heinze had managed to get hold of two of them for this mission.

Matthias had the other one.

Konrad emptied the entire thirty-two round magazine into the front seats of the vehicle, the deafening automatic weapon shattering the peaceful tranquillity of the admiral's home.

Matthias did the same from the opposite side.

The bodyguard fired back through the shattered glass, but Konrad's and Matthias's bullets tore through him like a hot knife through butter. The chauffeur fell forward and jammed his foot on the accelerator pedal as he died.

The Mercedes lurched forward and smashed into a tree at the side of the driveway as Konrad and Matthias reloaded and emptied another sixty-four rounds into the Mercedes.

Both the SS officers in the front were dead.

Michael and Heinze waited until the shooting stopped, and as soon as it did, they rushed to the rear door and threw it open. The admiral lay on the rear seats, his face ashen and covered in broken glass.

Michael dragged him out of the vehicle and dropped him on the floor. Ludsecke clutched his briefcase to him as though it were the holy grail, and he glared at Michael and gripped as tightly as he could.

"I know why you're here," he snarled. "You'll have to kill me for this."

"I have no problem doing that," Michael said. "Hand it over and there is no need for you to die this day."

Ludsecke's lips curled into a wild grin. "You've overestimated yourselves. The Führer increased security for all the senior officers. It is you who will die, traitor, not me."

As he spoke, another vehicle screeched to a halt outside the gates. Four men jumped out and threw themselves to the ground as they opened fire on Matthias and Konrad as they reloaded their MP 38s.

Konrad fell in a hail of bullets, and Michael saw at least three strike Matthias.

Heinze, shielded by the Mercedes, returned fire, catching one man in the head. Michael dropped the admiral and used the rear door as protection.

He fired, killing another. The two remaining alive spread out, one jumping into the bushes and the other hurling himself towards Michael.

The admiral rose to his feet and tried running to the house. Michael tripped him as he ran past, and he used the confusion to roll out from under the door and fire at the fast-approaching SS officer.

He was too late. The officer leapt on him, his SS dagger in his hand. Michael saw the whites of his eyes as his head connected with Michael's nose, cracking bone and sending his head spinning into momentary darkness.

The momentum of their fight carried them to the front of the Mercedes, right next to the rising admiral.

"Kill him," the SS officer barked, but Admiral Ludsecke ignored him. Instead, he stood up and ran for the house, clutching his briefcase as if his life depended on it.

Michael came to just in time. He saw the flash of steel rise in the air, and he whipped his head to the side as it sliced towards him.

He screamed as the blade caught the side of his head underneath the hairline above his ear, and as the knife thudded into the gravel, he pulled the trigger of his Walther PPK that was jammed into the officer's stomach.

The gunshot sounded muffled, and the SS officer let out a yelp before collapsing on top of Michael.

He pushed the man off him and set off at full speed after the much slower admiral. He couldn't see Heinze or the last remaining SS officer, but he could hear them fighting in the bushes.

The admiral was close to the steps when Michael closed the gap. He leapt into the air and landed on the older man, who dropped to the ground like a stone.

The air was knocked out of him, and he screamed someone's name as soon as he'd taken a breath.

"They're all dead, Ludsecke," Michael panted. Blood from his nose and head dripped onto Ludsecke's face, and Michael could see it angered him immensely.

"Do you know who I am?" the admiral spat at Michael. "I'll have you executed for this."

"No, you won't," Michael answered, looking around

for any approaching SS men they might have missed. "It'll be you who hangs for taking top secret documents home against the express orders of your demented leader."

Ludsecke snarled and tried to hit Michael, but he wasn't strong enough to hold back the younger man. Michael hit Ludsecke hard in the midriff, causing him to gasp in pain.

Ludsecke's grip loosened, and Michael grabbed the briefcase from him. He rolled away and pointed his gun at the admiral, who glared at Michael with the same level of hatred he'd last seen on the face of Karl Lutz in Munich.

He patted the admiral down and removed his pistol. "Your wife is tied up inside. I'm sure she'll appreciate you releasing her."

The admiral glared at Michael as he ran back to assist Heinze. As he reached the gate, a gunshot went off from the side of the bushes, followed immediately by another one.

Heinze stumbled out of the bushes and fell at Michael's feet. Ignoring him, Michael ran to the bushes to find his attacker.

He found him face down in the dirt. He was dead.

"Heinze! Heinze!" Michael shook his shoulder. "Are you alright? Are you shot?"

Heinze looked up. "I'm hit. Get out of here, and get those documents back to London. Don't let us die for nothing."

"You're not dying here," Michael said. He checked Heinze's injuries and saw he'd been shot in the stomach. He helped him to his feet and half-dragged him to the rear of the house and the back fence.

"What about Matthias and Konrad?" Heinze asked, his face as pale as a winter's moon.

“Dead,” Michael answered. “I saw them both fall in a hail of bullets.”

“We can’t leave them,” Heinze gasped.

“We have no choice. The SS and Gestapo, and probably even the Wehrmacht, will be here soon, and we must get away before they get here.”

“I’m slowing you down. Leave me and get away.” Heinze tried stopping but Michael was having none of it.

“I’m not leaving you here. I couldn’t help Eva, but I’ll be damned if I’m watching you die as well. Now shut up and get moving.”

Michael helped Heinze over the fence and then followed him. He emptied the contents of the briefcase into his rucksack and threw the empty briefcase into the woods.

Then he dragged Heinze to their vehicle, hidden in the foliage half a mile away.

Chapter 55

Heinze lay across the back seat moaning as Michael drove the Opel through Wannsee and Potsdam, taking care to drive slowly so as not to arouse any suspicion.

He was glad when they reached the country lanes in the dense woods north of Potsdam that would take them back to their farmhouse in Elstal.

It was dark when they arrived, and Michael parked the vehicle outside the house so he could help Heinze inside.

Heinze's eyes were closed, and for a moment Michael thought he was dead. His eyes flickered open and his hand, covered in blood, grabbed Michael's arm.

"Leave me. I'm done. Get out of here and save yourself."

"I'm not leaving you," Michael insisted. "Even if I have to drive you all the way to Hamburg myself, I'm not leaving you here."

"You're a stubborn man."

Heinze coughed up blood and Michael knew he probably wasn't going to make it.

He helped Heinze out of the vehicle and as he guided him towards the farmhouse, Heinze stopped him.

"We emptied the house. Everything is in the barn, including the medical kit. Take me there."

Michael turned Heinze around and helped him to the barn, where he sat against the boxes they had readied for their evacuation later. He rummaged through them, throwing everything on the floor as he searched for the medical kit.

"You need a hospital," Michael grumbled. "But I can't take you there. I'm not much good at this, but I'll do my best."

He found the kit and knelt in front of Martin Heinze. He opened the SS jacket and tore open his shirt, exposing the wound to the left of his abdomen. Blood oozed from it, and for a moment Michael was taken back to the wet grass at the side of a road near Munich where his brother had died from similar injuries.

Michael's breath caught in his chest as he wiped the blood with the SS shirt he'd torn off his own body.

David. I'm so sorry.

His vision blurred as he fought back the emotion, so he focused on Heinze to take his mind away from David.

The light in the barn was poor, but just about good enough to see what he was doing. He grabbed the green glass bottle labelled Lysoform, the German equivalent of Dettol, and poured it on Heinze's wound.

Heinze stiffened and yelled out as the Lysoform burned. The strong antiseptic smell invaded Michael's senses, reminding him of hospitals and doctors' surgeries. More than anything else, the invasive smell of cleanliness and hygiene reminded him of his mother cleaning his cuts and scrapes when he was a young boy.

After cleaning the wound, Michael carefully dried it

before plugging it with a gauze pad soaked in Lysoform. He wrapped it as best he could and then helped Heinze change into his own clothes.

"You still need a doctor, but this will do until I can get you to Hamburg, or at least out of Berlin."

"You're not taking me anywhere," Heinze protested. "We came here for Ludsecke's U-boat plans and they must be your priority. Don't let Matthias' and Konrad's deaths be for nothing."

"I'll get them back, but I'm not leaving you. That's final and we're not arguing about it. We'll stay here tonight and leave at first light."

Michael changed and took their SS uniforms to the corner of the barn, where he buried them under piles of old straw.

He gathered some useful supplies such as food, water, spare fuel, and maps, and loaded them into the vehicle, leaving the weapons handy in case they were needed, although there was no way the Nazis could know where they were, then he sat next to Heinze and threw a blanket over them both. "We're safe here for now. Get some sleep and we'll get out tomorrow."

Heinze grumbled, but his eyes closed. Michael used his torch to study the map and plan a safe route to Hamburg avoiding the bigger cities.

An hour later, he grabbed his rucksack and looked at the documents he'd stolen from Ludsecke.

These had better be worth it.

All told, Ludsecke had a stack of documents in different folders that were several inches thick. From what Michael could see, Konteradmiral Karl Dönitz was the man responsible for most of them, as his name appeared everywhere.

Grand Admiral Erich Raeder's signature was also

present, but Admiral Ludwig von Ludsecke wasn't mentioned anywhere, at least from what Michael could see.

The files were organised into different folders:

U-Boat Strategy and Organisation

Coordination

Concentrated Attacks

Diversion and Ambush

Retreat and Avoidance

The files went into detail about how the U-boats would work together in what Dönitz called Wolfpacks. How many U-boats the Kriegsmarine currently operated, as well as the ports they operated from was all included.

This was vital intelligence, and even to the untrained eye of Michael Fernsby, it was important enough to see that it could turn the tide of war in the Allies' favour.

The operation had been worth the sacrifice.

Michael's eyes were burning, so he replaced the files in the rucksack and closed his eyes. He'd learned from past experience that sleep was as important as action, and he had to grab it whenever he could.

Tomorrow would determine whether he would live or die, but for now, he was safe.

Five hours later, Heinze elbowed Michael and shook his arm. Vehicles – several of them – were approaching the remote farmyard.

Chapter 56

Michael leapt to his feet and grabbed his trusty Walther PPK and half a dozen full magazines. Sleep quickly faded as he realised what was happening. Heinze, too, struggled to his knees and grabbed a box of weapons and ammunition.

"We have to leave," Michael whispered. "Now."

"It's too late," Heinze whispered back. "I don't know how they found us, but they're here."

"Then we fight."

"Don't be stupid," Heinze's head was buried inside the box he'd dragged to his side. "There's too many of them."

"How do you know that?" Michael asked.

"Listen," Heinze said. "I can hear at least three vehicles. At least one's a truck, which I guarantee you is full of soldiers from the Wehrmacht barracks in the Olympic Village."

"Then we've failed," Michael said. "We die here and they'll get the files."

"Not all is lost," Heinze said. "I'll draw their fire while you get away. It's our only hope."

"I told you, I'm not leaving."

"We don't have time for this," Heinze snarled at Michael. "Look at me. I'm dying and we both know it. At least let me die my way, for the Germany I love. Eva is waiting for me and I'm ready to join her."

Michael wanted to argue but he knew Heinze was right. Martin's would be one more life sacrificed in his name. The nightmares would haunt him for the rest of his life.

Which wouldn't be long if he didn't act fast.

He grabbed the keys to the Opel from his pocket and fell to his knees beside Heinze.

"You are a brave man, Martin. Eva would be proud of you, and for what it's worth, I am, too. You will not be forgotten. If I get out of this alive, I promise to see that you are recognised when this war is over."

"It's been an honour. Now, get out of here before they burst in and kill us both."

Michael rose to his feet, grabbed his rucksack, and took one last look at Heinze. Then he ran for the rear door of the barn.

Before he got there, the main door burst open and at least twenty men rushed inside, all of them aiming their weapons at Heinze.

Michael threw himself behind a supporting wall that held up the hayloft and separated it from the rest of the barn. He was trapped!

"You must be Martin Heinze," a voice snapped through the frosty air. "Where's Fernsby? We know everything, so tell us where Fernsby is, give us the documents back, and I promise we'll treat you fairly."

Michael was stunned.

How do they know my name? How did they find us so quickly?

Michael's mind raced. Konrad and Matthias were

dead. He'd seen them fall with his own eyes, so what happened? Did someone betray them? Who?

There was no time to dwell on it. Soldiers swarmed into the barn, all of them aiming their weapons at Heinze. Michael couldn't see what was happening, but he could hear it loud and clear.

"I won't ask you again. Where are the documents you stole from Admiral Ludsecke? Does Fernsby have them?"

Heinze grunted and Michael got the impression he was playing on his injury. Although serious, he'd been more alert before the barn's invasion.

"How?" Heinze growled.

"Your good friend Konrad told us everything. He was barely alive when we found him, so we took him to the admiral's house and, well, Heinze, you were in the Abwehr. You know what we did to him to make him talk."

Michael ground his teeth at the man; obviously Gestapo.

Heinze remained silent, and Michael wondered for a moment if he'd succumbed to his injuries. If he had, then he, too, would be dead very soon.

"Heinze, are you still with me?" Michael heard the Gestapo agent kick him, and Heinze grunted in response. "You should have seen the look on the admiral's face. He was disgusted, but we got what we desired from Konrad. He sang like a bird and told us everything."

"What did you do to him?" Heinze asked.

"Hmm," the Gestapo agent grunted. "Do you really want to know?"

Silence.

"Very well then. It's surprising what a hot knife will do to a bullet wound. Your friend cried and screamed like a little girl."

Heinze shuffled on the ground. "Nazi bastards," he shouted at the Gestapo agent.

"We know all about your little group, and we picked up Hans and his girlfriend in Hamburg a couple of hours ago. What was her name? Kirsten, was it? She's a pretty little thing. It's a shame to think what our agents are doing to her right now as we speak."

The Gestapo leader was obviously trying to get a response from Heinze. He was trying to make him so angry that he'd lash out and give up Michael in an angry tirade.

The Gestapo man obviously didn't know Martin Heinze, because he remained silent, slumped on the floor.

"Your resistance cell is destroyed, Heinze. All your men, and the woman, are either dead or soon will be, some of them very painfully, I might add. Give me the admiral's documents and tell me where Fernsby is and I'll see to it that you die an honourable death."

"Where's Konrad?" Heinze asked.

"He's dead. I promised him medical attention after he'd told us everything, but alas, his injuries were far too serious. He died before we could get him to a hospital."

"Nazi bastards," Heinze said once again.

"There's nowhere for Fernsby to go." The agent ignored the insult. "Your cell in Hamburg is destroyed and Fernsby is alone. He'll never make it out alive. Give him up now and I'll make his death quick and painless."

"Liar," Heinze said. "Fernsby has already eluded you twice, so what makes you think you'll find him this time? You can torture me all you want but I won't give him up. I can't, because I never knew his extraction plan. None of us did."

"You're lying," the Gestapo agent growled.

"It's called operational security," Heinze answered. "Surely you know what that is?"

"You're lying, and you're going to regret it."

Michael heard the agent kick Heinze, and his pained grunts made his heart weep. He clenched his fists, fighting the suicidal urge to leap to his defence.

"Search the farm," the Gestapo agent ordered the soldiers. "He can't have gone far. He might still be here for all we know, although I doubt it. Cowards like him would be as far away from danger as possible."

The soldiers started moving about and Michael realised it would only be seconds before they discovered him behind the wall. The exit door was thirty or more feet away and there was no way he'd reach it without being seen.

He was trapped.

Chapter 57

Michael took a deep breath and readied himself to fight. Seven or eight soldiers approached the rear exit and as they neared, he placed his finger on the trigger.

He'd take as many as he could before he died in a hail of bullets.

As he rolled away from the wall, he heard – and then felt – a massive explosion that rocked the foundations of the barn.

Men fell, screaming in agony. A deafening roar thundered in Michael's ears, blocking the sounds of human suffering from his brain.

Clouds of debris rose high in the air, making it difficult to see what was going on around him. The wall he'd been hiding behind moments before was now collapsed in a heap, blown apart by the grenades Heinze had detonated in the barn.

Loose straw and dirt clogged his lungs, and Michael struggled to breathe. His back hurt where parts of the wall had landed on him, and he pushed them away so he could stand up.

He coughed, but barely heard himself. The ringing in his ears hurt and he sat on his knees, rocking back and forth in both pain and shock.

As his senses returned, he began to hear the noises of the wounded soldiers. Then it got worse as the clouds of dust settled and he could see what Heinze had done.

The boxes he'd been lying against were gone, obliterated by the grenades. Heinze was gone too, blown to the winds from the force of the blast.

Severed limbs shimmered in the dull light, and mortally injured soldiers squirmed on the floor, screaming in agony as they slowly died.

The barn doors were blown off, allowing cold, fresh air into the inferno that was the barn. Stacks of old hay were on fire, and it wouldn't be long before what was left of the barn followed suit.

Michael rose unsteadily to his feet and staggered towards the open doorway. Before he got there, he tripped over a writhing soldier and fell to the floor, landing in a pool of dark, thick liquid. The next thing he knew, he was on his knees throwing his guts up.

Two shadows entered the barn, both with weapons held high. One shouted something, but with the ringing in Michael's ears, it wasn't clear enough to hear what he was saying.

He threw himself to the ground and searched around for the weapon he'd lost in the explosion. He couldn't find it, so he grabbed a rifle from a severed arm and took aim.

The first soldier fell to his left, and as the second spun around, he pulled the trigger again, dropping him where he stood.

Michael lay still for a moment while he gathered his senses. He banged the side of his head, trying to clear his mind, and rose to his feet.

He had to get out before the entire Nazi apparatus descended on the barn.

He looked for the Gestapo agent, but he'd been closest to Heinze and suffered the full force of the blast. He found another pistol close by, grabbed it, and threw the rifle to the ground.

"Please, help me."

He looked down to see a soldier grabbing for his leg. The soldier's leg had been blown off above the knee, and the sight made Michael retch and throw up again.

He leant forward and took the soldier's hand in his. He didn't look much older than he was, and it brought home once again all the horrors of war. Michael knew his nightmares would be a lot worse after this.

"I'm sorry," he said to the soldier. "I'm sorry this had to happen to you."

"Help me," the young Wehrmacht soldier pleaded.

"I can't," Michael replied, feeling as helpless as he'd ever done. "There's nothing left for me to help you with. Sit tight, and someone will be here soon to help you."

"Don't leave me," the soldier cried as Michael stood up.

He took a deep breath and pried the soldier's arm from his leg. "I'm sorry," he said.

He ran to the shattered door and looked around for any signs of danger. All he heard was the moaning of the wounded behind him, and even that was waning as they succumbed to their injuries.

He ran to the Opel and started the engine. Before long the farm would be crawling with Nazis, and he had to put as much distance between them as he could.

He drove away from the farm, forcing himself to slow down before he ran off the narrow road and crashed into a tree. He knew the Gestapo would be on the lookout for him, and they no doubt knew what vehicle he was driving after Konrad's torture.

He drove north, neither knowing nor caring where he was going. All he wanted to do was get away from the farm and keep away from the bigger towns and cities.

He'd worry about getting to Denmark once he'd put some distance between himself and the angry mob that would soon be on his tail.

Chapter 58

SS Sturmbannführer Albert Kreise paced around the office in the Gestapo headquarters in Dusseldorf. He'd been there for over two hours, waiting to hear what his new orders were going to be.

Until two hours ago, he'd been pleased with himself for planning a successful sting on the British MI-6 intelligence agency, as well as the Dutch intelligence services.

Captain Sigismund Payne Best and Major Richard Stevens had been involved in a series of meetings with supposed German military and intelligence officers who were planning to overthrow Hitler and avert another major war.

In reality, the German officers were members of the SD. Following Kreise's plans, they had set up the meetings intending to discover the strength of British intelligence in Europe.

What followed was a masterclass of deception and subterfuge. The British fell for it hook, line, and sinker, and as a result, Kreise had orchestrated the dismantling of British SIS operations in Europe for years to come.

On the afternoon of November 9, 1939, Best and Stevens, along with members of the Dutch intelligence services, thought they were meeting a German general in Venlo, Holland, at a cafe close to the German border.

They were supposed to discuss peace terms once Hitler had been deposed, but in reality, it was an ambush. The SD kidnapped the two British SIS men and bundled them into a vehicle that sped across the border into Germany.

A Dutch officer, Lieutenant Dirk Klop, died in the incident, but as far as Kreise was concerned, all was fair in love and war. Even though Germany was not at war with the Dutch, Klop was a casualty of the war declared on Germany by the British, and his involvement proved the complicity of the two countries as they conspired against Hitler's Reich.

The Dutch and British were already squabbling, and a wedge was being driven between their intelligence agencies.

Now, in the early hours of the morning, Kreise was supposed to be interviewing the British MI-6 officers but instead, he'd been told there'd been a change of plans and he was to stand by for further orders.

He'd been waiting for more than two hours.

The shrill ring of the telephone stopped him in his tracks. Kreise stared at it as though it were an alien from another world.

What the—? Is that for me?

"SS Sturmbannführer Albert Kreise," he snapped as he answered the telephone.

"I believe congratulations are in order, Sturmbannführer Kreise."

Kreise froze. He'd recognise that cold, heartless voice anywhere.

"Obergruppenführer Heydrich," he stammered. "I wasn't expecting to hear from you at this early hour."

"The mission in Venlo went perfectly, and I'll see to it that you are recognised for your efforts. However, there has been a change of plan, and I am pulling you from the operation."

"Sir?" Kreise wanted to scream at Heydrich, but he knew better.

"You have been occupied with the Venlo incident, so you wouldn't have heard, but two seemingly unrelated events last evening changed everything."

"What happened, sir?"

"Do you recall our meeting in Berlin recently with Reichsführer Himmler, where we discussed the implications of your discoveries from the British shipping owner, Stourcliffe?"

"Of course, Obergruppenführer Heydrich. It was the greatest pleasure of my life to meet with you both there."

He was lying, but it was all he could think of to say. He'd thought long and hard about what Stourcliffe's revelations could mean, but there were so many possibilities, and he'd been too pre-occupied with the double-cross setup in Venlo to go into it any further.

He'd done his job by providing the intelligence to Heydrich. What he did with it was up to him.

"There was an attempt on Hitler's life in Munich last night." Heydrich's voice was flat and devoid of emotion.

"Is the Führer safe?" Panic rose in Kreise's stomach.

"Fortunately, and by a stroke of luck, he's unharmed."

"May I ask what happened, Obergruppenführer Heydrich?"

"The Führer was giving a speech at a beer hall in Munich to commemorate the terrible loss of our sixteen blood martyrs, who died in the 1923 Beer Hall Putsch in

Munich. Because of bad weather, he cut short his speech and left early so he could return to Berlin. Shortly after he left, a bomb exploded. The beer hall collapsed, and so far, at least seven good people are dead."

Kreise pursed his lips and exhaled loudly. "So, it *was* a British assassination attempt." It was more of a statement than a question.

"It would appear that way, yes, and if that was the only incident that occurred, we would wholeheartedly believe that it was connected to Stourcliffe's revelations. However, a second incident occurred last night, and this is one you won't hear on the radio or newsreels."

"What happened?" Kreise listened intently. If something overshadowed an assassination attempt on Hitler, it must be big.

"Yesterday, there was an attack on a Kriegsmarine admiral. Top secret documents regarding our U-boat strategy and operations were stolen."

Kreise was silent for a moment while he digested the information. "Sir, with all due respect. I know the implications and importance of the U-boats, and I'm sure they cannot be allowed to fall into British hands, but how is that related to Stourcliffe? We caught the MI-6 agents red-handed in Venlo, and the assassination attempt proves it."

"You're correct, Kreise, and to make certain, the British agents are to be transported to Berlin for further questioning. However, although the two events may be linked, I don't think they are."

"Why is that, sir?" Kreise was confused. It seemed to him as though he'd caught the MI-6 agents in the act.

Whoever they had working for them, after carrying out the assassination of Hitler, it made sense that they would require extraction, and one of Stourcliffe's ships in Denmark would be perfect for it.

"What else happened in Berlin, sir?" he asked.

"I'm glad we're finally getting to it." Heydrich sounded frustrated with Kreise's questions. "One of them was captured alive and he told us everything."

Kreise listened, hardly able to breathe.

"A resistance group from Hamburg was working with a British agent. They attacked the admiral and killed several of our men. The captured traitor told us where they were hiding and we sent a squad of soldiers to detain them. The one remaining German traitor blew himself up, killing every one of our soldiers and Gestapo officers."

Kreise remained silent. He still hadn't heard anything to connect the Berlin event to Stourcliffe's ship in Denmark.

"You don't sound convinced," Heydrich said impatiently. "The British agent they were working with got away with the Kriegsmarine's strategy and policy documents for the Atlantic war effort."

"I understand the importance, Obergruppenführer Heydrich. I just don't see how this fits with Stourcliffe's ship waiting for a British agent in Denmark. Unless they are collecting two of them – one from Berlin and the other from Munich?"

"I don't think so." Heydrich's voice was cold. "The official version of the assassination attempt will blame the British, but I don't believe they were involved. We arrested a man named Georg Elser at the border who confessed to it all. He insists he worked alone, and at this moment, I'm inclined to believe him."

"Is there something you're not telling me, sir?" Kreise asked.

"The British agent who got away is Michael Fernsby."

"What?" Kreise almost dropped the telephone. "Fernsby? Are you sure?"

"Are you questioning me, Kreise?"

Kreise immediately regretted his choice of words. "No, sir. Not at all. I apologise for my outburst."

"The traitor told us who it was, and from his description, we believe he was telling the truth. Fernsby is the agent your Stourcliffe is picking up in Denmark, and you will be there to stop him."

The hairs rose on Kreise's arms. *Fernsby!*

"Yes, Obergruppenführer Heydrich. I'll leave right away. What about the British agents we have here in Dusseldorf?"

"They're coming to Berlin for further questioning. You are relieved of your duties with them, and from now on you are to concentrate on capturing Fernsby. Those files must not reach London, do you understand?"

"Perfectly, Obergruppenführer Heydrich. What about Fernsby?"

"Kill him."

Chapter 59

Once he'd got a few miles between himself and the bloodbath at the farm at Elstal, Michael calmed down enough to think rationally.

Taking stock of his situation, he knew it would mean instant execution if he was found carrying top secret Kriegsmarine documents, especially after what had just happened. The German authorities would shoot first and ask questions later.

It wouldn't be long before the farmyard was crawling with Nazis, and they would be enraged when they found the carnage he'd left behind.

Martin Heinze's brave sacrifice had to mean something, not to mention Hans, Kirsten, Matthias, and even Konrad. Konrad may have given them up, but Michael knew he'd have resisted as long as he could before the barbaric torture became too much to bear.

Michael pulled over and stopped the car at the side of a country lane a few miles northwest of Elstal. He almost fell out of the vehicle, and he sat on his knees, taking big gulps of air.

He rocked back and forth, but no matter what he did, the pain in his chest would not go away. It wasn't a physical pain, but an emotional wound that hurt more than any bullet or blade could ever do.

So many people have given their lives for me, and yet I continue to survive. Why? Why am I alive and they aren't?

As his breaths got sharper and shallower, images of his beloved Mina calmed him down. He always saw the same vision; Mina leaning over him, smiling, her long blonde hair falling over her face and covering her eyes. He longed to reach out and hold her, and take comfort from her.

I'm never going to see her again! I don't even know where she is.

She might have called herself Elise, but he knew it was her voice he'd heard on the crackly radio.

Where is she? What has happened to her?

From what he could piece together, they must have been caught helping Jews escape. Her father was dead, but what about her mother and sister?

Where is she? She said she was broadcasting from a place that knows and understands freedom from persecution, so she couldn't be in Nazi Germany. His best guess was France, as it was the closest border to her home.

Wherever she was, Michael hoped she was safe.

He forced his mind to his current situation, and as soon as he did, the familiar chest pain returned. Ignoring it, he focused on what he had to do to get out of Germany with Ludsecke's U-boat plans.

The first thing was to ditch the Opel. There was no doubt in his mind that Konrad had given the Gestapo everything they'd asked for during his torture, including the vehicle they were using.

Roadblocks would be everywhere, and anything remotely resembling a black Opel Olympia would be stopped and searched. He wouldn't make it very far, and if he didn't get rid of it, he'd be dead before daybreak.

The next thing he had to do was inform London of the success of the operation so they could arrange for one of Stourcliffe's ships to meet him at the port of Esbjerg in Denmark.

For that, he needed a radio, and now that Kirsten was out of the picture, he was going to have to relay the message himself. After that, it was a matter of avoiding detection until he crossed the border into neutral Denmark.

Easy!

He drove the Opel a short way until he found a dense copse of trees off to his left. He turned onto a narrow lane and buried the vehicle as deep into the undergrowth as it would go.

Once he'd concealed it as best he could, he used his torch to retrieve three bottles of water, a map of Germany, and as much food as his already full rucksack could carry.

Then he set off on foot with only one thought on his mind: Get to Hamburg.

It wasn't long before he entered the outskirts of a town called Nauen. Surprisingly, several streetlights could be seen ahead, which told him they were not expecting any air raids from the British or French air forces that evening.

It was a fair assessment, and Michael was glad of the lights as they guided him towards the town and the possibility of either a train station or another vehicle he could steal.

He kept to the shadows as he approached the town centre. Up ahead, lights and movement caught his eye. Men were running around in the headlights, and at least a dozen vehicles blocked the road.

It's a roadblock!

Michael threw himself to the ground, glad that he'd ditched the car. The Nazis were acting rapidly. He'd expected at least a few more hours to put distance between them, but they were already onto him.

Using back alleys, he jumped over walls and ran through cul-de-sacs to avoid the roadblock. He found the train station, but it was crawling with soldiers.

Now what? I can't use a train, and I daren't take a vehicle because there'll be roadblocks everywhere. I'm trapped.

He huddled behind a dark, empty factory building, thankful that it wasn't operating a night shift. He had about two more hours before daylight, and whatever else he did, he had to find somewhere he could shelter out of sight for the day.

As his eyes adjusted, he spotted a bicycle propped against the wall beside a door, probably belonging to a night watchman. Michael looked at it as a wild idea formed in his mind.

He'd ride all the way to Hamburg! It might take a long time, but he could cycle at night and hide during daylight hours. It was too dangerous to travel by rail, and even more dangerous to steal a vehicle, so it was either walking or bicycle.

Michael crept up to the bicycle and shone his torch, using the red filter to avoid any white light that would be a dead giveaway.

The bicycle looked to be fairly new and it was in good shape. The frame was a little small for him, but it would have to do.

There were no markings on it, but it had handlebars that swept upwards for riding comfort, large mudguards, and a rock-hard leather seat that was going to hurt.

It was single speed, a popular choice for towns and

cities, but that didn't bother Michael. He donned his rucksack and grabbed the bicycle, jumping on it as he gathered speed.

Keeping to side streets, he avoided the roadblocks and soldiers, and headed northwest towards Hamburg and the North Sea, almost two hundred miles away.

Chapter 60

The blanket of darkness was lifting by the time Michael reached the village of Hertefeld, so he pulled off the road into a hedgerow and hid the bicycle under as much foliage as he could muster.

Then he clambered inside a thick clump of bushes and tried to rest. So much had happened since the attack, and he needed time to take stock of everything, but more than anything else, he needed rest. Without sleep, he'd never make it to Hamburg, never mind Denmark, so he ignored the cold November dawn and closed his eyes.

An hour or so later, he awoke with a start. The hedgerow was at the opposite side of a field from a main road that ran close to the village, and the sound of heavy trucks and military vehicles disturbed the tranquillity of the morning.

Michael watched as trucks full of soldiers thundered down the road, all heading toward Elstal, and probably the Olympic Village barracks, for further orders.

What made him more nervous were the Volkswagen Kübelwagens that followed behind. He called them bathtubs, because their shape made them look like bathtubs on wheels.

The bathtubs had caused Michael severe problems on his previous adventures in Germany, and whenever he saw one, he knew trouble was not far behind.

This time, at least, they drove past and continued on their way.

He settled down again, but by early afternoon he'd had enough. It had started to rain, and he was cold, wet, tired and hungry. He ate a mouthful of jam on a stale piece of bread and headed out.

He had a long way to go, and he had no time to lose.

Seven hours later, he found himself in the middle of dense woods close to a town called Lenzen. He'd followed the nearby River Elbe to reach Lenzen, and if he kept with it, the river would ultimately lead him all the way to Hamburg.

After a short rest, he continued his long journey under the cover of darkness.

By now, his rear end was on fire. The seat was about as hard as a lump of concrete, and his posterior hurt as soon as he straddled the bicycle. Although he was physically fit from running, he'd never spent a lot of time cycling, at least not since he was a young boy.

His knees ached, and his calves were burning. Even so, he kept going, ignoring the pain and discomfort.

The rain came down in sheets, soaking him to the skin. He shivered as he rode, and his hands were freezing.

By midnight, he was feeling sorry for himself, and he wasn't paying attention to his surroundings. Still staying close to the Elbe, he went through the village of Laake.

A mile farther on, he stopped at a junction in the middle of nowhere, and as he was about to turn left, a pair of headlights turned on, blinding him in the bright, unexpected light.

He wobbled and fell sideways off the bicycle, in what would have been a comical event under different circumstances. He sat in a puddle of water in the middle of the road, staring at the blinding headlights ahead of him.

"Halt!" a man's voice shouted at him, which was a ridiculous command given his current situation.

Michael threw his hands in the air and rose to his feet. Two shadows appeared in front of the headlights, both of which aimed rifles at him.

"Papers."

"In my rucksack." Michael answered. "Can I get them?"

"Ya, hurry."

As rain poured down on them, Michael was glad the admiral's documents were buried at the bottom of the rucksack underneath his food and water supplies.

He rummaged around, pretending to search for his identification papers. In reality, he was scanning the surroundings, trying to work out how he was going to get out alive.

With two men pointing rifles at him, there wasn't an obvious way to escape, so he shivered and pulled his papers from the rucksack.

"Name?" one of the soldiers demanded as he grabbed Michael's identification papers from his outstretched hand.

"Gerhard Hoffmann."

The soldier shone his torch on the soaked papers and studied them for a moment. He looked Michael up and down before handing them back.

"What are you doing here this late at night?"

"Ever since I came home from Poland, I cannot sleep." Michael said the first thing that entered his mind. "I'm a medic, and since the Führer's glorious victory, I'm unable to get the images of battle out of my mind. As odd as it may sound, I find riding my bicycle in the rain, especially at night, to be therapeutic and calming."

"Where are you going?" The soldier eyed Michael with suspicion, and Michael knew he didn't believe him.

"Nowhere in particular," Michael lied. "I'm just riding around until I get tired enough so I can sleep."

"It says here that you live in Bocholt," the soldier said. "What are you doing here?"

What was the name of that town I rode through?

"My uncle lives in Lenzen," Michael said. "I'm visiting him before returning to my unit."

"You cycled from Lenzen to here in this rain?" the soldier questioned, his voice a few decibels higher than it had been moments before.

"As I said, I can't sleep."

"The war must have really messed you up," the soldier said. "Come, we'll take you home."

"There's no need," Michael answered. "I'll ride home when I'm ready."

"I insist." The soldier aimed his rifle at Michael. "Nobody should be out in this foul weather."

Michael had no choice other than to comply.

"Are you armed?" the soldier asked as Michael picked up his bicycle and wheeled it towards the glaring lights.

"No." He hoped the man didn't search him.

He stopped dead when the soldier opened the rear door of the vehicle outwards. It was a bathtub! Michael shivered and stepped back.

The barrel of the rifle poked his back and he threw his hands into the air again.

The bicycle clattered to the ground.

"Keep your arms up," the soldier demanded.

Michael faced the bathtub while the soldier ran his hands through his pockets and around his belt area. It would only be a matter of seconds before he found the weapon hidden in his right sock.

The second soldier disappeared from view on the far side of the bathtub and Michael heard him opening the driver's door.

The soldier behind him pulled his rifle back and grabbed the rucksack, snatching it from Michael's shoulders. Then he dropped his hands and began patting down his leg.

It's now or never.

In an instant, Michael spun around and snatched the rifle from the soldier's left hand. At the same time, he grabbed a handful of hair, and as the man screamed for help, Michael rammed the barrel into the soldier's head, knocking him backwards onto the ground.

His companion leapt out of the driver's seat on the other side of the bathtub, but not before Michael smashed the rifle's headstock into the soldier's head on the ground.

Blood oozed from the head wound and trickled lazily into a puddle of water, where it quietly disappeared. Michael grabbed the weapon from his sock and threw himself to the ground.

The other soldier charged around the front of the bathtub, screaming at the top of his lungs. He aimed his rifle and was about to fire when Michael pulled the trigger.

The soldier dropped like a stone, dead before he hit the ground.

His companion was coming to his senses and struggled to his elbows. Michael quickly rose and kicked out at the injured man, catching him in the head.

The soldier screamed, and with a strength that surprised Michael, he rolled over, got to his feet, and kicked Michael hard in the groin, sending him to his knees as lightning bolts of pain jolted his body.

The soldier grabbed Michael's hair and yanked his head back. Then he snatched the gun from Michael's hand and tossed it aside.

"Now I kill you, traitor. Our orders are to take you dead or alive, and you are a dead man."

Michael reached into his left sock and grabbed the knife he'd stowed there during his bike ride. In one flowing movement, he rammed it as hard as he could into the soldier's boot. It pierced the leather and embedded itself in his foot.

The soldier screamed and leapt away from Michael, who flew after him. He shoulder-barged him to the ground and hit him in the throat, giving himself time to grab the knife and pull it from the soldier's foot.

As the soldier screamed, Michael thrust upwards below the rib cage, forcing the knife through soft flesh into his heart.

The soldier exhaled deeply, his eyes wide with fear and shock.

"I'm sorry," Michael said. And he meant it.

He held the soldier's head in his arms while he died, and when he did, Michael hit his fist on the ground several times in anguish.

After making sure both men were dead, Michael ran to the side of the road and bent double while he vomited for all he was worth. It didn't matter how many times he did this, it always left him with more guilt than any human should ever have to endure.

This incident would now be added to the growing list of others, and the nights would be a lot longer because of it.

He gathered himself and dragged the dead soldiers to

the bushes at the side of the road. He stared at the bathtub trying to work out what he was going to do next.

It wouldn't be long before the soldiers were missed, and once again, the area would be flooded with soldiers and Gestapo.

With all his heart and soul, he didn't want to get inside that vehicle, but he wouldn't be able to get far enough away in time on the bicycle. Reluctantly, he dragged the dead soldiers to the rear doors and threw them onto the back seats.

He dumped his bicycle on top of them and jumped into the driver's seat of the vehicle he hated more than any other.

Chapter 61

The rear-engine, air-cooled Kübelwagen roared into life, making far too much noise for Michael's liking. He was glad the top was up, as he was sopping wet, freezing cold, and filthy from the fight in the puddles.

A dull pain thudded in his groin, but he cast that aside and concentrated on getting control of the bathtub. He thrust it into gear and lurched forward.

He turned the vehicle around and headed towards Hamburg as fast as he could. He knew he wouldn't get far in such an obvious vehicle, and as soon as the Wehrmacht realised it was missing, they'd be looking for him, but he'd put as many miles between them as he could, while he could.

He drove in silence for an hour, trying, and failing, to stop reliving the nightmare events of the evening.

He'd gone about as far as he dared with the bathtub, and now it was time to ditch it, along with the two dead bodies in the back seat.

The Elbe was on his left, so he turned down a narrow lane with a sign indicating a boat with an arrow pointing towards the river. He followed the winding road until it ended close to the riverbank.

Heavy rain hammered the windscreen, and even stationary, the wind whipped around the vehicle, buffeting it from side to side.

Michael exhaled, opened the door, and was met with freezing, driving rain as soon as he stepped outside.

Ignoring the foul weather, he grabbed the torch from his backpack and searched for a medium-sized rock. After finding one, he retrieved the bicycle from the rear of the Kübelwagen, and dragged the body of the soldier who'd attacked him out of the vehicle.

Rigor mortis hadn't yet set in and the body was still flexible. Michael avoided shining the light on the soldier's face, because he knew from the bitter experience with his brother that by now, it would have turned unnaturally pale, which was a sight he never wanted to see again.

The soldier was bigger than he was, but not by much. Michael forced back his feelings of disgust and stripped the soldier to his underwear.

He took off his own clothes and threw them into the back of the vehicle. The uniform was loose, but it would pass for now. Michael pulled the man's identification papers from the inside pocket of the jacket and shone his torch on them inside the open door of the bathtub so the rain wouldn't ruin them.

Joachim Hopp, D.O.B. May 3, 1920.

Michael was now Joachim Hopp and he forced back the bile from his throat as he dumped the real Joachim back in the vehicle.

He took the heavy stone, and after starting the engine and ramming it into gear, he jammed the stone over the accelerator pedal, forcing it all the way to the ground.

The Kübelwagen lurched forward, and Michael barely

had time to jump out of the way before it flew off the riverbank and splashed into the raging river that was swollen from the heavy rains.

Michael watched as the bathtub filled with water and slowly sank beneath the dark, murky water. The engine spluttered and then died, leaving him in silence once again.

He clasped his hands together and looked up into the rain-filled sky.

After one last look at the rushing river, he donned his rucksack, grabbed his bicycle, and went back to the road.

He had another forty miles to go.

Chapter 62

Every hundred yards he pedalled into the gale felt like a mile. The rain stung his cheeks, and by the time he reached the outskirts of Hamburg, it was almost six am.

He was exhausted, soaked, freezing cold, and hungry. But he was happy to have made it this far.

Luckily, the house where he'd planned the operation with Heinze and the others was on the eastern side of Hamburg, so he didn't have to go through the city streets to get there.

Riding from memory, he stopped two streets over from Griesstrasse, where the house was located. He hid the bicycle in a clump of bushes and made his way to the rear of the house.

Kirsten and Hans were in the custody of the Gestapo, so Michael was under no illusions that the house hadn't been searched. However, the resistance units closely guarded their radio sets, and Kirsten would have hidden it well when it wasn't in use.

And Michael knew where it was.

The Gestapo had no reason to believe Michael would

return to the house in Hamburg, and it was probably the last place they'd expect him to be. They would have gone through the house with a fine-toothed comb already, so there was no reason for them to still be there.

At least that was what he hoped as he climbed a tree across the alley at the rear and waited until daylight so he could see for himself.

The wind finally dropped, and as dawn broke over the horizon, the rain slowed, revealing dark clouds overhead as the heavens threatened to open again at any moment.

Michael shivered under the soaked Wehrmacht trench coat. His eyes were heavy with fatigue, and he fought back the sleep that threatened to wash over him.

The dull, grey morning revealed nothing other than sullen silence, so as soon as he was satisfied the house was deserted, he climbed down from the tree and slipped through the fence at the rear of the house.

Crouching low, he ran to the wall between the door and a window and knelt for a moment while his heart rate slowed enough to hear anything above the crashing in his chest.

He listened for a few minutes, and as his heart slowed, he picked up the sound of voices inside the house. At least two men were talking, and Michael's heart rate spiked again when he realised the Gestapo were still inside the house.

Why? What were they still doing there?

Then he realised. They still hadn't found Kirsten's radio set, and they needed it to get the codes they had been using so they could break the rest of the resistance group.

Damn it!

Michael quickly jumped over the fence and ran back to the tree where he'd hidden his bicycle.

Now what do I do?

He'd relied on getting the radio set, and now he couldn't retrieve it. He was lost and alone in a sea of enemies intent on his destruction.

He briefly considered going in with all guns blazing and taking out the Gestapo agents so he could retrieve the hidden radio set, but quickly dismissed the stupid, suicidal idea and cast it aside.

Leaving the bicycle hidden in the thicket, he joined the growing throngs of men and women making their way to work. School children giggled and played as they walked to school, and Michael marvelled at the normality of it all.

Don't these people know there's a war going on?

A powerful urge to be back home with his mother and father gripped him, and for a moment, he lost himself in thoughts of what they would be doing right then.

He pushed the thoughts to the back of his mind and concentrated on what he had to do, which was to be vigilant and not do anything that attracted attention.

The military coat was filthy and soaked, and Michael knew it was time to ditch the uniform. Enough people had already glared at the bedraggled soldier walking amongst them, including more than a few military personnel.

He stopped in an alley between a row of shops and retrieved some German Marks from one of the hidden compartments in his rucksack.

He found a clothes shop and after explaining that he'd slipped on the walk from the Bahnhof and covered himself in mud, he bought civilian clothes, along with an umbrella.

He changed in the alleyway, discarding the uniform in a rubbish bin behind the shops.

Feeling better to be out of the dead soldier's uniform, Michael bought a street map of Hamburg and caught a bus to Ohlsdorf Cemetery.

The umbrella wasn't just for rain protection. By

holding it low over his head, it prevented anyone from getting a good look at his face, which, by this point, was vital. Just about every Gestapo officer in the country would be on the lookout for him, not to mention the Wehrmacht, who by now would be searching for the two missing soldiers and their bathtub.

Once again, Michael was the most wanted man in Nazi Germany. He couldn't keep riding his luck with this, and he had to get out as soon as he could.

He hoped the Nazis were concentrating their efforts along the Rhine where he'd made his previous escapes, but in wartime, nothing was certain, and Michael wasn't taking anything for granted.

Under the gloomy skies, he quickly found Marlene Braun's overgrown grave and sat under the cover of trees while he wrote his coded message to Sanders back in London, who by now must be wondering what had happened to him and the mission.

He kept the note brief.

Operation Harbour successful. Will be at the rendezvous three days hence.

Harbour.

November 12, 1939.

The flat tin box he'd previously used was buried behind Marlene's gravestone. He placed the new message into it and reburied it, hoping the SIS agent was still around and hadn't been captured by the Gestapo.

Taking one last look at the sad inscriptions on Marlene's gravestone, Michael walked away.

He stopped, realising there was nowhere more secluded in Hamburg than where he was right then. So, he wandered into the dense woods and made a place for himself to rest, sheltered from prying eyes.

Satisfied with his hiding place, Michael closed his eyes and fell fast asleep.

Chapter 63

Michael woke with a start. For a moment, he didn't know where he was, and he stared at the overhanging branches above him as his senses returned.

Cold water dripped down his neck, and he was drenched from the soaking ground. He shivered and rubbed his hands together to get some circulation going, listening intently for signs of human activity; there were none. He doubted anyone ever came to this part of the cemetery, which suited him fine.

Then he heard it. Faint sounds of scraping as soil was being removed. He parted the branches so he could see, and watched as a man in a long raincoat and a fedora hat crouched behind Marlene's gravestone.

It was either the SIS or the Gestapo! Michael hoped it was the former.

He watched the shadowy figure disappear from view, carrying the message that would hopefully get Michael safely back to England if he could make it to the port of Esbjerg in Denmark.

Checking his watch, he was shocked to find he'd been

asleep most of the day, so after grabbing the last of the jam and stale bread from his rucksack, Michael re-joined the throngs of people making their way home after a day of work and blended in as best he could.

He took the bus back to where he'd left the bicycle and walked past it a couple of times to make sure it was undisturbed.

A cafe was nearby, so he took advantage of a pleasant spot to keep an eye on the thicket while he warmed up and ate a hearty meal consisting of a Wiener Schnitzel, washed down with several cups of steaming hot coffee.

This was the first proper meal he'd had in a long time, and he immediately felt better as it settled in his stomach.

He purchased bread, hard cheese, and sausage from a shop on the corner of the street and waited in the cafe for daylight to fade.

As dusk approached, it was time to move. Michael had a long, hard night ahead of him, and he hoped the weather would be kinder than it had been the night before.

His legs ached from the almost two hundred miles he'd already cycled, and the thought of another hundred and twenty did little to ease the rising dread in his full stomach.

His backside hurt like never before. Even sitting on the seat in the cafe had been agony, and he'd constantly switched between cheeks to alleviate the pain.

His muscles hurt everywhere, even in places he didn't know he had them, and the last thing he wanted to do was ride all night to the Danish border.

But that was what he had to do, so he berated himself for whining and stepped outside.

At least it wasn't raining right now.

Chapter 64

For the next six hours, Michael headed north as fast as his body allowed. After the first thirty minutes, the muscle stiffness eased, and he could pedal harder.

His rear end hurt more and more, and no shift of sitting position helped. He took to standing on the pedals to give his cheeks a rest, but as soon as he sat down again, the pain and tenderness came right back.

What I'd give for a soft cushion!

Blisters formed on his hands from gripping the handlebars, but the most discomfort, other than his buttocks, came from his inner thigh and groin area.

Although the pouring rain had thankfully ceased, a light drizzle had persisted most of the evening, so his wet trousers rubbed and chafed his skin, causing ever-increasing soreness as he rode north.

Around midnight, he pulled over into the woods just south of a town called Kropp. So far, the back roads had been quiet and free from roadblocks, which he'd expected this far north of Hamburg.

But he wasn't taking any chances.

He pulled the bicycle out of sight of the road and crawled behind a thick bush. Raindrops dripped down his neck, making him shiver as they froze his already ice-cold body.

He'd filled a bottle with water from a stream a few miles back and now gulped down a pint or more in one sitting, knowing he was dehydrated and wouldn't make it to Denmark if he didn't drink enough water.

Once he'd eaten the sausage and a chunk of the bread and cheese, Michael took his torch and risked the white light for a few moments while he inspected his aching body.

His thighs were on fire, and every pedal rotation had been agony. The torch revealed a large area between his legs that was rubbed raw and blistered. It hurt to the touch, and he knew it would get a lot worse before the night was over.

He groaned as he pulled his trousers up again, and sighed as he tried making himself comfortable.

Don't think about it.

That didn't work, because every time he moved, even an inch, pain shot through his inner thighs like a thousand pinpricks all at once. He was in trouble, and he knew it.

Michael fell into a restless slumber, and for the next two hours, he lay as still as he could to allow his body to recover, if only a little.

Around two am, he reluctantly gathered his rucksack, checked the map one more time, and struggled out of his hiding place.

His whole body screamed at him, but his inner thighs complained the most. Every step he took towards the road was torture and his mind demanded he give up and lie down again.

Ignoring the pain, he mounted the bicycle and headed

north. Immediately, his rear end felt like it had been rammed by a rhinoceros, and his thighs burned.

I'm never riding a bicycle again.

Doing his best to ignore his damaged body, Michael skirted the town and headed into the darkness beyond.

Three hours later, a tired and broken Michael reached the town of Ellund. The border was less than ten minutes away, so he pulled over for another quick break to ready himself for what was to come.

He needed to get clear of the border towns in Denmark as soon as possible to avoid any possibility of Nazi guards or spies, and figured that if he went farther into Denmark, he would be less likely to encounter any German units.

After slaking his thirst, he remounted and headed up the smallest, narrowest country lane he could find. Five minutes later, he approached a sign telling him he was leaving Deutschland and entering Denmark.

Normally, this type of road would be empty and free of traffic, and certainly free of guards and roadblocks, so Michael was shocked when he saw lights ahead and heard the unmistakable sound of a bathtub.

Another one! I can't get away from the bloody things.

There was no tree cover he could use to box around them, so he left the road and, dragging the bike alongside him, tramped through ankle-deep mud in the fields to avoid them.

As he got close, he retrieved his weapon, just in case. He was around one hundred yards from whoever was guarding the border, and he could hear voices, but couldn't tell what they were saying.

He dropped his bicycle and crawled through the mud to get closer. The chafing and aching were forgotten as he wriggled on his stomach, closer and closer.

Two soldiers guarded the deserted lane, and they were complaining bitterly about being sent on such a useless stag duty.

"There's as much chance of the moon falling out of the sky as there is of the British spy coming down this lane," one soldier complained.

"I know. It's pointless, like much of what we do," his partner answered.

"If he does come here, I'll kill him with my own bare hands," the first soldier added. "This is a waste of time. We could be nice and warm in our bunks, but instead, we're sent to the middle of nowhere to do nothing but stand around all night freezing our arses off."

"They said he's carrying something that can't get out of Germany," his partner said. "Whatever it is, it must be important, because you heard them. They told us to kill the Englander, but we can't look at whatever he's carrying or the SS will arrest us!"

His friend shrugged. "Who knows?" he asked. "We just do as we're told."

Michael lay in the wet, muddy field, silent and stunned. They were obviously looking for him, but why? What were they doing, barricading even the most remote country lanes along the border with Denmark?

He'd assumed they were looking for him along the Rhine, not far to the north at the border with Denmark.

It must be a precaution. They have no way of knowing I'm coming this way.

None of the captured resistance members knew his escape route for this very reason, so he knew the information hadn't come from them.

His mind cast back to Maureen Ingram and her final words at the golf course in Sandwich after his last mission with Gustav Adler.

You are all so stupid. The wolf was at your door, and all you did was open it and let him in.

Was there a spy in the higher echelons of British intelligence? Sanders had assured him that Maureen was the wolf, and that there wasn't a highly placed spy in their midst.

So, how does that explain two soldiers guarding a remote border crossing in the middle of nowhere? They were clearly looking for him, so where did they get their intelligence from?

He cast aside his worries temporarily. He would need to be cautious when he entered Esbjerg in case the Nazis were waiting for him, but for now, he had to concentrate on getting Ludsecke's U-boat plans past the guards and into Denmark.

Chapter 65

Michael crawled back to his bicycle and carefully boxed his way around the soldiers. Once he was out of sight, he returned to the road and jumped on the bicycle.

Daylight wasn't far away. He was caked in mud again, and his appearance would give him away to the first person who clapped eyes on him. He rode a short way to a village he didn't know the name of, and turned towards a copse of trees he could make out in the shadows of the breaking dawn.

A few hundred yards down the lane, he came across an isolated house on his left. He slowed and pulled over to investigate further to see if it was a suitable place to stop for the day.

The house was in darkness, but that meant nothing as it was still early. Wary of dogs, or other animals that would alert any occupants to his presence, Michael left his bicycle resting against a tree and cautiously approached the house.

The property was large and comprised of three buildings in a U-shaped setup. Michael ignored the main house and scurried towards the building to the right of it.

From what he could see in the dim light, it appeared to be a smaller house that was detached from the larger one to its left.

He went around the back. A thicket of trees stood no more than thirty feet to the rear, so he ran back for his bicycle, pushed it to the trees, and hid it in the centre of the thicket.

He climbed a branch and sat, watching and waiting to see if anyone was home.

As dawn broke and the dull, grey skies promised more of the same weather, his eyes strained as he scanned for any movement.

By nine, he still hadn't seen any signs of life, so he took a chance, jumped from the tree, and approached the rear of the house.

Keeping to the shadows as best he could, he crawled around the side of the building, being careful to avoid any windows. There was still no sign of activity from either house, so he crept around the front, prepared to run at the first hint of trouble.

Nothing. Silence prevailed, so he cautiously tried the door handle, but it was locked. He felt around, but there was no key.

Assured the place was empty, he checked the third building, to the left of the main house. This was a large barn the owners used to store farm equipment.

The barn reminded him of Ryskamp, and for a moment, his mind drifted back to Mina.

Where is she?

His heart ached at the thought of her voice on the radio. The very real possibility that he would never see her again crossed his mind, but he quickly forced it away.

Let me get home with the U-boat plans. Then I'll worry about Mina.

He left the barn and returned to the main house. Feeling the ledge around the stone doorframe, his fingers closed around a cold piece of metal.

A key!

The door creaked as it swung inwards and a musty smell told Michael that nobody had lived here for a while, so he entered and locked the door behind him.

The house consisted of two floors and several rooms. Most were empty and after checking every room, he entered the kitchen and tried the light switch, which surprisingly worked.

Everything in the kitchen seemed to work, and he crossed his fingers as he turned on the taps to see if fresh water ran through the pipes.

It did.

Then he went further and turned the knob on the gas stove, hoping against hope it worked. It did, but he turned it off while he took stock of his situation.

Whoever owned the house had clearly not lived there for a while, but it wasn't abandoned. Perhaps it was a summer home for a family in a city, but whatever it was, it worked perfectly for Michael right now.

He explored the few rooms that were furnished: a sitting room had a couch and a chair, and a bedroom with a double bed and a wardrobe.

A few clothes hung inside the wardrobe, one side for a man and the other for a woman. He rummaged through the man's clothes, and although they were presentable, the owner was much shorter than he was.

He couldn't use them.

He went back to the kitchen and opened the cupboards, that were mainly bare. One of them had a few cups and a couple of pans, but that was all.

Filling the pans with water, Michael turned on the

stove and brought them to a boil. There was no running hot water, so he used his shirt to bathe himself from head to toe.

He filled the sink with water, took off all his clothes, threw them into the sink, and scrubbed them as best he could with his hands to remove as much of the filth as possible.

After laying them over the couch, Michael donned his wet underwear, grabbed a cup of steaming water for a hot drink, and sat at the table to eat more bread and hard cheese.

After breakfast, he collapsed his sore, exhausted body onto the couch and fell into a deep sleep.

Searing pain in his inner thighs woke him a few hours later. He looked in dismay at the raw, red rash that had spread halfway down both legs.

The agony was driving him crazy, so he grabbed a shirt from the upstairs closet and soaked it in cold water before pressing it onto his burning, chafed, and blistered legs.

The relief was instant, but short-lived. As soon as he removed the shirt to re-soak it in cold water, the burning pain returned. He cringed at the thought of his mother telling him to pour Dettol on, and shuddered to think how painful *that* would be.

He patted the area dry, and then a short while later, gave in to the agony and covered it once again with the wet shirt but by the afternoon, he had to sit in a cold bath upstairs to enjoy a few minutes of relief.

Eventually, before it was dark, Michael spread his map on the table and worked out how he was going to get to Esbjerg. His mind focused on the border crossing, and he worried about what was waiting for him at the docks.

There was no other plan of escape, so it was Esbjerg or

nothing. He'd just have to be vigilant and hope that nobody recognised him.

He slept on the couch, using a pair of curtains that weren't hung for a cover, and before dawn broke, he was up and getting ready to leave.

His clothes were still damp from the wash he'd given them, but at least he looked presentable and shouldn't get a second look as people walked by.

The moment he pulled wet trousers on, his raw thighs started burning all over again. Gritting his teeth, he forced himself to concentrate on what was ahead of him and tried to push the pain to the back of his mind.

It's going to get worse before it gets better.

It was still dark when he retrieved his bicycle and started pedalling. The house was left exactly as he'd found it, and the owners would be hard pressed to tell that someone had ever been there.

His rear end protested as soon as it hit the seat, and between that and his chafed thighs, Michael felt miserable as he left the house behind him.

At least the rain had subsided, although as dawn broke, the clouds were dark and oppressive.

He'd decided to cycle another thirty miles into Denmark, to a small town called Agerskov, before finally ditching the bicycle. That should be far enough into the country to avoid any Nazis looking for him.

Three painful, but uneventful hours later, he reached his destination.

Chapter 66

Michael stopped by a copse of trees near some houses on the outskirts of town. He threw the bicycle into the trees, silently thanking it for carrying him so far.

To say he was relieved to be rid of the bicycle was an understatement, and as he threw it into the trees, he vowed never to ride one again.

He pulled his wad of Dutch Krone from the hidden compartment in his rucksack, and headed into town on foot, trying his best to walk normally with his thighs on fire.

After reaching the small town, he quickly found the bus stop. Opposite was a small cafe, so he went there and ate a hearty breakfast of rye bread and eggs, washed down by several cups of steaming hot coffee.

Feeling refreshed, he waited for an hour before boarding a bus heading northwest. The conductor spoke German, so Michael asked him the best way to reach Esbjerg on a bus.

The conductor was more than helpful and took the

time to write down the stops he would have to make to reach his destination, which was less than fifty miles from Agerskov.

Luckily, the conductor didn't ask what he was doing in Denmark and Michael didn't offer any information. After paying for a ticket all the way to Esbjerg, he settled into his seat and watched the rain splattering against the windows, glad of the fact that he was no longer on the bicycle.

After changing buses twice, he reached Esbjerg in the early afternoon. Aware of the fact that the Nazis were probably waiting for him, Michael checked into a guest-house using the Dutch identification papers he was supposed to have ditched before he'd entered Germany.

He'd bought a new set of clothes before checking into the guesthouse, and after taking a long bath to soothe his aching body and sore thighs, he set off for the docks and the ships moored in the harbour.

Worried in case SIS hadn't received his message, he scoured the docks, hoping Stourcliffe's ship was there.

Pulling the cap he'd bought over his eyes in the hope he wouldn't be recognised, Michael strolled up and down the harbour, and at the far end, tucked away from all the other ships that were docked, he saw a familiar sight that made his blood boil.

The SS Kingfisher sat silent, her grey hull matching the surrounding skies perfectly. The red ensign of the Merchant Navy fluttered in the wind, the Union Jack in the top left corner a visible sign of British registration.

Stourcliffe's white flag, with the Union Jack in the top left corner, flew underneath the red ensign. The unmistak-able SSL lettering embroidered in gold thread in the centre ensured the world knew who owned the ship.

Michael scowled when he saw it.

"Stourcliffe Shipping Line," he snorted out loud.

The SS Kingfisher had once belonged to his family, and he and David had spent many a happy hour running and playing on the decks when they were young boys.

"Stourcliffe." Michael once again spat the words from his mouth. Of all the people he would have liked to rescue him, Sir Robert Stourcliffe was the last one he'd have chosen.

No cargo was being loaded or unloaded and there was no activity around the ship, although Michael assumed that would change either later that evening or first thing the next day. Then the ship would be a hive of activity, with people and goods coming and going for a frenzied few hours before it left the harbour and headed back to England.

That would be the perfect time to board, so Michael turned around and headed back towards the guesthouse. He took a different route, constantly double-checking and changing direction to make sure he wasn't being followed.

Happy he wasn't, he found a quiet restaurant where he enjoyed fresh seafood before returning to the guesthouse for the night.

Butterflies performed a symphony inside his stomach, and he felt strangely tense as he settled down to sleep. Something didn't feel right, and it was all down to the two soldiers at the border crossing.

The Nazis can't possibly know I'm here unless someone in London told them. But who?

Michael didn't know, but he was determined to get to the bottom of it if he managed to get home safely.

He closed his eyes, but sleep wouldn't come, so he tossed and turned, dozing off for thirty minutes before waking with a start. He was soaked with sweat, and his thighs burned.

Eventually, he gave up and sat by the window, staring

into space, thinking about nothing other than how he was going to get on board the SS Kingfisher the next morning.

Chapter 67

The next morning, filled with a growing sense of trepidation, Michael stepped out into the crisp November air with his collar pulled up and his cap pulled down as far as he could without blocking his vision.

He joined the hustle and bustle of a city preparing itself for the day ahead. Men and women rushed everywhere, trying to get to work on time. Children ran to school with parents close behind, trying to keep up.

To all intents and purposes, this was another ordinary day for the citizens of Esbjerg. But it wasn't for Michael Fernsby.

The rucksack on his back, unnoticed for the previous three hundred miles, suddenly felt as if it held heavy gold bars, such was the burden of the U-boats' strategic plans. Men and women had died for these secrets, and Michael was sure his ordeal was not yet over.

He closed his eyes and took a large gulp of air. I hope I'm wrong, he thought.

But the oppressive feeling stuck in his gut, and if there was one thing he'd learned about himself over the last year, it was that he needed to trust his gut instincts, as they had saved his life more than once.

The harbour was busy that morning, with fishing boats unloading their catches and merchants haggling over whatever they were arguing about.

Larger merchant ships loaded and unloaded their wares, and as he weaved between the throngs of people, Michael kept a watchful eye all around him as the butterflies in his stomach turned into seagulls.

The SS Kingfisher came into view. Unlike the day before, when the scene was calm, this morning the ship was all business; men were at work loading the ship with whatever goods were heading back to Britain.

Michael was glad of all the activity, because it would allow him to slip aboard unnoticed. Once on board, he would seek the captain and tell him who he was in the hope that Stourcliffe had briefed him.

But knowing Stourcliffe wouldn't miss the opportunity to cause a Fernsby as much misery as he could, he was expecting to have problems once on board.

Movement to his right caught his attention. Several men, at least a dozen or more from what he could see, were pushing their way towards him. All of them were staring at him, and Michael immediately knew they weren't friendly.

He turned to run, but stopped dead when a familiar voice spoke in his ear.

"Move, and you're dead."

Kreise!

Michael was stunned. How had he missed this?

The barrel of a gun pressed into his back, and as the men closed in around him, Michael knew it was over.

"Die now or later," Albert Kreise said. "The choice is yours."

His mouth was so close to Michael's ear that his hot breath tickled his neck. He shuddered and held his hands in the air.

Kreise grabbed the rucksack and shoved Michael roughly. He patted him down and removed the Walther PPK and the knife tucked into his socks.

"I'm guessing the documents you stole are in this rucksack?" he asked.

Michael ignored him.

"Your silence tells me everything I need to know," Kreise barked in his ear. "Move." He prodded Michael in the back with his gun.

"Where are we going?" Michael asked. He looked around for anything he could use as a distraction, but there was nothing. People were far too busy to notice the altercation, and even if they did, they'd probably not want any part of it.

"Somewhere we can talk without interference," Kreise hissed.

Michael knew full well what that meant, but even if he died in a pool of blood in the harbour, he would not allow himself to be taken for interrogation by the German SD.

The men led by Kreise herded Michael towards some buildings at the rear of the harbour on the far right as Michael stood. One was probably empty, waiting for blood to be spilt as Kreise took pleasure in torture and death.

Michael closed his eyes for a moment while he collected what was left of his strength and courage.

This is it. This is where I die.

"You have caused me more anguish than anyone I've ever met," Kreise said. "For that, I commend you, but now it's over. I won. I always win. Did you think you'd get away with our U-boat strategies? That was never going to happen, Fernsby, no matter how many German traitors you sacrificed to do it."

"I got away with Adler's documents," Michael retorted. "And I'll get away with these too. We'll win this war just as we won the last one. Whether I die or not is irrelevant. There's plenty of men better and braver than me, and they won't stop until you're defeated."

"Brave talk from a worthy enemy," Kreise said. "Now stop talking and move." He shoved Michael hard in the back.

Michael had used the exchange to look for a way out, but he was surrounded by SD agents and for now at least, there was no escaping.

Kreise had the rucksack that held Ludsecke's U-boat plans, and as long as he had that, Michael wasn't going anywhere. Otherwise, the entire operation would have been for nothing, and Heinze and the others would have died for a lost cause.

The crowds of workers fell away as they neared the buildings. By the time they were thirty feet away, they walked alone. The SD agents, led by Kreise, became more aggressive and shoved Michael harder.

He resisted as best he could, slowing down and stalling for all he was worth. Whatever escape he was going to attempt, it would have to be from inside the building while the men were getting ready for the interrogation.

Michael steeled himself for what he was about to do. He pushed all thoughts of his own welfare from his mind and shackled his emotions as best he could.

A massive explosion suddenly ripped through the bleary morning. A building to the right of the one Kreise was aiming for shattered into a million fragments, sending metal and dirt high into the air.

Most of the SD agents threw themselves to the ground.

The three or four that didn't circled around Michael and Kreise.

Men, at least two dozen, emerged from the cloud of debris, their weapons aimed and ready to fire. The SD agents, realising what was happening, leapt to their feet and opened fire.

Men from both sides fell as gunfire was exchanged.

Michael spun around in a flurry of controlled aggression and got his first look at Kreise. He was just as he remembered him from their last altercation, and he smiled when he noticed the fading scar on the bridge of Kreise's nose.

Kreise reacted at the same time, raised his gun, and smashed Michael over the head with the butt. Michael's legs collapsed from under him, and he fell to his knees, momentarily shorn of his senses.

He grabbed Michael by the scruff of his collar and dragged him to his feet, ramming the barrel of his gun into Michael's ribs.

"You're coming with me," he said.

As Michael's senses returned, he looked at the carnage all around him. Although it had only taken a matter of seconds, the entire ordeal felt as if it was happening in slow motion.

SD agents lay on the ground, either dead or dying from their wounds. A few feet away, more men lay where they'd fallen. There must have been over twenty men on the ground.

Those still standing were fighting, and Michael's jaw nearly hit the ground when he recognised two of the people fighting against the Nazis.

They were the two men Sanders had introduced when he first entered the underground war rooms in London.

What were their names? The fog in his head lifted just enough for him to remember.

Richard Keene! The name rushed to him as Kreise dragged him away from the melee towards the crowds of workers and civilians stood watching the commotion with a mixture of fear and confusion on their faces.

Keene. I thought he was in Poland.

Clearly not. The other was Lieutenant John Palmer, the liaison officer who worked for Sanders.

What are they doing here?

He didn't have time to think because Kreise was in a hurry. He pulled, dragged, and kicked Michael at gunpoint, away from the fight as fast as he could.

Michael had no choice other than to comply, so he offered no resistance. Kreise was steering him towards the water's edge at the eastern side of the harbour on the opposite side to where the Kingfisher was docked.

As they approached, Michael saw a small boat, no doubt waiting to whisk them out to a bigger one somewhere out to sea.

He *couldn't* get on that boat.

The workers in the area had vanished, leaving it deserted except for the men fighting for their lives. A couple of buildings stood to their left, and Kreise tried steering Michael away from them as they neared the small fishing boat.

Screams and shouts behind them caught everyone's attention, and another loud gunshot echoed in the dull morning air. Michael felt Kreise's grip loosen slightly as he turned to see what was happening.

Michael seized the opportunity.

He spun around rapidly, knocking the pistol out of Kreise's hand. He headbutted him on the nose, making Kreise see stars and knocking him momentarily senseless.

Kreise's broken nose erupted, blood spurting everywhere, including all over Michael. He staggered backwards and Michael, now recovered, kicked him as hard as he could in the groin. Kreise crumpled to the ground.

Michael grabbed the rucksack and snatched the gun from the ground. He turned to shoot Kreise, but as he did, gunfire erupted from the fishing boat.

The bullets narrowly missed, and Michael ran, dodging and weaving to avoid the bullets pinging the ground all around him. Kreise got to his feet, and with another gun in his hand, chased after him.

Michael ran fast towards the men who had come out of nowhere to save him. Kreise wasn't far behind and started shooting.

Michael knew he'd be dead if he continued running and he was too far away for Keene or Palmer to help him. In any case, they were still fighting with the SD agents, although from what he could see, they, along with the men they had with them, had got the better of the Nazis.

Crowds of people had gathered to their left, all watching with morbid fascination as the battle played out in front of them. Michael didn't want to put the bystanders in any danger, so he veered towards the two buildings that were now off to his right.

The building he entered was dark inside and it took a moment for his eyes to adjust. When they did, he found himself in a warehouse full of the smells of the fishing industry.

He raced behind a stack of equipment and pallets, finally crouching where he could watch the entrance. Kreise rushed in and took shelter behind a pile of packing material for the transportation of the fish.

"You're not getting away this time, Fernsby." Kreise sounded furious.

Michael didn't answer. He knew Kreise was trying to locate him, and he wasn't going to make it easy for him.

Two men rushed into the warehouse, and for a moment, Michael thought it was Keene and Palmer. His heart sank when he heard them shouting in German.

"Where is he?" one of them shouted.

He was close by. So close he'd almost stepped on him. Michael raised his weapon and shot him between the eyes.

The other man rushed towards them, and as he got a few feet away, gunfire from the open doorway stopped him in his tracks. The Nazi fell dead on the floor.

Michael peered around the equipment and saw Palmer standing with his gun aimed at the dropped SD agent. The next moment, another hail of bullets erupted from behind the packing gear. Palmer screamed and fell, clutching his chest.

Kreise ran out of the warehouse.

Michael chased after him, and as he reached the entrance, he ran into Keene, approaching from the other direction.

"What happened?" Keene asked.

"Palmer's hit," Michael shouted back. "In there." He nodded towards the area where Palmer had fallen.

Without wasting another second, he gave chase to Kreise, who had a head start on him. To his right, a handful of men stood over the fallen SD agents. Kreise was running the opposite way towards the fishing boat, and his way out of Denmark.

Michael gave chase, but as he got closer, gunfire erupted again from the vessel, stopping Michael in his tracks. He was no match for their firepower, and he would never get close enough to shoot effectively.

He backed off and watched Kreise jump on board. The little boat set off as soon as his feet hit the deck.

"Kreise!" Michael screamed at the top of his lungs.

Albert Kreise stared at Michael and their eyes locked for a few moments until the fishing boat turned and powered away.

There was no doubt in Michael's mind that he was fighting two wars. One was for his country, facing the might of Nazi Germany. The other was a personal, one-on-one battle with Albert Kreise. One or both of them would not survive this war.

Michael vowed that Albert Kreise would die if it was the last thing he ever did.

Chapter 68

Sirens wailed in the distance as they closed in. Michael ran back to the warehouse, where he found Richard Keene pumping Palmer's chest and giving him mouth-to-mouth resuscitation.

Michael dropped to his knees and helped pump Palmer's chest.

"It's no use," Keene said after another few attempts. He felt for a pulse, but there was none. "He's dead."

"The Danish police are here," Michael hissed. "We've got to go before they get hold of these." He pointed to the rucksack on his shoulder.

Keene nodded. "Help me with him."

They lifted Lieutenant Palmer up and took a shoulder each as they carried him outside. A group of men waited for them, and Michael stood patiently while Keene had a conversation in Danish with one of the men.

After it was over, the men took Palmer and carried him off behind the buildings and away from the harbour.

Police vehicles screamed in from the far side of the

harbour and several bystanders pointed towards the carnage.

"Follow me," Keene said, and set off running.

He led the way, following in the footsteps of the men he'd just spoken to. The Danish police stopped and looked at the dead men outside the destroyed warehouse. From what Michael could see, there must have been at least thirty or forty dead, which was the most he'd ever seen.

He didn't have time to allow his feelings to take over, although he knew the dead Danish men would be added to the long list of brave men and women who had made the ultimate sacrifice so he could live. It was a heavy burden, but this wasn't the time to dwell on it.

Keene ran across a road outside the harbour, made several left and right turns, and came to a stop at a black Volvo PV51 parked at the side of a road.

Keene opened the driver's door, jumped in, and leant over to open the passenger side. He gunned the engine and drove off, keeping to the speed limits so as not to garner any attention.

There were more motorcycles and bicycles than cars, so Keene tried his best to blend in as much as he could. He kept to the side roads on a route he'd obviously previously rehearsed.

"Where are we going?" Michael asked. He had questions, lots of them, but this wasn't the time to ask.

"Home."

Keene drove in silence, slowing down for horses and carts as often as he did for pedestrians and cyclists. Michael was relieved when they left Esbjerg behind them.

"I thought the Kingfisher was taking me home," Michael said as they drove northwest towards what he presumed was the coast.

"Change of plans," Keene replied. "I'll explain everything later once we're safely out of here."

Richard Keene, with his distinct northern accent, was a man of few words. Michael's stomach tied in knots as he tried to make head or tail of what had happened.

I've been right all along. Maureen Ingram was not the Wolf at the door. Someone else, high in British intelligence, betrayed us.

But who? And how did Unit 317 find out? Obviously, Sanders sent Keene and Palmer to Denmark to rescue Michael, but the burning question remained, how did they find out about it?

Michael remained silent as Keene navigated his way to the small town of Vejers, about twenty-five miles north of Esbjerg.

Keene stopped at the end of a narrow lane by the beach. He locked the doors and tucked the keys on the driver's side front wheel. Then he beckoned Michael to follow him.

From the beach, Michael saw a small vessel, possibly another fishing boat, moored a short way out to sea. Keene waded into the water with Michael right behind him.

He held the rucksack above his head as the water got deeper. It was freezing and shocked his system as he waded deeper and deeper. When it was almost to his chin, they reached the fishing boat and firm hands pulled them over the sides.

The moment they hit the deck, the engine roared and the boat turned out to sea. Michael slumped next to Keene and looked him in the eyes.

"I've got questions, and I want answers."

Chapter 69

The coastline of Denmark vanished over the horizon as the fishing boat took them farther out to sea. After about an hour, they made a rendezvous with a Royal Navy Black Swan-class sloop ship.

The HMS Flamingo, designed to be a convoy defence vessel, looked brand new, and she shimmered in the late morning gloom. Alongside the three-hundred-foot-long ship, the fishing vessel felt small and insignificant.

A rope embarkation ladder was thrown down to the fishing boat, and Michael followed Richard Keene up to the deck. Once on board, the first person to meet them was Tony Sanders, and he greeted Michael like a long-lost brother.

"Welcome aboard, Michael," he said as he shook his hand vigorously. "Richard, I'm glad to see you too." He peered over the side, expecting to see Palmer clambering after them. "Where's John?"

"He didn't make it," Keene said, shaking his head.

Sanders closed his eyes and took a deep breath. "Come, we have much to discuss."

Michael and Keene followed Sanders to a cabin at the rear of the ship. "This is the captain's cabin, but he's kindly loaned it to us so we can talk in private."

After warm blankets and hot coffee were handed to the two soaked men, they got down to business.

"What happened?" Michael asked. "How did the Nazis know I was in Denmark? I thought I was supposed to go home on one of Stourcliffe's ships, so why this? And why were you here to rescue me?"

He directed the last question at Richard Keene.

Sanders held his hands in the air. "I'll explain, but first, tell me what happened to John Palmer."

Michael sighed. "He ran into a warehouse to help me. He killed an SD agent before Kreise shot him. Richard and I tried to revive him, but he was gone."

"Where is he?" Sanders asked.

"The resistance group I've been working with took him," Keene answered. "They promised to give him a proper burial."

"Who were they?" Michael asked. "And what were they doing there?"

"Please," Sanders said. "A lot happened after you deployed, and there's a lot you don't know."

"I'm listening," Michael said, staring Sanders in the eyes.

"Stourcliffe was compromised," Tony Sanders started. "The SD were blackmailing him after one of their lovely ladies set him up. They photographed everything."

"Stourcliffe was caught with a woman?" Michael almost wanted to laugh.

"It would be funny, except they used him to extract information that caused a lot of damage to Britain and the deaths of many good men," Sanders said. "It's funny you mentioned that Albert Kreise was in Denmark, because it was him that cornered Stourcliffe and put the pressure on him to betray his country."

"That explains how they knew I was in Esbjerg," Michael said. "But what else did he do that could harm Britain?"

"Kreise knew that reputation was everything to a man like Stourcliffe," Sanders said. "He set him up in Rotterdam and threatened to release the photographs to the newspapers in England. Stourcliffe panicked and agreed to pass on information regarding our merchant ships."

"Two ships were sunk by U-boats because of him," Keene interrupted. "Not only did we lose valuable ships and cargo, but hundreds of men lost their lives because of his treachery."

Michael grimaced. "How did you find out about it?"

"Guilt and remorse eventually got to Stourcliffe, so he approached Colonel Z and confessed everything," Sanders said.

"Including the fact that he'd told the Germans he was meeting me in Esbjerg?"

"No, from what he told Dansey, all the Germans knew was that he was picking up a member of SIS. He swore there was never any mention of your name."

"Kreise knew I would be there," Michael said. "They sent him, because he knows me better than anyone else. Someone told him my name."

"Stourcliffe swears it wasn't him," Sanders replied. "And from what I gather, he came clean about everything else, so I don't see why he'd lie about that."

Michael's eyebrows shot up. "Wait, I think I know."

He told Sanders and Keene what had happened to Heinze and the other resistance members, including Konrad being wounded and interrogated by the SS.

"There's your answer," Keene said. "You can hardly blame him, but I can guarantee it was Konrad who gave them your name."

"Now that is out of the way..."—Sanders looked at Michael's rucksack—"Did you get them? I hope so, or all of this was for nothing."

Michael opened the rucksack and pulled out the files he'd taken from Ludsecke's briefcase.

"All present and correct, sir."

Michael passed the files to Sanders. All told, there were five thick folders, each with a header that informed the reader of its contents:

U-Boat Strategy and Organisation

Coordination

Concentrated Attacks

Diversion and Ambush

Retreat and Avoidance

They all stated that the contents were top secret, and the signatures of Erich Raeder and Karl Dönitz were in evidence everywhere.

Sanders leafed through the folders, one at a time. He whistled at the information they contained and smiled up at Michael.

"Bravo, Michael. Once again, you have proven your value to us. The information in here will put the U-boat campaign back months, if not years. I can see another commendation coming for this."

"I don't want another commendation," Michael said. "I just want people to stop dying for me, that's all."

A sombre silence fell on the three men as they remembered all those who had fallen in support of Michael's vitally important mission.

"How did you get involved?" Michael broke the silence. "I thought you were in Poland?"

"Me?" Keene asked. "I was. I'd not long returned when the Stourcliffe storm erupted. Tony asked me to help, and I was only too willing to oblige."

"What happened with the building that exploded?" Michael asked. "Was that deliberate?"

"It was." Keene nodded his head. "We were going to force the Nazis into it before blowing it up, but when we saw what Kreise was doing to you, we used it as a distraction."

"I'd say it worked." Michael raised his eyebrows in acknowledgement. "Who were those men you brought with you?"

"Before Poland, I'd been in Denmark working to recruit and train the resistance in anticipation of an expected Nazi invasion. The ports are of strategic importance to both sides, and we need a strong resistance in the event the Germans do attack."

"You're expecting them to invade Denmark?" Michael asked. "I thought they were neutral."

"So are the Netherlands, and how safe are they?" Keene replied. "The Danish and Norwegian ports are too important for the Germans to ignore. If they fell into our hands, we would control the waters around Germany, and they won't allow that to happen."

"What's going to happen to Stourcliffe?" Michael asked.

"That's the big question, isn't it?" Sanders replied. "I don't have the answer, but he's committed treason of the highest order that resulted in the loss of hundreds of lives. He compromised a highly sensitive SIS operation, so at the very least, he should face serious jail time."

"That's all?" Michael asked. "Anyone else would face a firing squad."

"He *may* end up facing a firing squad," Sanders said.

"All I know is that he's under house arrest and his case is being discussed at the highest levels of government."

"He's under house arrest?" Michael snorted. "Our system is a disgrace if he gets away with this."

"He's highly connected and has the resources and influence to get off lighter than most others would," Sanders said. "But I'd be surprised if nothing happened. I just can't see it."

"We'll see," Michael said, shaking his head.

Chapter 70

A week later, Michael was summoned to Dansey's office in the war rooms. Tony Sanders was already there, sipping a hot cup of coffee from Dansey's personal stash.

Michael took his seat in the chair beside Major Sanders and waited for Dansey to break the silence.

"Well done, Captain Fernsby," Dansey began. "Once again, the information you obtained may well turn the tide of war in our favour. On behalf of His Majesty's government, I offer you our gratitude and congratulations."

"Thank you, sir," Michael replied. He always felt awkward receiving praise or accolades, especially after so many good people had died for the cause.

"It wasn't just me, sir. Good men and a brave woman died for those U-boat plans, so I'm glad their sacrifice wasn't for nothing."

A solemn silence chilled the air as all three men reflected on what it really took for such a mission to be successful.

"Yes, indeed." Dansey broke the silence. "May the brave men and women who lost their lives rest in peace."

"Amen." Both Michael and Sanders spoke at the same time.

"The admiralty has a lot to work on, thanks to you." Dansey's expression brightened. "The First Lord of the Admiralty, Winston Churchill himself, sends his congratulations to you for a job well done."

"Please tell him I'm flattered and grateful," Michael replied.

"I was going to send you off on well-deserved leave, but something came up that I thought you might want to know first."

Michael's heart juddered in his chest. Surely, they weren't sending him somewhere else? He'd only just got back, and he needed some time alone to recover, both mentally and physically.

"Did you really cycle three hundred miles to the Danish border?" Dansey asked.

"I did, sir. I felt it was safer than travelling by either rail or vehicle, which is what the Germans would have expected me to do."

Sanders shook his head. "You never cease to amaze me, Michael. What you pulled off was astounding, and after this war is over, if your story ever gets told, it will be the stuff of legends."

"I doubt that." Michael's face turned red. "There are plenty of men and women out there much braver than me."

His thoughts turned to the voice on the radio, sending messages of hope and truth throughout Europe.

Mina, for one.

"You are a great asset to our organisation, Captain Fernsby..." Dansey continued the flattery. "You'll be relieved to know that you're going home but stay close to the telephone because I'm sure you'll be needed again soon."

"Thank you, sir," Michael said, blowing out his cheeks. "I thought you were going to send me somewhere else."

"In your condition?" Dansey retorted. "I've read the doctor's reports, and that rash needs time to heal."

Michael's face turned red again.

After some light humour at Michael's expense, Dansey's face turned serious again.

"Tomorrow morning's newspapers will be filled with what I'm about to tell you, but we held them off while we got our story straight."

"What happened?" Sanders asked.

Michael stared at Dansey, hoping the news wasn't personal to him. He couldn't stand much more, not right now.

"You both know about Stourcliffe's treason. What you don't know is how remorseful he was for what he did. He changed an entire lifetime's behaviour after the unfortunate event that ruined his life."

"The unfortunate event that ruined his life?" Anger rose in Michael's chest. "Sir, he betrayed us. His actions led to the death of hundreds of innocent sailors, all of whom had wives, children, parents, and loved ones. Not to mention that he jeopardised my mission and almost got me killed."

"I'm aware of all that, Fernsby," Dansey snapped. "And I wasn't making excuses for him. He deserved everything he had coming to him."

"What's going to happen to him?" Michael asked.

"Nothing now. He's dead."

"What?" Sanders beat Michael to the question. "What happened?"

"After he came to me and confessed, we worked

together with MI5 and Special Branch. With his help, they arrested an entire German spy network in this country. The PM considered a pardon, but other forces prevented it," Dansey answered.

"Stourcliffe was abrasive, and he'd upset a lot of powerful people over the years," Sanders said. "I'm not surprised there were voices of dissent."

"He didn't deserve to be pardoned," Michael said. "Not after what he did. How did he die?"

"I'm getting to that," Dansey said. "Whether he deserved it or not, we can all agree that he made a grave mistake in Rotterdam. A mistake that ultimately cost him his life."

Michael shrugged his shoulders. After the way Stourcliffe had treated his father over the years, he had little sympathy for the obnoxious aristocrat.

"None of what I am about to tell you will end up in the newspapers. They will report that Sir Robert passed away peacefully at his desk while at work."

"So, he is getting away with it!" Michael asserted, annoyed that Stourcliffe continued to get preferential treatment even in death.

"In a fashion, yes. Although Sir Robert was under house arrest, he ventured out yesterday and ended up at his office overlooking the Thames." Dansey clasped his hands and took a deep breath.

"From what I can gather, he sent his secretary home with an envelope he instructed was not to be opened until this morning. Imagine her surprise when she found he'd written her a cheque for five thousand pounds."

Michael's jaw hit the ground.

"Apparently, she passed out and hit her head on the floor. In his note, he apologised for treating her so poorly over the years, and he hoped she would forgive him for his sins when everything came out, which it will tomorrow morning."

"Good God," Sanders said. "No wonder she fainted. That's a fortune by any standards."

Dansey nodded.

"What did he do?" Michael asked again.

"After his secretary left, he locked the door and drank a bottle of brandy. Then he took a gun and shot himself."

Sanders sighed, but Michael just stared at Dansey.

"What about his family?" he asked. "Robert Junior and I may not see eye to eye but he doesn't deserve the shame that is about to fall upon him. Nor does his wife."

"Oh, his wife had already left him," Dansey said. "She moved to their estate in Scotland as soon as he confessed. Their marriage was over."

"What happens to his shipping empire?" Sanders asked. "Wasn't he Britain's wealthiest man?"

"Indeed, he was," Dansey replied. "And now all that passes down to his son."

"His son's already insufferable," Michael said. "I can only imagine what he'll be like now he's inherited all his father's wealth."

"On the contrary, Captain Fernsby. Young Robert shunned his father after his confession and joined the army. He's in officer training right now at Sandhurst, although I'm sure they will allow him compassionate leave to be with his mother."

"What happens to his ships and all his other assets?" Sanders repeated his question.

"For now, his board of directors will oversee the shipping business, but I'm sure the government will insist on changes. Not to mention his competitors who lost men and ships because of his actions."

"I feel sorry for his family," Michael said. "But Sir

Robert doesn't deserve much sympathy. Am I free to leave, sir? I would like to inform my father of this before he sees the newspapers or hears the radio tomorrow morning."

"You're free to go, Captain. I want you back here fit and healthy."

"Yes, sir, thank you."

Michael rose from his chair to leave. Tony Sanders rose with him and offered his hand. "I'll speak to you soon, Michael."

"One more thing, Captain," Dansey said as Michael reached the door.

"Sir?"

Dansey reached into his desk and pulled out an envelope. "This was addressed to your father. It's from Sir Robert, and as you can see, he requests you don't open it until after the news breaks tomorrow."

"For my father?" Michael took the envelope, confusion clear on his face. "What does he want with us?"

"Maybe he left you five thousand pounds as well," Sanders said. "It's not like he couldn't afford it."

"I don't want his money."

Michael put the envelope in his pocket and left Dansey's office.

Chapter 71

The train arrived in Sandwich as daylight fell and the blackout began. Michael once again felt as if his life was in the balance as he dodged the vehicles and cyclists who couldn't see him as he walked home.

He made it safely and banged on the heavy oak front door. Warhurst was shocked when he opened it.

"Master Michael, what a pleasure," the butler said, shaking his hand vigorously and standing aside so he could enter. "Are you injured, sir?"

Michael smiled. It seemed every time he came home after an absence that he was injured in some way. "Nothing that won't heal."

"Wait in the sitting room and I'll inform your mother and father."

Michael did as he was told and entered the family sitting room. He was immediately drawn to the sideboard and the family photos from happier times when they were all together.

His eyes centred on a picture of him and David smiling at the camera. His heart melted when he remembered the good times they'd shared, and his eyes misted at the thought of it never happening again.

"Michael!" His mother raced into the room and threw herself on him. "Michael, it's so good to see you."

Gigi soon followed, and after they fussed over him for a few moments, he pulled away and watched his father limp into the room on his cane.

Michael flinched seeing how his father, at only forty-two years old, looked and acted as though he was in his seventies. The accident had taken a serious toll on him and it broke Michael's heart to see him suffer this way.

They stood in the centre of the room and shook hands. "Son, it's great to have you home. I guess you can't tell us where you've been?"

Michael shook his head.

"You're home now and that's all that counts," Dorothy said, clinging onto her only surviving son.

"Did you find any more lost treasure?" Gigi asked jokingly.

Michael laughed and shook his head. "No, sorry. Not this time."

"So much has changed since you left," Gerald said, struggling to sit down in his Victorian armchair. "So many men have signed up and gone to war. Everyone I know has children who have volunteered, and I couldn't be prouder of you and what you are doing for Britain."

"There's a war to be won," Michael said. "Everyone has to do their part or we'll be overrun with Nazis. Where's Judith?"

"She's staying with a friend for a few days," Dorothy answered. "She'll be delighted to hear you are home. I'll call her tomorrow and Warhurst will pick her up. I don't want anyone going out in the blackout. There's no telling what will happen."

"I'm sure," Michael said. "It was quite an adventure just getting home from the railway station."

The room briefly fell silent. Gerald looked as if he was in pain and his mother and Gigi stared at him as though he were about to announce he was leaving again.

"There is something I want to tell you," he said.

"I was waiting for that," Dorothy said. "I could tell by your face. You're leaving again, aren't you?"

"No, Mother, not yet."

"What is it then?" Gigi asked.

"It's about Robert Stourcliffe." Michael pulled the unopened envelope from his pocket.

"What has that pompous ferret done now?" Gerald's eyes lit up at Stourcliffe's name.

"He's dead."

Stunned silence filled the room.

"What happened?" Gerald asked.

Michael told them the gist of what Sir Robert had done, leaving out the part where he was involved.

"Good gracious!" Gerald blew out his cheeks when Michael was finished. "I knew Sir Robert to be many things, but a traitor wasn't one of them."

"He panicked when the Nazis set him up," Michael said. "They knew how vain he was and they played it to perfection. He changed his ways and apparently left his long-suffering secretary a lot of money before he died."

"Good for her. He treated her terribly," Gerald said. "I saw it for myself when I had the misfortune to meet him at his offices."

Michael hesitated. "He left something for you as well."

More stunned silence.

"What would Stourcliffe leave for me?" Gerald looked confused. "He hated me."

"I don't know." Michael passed the letter to his father. "You open it."

Gerald took the envelope and shook it. "It doesn't appear to have any money in it," he joked.

Michael watched his father's jaw drop as he read the contents. When he'd finished, he looked over at Michael, his eyes wide with shock.

"What did he do to you, son? It must have been something bad if he felt this way over it."

Michael took a deep breath. "What does the letter say?"

"What did he do to you?" Gerald pressed.

"He told the Nazis where I was. As I was on sensitive business for the government, it wasn't an ideal time. A lot of men were killed because of his actions, and I only escaped because I had help."

"That bastard," Gigi spat. "I know we shouldn't speak ill of the dead, but he always hated this family."

"Well, he tried making amends at the end." Gerald looked around the room, his face pale as he met his wife's eyes.

"Dorothy, you won't believe this."

"What?" she asked.

"Stourcliffe left us four of his ships. He wishes them to be returned to us at no charge. He already signed the paperwork, and the ships are in Ramsgate awaiting transfer to me."

Gerald dropped the letter to the floor and looked at his wife. "After all he did to us. All the embarrassment and all the hurt. His very last gesture was to give us back our ships. Dorothy, I don't know what to say."

Dorothy ran to her husband and cradled his head in her arms.

"I guess that means we're back in the shipping business," Gerald said through moist eyes to Gigi and Michael.

Michael shook his head. He didn't know what to say.

"He changed his ways at the end," Dorothy said. "I'm lost for words."

"How are you going to cope with this, Gerald?" Gigi asked. "You can barely get around as it is. You have the brewing business to contend with, and now you have your ships back."

"I'll have to hire people," Gerald said. "Michael will be back once the war is over, but until then, I'll hire someone who can help."

Everyone looked at Michael.

"When this war is over, I promise I'll help all I can. I won't let you down."

Michael couldn't believe what Stourcliffe had done, and although he'd escaped justice by killing himself, his deeds proved that he'd done a lot of soul searching before taking his life.

He wondered how Robert Junior would take the news that his father had given the hated Fernsbys their ships back. No doubt he'd hate them even more.

Michael didn't care. Losing the shipping business to Stourcliffe was the worst thing that had ever happened to his father, even more so than the accident that almost took his life.

Now he'd got them back, Michael hoped his father would recover his will to live and make a full recovery. After all, he was young enough.

He lay on his bed, going over everything that had happened since the last time he was at home. The one overriding event was hearing Mina's voice over the radio.

He reached down and fiddled with the dial, hoping to

hear her voice once again, but to no avail. Wherever she was, she wasn't broadcasting that evening.

I'll find you, Mina. Stay safe, and I'll find you.

Chapter 72

SS Obergruppenführer Reinhard Heydrich sat in the rear of his luxury Mercedes as his convoy sped towards the sprawling mansion in the upscale Dahlem area southeast of Berlin.

The vehicles in front and behind were full of well-trained Gestapo, SD, and SS men, all eager and willing to carry out his orders without question.

Heydrich didn't bother himself with menial day-to-day arrests, but this one was special, and the look on the pompous aristocrat's face when he saw who was at the door would be worth the drive alone.

Anyway, he was fulfilling a promise. Some would say it was a threat, but Heydrich didn't see it that way. He had merely told Admiral Ludsecke that if the rumours of him taking top secret Kriegsmarine documents home against the Führer's express orders were true, then he would personally go to his home and arrest him.

After the recent shambolic events in Berlin and Denmark, there was no doubt the rumours were true.

Ludsecke had damaged the Reich and embarrassed the

Führer. Now Heydrich would show the admiral what happened when he got on the wrong side of the SS.

Heydrich had heard stories of the grand three-storey villa tucked away in the woods, but he'd never seen it before. He pursed his lips in approval as the view through the ornate wrought-iron gates showed what lay beyond.

After the demise of the original guards, Heydrich had personally chosen the new ones who guarded and protected Ludsecke and his imposing mansion. These guards were loyal to him, and the slightest movement by the admiral was reported immediately.

If the pompous old fool thought he could sneak out of Germany, he was badly mistaken.

The SS guards opened the gates as Heydrich's vehicle came into view. The flags flying on the front told anyone looking who was in the rear seat, and anyone with half a brain stood back and saluted.

Nobody wanted to cross the Blond Beast.

The SS guard threw his right arm in the air in the Nazi salute as the vehicle glided into the lane between perfectly landscaped gardens and hedgerows.

A swastika flew alongside the sharp, white double S signs on a black background that was the fearsome symbol of the SS, and as it drove slowly down the driveway, more and more SS guards stood to full attention and raised their arms.

The front two vehicles had already arrived and the occupants stood on the steps leading up to the grand mansion, waiting for Heydrich to lead the way.

Heydrich climbed out of the rear seat and strode purposely up the steps. He stopped at the top and turned around to survey the impressive sight.

He spun around and marched through the open door.

"Where is he?" Heydrich snapped at the SS guard holding the door.

"In his study, Obergruppenführer."

Heydrich, followed by a dozen armed men, marched up the stairs to the closed door, where another guard stood to attention.

"Is he in there?" Heydrich asked.

"They both are, sir."

"Open it."

"I'm afraid I can't, Obergruppenführer Heydrich." The guard looked pale as he spoke to the SS chief. "The admiral locked himself and his wife inside and we don't have a key."

"Then break it down!" Heydrich was in no mood for Ludsecke's games. He was here to personally arrest the old fool and nothing was going to get in his way.

"Yes, Obergruppenführer."

Several men started beating at the door, yelling for the admiral to open it.

The admiral ignored their calls, so the SS men started kicking the door down. Heydrich paced up and down impatiently while the men broke through.

Eventually, the door broke off its hinges and the men forced it open. Heydrich pushed past them and marched in with his mouth open, ready to give the order that would end Ludsecke's life.

Or at least it would after he'd been tortured and confessed his crimes.

Admiral Ludsecke sat slumped over his desk. His head lay on his outstretched arms and several stacks of papers were scattered over the floor, presumably knocked down during Ludsecke's dance with death.

Katharina Ludsecke, the admiral's long-suffering wife,

was seated on a couch. Her head lolled back and her eyes were closed.

Heydrich yanked Ludsecke's head up by the hair and stared at his face. Spittle ran down the side of the admiral's mouth, as it did Katharina's.

Admiral Ludwig von Ludsecke and his wife Katharina were dead. They had both taken cyanide rather than face the wrath of the SS.

Heydrich stormed out of the mansion, his face like thunder. "You were supposed to be watching him," he shouted at the officer in charge of the SS troops guarding Ludsecke.

The officer bowed his head. "My apologies, Obergruppenführer. The admiral and his wife locked themselves in the study before my men could get to them."

"I don't accept failure." Heydrich's voice was cold and emotionless. "Report to my office at eight sharp, Obersturmbannführer. Your orders were to make sure Ludsecke remained alive and in place until he was arrested."

"My apologies, Obergruppenführer Heydrich. The men responsible will be dealt with."

Heydrich threw an icy stare at the SS officer quaking in his boots before him. "Tomorrow morning, Obersturmbannführer. Eight sharp."

Heydrich stomped down the stone steps, not giving the SS officer another glance. He would deal with him in the morning.

"Where to, sir?" his driver asked.

"Back to my office."

Heydrich had one more thing to do before he put the whole sorry mess behind him.

Chapter 73

SS Sturmbannführer Albert Kreise nervously entered the RSHA offices in Berlin. He'd been summoned by an angry Heydrich after the failure in Denmark, and Kreise was worried that the Blond Beast was about to do to him what he'd done to many others, including one just a few days earlier if the rumours were to be believed.

Heydrich's secretary looked disapprovingly at the fading bruises around Kreise's eyes and waved him through without a word.

That's an ominous sign.

Albert Kreise gulped and took a moment to compose himself before knocking and entering. His stomach was doing the dance of a thousand infernos as he stepped into the lion's den.

Heydrich sat behind his opulent, ornately carved desk at the opposite end of the large office. His unsmiling face looked tired and angry, which didn't bode well for Kreise.

"Obergruppenführer Heydrich, it's good to see you again," Kreise lied.

"I trusted you, Kreise." Heydrich got straight to business. "I personally vouched for you when you transferred from the Gestapo to the Sicherheitsdienst."

Kreise looked away from the piercing eyes of the Blond Beast.

"You failed me!" Heydrich slammed the palm of his hand onto the desk. "Your job was to kill the British spy and retrieve the stolen Kriegsmarine plans. Instead, you caused a major international incident and allowed the spy to get away with the U-boat files."

Kreise gulped a lungful of air and looked up at the man who literally held the power of life and death in his hands.

"Stourcliffe confessed, Obergruppenführer Heydrich. The British knew we were there. They were waiting for us with a group of Danish resistance men."

"Danish resistance?" Heydrich roared. "What are they resisting, Kreise? You? Me? The Führer?"

"Sir, from the information my intelligence gathered, the British Secret Intelligence Service, mainly their MI6 and the shadow unit they call Unit 317, sent agents over there to recruit and train in the expectation of a German invasion."

"Your intelligence?" Heydrich glared at Kreise. "That is a trait sadly lacking in you, Kreise. Ribbentrop has been busy putting out diplomatic fires ever since your failed mission, and I can't even begin to tell you about the turmoil in the Kriegsmarine headquarters right now."

"My apologies, Obergruppenführer Heydrich. I wasn't expecting a British-led reception. I had Fernsby in my custody, and I was leading him to the boat so he could be interrogated after we retrieved the U-boat files. All hell broke loose, and a firefight erupted, leading to the deaths of our men. Regrettably, Fernsby got away, along with the U-boat files."

"You were the only member of your team that got away, right?" Heydrich asked accusingly.

"I don't know what you are trying to imply, Obergruppenführer Heydrich, but I didn't run away, if that is what you are getting at."

The burning bile in Kreise's stomach rose to the surface. If he was going down, he wasn't going on all fours, grovelling to this inhumane beast with no conscience.

"I've read the report, Kreise. I know what happened."

"Whose report, sir?" Kreise asked. "Mine? As you said, I was the only one who got away."

"You're forgetting your colleague who operated the fishing boat," Heydrich retorted. "He witnessed everything, and it is only because of his report that you are not being executed for cowardice."

Kreise sighed and relaxed his shoulders. He'd been fully expecting the doors to be burst open by a squad of black-clad SS coming to drag him out to his death.

"I had high hopes for you, Kreise." Heydrich's voice returned to its normal, monotonous pitch. "You did well to recruit the British shipping magnate, and you have served me well until now."

"Thank you, Obergruppenführer Heydrich. I'm sorry I let you down."

"You will report to the SD office in Bonn, where you will carry out administrative duties for the agents. You are no longer trusted, and you should be thankful I have shown you mercy here today."

Mercy? Heydrich didn't know the meaning of the word.

"Yes, Obergruppenführer Heydrich. Thank you."

"Now, get out of my sight. I don't want to hear your name again."

Kreise snapped his heels together and threw his right

arm in the air. "Heil Hitler!" he bellowed at the top of his voice.

"Heil Hitler," Heydrich replied.

Kreise turned and walked out, half expecting Heydrich to put a bullet in his back as he did so. But then, the Blond Butcher didn't do any of the dirty work himself. He always had some other willing soul to do that for him.

Albert Kreise left Berlin an angry man. Clerical duties for an out of the way SD office were Heydrich's way of belittling him. That was the job of the junior agents, and he, SS Sturmbannführer Albert Kreise, was one of the brightest minds in the whole of the German Intelligence community.

I will return. I'll show Heydrich that I am the best out there.

As he watched the world go by from the window of the train heading west, he reflected on his growing rivalry with Michael Fernsby. So far, Fernsby had outsmarted him at every turn, either by cunning or sheer luck.

Mainly sheer luck.

Fernsby had proven to be the bane of his life, and the next time they met – and he was sure their paths would cross once again – he would get his revenge on the young British spy.

One of them would not survive this war, and Kreise vowed to himself that he wouldn't be the one who failed.

Of that, he had no doubt.

The End.

Author Notes

After all the atrocities committed by the Nazis, it might be hard to believe that the sinking of the Athenia on September 3rd, 1939, would cause any consternation in the higher echelons of power in Berlin.

At the heart of Ludsecke lies a pivotal moment in history, one that shaped the course of World War II and the lives entangled in its wake. The sinking of the SS Athenia, mere hours after Britain declared war on Germany, marked a tragic start to the hostilities, underscoring the brutal unpredictability of war.

This event, though a single note in the symphony of a global conflict, encapsulates the initial reluctance of both sides to repeat the catastrophic engagements of the First World War.

Adolf Hitler, at the onset of the conflict, purportedly sought to avoid the mistakes that had previously drawn the United States into battle, keenly aware that the sinking of the Lusitania had been a turning point in World War I. His reaction to the Athenia's sinking—fury and frustration—reflects a complex figure trying to navigate the early stages of war under the guise of a "gentlemanly" conflict, a notion that would rapidly disintegrate as the war progressed.

The real-life figures of Karl Dönitz and Erich Raeder, architects of Germany's naval warfare strategy, stand in contrast to the fictional Admiral Ludsecke, a creation of my imagination designed to explore the moral and strategic dilemmas faced by military leaders.

Dönitz and Raeder, each with their own perspectives on how the Kriegsmarine should conduct itself, provide a factual backdrop against which Ludsecke's fictional actions unfold, highlighting the tensions and decisions that shaped the naval conflict.

Ludsecke diverges from history not to rewrite it, but to offer a lens through which we can examine the complexities of war, the human spirit, and the choices that define us in times of turmoil. It is a tale woven from the threads of both fact and fiction, intended to honor the truth while exploring the "what ifs" of history.

I hope you enjoy the story.

J.C. Jarvis

Get a FREE Book!

Please Leave A Review

If you loved Ludsecke and have a moment to spare, I would really appreciate a short review.

Your help in spreading the word is gratefully appreciated and reviews make a huge difference to helping new readers find the series.

Thank You!

More Books by JC Jarvis

Fernsby's War Series

Ryskamp

Alderauge

Ludsecke

Rotterdam is available for Pre-Order NOW!

The John Howard Tudor Series

John Howard and the Underlings

John Howard and the Tudor Legacy

John Howard and the Tudor Deception

About the Author

J.C. Jarvis is the author of the breakout Fernsby's War series.

He makes his home at www.jcjarvis.com

Email: jc@jcjarvis.com

Made in United States
North Haven, CT
28 June 2024